I0760535

PRAISE FOR BEAST HUNTER AND OTHER FAIRY TALES

"*Beast Hunter* sweeps you up in a rousing tale that twists the fairy tale world on its head. Quick to read, but sticks with you and makes you eager for more."

—H.L. Burke, award-winning and bestselling author of over twenty eclectic fantasy novels

"*Beast Hunter* captivated me! From the first page, I was sucked in, unaware of all sense of time, and had to know what was going to happen next (even if it took reading into the wee hours of the morning to find out). Ro is such an admirable character, and seeing her courage through all the plot twists Michele wove into this engaging story, it left me desperate to get my hands on its sequel, *Kill the Beast*, as soon as possible to continue Ro's adventures!"

—Laura A. Grace, author of *Dear Author* and *Team Lines* and *Gathering Faith*

"*Beast Hunter* is an absolute must-read for those who love twisted fairy tales with strong female leads. Family drama, mystery, shadowy characters, and a heroine you can't help but root for, what's not to love? I was hooked immediately and now can't wait for the rest of Ro's story to unfold."

—Dawn Ford, award-winning fantasy author

❧

"Clever and fresh, with a compelling, relatable heroine, *Beast Hunter* is a fitting prequel to the Beauty and the Beast story, *Kill the Beast*. A potent little novella that will leave you eager for more!"

—Janeen Ippolito, author of the Star-Crossed Fairy Tales, including the award-winning Cinderella retelling *Met By Midnight*

❧

About the Book:

Two children lost in the woods.
Red shoes that won't stop dancing.
An innkeeper harried by the ghosts of her past.
Fey-made clothing that only the worthy may see.
A man with a beard as blue as his temper is hot.
The legend of the great white wolf.
And the hunt of a lifetime.

Beast Hunter and Other Fairy Tales turns beloved stories inside out, shatters expectations, and offers new adventures, delightful twists, and unexpected endings that will keep you coming back for more.

❧

Beast Hunter
and Other Fairy Tales

Laura Hollingsworth

Beast Hunter

and Other Fairy Tales

Michele Israel Harper

Love2ReadLove2Write Publishing, LLC
Indianapolis, Indiana

Published by Love2ReadLove2Write Publishing, LLC

Indianapolis, Indiana

www.love2readlove2writepublishing.com

Ebook ISBN: 978-1-943788-70-5

Hardcover ISBN: 978-1-943788-69-9

LCCN: 2023944213

Library of Congress Cataloging-in-Publication Data is on file at the Library of Congress, Washington, DC.

Cover Design by Laura Hollingsworth

All fairy tale quotes are from the public domain and translated from English into French by Michele Israel Harper. All mistakes are the author's.

ALSO BY MICHELE ISRAEL HARPER

Wisdom & Folly Sisters:

The Complete Story

Candace Marshall Chronicles:

Ghostly Vendetta

Zombie Takeover

(Coming Soon)

Vampire Feud

Mummy Resurrection

Beast Hunters Series:

Beast Hunter: A Prequel Novella

The Lost Slipper: Cosette's Story

Kill the Beast

Silence the Siren

(Coming Soon)

Quell the Nightingale

Slay the Wolf

Stop the Snow Queen

End the Fey

Coming Soon:

Standalones:

Queen of the Moon

Dreamworld

Stars Collide

The Ravens

Altered Time Saga:

The Lady Bodyguard

The Lady Spy

The Lady Assassin

Altered Time Novellas:

Lady in Hiding

Making of a Lady

Lady Out of Time

Tales of the Cousin Kingdoms:

Ruby Dragon Kingdom

Diamond Unicorn Kingdom

Sapphire Griffin Kingdom

Emerald Pegasus Kingdom

Time of the Dragons

To my coffee club members,
Sophia H. and Bethany L.
Thank you from the bottom of my heart for fueling the writing so that I could make this book a reality!

BEAST HUNTER

Le Petit Chaperon Rouge
"Little Red Riding Hood"
—Charles Perrault—

Little Red Riding Hood set off at once for the house of her grandmother, who lived in another village.
On her way through a wood she met that sly fellow, Mr. Wolf. He would have very much liked to eat her, but dared not do so on account of woodcutters nearby in the forest.

Le Petit Chaperon Rouge partit aussitôt pour aller chez sa grand-mère, qui vivait dans un autre village.
En traversant un bois, elle rencontra ce homme rusé, M. Loup. Il aurait beaucoup aimé la manger, mais n'a pas osé le faire à cause des bûcherons à proximité dans la forêt.

Laura Hollingsworth

1

Toes frozen, Rose sucked in a breath as the castle materialized before her and stretched far above her head. Moonlight blazed on the barren trees, lighting the forest as if it were midday.

It was time. The one night of the year she could see the castle—the castle no one else could.

Please! What are you doing in there? Can't you see what's going on? Can't you save us? her heart pleaded, but of course he couldn't hear her silent desperation, no matter how often she wished otherwise.

Rose sighed and dropped her gaze, her eyes darting around the too-silent woods. Cosette huddled nearby, complicit in this yearly excursion, even if she couldn't see what Rose could. Cosette gathered sticks and twigs—what was left of them—unhampered by the lateness of the hour thanks to the glaring moonlight.

Rose's eyes drifted uneasily over their surroundings.

Decay blackened everything and filled the landscape with its pungent odor. Rose struggled to remember what greenery looked like. It was the same night or day—black as far as the eye could see.

Cursed. Her land and everything in it. And there was nothing she could do about it.

Wait. No one was near them. Rose's breath caught. They were too far away from the huntsman. The huntsman they'd dragged farther into the woods than he'd wanted to go, later than he'd wanted to be out, simply because Rose had to convince herself yet again that she wasn't imagining the château. And he'd left them.

Rose growled low in her throat. Typical.

"Cosette! Come closer, love. I don't see . . . him." Whatever his name was this time.

Cosette nodded and picked up her basket, her weary sigh nearly silent, but like a gust of wind to Rose's ears. The quietest of noises revealed themselves to her like a crack of thunder at the oddest of times.

Rose looked for the huntsman once more, though she knew it was futile. What was his name? She never knew any of their names. Huntsmen streamed through her town, always on the prowl for the biggest catch. The highest reward from the steward. While she and her sister were forced to scrounge farther and farther away from the protection of the community. There was no food. No fuel. Commerce had all but ceased.

The huntsmen said it was the same all over the kingdom. Rose refused to believe it. The prince's people couldn't all be starving. They couldn't.

Her shoulders drooped. But they were. The prince's people were starving. The palace was inaccessible. Completely forgotten by all but her. And no one knew what to do. Least of all, her.

The villagers' eyes oft strayed to the silent castle, though not one of them could see it. If Rose questioned them, asked what they were looking for, they would blink as if coming out of a trance and laugh uneasily, clearly at a loss.

Not one of them believed Rose when she said it was still there. That it had ever been there.

She was swiftly taking Madame Savon's place as the town's lunatic.

Cosette settled her basket closer to Rose and began gathering twigs for their hearth once more. "We'll need to go soon, Rose."

"I know. Just a few more."

Rose moved to the next trap and checked it. Empty. Of course. She plodded to the next, eyes drifting to the castle. A smile hovered about Rose's lips as her favorite daydream replayed itself.

The prince riding through her once-prosperous village. Before the silence. Before the riots. Before people withdrew into themselves, weary with hunger and hopelessness. Before the merchant ships sank. Before she'd lost her mère, and her père had lost himself.

A young Rose had been cheering, waving a little flag with a blood-red rose on it, dancing in circles. She'd stumbled and fallen—right in front of the prince's horse.

She remembered the cries, the gasps around her while the rest of the crowd remained oblivious. The horse had reared. The prince had barely maintained his seat. And Rose had been certain she was about to die.

Père had snatched her away from the horse's hooves and cradled her close. He'd straightened and eyed the prince boldly when he'd brought his mount toward them.

The prince's ice-blue gaze had seared itself into Rose's memory. She couldn't look away then, and she couldn't look away now. Even though it was just a memory.

His entourage and guards had raised a fuss—to this day it reminded her of the hens clucking in their coop before plague had taken them all. But the prince had raised his hand, silencing the chatter.

"Your name?"

She'd spoken at the same time as Père.

"Rosette."

"Her name is Rosette."

Warmth never entered the prince's eyes. His perfect face had been carved with a bland look Rose couldn't place. It both terrified and intrigued her. But he'd held out a single red rose.

"For the brave young lady, worthy of such a name."

Rose beamed. Père relaxed. The cheering near them resumed.

The prince had given her a bow from his seated position astride his horse and then had urged his mount on.

And Rose's heart had never been her own since.

Although her père had snatched her from under the horse's hooves that day, to her, the prince had saved her. He hadn't demanded punishment. He hadn't scolded her. Instead, he'd handed her his most prized possession. A beautiful, lush rose from his esteemed gardens.

A perfect rose for little Rose.

Even now the memory brought a smile to her blue lips. But memories were hard to hold on to when one's belly ached and vision blurred.

And no one had called her Rosette since Mère died. Her smile faded, and she forced her thoughts back to the prince and the silent castle.

Maybe the prince couldn't save them this time. It had been so long . . .

Rose's jaw tightened. *Non!* He would save them. He *would*. She just had to wait a little longer.

Rose blinked. All the daydreams in the world wouldn't put food in her stomach or a fire in their stove. She sighed, checked to see if Cosette had followed her—she had—then bent to peer into the next trap. She paused halfway, arm outstretched. She propped her hands at her waist, still bent over, and tried to take a deep breath.

She couldn't.

Through her dress, she plucked at the stays that held her captive. If only her sisters didn't insist on strapping her in so tight!

Fire lit in her. Her sisters. If only she had the strength to . . . non. The only one who mattered was Cosette. Only ever Cosette. The youngest, the one Mère had begged Ro to watch over before she'd slipped from this earth as silent as a shadow.

If she kept Cosette safe, it didn't matter what the rest of their older sisters did. All five of the greedy little twits.

She tugged at the stays again, still shocked by how small her waist was now. Her sisters lounged and complained while she and Cosette worked their fingers to the bone and wasted away.

She thought about straightening, but it was too much work. She eyed the slender branch no longer propping open the trap's door. It was just out of reach. And it was beginning to get too dark to see it, thanks to a few clouds beginning to obliterate the glaring moonlight.

Bless Cosette for following her on this night, when they should've been safe at home. Black spots swam in her vision. If only she had something to eat. If only she could breathe.

If only. Always, ever, *if only*.

Her eyes darted around the nearby forest. Cosette's bright-red cape—the only thing left to them that was made by their mère—shone through the barren trees, the moonlight hitting it just so. How had she gotten so far away?

A low snarl did for Rose what she hadn't the strength to do for herself. She snapped upright and spun toward the growl, her world tilting dangerously.

A lone wolf, ribs straining against its patchy coat, swung its head between her and her sister.

In a flash, every feature brightened, sharply illuminated, and Rose could see its entire being as if lit by a flame. Its matted, filthy fur. Eyes ravenous with hunger, near insanity. Every muscle straining to hold perfectly still. One chipped tooth. Eyes catching the moonlight and throwing flashes of reflected light back at her.

Rose blinked, pulled the dull blade from her pocket, and shifted forward, crouched, ready to spring.

The rest of the woods dimmed further, but the wolf stayed brightly lit. The wolf and Cosette's red cape. What in all the realms?

The wolf eyed her, teeth bared, ribs heaving. Rose slid to the side, anticipating its every move, desperate to block the path to her sister. She instantly saw the path the creature would take and its outcome, and she staggered from its weight.

Cosette shredded, lying still in the crimson snow.

She blinked rapidly and tried to stay upright, only to find the wolf still crouched, ready to make its move.

Pick me, pick me, she silently pleaded. Desperate. Horrified. What had she just seen?

The wolf chose her sister.

She lunged. But she wasn't fast enough.

The wolf bounded through patches of snow and black leaves, skirting Rose easily, on a path that led to the end of Rose's world.

She ran. She'd never make it in time. She was too far away, and the wolf outpaced her with every footfall.

"Creator! Help me!"

She flung herself after the creature. Cosette's head jerked up at her cry. Rose jumped on a fallen log and launched herself at the wolf.

Impossibly, she landed before the wolf—between the wolf and Cosette. She had time for half a blink, then it toppled her. She plunged the dagger deep into its chest, the handle disappearing as they went down.

Her head cracked against something hard, and her scream cut off as the woods vanished.

❧

"Rose. Rose! Please, wake up. Rose!"

Rose's eyes slowly opened. Cosette tugged at her, her strength pitiful. Rose couldn't move. Why couldn't she move? It was so warm . . . Her eyes drifted shut.

"Rose!"

Her eyes snapped open. Foul stench assaulted her at the same time she realized she still couldn't breathe. She hefted the wolf off her and tossed it to the side. The thing lay still and dim. No unnatural color about him at all. Rose cursed.

What in all the realms had just happened?

Cosette stared at her with wide eyes.

Rose jumped to her feet, then doubled over, struggling for breath. "Curse that blasted huntsman for leaving us to fend off the wolves ourselves!"

"It's better than what some of them try to do."

Cosette's quiet words washed shame over her.

Rose gasped for another breath. Didn't she know it. But thanks to her brothers teaching her to grapple and to evade grasping hands, not one of the huntsmen had succeeded with either of them. And they never would. She wheezed.

"What is it? What can I do?" Cosette cried.

"My"—she gasped—"corset." Rose clawed at her chest. "Get. It. Off."

Cosette stared at her in horror for one moment before spinning her around and unlacing her apron, her dress, her overshift.

Rose tried to help, her attempts feeble. How had she just thrown a wolf as if it weighed nothing, yet she couldn't help her sister with her own stays?

And how had she jumped in front of the wolf at such a distance, not brushing one of the trees that stood between them, for that matter? She couldn't wrap her mind around it.

Cosette's cracked fingers were deft, and she soon had the threadbare garments over her sister's head and began unlacing her stays.

Rose gasped a full breath, then two more, just to remember what it felt like. "Don't . . . ever . . . wear a corset. Ever."

Cosette's mouth dropped open slightly—she was a lady through and through. At least, she would've been, had she been given the chance. Unlike her sisters. Snobs, the lot of them. Cosette's concerned look jolted Rose to the present.

"Rose, surely you don't mean that!"

"Promise me."

Cosette often did what Rose asked without question, but she searched Rose's face before slowly nodding. The panic hadn't quite left her eyes. "Your color's returning."

Rose turned and stared at the wolf. The Creator had heard her. He'd saved her Cosette. Then why hadn't He saved Mère?

Her mouth hardened into a grim line.

She jerked away from the thought and attempted a smile for Cosette's sake. "What do you say we take this back to the village? The huntsmen will be glad to know, and we might even get some meat."

She shivered, the cold blasting through her undershift.

Cosette's eyes widened. "Not until your clothes are back on!" She stuffed Rose back into her dress and hid the corset under a pile of black leaves. "Besides, we may not be able to get our teeth through whatever meat's on him."

Cosette eyed the wolf doubtfully, but Rose could see the hunger in her eyes. The creature would be picked clean, what with seven sisters, two brothers, and a père who may or may not be present.

"Rose, how are we going to get him back to the village?"

Rose glanced at the pile of blackened leaves, then at Cosette's tiny waist, then at the abandoned cloth peeking out from under a mound of leaves.

A slow grin spread across her face. "I have an idea."

2

Torchlight flickered as the huntsmen listened to her tale with apparent boredom, but the fire of greed lit their eyes. Scraggly though the beast was, it would still bring a handsome reward from the steward.

Rose was counting on it.

She shivered as a blast of freezing wind swept through their small town of Champagne, danced around the shabby houses, then howled off into the trees.

"You expect us to believe you killed a wolf singlehandedly. You."

The huntsman in charge eyed her. He clearly didn't believe her, nor did any of the others. Though the three men's eyes never strayed far from the carcass she and Cosette had hauled back on the makeshift litter made with their stays and aprons.

Cosette would've died had anyone known the stiff material wrapped around the two poles, hiding beneath their large aprons, was their undergarments.

Rose bristled and stepped forward.

Cosette laid a gentle hand on her arm. "Monsieur, I

assure you, every word my sister says is truth. She would not deceive you."

Rose relaxed. Her sister may have been the only person left in the world who believed in her, but oh, it felt like warmth and sunshine had returned to their world.

Madame Savon shuffled past, her stench and incessant muttering identifying her in the moonlight that struggled against the clouds. "You should've let the wolf have her, girl. One less mouth to feed. One less person to watch starve."

Never! Rose lunged with a low growl in her throat. Cosette whimpered. Rose drew herself up short from actually attacking the old woman, and glanced at her shaking hands. Was her self-control slipping so easily? Her hands twitched as she lowered them. But how dare the madwoman say such things about Cosette?

Madame Savon continued by without another glance in their direction, muttering about wolves, witches, and troublemakers. Rose wasn't certain which of the last two categories Madame Savon considered her. Maybe both.

Rose clamped down on the shout wanting to escape her mouth. Cosette would never be harmed. Not if she had any say about it.

One of the huntsmen started to speak, but a town crier called out at that moment. All turned to listen, hanging on to every bit of news possible. His horse's hooves pounded through the town as he repeated his message.

"The Mesdemoiselles of the Mountain are coming this way! Bring yer valuables. The Mesdemoiselles of the Mountain are on their way! Three months."

Rose's heart leaped. Food! The three women chilled her to her core, but they brought food. Somehow. Not a thing would grow in the entirety of France, yet they had food to barter and sell every couple of months.

Lights flicked on throughout the village, following the

crier's path, then quickly extinguished as people saved their precious candles. Several came out of their homes.

The crier thundered out of the small village, off to the next.

Rose spun back to the huntsmen. Her eyes sought the one who'd started to speak, and her eyes demanded he continue.

"I can give you eighteen livres for the wolf's fur, and another five for the meat." He shrugged, looking apologetic. "Though there isn't much there, and it'll be tough as bark."

Rose stared at the huntsman, eyes wide. That much? She'd expected him to swindle her. The meat was worth half that. Less, perhaps.

After too long a moment of silence, the burly man broke it. "Fine, I'll give you a hindquarter of the meat as well. But only after the steward has seen it. Deal?"

Rose nodded, her mind spinning with possibilities. If she made money from bringing in wolves . . . Could she do this for a living? Become a huntress?

Cosette would never be hungry again. Her family could eat. Her eyes trailed after the town crier. Maybe she could travel with the Mesdemoiselles' wagon . . .

He leaned forward. "But you will tell no one the huntsman wasn't with you. You will tell no one you killed the beast yourself. Understood?"

Rose's jaw clenched, but she nodded. She'd just have to kill another and take it to the steward herself.

Her eyes drifted to the huntsman who'd deserted them, but he busied himself looking off into the darkened forest beyond the flickering light.

She ensured he felt the heat of her glare, however.

Rose turned back to the lead huntsman once the nameless huntsman started to squirm.

She held out her hand, her mind spinning with how

much she was being paid for the wolf—how was that even possible?—and a weighted bag was placed there.

She poured the coins into her hand and carefully counted each one.

Then she was running. As she passed her sister, she grabbed Cosette's trembling hand and hauled her toward their cottage.

Wait until her brothers saw this! Her père! Her sisters! They would survive.

Rose waited all that night. All the next morning. Past when the rooster would've crowed were he still alive, past when the sun peeked over the horizon, past when it blazed in the sky above, muted by thick, dreary clouds.

And still they all slept.

Rose paced. How could her family sleep all day, then complain about the candles wasting away when they were up most the night? They may have made and sold them, but they couldn't afford to waste even one candle. There was never enough, but their laziness made it worse.

A knock at the door sent her bolting toward it. She paused, then scrambled to hide the money pouch. Surely a thief would kill for the number of coins she'd received the night before.

Then she turned and bolted toward the door once again.

Cosette calmly answered before she reached it, tossing a reprimanding look so much like Mère's, a pang shot through Rose's heart.

"Oui? Oh, merci. I can't thank you enough. You are too kind."

Rose peeked over Cosette's shoulder. Her face fell. Oh. The huntsman they'd spoken with earlier. She'd hoped Père might come home. Then fear flared in her gut. Did he want the money back?

Rose clenched her fists and prepared to fight. Well, he couldn't have it. Her family wouldn't survive without it.

The hunstman jerked his head toward the carcass dangling down his back, turning so they both could see it. "Where do you want it?"

Rose's mouth fell open. The entire wolf, gutted and stripped of his patchy coat, hung down the man's back, dripping blood.

Cosette opened the door wide and waved him toward their table. "So much meat, Monsieur? I thought we were to receive a portion?"

He stalked past her sister and slammed the bloody meat onto the wooden planks. The huntsman's eyes sought Rose's. "It seems tales of the Mademoiselle's bravery reached the steward before I did. He said to give you the meat with his blessing."

Rose snorted. He could keep his blessing. It was because of the steward their land was stripped of remaining resources so quickly. She wanted the prince back, not some upstart steward whose name she didn't even know.

She wanted her people to remember what they'd lost.

The huntsman slipped an axe from his belt and deftly started hacking the animal into more manageable portions. It didn't take him long to finish.

Must've been a gift from the steward as well.

Cosette spoke in low tones the moment he stopped, her gracious manner a rival to any Mademoiselle who used to grace the prince's court. "How lovely of him. Thank you for bringing it to us. There is freshly made mead in the kitchen, should you want any."

Rose shivered. Nasty stuff. She missed wine and fresh water and milk.

The huntsman grunted, his axe now back at his waistband, and headed that way, his eyes darting around the inside of their home.

Defensive about the hovel, Rose wanted to object, but Cosette lifted a warning hand. Rose grudgingly admitted to herself all the cottages on this side of the village were the same, thanks to unimaginative and lazy builders.

Rose started to whisper, but Cosette spoke over her, moving away. "Thank you again. I will always remember your kindness."

Rose rolled her eyes. Kindness, her foot. The huntsman was only there seeking a smile from any one of Rose's lovely sisters. Too bad the entire horde was in bed.

She and Cosette were not nearly as lovely as the rest of the girls who didn't work. Rose's fists clenched.

She glared at the man who was supposed to offer protection, yet let two starving girls do his job. Mead trickled down his beard. He looked like a fool. She rather enjoyed it.

Cosette shook her head at Rose, then smiled at the departing huntsman before she shut the door softly. Rose stalked to her side and eyed the slab of wolf. If the shrunken thing could be called that.

"Do you need any help?" Rose asked her sister.

Cosette stifled her horror a moment too late. "Um, non, dear." Her smile turned impish. "I'd like there to be a little meat left when I'm done with it."

"I won't drop it this time. Promise."

Cosette shook her head. "I was more concerned it might go up in flames. It has to last as long as possible, you know."

Rose flushed. Cosette lifted on her toes to drop a quick kiss on her sister's cheek, then hefted the haunch of meat in her slender arms, leaving the rest behind.

Rose stood in the center of the room, tapping her toes. She glanced out the window for the hundredth time, trying to gauge the position of the sun through the clouds. "That's it."

She darted out of the room and tugged her two brothers from their shared bed. They were lucky there were only two of them, not seven. Their new cottage was far too crowded.

Rose started to miss her old home—in the wealthy part of town—but jerked herself away. Such thoughts only caused agony.

"Claude! Pascal. Wake up! Come see."

Groans met her urging, but she prodded them the entire way to the table anyway, now cleared of the wolf.

Rose plunked the small bags of coins on the rough-hewn surface and waited. The sleep drained away as her brothers' eyes widened. She smiled.

Exactly the reaction she was looking for.

She overturned the bag and let a few coins scatter across the part of the table not smeared with blood, then peeked behind her. Cosette was busily preparing the meat in the kitchen, out of earshot.

She turned back to her brothers and leaned forward.

"I can trust you. Right?"

Nods and half-awake mumbling met her stern glare.

"This is for Cosette. Not Père. Not Bernadette, Yvette, Reinette, Nicolette, or Lynette. Just Cosette. She doesn't starve, and she never goes into the woods to check the traps. Understood?"

"Aw, Ro," Claude said. "We don't even know when the wagon comes back through—"

She cut him off. "Three months. They will be here in three months. Buy as much as you can. You know the food never goes bad." Her eyes narrowed. "Somehow . . ."

Pascal slumped. "And to think I could still be sleeping. You buy it." He turned to go.

Rose latched on to his arm and hauled him back. She waited until her disgruntled brothers met her gaze. She eyed them both, her gaze intense.

"I won't be coming back."

Pascal blinked. Claude's mouth fell open. "What?"

She nodded. "I'm going to go with the wagon. Find out if there's work hunting wolves. Or working the Mesdemoiselles' garden. Anything. I'll not stay here and watch our lives disintegrate into ash around us."

"Ro—"

"I don't want to—"

Her brothers' protests were cut short when she snatched up the bag and started shoving coins back into the leather pouch, her jaw clenched.

She was done begging. She knew what she had to do.

They both jumped forward at the same time.

"All right, all right!"

"Fine!"

"Whatever you say."

She let the bag fall back on the table with a dull *clack*. Claude snatched it up, Pascal's fingers too slow. They scuffled over the bag, their eyes bright when they stopped fighting long enough to take in its contents.

It may have only been livres, but it was more than any of them had had in a long time. So long. She turned to go.

"But how—"

"Where—?"

"Why?"

She spun and pierced them with a glare. "It doesn't matter how I got it. Cosette eats. She wears shoes again. Warm clothes. And she works here, in the house, away from those dreadful huntsmen. I'll worry about where the money comes from. Do those things, and you'll have plenty."

She hoped.

Pascal looked dubious, but Claude's eyes shone. It wouldn't take Claude long to convince Pascal of their good fortune. Anything to get out of work.

A few more words should persuade them both.

"Do those things, and you'll have enough. More than

enough. If I find Cosette is missing one of those things—just one!—you'll have to find a way to earn the livres yourselves."

Their eyes widened with every syllable of her tirade.

"But, Ro . . ."

The feeble objection faded into nothing.

Rose turned and strode from the room, each step singing of confidence.

Ro, she rather liked that name. Much better for a huntress than Rose. Yes, Ro. She could get used to that. She could—

Cosette peeked at her from the kitchen, a question in her eyes. Rose ducked her head and sprinted for their attic room. Three months. She had to keep the secret from Cosette for three months.

Or she'd never have the strength to leave her sister behind.

3

"Claude! Pascal! Come quickly!"

Ro's head lifted from the book she was devouring, and a frown puckered her forehead. Was that Père? Shouting?

"Oh come, my daughters, come! Bernadette! Yvette, Reinette, Nicolette, Lynette! Come at once! Rosette—my darling little rose. Cosette! My pet. Make haste!"

Ro bolted the moment she heard her name. Père hadn't spoken it in so long. She collided with a tangle of sisters at the top of the stairs, the lot of them staring down the steps as though some madman had broken into their home and now threatened their very lives. Ro rolled her eyes.

Pascal and Claude pushed their way through the girls, and Ro followed in their wake.

The girls clomped down the stairs but refused to step off, once again clogging the pathway.

Père stood in the front doorframe, letter in hand, beaming, his loose, now-gray hair blowing wildly in the blustering breeze. Ro's gaze jumped between the letter and the smile on his face.

He was smiling. Really, actually smiling.

She must be dreaming. She couldn't allow hope to blossom, not yet, but her traitorous heart beat wildly in her chest.

Her eyes sought Cosette's while her brothers demanded to know what the letter said. Cosette stood in the doorway, arms full of dried candles, blue eyes wide.

The straggling sunlight shone through the window behind her, illuminating her gorgeous blonde hair for a glorious moment and making her look like the angel she was.

Cosette shrugged, a hopeful smile tugging at her lips, and they returned their attention to Père.

"Quiet now! Quiet now. It says"—he perched a pair of spectacles on his nose—"'Monsieur Michèl-Pierre Reynard the third, we make haste to inform you that your cargo vessel, the Jacqueline Rose—'"

Ro's heart squeezed at the mention of Mère's name. They may have lost everything, but the loss of that one ship was more painful than any other loss. Père had never been himself since that day. Well, not till today. She shook herself and paid attention.

"'—therefore we ask you to hurry to *le Port de Calais* and claim her fortunes. The ship is full to bursting, its cargo and crew intact.'"

Everyone cheered. Except Ro. A small smile blossomed on her face. Dare she hope?

Her sisters flung themselves at their père, and her brothers linked arms and started singing and dancing in circles like the fools they were.

Père extracted himself from his children's hugs and blustered around, accomplishing nothing at all. "I must away at once. My horse. Where's my horse?"

"I've got it, Père." Claude dashed away.

"And I'll make sure your saddlebag is packed for a long journey." Pascal followed his brother.

Reinette squealed, her wheat-blonde curls bouncing, and called after her brother. "He doesn't need anything for a long journey, halfwit. He's coming back rich!"

"Ooh, ooh, ooh!" Bernadette pushed her way forward. "Bring me a gown, Père. A ballgown. Dripping of lace, the best you can find."

As the oldest, Bernadette thought her word was law and the rest of them had to obey her merest whim. Ro snorted. She may have shared her eldest sister's dark hair, crystal-blue eyes, and willowy build, complements of their père, but that was where the similarities ended. She hoped. Bernadette was the worst snob of them all, and Ro dearly wanted to take her down a few pegs.

The rest of the girls shared variations of Mère's golden-blonde hair and lovely blue eyes, but Cosette was the only one who retained her gentle spirit. All the bickering? Well, Ro had no idea where that came from.

"Bring me diamonds!"

"And ruby slippers."

Bernadette shot Reinette a scowl. "They don't make those, halfwit."

Reinette's deep-blue eyes flashed. "Chantrice had a pair at the last dance we attended in Paris, and I want ones just like them. Non! Better. Diamond slippers! Teach her to stick her nose up at me."

"Bring me pearls, Père."

"Ah! I know. A peacock fan. Ten of them!"

The girls' voices joined as one, and they tried to outshout each other as they asked for the most ridiculous and expensive gifts they could think of. Things that had once been commonplace.

Père broke away, eyes on Ro. Her heart stuttered, and she drank in the sight of his smile, his lucid eyes, his attention on her.

"You have not yet said what you wanted, little Rose."

Her mind went blank, and she blurted out the first thing that came to it. "A rose," she squeaked.

Her sisters laughed, and Ro ducked her head.

"A rose? Simpleton. He could bring you a thousand roses!" Bernadette laughed, always the most outspoken and cruel of the sisters. Whether she meant to be or just didn't realize how she sounded, Ro wasn't sure.

Père gently lifted Ro's chin. As soon as their eyes connected, tears filled hers.

"A rose, dear child? Are you sure that's all you want? I could bring you so much more."

She choked and nodded. All she really wanted to do was to fling her arms around him and sob. How her heart ached at the sight of him!

Before she worked up the courage to slip her arms around Père, whom she feared might brush them aside in the next instant, or to show her sisters the depth of her feelings, who would most definitely mock her for years to come, he moved on to Cosette.

Ro wrapped her arms around herself and turned away from her sisters, pretending to watch his exchange with Cosette. She didn't want her sisters to see the tears spilling down her cheeks. Her entire being ached to feel his arms around her again.

"And what of you, dearest Cosette? What can I bring my little pet?"

Cosette wrapped her arms around his waist and stared up at him with adoring eyes, the loveliest blue of all. She didn't care what her sisters thought. Ro envied her. "Only you, safely back from your trip. There is nothing more I want in the world."

Ro shook her head. Only Cosette could forgive the last fifteen years in an instant.

The jeers and heckling from her sisters started at once, but now they sounded much more poisonous.

"Well, of course she does. Pretty dresses wouldn't look fetching on her anyway."

"Thinks she's better than us, more like."

"Well, I think she's a snob."

Ro's eyes flashed. Her sister was the prettiest of them all. Well, she had been. And the kindest. She'd only taken two steps, rage boiling, when Cosette's hand wrapped around her arm.

She looped her arm through Ro's and pulled her away, lowering her voice so only Ro could hear.

"Let's not give any of them a black eye today, dearest. Let Père's memory of his departure be a happy one."

"They shouldn't say such things about you."

"Non, they shouldn't. But they do. You have to learn how to let it go, love. You can't control anyone but yourself."

"Yes, Mère."

Cosette's eyes glistened. "It's wonderful her ship was found, isn't it?"

All the fight vanished from Ro. Her heart ached with longing. "I'd give anything to have her back with us."

"Me too, dearest, me too."

"Well, I must be off!" Père beamed at them all, taking time to kiss each daughter's cheek and shake his sons' hands. Pascal held the horse still while Claude handed him his saddlebag. Their père thundered away, pausing at the gate to wave.

"Don't forget my dress!"

"Or my diamonds!"

"Who cares about you? Remember my pearls, Père!"

Cosette shook her head, and Ro directed a glare her sisters' way that was promptly ignored.

Père disappeared, and the siblings took their time to make their way back into the house, even with the frigid air that should've been warm and full of spring. Ro took a deep breath. Snow was on the wind.

Cosette clapped her hands. "All right, dear ones. Claude, Pascal, the barn still needs to be mucked and the animals fed. Girls, let's clean this house from top to bottom to prepare for Père's arrival."

Lynette yawned and sprawled across their threadbare couch. "Why should we? He'll be months in returning, and by then we'll have servants to attend us. As it should be."

Her twin sister Nicolette joined her, shoving her sister's feet to the side and plopping down in the available space. "Yeah, who made you our boss all of a sudden, Cosette?"

Both had honey-blonde hair and cornflower-blue eyes and had made quite a stir at balls in times past with their petite figures, demure smiles, and mischievous twinkles in their eyes.

They could've been such fun, Ro was sure of it, had they not followed Bernadette in everything she said or did.

Cosette's eyes sparkled, and she gave them a good-natured wink. "Père did, of course. Just as he does each time he goes away."

Bernadette pushed into the room, displacing Reinette and Yvette, who were lounging against the doorframe. "I'm the eldest. I should be in charge."

Cosette offered her the basket full of freshly made candles she still held. "Then would you be a dear and finish storing the candles? I have no problem sweeping the room in your place."

Bernadette pulled away from the candles and wrinkled her nose. "And smell as you do? Never! Why we can't have beeswax instead of that awful-smelling tallow, I'll never know."

Ro crossed her arms, mimicking her brothers' poses. They grinned and said nothing, enjoying the bickering. Ro wasn't so laid back. Unfortunately. Each flung word filled her with more and more tension until she feared she would burst. Maybe a little teasing was in order, instead of the sharp retort she wished to fling her sister's way.

Ro smirked. "You mean since the bees all died? Or when the flowers stopped growing?"

Bernadette shot her a glare. "Thanks to you, Père's trip will take longer. He'll have to scour the entire countryside to find a rose."

Ro's heart dropped. Bernadette was right.

Reinette's face only held curiosity. "Why did you ask for a rose? Because of your name?"

She flushed. More like because of Mère's name. "I-I haven't seen one in so long. I wasn't thinking—I'm sorry—"

"Oh, hush now." Cosette bustled around the room, cleaning things that were already clean but so threadbare, they might fall apart any second. "If Père truly has his fortunes restored, he can hire someone to hunt for a rose."

Bernadette huffed and crossed her arms. "You know he won't. Anything for his precious Rose."

She sent a glare Ro's way. As if Ro could be responsible for her own birth.

Pascal interrupted. "I can't believe you didn't ask to go with him, Bernadette, and acquaint yourself with your former beaux."

Only Ro saw the teasing glint in his eyes.

Bernadette gasped. "Oh non! Now why didn't I think of that?" She ran around the room graced with white-and-yellow décor, doing nothing of value, very much like Père had just done. "Quick! Help me get ready. Do you think I can catch him?"

Claude laughed. "Do you intend to walk the whole way, ma chère?"

Bernadette stilled, her glare back in place, and huffed. "Do I look like someone who would do that?" She tilted her head. "Why do you ask?"

Pascal shrugged. "We only have the one horse, he is old, and Père needs to ride. By all means, run after him, but you'll have to walk the whole way to the Port of Calais."

"Oh, phooey!"

The boys looked at each other, then burst into laughter. Ro chuckled. She got the brunt of Bernadette's glare.

"Well I hope you are satisfied when Père searches the whole of France then dies when he can't find the one thing you asked for." Bernadette stomped out of the room and up the stairs, temper in full swing.

Ro raised an eyebrow as Cosette cried, "Now, that isn't kind! Come back and apologize this instant!"

Did Bernadette listen? Of course not. Ro wondered why Cosette even tried.

"Let her go, little pet. The room will be better for it." Claude winked at Cosette.

Lynette scrambled up from her sprawled position on the couch. "Wait! Dies? What about my pearls?"

Cosette raised her hands, exasperation close at hand. Ro leaned forward, almost hoping her angelic sister would lose her composure. It would be a nice change from the even, levelheaded saint who lived among them. Then again, she rather enjoyed having at least one sister who wasn't full of spite.

"Now listen, all of you. We do not know for certain that Père's fortunes are absolute. He may get there only to find the money gone."

Bernadette's stomping footsteps on the stairs halted. All chatter ceased. Each sister stared at Cosette with an expression of disbelief plastered on her face, including Ro.

The explosion of noise was almost painful.

"What do you mean?"

"How could you possibly say that?"

"First Bernadette wishes him dead, now you wish him—

and us—destitute? What cruel sisters you are!" Yvette burst into tears.

Her looks, somewhere between Cosette's and Reinette's with golden-blonde hair like Cosette's yet deep-blue eyes like Reinette's, belied a certain sweetness that was no longer present, thanks to constant bickering—her sisters' favorite pastime.

"Hush, everyone! Now wait a minute. Nicolette, Reinette—listen to me." Cosette tried to calm the room to no avail.

Ro let loose an ear-piercing whistle. Cosette cringed, but Pascal gave her a nod. "Nice."

Claude shook his head. "My sister. The greatest tomboy I know. I'm so proud."

Pascal chuckled. "At least she's the only normal one of the group."

Claude shrugged. "Except Cosette, of course."

Pascal snorted. "Anyone that calm can't be normal."

Both boys snickered. Yvette shot them a glare.

"That's quite enough out of you two," Cosette interrupted.

She turned to the girls, raising her voice to ensure Bernadette heard, even though Ro was certain she was hanging over the banister.

"Of course we don't wish those things. We'd be thrilled if he returned in perfect health and a little money besides. But the money is trivial. And not definite. We must prepare ourselves in case our fortunes do not come to pass, and we must work hard in order to survive until he does return."

Footsteps clomped back downstairs, and Bernadette entered, shaking with fury. She shoved a finger in Cosette's face. "I, for one, am sick of living this way. I want my servants back. I want my own room. And I want it now."

Reinette let out a loud sigh. "Here we go again."

"I am not lifting a finger until Père returns with all of

those things. Do you hear me? If you want to work your fingers to the bone, then *you* can be *my* servant."

She stomped out of the room, pounding up the stairs much louder than necessary, then slammed her door.

The sisters sat in silence, one brother staring at the ceiling, the other at the empty fireplace.

After a few seconds, Bernadette's door opened, then slammed again, rattling the windowpanes in the shabbily made home.

The siblings glanced at each other, then burst out laughing.

If there was more stomping after that, Ro couldn't hear it over the noise of their mirth.

4

Ro counted the days until Père's return—and until the Mesdemoiselles of the Mountain arrived. Just in case.

Cosette confiscated the little pouch of livres from their brothers and hid it well until the day they could buy plenty of food, material for one new dress each—a working suit for the men, of course—and luxuries they had long been without, such as thread, needles, and wax.

If they even needed to do so after Père returned.

The other girls chatted endlessly of the mounds of things he would bring them, but Ro and Cosette never spoke a word of it, except to kneel in the little alcove used for prayers and implore for Père's safe return.

It was as if they spoke of it, their anticipated happiness might burst like a soap bubble.

Even Ro prayed. But if it shocked anyone, they never mentioned it.

As she scrubbed dishes, made disgusting meals out of roots and scraps gained from the meager income of their candles, and mucked out stalls alongside her brothers, Ro's mind drifted often to her yearly trek, and how this year had been different than any other. How she'd left before the château vanished with the rising of the sun.

How the wolf had blazed to life in the middle of the night, and how she'd been able to defeat him when it wasn't possible. But she never spoke of it, not to anyone.

And she tried numerous times to make something light up in the dark, all of its own. It never happened, and she never saw events play out in her mind before they came to be.

Must've been a one-time thing to save Cosette from the wolf, she thought, though it didn't keep her from trying to make it happen. Often.

Magic smiled as the man blinked several times, trying to take in the splendid sight before him. He stepped from the frozen, snow-laden ground onto the warm spring path, crossing from the forest into the palace grounds.

Exactly where Magic wanted him. She waited until he was inside to close the palace gates. Of course, the old man took his time, staring at each orange tree, reaching out to touch leaves, then snatching his hand back as if he could erase the mirage with one touch of his finger.

Magic didn't care what he did once he got inside—the servants would be more than willing to take over. Simpletons. He could be there to murder them all, and they would still care for him as if he were the prince himself. It was sickening.

Magic told herself she didn't care what happened once he got inside the castle, but she couldn't help following him at a distance anyway. And even though each act of kindness from the servants disgusted her, she dared not interfere. His time here had to be perfect.

He enjoyed a splendid meal. A nap. Exploring the castle,

each facet revealed to him as it had been in its days of glory. Another meal. Another nap. More exploring.

Magic wanted to beat her head against the wall. Maybe set something on fire, watch him scream and run. But she controlled herself.

Night came, the man slept, and morning rose over the castle wall, calling him to wake. And Magic sat in her stronghold and watched, head propped on her hand, bored out of her mind.

This could not be over fast enough.

After breaking his fast, the old man once again explored the castle. Magic tracked him at a distance, trapped in her room yet able to follow him in spirit, certain she would throw her plan to the wind if she had to watch every minute detail of his exploration.

But wait. Something was different.

She sat forward. A gleam had entered his eye. He no longer touched things hesitantly, or explored as if he were on someone else's property; now he walked confidently through the rooms. He touched things with a sense of . . . ownership. He strutted about as a titled nobleman might, not a guest.

Magic sat back, a smile gracing her face for the first time since he'd entered the castle. Perfect. Her plan was about to be set into motion. Ah, how she loved greed in any form.

It was exactly what she needed.

He flew down the staircase, shrugged on his coat, and ran for the stables. Magic rushed to wake the beast. She only hoped she'd be in time.

❧

"Roses. Ah, yes. I need a rose for my Rosette."

Magic stood behind the man and his mount, pointing her staff to one of the roses. Though he couldn't see her, his eyes tracked down the long staff and halted on the flower.

"Ah, yes. Of course."

Magic smiled. Perfect. He grinned and plucked the flower from the vine, moving to tuck it in his jacket's lapel. Magic stepped aside as the beast let out the most frightful bellow. Magic laughed. Oh, the look on the poor man's face was priceless!

"How dare you touch my roses! And who gave you permission to pick one? I let you stay in my palace, gave you the best hospitality known to man, and this is how you repay me?"

Magic smiled. The beast was too deliciously cranky when he'd just woken up.

"For your insolence, you shall die!"

Magic rolled her eyes. Well now the beast was just being dramatic.

The man fell to his knees, crying and begging and pleading, telling the ridiculously boring story of his children, his misfortunes, and his daughter's request for a rose.

The beast froze at one portion of the story, just as Magic knew he would.

"I will forgive you your impertinence on one condition."

"Anything! Anything at all. Name it, and it is yours."

The beast grinned, revealing fangs and saliva and too many grotesque things to name. Magic shuddered.

"Your daughter. Bring her to me."

"I—uh—what?"

The beast scowled. "Give me your daughter in exchange for the rose, and you shall not die."

"I'm sorry. Wait. Which one?"

The beast snarled and threw out his hands. "Does it look like I care? Bring me the one who asked for the rose!"

"Oui."

The beast lost some of his ire and stammered. "Y-you agree? Just like that?"

"Oui. Quite right. Very well."

Even Magic's eyes widened. Would a père truly care so little for his offspring? Her eyes narrowed. He must have something else in mind.

Nodding too many times, looking to be the complete fool that he was, the man scrambled to his feet and backed away. "So . . . I am free to go?"

The beast marched forward, grabbed the man's collar, and lifted him into the air. Magic winced from the man's shrieks and gripped her staff tighter. This should be good. If only he quieted down.

"Know that you cannot escape your promise. Know that I will find you wherever you try to run—wherever you try to hide. Know that you are no match for me, mere mortal. And if you do not return with the girl, a curse shall befall you the likes of which you have never before seen." He threw the man. "Now go. And return with your daughter in two months' time."

Sobbing, the man scrambled away. He stilled. "Y-you mean, I-I-I have to come with her?"

"Go!" the beast bellowed.

The horse bolted down the long drive, and the man took off after it.

Magic approached the beast, who was staring after the man and his horse. "Well that was rather harsh, don't you think?" Of course the beast didn't answer her. "I wonder . . . can you even make good on your threat?"

She watched the beast carefully. The air surrounding him tasted of worry and hopelessness and despair. Exactly what she liked.

She smiled. "Didn't think so. I wonder. Will you ask me for help when the time comes?" Her smile grew. "And the better question: Will I give it?"

She studied him. No change. Shoulders slumping, he trudged away. Magic laughed. The girl would never rescue him, no matter how hard he tried to find her from the confines of his magical cage.

How she loved to tease him with hope, then plunge him back into despair.

No girl would come, no girl would set him free, and no prince would ever emerge from the beast.

5

Ro sat in the alcove, her book nearly plastered to the scrubbed-clean window. Cosette had promised her as much time as she wanted to read in exchange for scrubbing all the windows.

Cosette knew exactly what it took to get something done in the least amount of time possible.

Ro huffed and dropped the book in her lap, rubbing her eyes. The muggy light was just so horrible! She couldn't use a candle, and she couldn't trust the sun to shine. She glared at the heavy clouds, a constant for far too many years. Curse whatever had brought this blight upon their fair land! She just wanted to see the sun shine again. To see something green and *alive*. To read without nearly going blind.

Her eyes dropped to the gate. It swung open, slowly, as if shifted by the wind. Ro grumbled and stood. And curse whoever had left the gate open, for the thousandth time, for vagabonds and pests to enter at whim!

A man in rags stumbled through. Oh, great. Just what she needed. To watch Cosette feed someone what they couldn't spare and then end up manhandling the beggar off the property herself.

She squinted as something odd scratched at her through her anger. He seemed . . . familiar.

"Père! He's home!"

Ro jumped at Claude's shout above her head. She spun around to see him fly out the door. She had no idea he was standing right behind her!

Siblings who'd made themselves scarce since his departure, hoping someone else would do the many chores around the crumbling home, scrambled to the front door and crowded the doorway, trying to see what Père had brought.

Ro backed away. Something was terribly wrong. Why did he look like that?

He wasn't riding. In fact, his horse wasn't with him. His coat, threadbare and tattered, was wrapped tightly around him, and he trudged forward as if he carried the weight of the world on his shoulders.

Cosette scurried out of the kitchen, face bright. Her eyes connected with Ro's, and her face dimmed. She immediately rushed to Ro's side and took her arm.

They stood like this, silent and waiting, both steeling themselves for what was to come.

Ro had always thought her sisters were stupid—well, except for Cosette, of course—but this was ridiculous. Not one of them noticed how Père looked. The state of his dress. His empty hands. True, it wasn't much different than before, but still. He should have blazed through the gate with finery such as they'd only dreamed of for so long.

"Where are they? Where are my pearls, Père?"

"Diamonds! Did you bring diamonds?"

"Are you vapid?" Bernadette pushed her way to the front. "Where is my ballgown, Père? I demand to be introduced to society. No wait. A new society. I want new friends, not those false people who abandoned us at the first hint of misfortune." She strained to see past him. "Where are the servants? Do they bear your luggage?"

Père pushed past them. Claude and Pascal stepped back from the mob of girls, staring at him with pale faces, tight jaws, and wide eyes.

Cosette and Ro stepped back as their père came toward them, steps dragging, the dead look back on his face. He paused, staring at nothing at all. Fear enveloped Ro's being. Oh no. It couldn't be. He—he wasn't himself. Again.

Her heart shriveled and turned cold.

Ro studied his face, hoping for a change. But non, nothing.

Cosette gripped her arm, fingernails digging painfully. Ro didn't care. Nothing mattered anymore.

He continued forward, then paused next to Cosette. His eyes stared past her, seeing nothing. "You have your wish, little pet. I am home. For all the good it will do you."

Cosette's eyes filled with tears, but she lifted her chin. "Nothing in the world matters more."

He didn't seem to hear her. He shuffled forward a few steps, then stopped next to Ro.

He shoved something into her hands, but she couldn't look at it, not while that blank look was on his face. Something sharp pricked her finger, and dizziness consumed her, but she didn't care. She couldn't stop staring at his face.

"Your rose. You have no idea how much it cost me."

He stumbled into the sitting room, lowered himself into his chair, and stared into the fire. Just as he'd done nearly every day since Mère died and his ships were lost at sea.

Fury started to build. How dare he be so weak! How dare he not face what was happening—force his children to face it in his stead. Force *them* to care for *him*. He was no man. Not one she could respect, anyway.

She opened her mouth to tell him just that—she was done waiting and wishing and hoping for his return—when her sisters surrounded his chair.

"What happened?"

"You must tell us immediately!"

Pascal cleared his throat, a sheen in his eyes, "Oui, mon père, you must. What happened to you?"

That was the question burning in Ro's soul. What had happened to him? How did a person get to the point that he gave up and left, even though he was sitting right there? Ro's jaw clenched.

She didn't understand it. And she would never forgive him for it.

Cosette, always so in tune with Ro's every thought, squeezed her arm. "Patience, my love."

Ro growled. "I have been patient. Enough is enough."

Cosette shot her a concerned look the same time Pascal did. Claude moved closer to Père. "What of the gold? The treasure? What happened to our—your ship?"

Silence seized the room in its choking grip. The weight of the next few moments crushed Ro, driving the breath from her. Père's voice was so weak, so distant, she struggled to believe it was actually him speaking.

"Lost. All of it. Gone."

Questions exploded in a flurry around him.

"Quiet!" Pascal nodded at their père, though the man never looked Pascal's way. "Tell us of your journey, Père."

His voice was tender, gentle. Revealing the heart of gold he tried to hide under a carefree and teasing manner.

Ro waited so long, she was almost certain he wasn't going to speak. But she also wasn't leaving the room until she heard his tale.

"When I got there, the ship's goods had been dispersed. The crew had split the large profit brought in and had gone in search of their homes."

"Large profit?"

"Without contacting you!"

Claude silenced his sisters with a look.

Ro was glad. She was quite certain her fist would've caused more noise, not less.

"They thought me dead. Only the clerk at the shipping yard knew of my whereabouts, and he said he was too afraid to say anything because of how desperate the people were for the goods."

Another sister opened her mouth, but Claude quelled her with a fierce look. Bravo. Ro silently cheered him on. Now he just needed to direct that look at the lot of them to make them mind.

"I tried to track them down, but people are fearful. Willing to kill for a crust of bread. So, after several months, without any luck at all, I set off for home. A storm such as I've never seen arose, and I sought shelter."

Ro wondered how a voice could sound so dead when so many words were pouring from it. More words than he'd spoken in years. His eyes flew up and latched on to hers. Her breath caught at the intensity of it.

"I found a castle. In the woods."

Ro's heart skipped a beat. He *what*? Surely he hadn't said what she thought he had. Excitement filled her.

"Oui! Yes, I know! With eight turrets and a lined drive full of orange trees, bursting with blossoms and fruit. And the fireworks! Oh, it's so beautiful, isn't—"

Ro snapped her mouth closed. Everyone stared at her. She ducked her head, and her face filled with heat. Here came the teasing.

Père regarded her solemnly. "Oui. Beautiful. And it rose out of the mist, absent one moment and there the next, just as you said."

Ro soaked in his words, for once not feeling as if she were losing her sanity as everyone said. Someone else had seen it. Someone else had seen it! Her heart beat wildly.

"A castle? What do you mean there was a castle in the woods? What castle?"

More than one person shushed Bernadette this time.

"The minute I stepped through the gates, the storm abated. Snuffed out like a candle." His eyes drifted away. "Such loveliness. Such wealth! I was well taken care of." He moaned. "Oh, the meals! Such rich food as I haven't tasted in an age. I stayed until I felt like myself again, then I sought out my kind host. Finding no one, I was certain the castle was meant for me, and I was determined to claim it for us all."

Reinette interrupted, her voice small as she trembled under the combined glare of her brothers. "Dearest Père, could it have been a dream?"

He was quiet a moment, and Ro shot her a "thanks a lot" look. Fortunately, he started to speak again.

"I wondered that myself. How could anything so beautiful be real?"

Ro's eyes widened. They'd called her crazy for saying she could see it! But she could. Had been able to for a long time. Well, since it had disappeared. Now Père had seen it. That's why she dragged Cosette into the woods every year.

It came to life at night, then dispersed with the rising of the sun. She would dream of happier times. And wish for the prince. Wonder what had happened to him. Why he wasn't helping her people.

But . . . the castle, though beautiful still, was only a shadow of its former glory. Yet no one believed her, no one remembered the strong prince and the kind king and beautiful queen who had once ruled. She was left to wonder if it was all a fantasy she'd made up in her head.

But non. The memories were too real.

And somehow the entire kingdom had forgotten they once had a ruler.

"As I was leaving, I found a rose." He nodded to the flower still clutched in Ro's hand, and she looked at it for the first time. She gasped. She'd never seen a lovelier rose!

White, impossibly glimmering as with a hidden light, lush and full of life, as large as her brother's hands side by side. Never had she seen something this beautiful, even when roses still grew in France.

"A—a terrible, monstrous beast sprang at me. Told me I would die for stealing his rose."

Cosette gasped, and each of her sisters looked stricken. Ro tensed. Well, that had done it. Any hope Ro had held that her sisters would believe she saw a castle in the woods vanished. She could see it in their eyes.

Perhaps he'd been too long in the woods, out in the cold, exposed to the elements. Perhaps he'd had a dream. Perhaps his sanity was slipping. Ro's shoulders sagged.

But still—there was a beast in the castle? Was that why the prince had never been heard from or seen again?

"Surely he was dreaming?" Yvette whispered. Reinette ignored her.

"I begged for my life, told him of our plight, and . . . h-he told me—" He trembled and placed his hands over his face. "Oh, mon Dieu! What have I done?"

"There, there, dear Père!" Cosette rushed forward and put her arms around him. She lifted tear-filled eyes to Ro as if to ask what to do.

Ro shook her head. She had no idea.

"The horrid beast told me I had to give one of my daughters' lives in exchange for the flower. Only then could I repay my theft. Only then would I stop a-a *curse* from befalling our family."

The color drained from Ro's face, leaving her feeling lightheaded. Another curse?

Claude and Pascal stiffened instantly. Pascal was quick with a response. "We won't let that happen, Père. You can count on it."

But Père once again acted as if he were alone in the room, talking to himself. "I tried to give it back. At least, I think I did. He wouldn't take it. Only told me to go and bring her back with me. Soon. It was soon, wasn't it? He laughed at me, didn't he? Or was it a woman? I swear I heard a woman laughing . . ."

Cosette and Ro stared at each other, eyes wide. What could they do? Could they believe any part of his tale? Ro glanced back at Père, and his eyes sought hers. She jolted at the force of his gaze.

"And the daughter to whom I gave it would pay the price."

All feeling abandoned her, leaving her numb. Had she truly heard him?

"You must go to the castle, little Rose. You must pay my debt. You are the only one who can stop the curse. It is written in the stars."

Ro jerked back as if she'd been slapped.

Fury glimmered in Pascal's eyes. "We *won't* let that happen." His words were a promise.

Ro shot him a grateful look, then her stunned gaze returned to Père.

She opened her mouth to ask a question, but his eyes drifted away, and he was lost to them all, unmoved by further questioning.

Cosette cried out, and Yvette burst into tears, followed soon by the twins. Her brothers shouted, protesting, declaring Ro would never go, but it all faded away.

Ro stared at the rose in her hands, oblivious to the noise, and wondered what in all the realms he could mean.

Then rage filled her. Rage such as she'd never felt.

How dare her père bargain his life for hers? No one controlled her destiny. Not her père, not the stars, not a magical beast, not some flower, not any *curse*. She crushed the rose in her hands, the thorns pricking her palms until blood dripped on the carpet.

"Rose?" Cosette's voice was filled with enough alarm to penetrate the haze she floated in.

"Non."

The noise in the room ceased. Ro faced her père.

"Non."

His dull eyes met hers, and she continued, whether he heard or not.

"I owe you nothing. I will not pay your debt, I will not be your scapegoat, I will not allow you to hurt us any longer."

Silence for a heartbeat.

He bolted out of his chair and slapped her. "How dare you."

Ro blinked, the pain crushing her heart more vibrant than the thorns embedded in her palm. She shook her head, trying to convince herself it hadn't just happened. To convince herself he still loved her.

Fear crashed all around her, and she couldn't think. Couldn't fathom what had just happened. He'd never struck her before. Not once.

Père took her hands, gentling his tone. "You must go. Don't you see, child? You will curse us all! There was magic in that castle such as I've never felt. What do you think will happen if I do not fulfill my promise? You *must* go."

"Non, mon père. You cannot mean it. You don't mean it. I know you don't."

"I do, and you will." He grasped her shoulders tightly.

Pascal stepped forward, then hesitated. Père leaned close, and Ro's only thought was how bony his fingers felt now. How thin he was.

"Don't you see? You can save us all! He will not kill me. He will not curse your sisters. We can live!"

"You call this living?" Ro shook her head, feeling all but five years old again. She would save them, but not how he wanted. "Non. I cannot do what you want. I will not."

He shoved her away, and Ro stumbled, catching herself from falling by grabbing his chair.

Instantly, Pascal's arm came about her shoulders and Claude stood close to her other side, one hand on her arm.

Something filled Père's face that crushed Ro more than his slap, his neglect, or his words.

Hate.

"Then you are dead to me. Get out of my sight." He turned and headed to his study. He paused and pointed one finger at her. "Don't come inside my house again. You are not welcome here."

Then he slammed the door behind him.

Ro touched her fingertips to the throbbing welt on her cheek.

Claude's voice was raspy. "Surely he didn't mean it."

"Curse us? What does he mean she will curse us?" one of her sisters wailed.

Cosette reached for her, sobbing. "Rosette . . ."

Ro shrugged off her brothers' touch and fled. Out the door, over the fence, across the field.

And she didn't stop running as heavy snowflakes began pelting her from the sky.

6

Ro dropped to the ground, sucking in each breath. Even though she couldn't breathe, she began sobbing, only there wasn't enough air to do both. She cried and cried, whimpering, trying to get enough oxygen to her air-starved lungs.

She cried for her mère. Her père. Her sisters and brothers. Her Cosette. She sobbed for everything she'd known and everything she'd lost. She cried until she couldn't cry anymore and found herself staring up at the sky, the frigid breeze gentle in the barren branches for once, snowflakes collecting on her eyelashes. Her breath poofed in silent clouds above her face.

"Oh, Mère, how I wish you were here." She hiccuped between words. "Père would've never done such a thing."

She sat up, black leaves sticking to the side of her face and hair, and began shivering uncontrollably. She'd forgotten how cold it was. Though she was certain the trembling wasn't only from the temperature.

She'd been betrayed in the worst way, and by the one who should've protected her. Loved her. By the one she'd once treasured as Mère had.

Had he ever even treasured her? His own daughter? Oui. Long ago. Now hate filled the oft-vacant eyes where love and tenderness once resided.

She shook her head, desperate to quiet the thoughts that plagued her. Where was she? She glanced around, her breaths shuddering. Her eyes riveted on a familiar gate, a long, winding drive disappearing into overgrown trees. Her old house lay beyond, out of sight. How in all the realms had she run so far?

She eased forward and reached out a hand, then froze. She couldn't. Not after what she'd just lost. Too many painful memories were buried there.

She eased away from her former home, where she'd been so happy with Mère—where they'd all been so happy—and slipped back into the trees.

Her footsteps swiftly took her to a spot more familiar than any other place she knew. Her treehouse. Supposedly built for her brothers, Ro had made more use of it than they had. It was her hiding place. Her sanctuary.

Her hands remembered the handholds without her having to remind them, and she scaled the tree, soon settling inside the structure. She looked around in awe and swiped bits of bark from her hands.

Just as she'd left it. Frozen in time. She fingered the heavy pelt left there for late nights and chill weather.

Resolution filled her. There was but one path left to her.

She would hunt wolves. And she would find the Mesdemoiselles of the Mountain, first chance she got. She'd heard the rumors since they'd first offered food to her starving village, though even she admitted she didn't pay as much attention as she ought. How could she? Her head was nearly always filled with the latest book she'd immersed herself in. But she'd heard enough.

They lived on a mountain and granted wishes. Yet their dwelling couldn't be found, not unless the Mesdemoiselles allowed it. Then they would grant one wish to the person desperate enough to find them.

And Ro would be that person. And she would become the best huntress this land had ever known, better than any of the huntsmen.

All of a sudden, her eyelids were too heavy to keep open. Without really thinking about it, she pulled the pelt over her shoulders, lay on her side, and slept.

❧

"Ro? Ro, wake up. Ro!"

Someone prodded her side. Ro bolted up, eyes wide, senses reeling, trying to focus.

"Geez, it's just us, mon chou."

"Yeah, you look crazy enough to scare a rabbit."

One of them poked the pelt. "Non, a wolf."

"Non, a whole pack of wolves."

Her brothers snickered. Ro rolled her eyes.

"What do you want?"

Their laughter faded, replaced by the most somber expressions she'd seen on their faces. Ro realized with a jolt that such looks had always been present, only they covered it with mirth. She shivered as the wolf's pelt slid down her shoulders, revealing the threadbare dress beneath.

"We thought you might come here," Pascal said quietly, slipping off his jacket and wrapping it around her.

Claude nodded. "Yeah. You all right?"

Ro just stared at them, feeling completely dead inside. "What do you think."

Pascal winced. Claude glanced away.

"Désolé." She rubbed a hand over her face. "It's not your fault."

Pascal's look was fierce. "We won't let him take you, you know."

Her half-smirk didn't reach her eyes, though her heart melted a little. "I know."

"Do you still want to go with the Mesdemoiselles of the Mountain?" Claude asked.

Ro blinked, her mind thrown into another whirlwind. *Oui! Ah, oui.* She nodded.

"Good." Pascal dropped a satchel she hadn't noticed he carried in front of her. "They'll be here today."

Ro blinked again. It seemed the only thing she could do when stuff was thrown at her at such a rapid-fire pace.

"Stop doing that. You look like a scared rabbit."

Her face flushed, and she scowled. "Doing what?"

"Yeah, that scared-rabbit blink you've got." Claude snickered again.

"Rabbits don't blink, you idiot," Ro growled.

"Sure they do. And they look just as stupid as you do."

"Shut up!"

"Pay attention!" Pascal didn't care to be sidetracked, though he had no problem doing it to others. "Everyone will be gone today—Cosette plans on using all those livres—the ones you left *us*, by the way."

Ro shrugged. "I'll get you more."

Claude nudged her and winked. "You'd better."

Surely he was joking? Ro couldn't tell.

Pascal continued as if they hadn't spoken. "And the girls are mad for shopping, so you can sneak back in and get anything we missed." He nodded at the bag.

"Yeah, we didn't want to touch your unmentionables," Claude cut in.

They both guffawed this time.

"Get on with it," Ro growled, her face once again uncomfortably hot.

Pascal shrugged. "Père left again, so we'll get the girls away—"

"I want to see Cosette."

"—except for Cosette—"

"And I don't want her to know I'm leaving."

"—and we won't say a word about you leaving. Geez, is that all?" Pascal looked cross again.

Ro smiled innocently. "That's all."

They nodded and opened the trapdoor in the middle of the floor. Claude pushed the rope ladder out, and it swung crazily as he stepped down on the first rung.

Claude pointed at the bag. "Oh, and use some tooth powder. Cause, woo-ie, do you need it."

Ro tried to smack him, but Claude scurried down and disappeared, his laughter ringing in the trees. Pascal chortled, blocking her swing at him.

He stepped onto the ladder but paused, his head and shoulders still in the treehouse. That serious look crept back on his face, and Ro's heart dropped. Would she see them again? Talk to them before years passed?

After a moment's hesitation, he reached into his pocket and produced the rose. Ro gasped, another sucker punch to her gut. It was just as lush and beautiful as when she'd first seen it, not crushed in the least, and the white flower still glowed with an inner light. He held it out to her.

"Get rid of it," she hissed.

Hurt flashed on his face, but he covered it quickly. "I think you're going to need this."

She shook her head. "Non."

He gently laid it before her. "Just think about it. I can't explain it, but you need this flower, especially if you seek the Mesdemoiselles of the Mountain." He shrugged. "Maybe you can trade it for their help."

She just looked at him.

"Be there as soon as you can. I can't guarantee Père won't be back soon."

Ro nodded, her jaw tight. "You can count on it."

7

Claude stood in the yard with a rake. But of course he wasn't using it. Just leaning on it while he watched for Père's return. Ro shook her head. Typical.

Ro waited behind the stable. "Ro. My name is Ro," she muttered to herself.

Today was the day. The day she would leave her village, Rose no more. Ro, a strong, vibrant huntress who answered to no man.

Pascal left their house and hurried toward her, Cosette at his side. He waved Cosette on and stayed in front of the barn, where he could easily see the other side of the cottage.

Ro frowned. Père must've unnerved them all last night.

"Rose!" Cosette flung herself at her sister and held on tight. "Oh, I am so sorry. Are you all right?" She pulled back and searched Ro's eyes.

"I'm fine." She tried to smile, but it stuck somewhere in her throat, and she swallowed hard instead. "Really, I'm fine."

"Non, you're not." Her voice turned soft. "He should've never hit you."

Ro's eyes turned flinty. "Non, he shouldn't have."

Cosette's sympathy instantly turned to concern. "What will you do?"

Ro shrugged and looked away.

"I see."

Ro glanced back, alarmed. Did she?

A bright smile replaced Cosette's frown. "I'm sure Père didn't mean it. He must've been tired from his trip. Disheartened. We'll talk to him. He'll apologize. You'll see."

Ro shook her head. Wasn't that just like Cosette to try to find the positive side of everything?

Cosette squeezed her hand. "Wait here. I'll go get the baskets." She hurried toward the little cottage.

Ro soaked in her sister's every step. Memorizing every detail. She shook herself from staring once Cosette disappeared around the corner. She took a deep breath and leaned against the barn, closing her eyes.

"I'm Ro. Ro. Bonjour, my name is Ro. Nice to meet you. I'm Ro." She groaned. She needed to sound strong, confident, not like she was scared out of her mind. She squared her shoulders and stared at the stone fence bordering their property. "Bonjour. I'm Ro. Hunter. Huntress. Of things."

Someone bumped her shoulder. "Just keep talking to yourself, mon chou. People will think you're as crazy as Madame Savon."

She gasped and jerked toward the voice. "Claude! Aren't you keeping watch?"

He shrugged. "It's more entertaining to watch you talk to yourself."

"I am *not* talking to myself."

Claude raised an eyebrow, and his eyes blazed with mirth. "Oh? Perhaps you *should* take Madame Savon's place. Before people start to talk . . . of things."

She slugged his arm and started to give a sharp retort, but Cosette was back, smiling at her, two large baskets over both arms. "Of course they won't. She's a dear."

Claude snorted.

The tiniest smile materialized on Ro's face.

Cosette waved, her movement hampered by the baskets. "I've got to get there before all the goods are gone. See you when we get back from the village!" Her eyes held a promise. "We'll talk then."

Ro held her smile in place by the sheerest of willpower. *Non, we won't.*

The smile vaporized the moment Cosette's back was turned. Ro watched Cosette, flanked by Claude and Pascal, walk away. Pascal glanced back at Ro, brow scrunched, eyes sad.

Ro gave a firm nod. He sighed and turned back around, and the three disappeared around the bend.

Her eyes sought the void where the château should have been. "Give me strength," she prayed to no one in particular. Maybe the Creator still heard her. Maybe not.

She darted inside and gathered what she needed quickly, before her sisters came back or Père caught her in his home. If he even bothered returning from his aimless wanderings. One thing was certain: she wouldn't be coming back.

She took a leather strap and tied back her hair. She changed into her brother's trousers, grabbed Père's old crossbow, and stuffed anything else she needed in the bag her brothers had given her. Then she took the same trail as her siblings, soon gaining on them in her haste.

She crouched behind a cluster of barrels—once holding the finest wine in France, now cracked and dry—and waited until her siblings were done at the market and heading home. The rest of the town square bustled with townspeople trading for much-needed goods.

Cosette's voice rang out, and Ro tucked herself tighter into her hiding spot.

"Can you believe it? Look at all we were able to buy! Wait till Rose sees!"

Ro peeked as her sister pranced past her, capturing the joy on her sister's face in her memory forever. "I will never forget you," she whispered.

Soon Cosette's happy chattering faded and disappeared entirely.

Ro took a deep breath, stood, and made her way to the Mesdemoiselles' wagon. Her heart clenched at the thought of having to face the three women. They made her skin crawl. But Cosette was worth it.

She glanced up and froze. An old man, tall and still full of vibrant life, though his hair was peppered with gray, handed out vegetables in the Mesdemoiselles' place.

She blinked. Who was he?

She waited, invisible in the crush of villagers whose only goal was to trade for enough food to last until the Mesdemoiselles' wagon came again. But where were they?

Not one else appeared. Just the old man, working by himself. Someone called him "wagon master." Ro took a deep breath. Then he was the one she needed to ask.

Ro made her way forward, slipping through the throng, and stood tall before him. She met his eyes without a flinch.

"I wish to see the Mesdemoiselles of the Mountain."

She expected the wagon master to object. He simply eyed her for the briefest of seconds, then jerked his grizzled head toward the covered wagon. "Get in."

He then continued distributing vegetables in exchange for any valuables the people of Champagne had left.

Ro swallowed and peeked inside the enclosed wagon, expecting to be greeted by the haggard women she so loathed to see. Nothing. Just vegetables, lush and ripe. Apparently she would meet the Mesdemoiselles elsewhere.

She slipped past the mounds of food and settled in the ever-widening empty spot, thankful the flaps would hide her should her sister decide to come back.

While she waited, her gaze strayed to the castle, where it

should've peeked through the flaps. She moved one aside to see better. Nothing. She settled back to wait. And hide. Her eyelids grew heavy.

She jolted awake, and the wagon dipped, swaying gently as it rumbled away from her village. Moonlight beamed brightly all around the wagon, the noises of trade and haggling having died away.

The castle, glaring white in the vibrant moonlight, arrested her full attention.

She wanted to capture the sight forever, but the desire to do so slipped away. The prince hadn't saved them. Père hadn't rescued her. The Creator hadn't restored her mère or her land. She was leaving her home, the sister she loved, to track wolves like a common huntsman. Her jaw clenched.

But wait. How could she see the castle again so soon? It hadn't yet been a year.

A voice whistled through the trees, carried on the breeze. "Huntresssss . . ."

She jolted awake, the noise of trade drowning out the dream. Murky light from an overcast sky greeted her, and she pulled back one of the flaps. Still in her village. Still daytime. Yet the horror of that one word stayed with her.

She eased back into her spot. Chatter came and drifted away as customers procured their coveted goods.

No matter that it had been a dream, every bit of it was true. She could trust no one but herself.

She had no idea how long she sat there and seethed, but the wagon master soon emptied his wagon of vegetables, now piled high with furniture and trinkets instead, climbed into the seat, and set the cart in motion.

Anger slid through her as the towering castle in her mind faded from view. She would never wait for someone else to rescue her. She would never wait for a prince to save her, not again.

She would never be helpless. She would become the huntress, Ro, and she'd be good at it.

A town crier thundered through the village, shouting something about a Gautier, though Ro couldn't make out what. Cheers followed the announcement.

The cart exited the village, rocking from side to side to the cries of "Gautier! Gautier will save us!"

Ro clutched the sides of the wagon as it swayed. Gautier be hanged—whoever he was.

She couldn't escape fast enough.

❧

Ro tossed in her sleep. She knew she was asleep. She knew she dreamed. But no matter how hard she tried, she couldn't wake up.

She fought harder.

Three witches on broomsticks circled her, black cloaks flapping in the wind. Their screeches and laughter filled the air; they laughed at her. They were bent on tormenting her. And Ro had no idea why.

Ro had never been so terrified in her life. Yet she still couldn't make herself wake up.

Ro stood frozen below them as they circled her, taunting her. Their twisted faces, vicious sneers, and hate-filled eyes washed over her, and her knees shook. Why couldn't she move?

Then the first dove at her. She had just enough time to see the second and third follow their leader before she turned and fled.

She could move. Finally!

She ran and ran, but she never covered any distance.

Something hit her from behind, and she slammed into the ground.

"Non!" she cried.

"Yesss . . ." a wicked voice hissed in her ear.

She tried to scramble to her feet, but a broom handle pinned her to the ground. Two more swiftly followed.

The more she struggled, the more they laughed. Her back ached in pain.

Ro was too scared to sob, too frightened to make a noise. She opened her mouth in a silent scream and clawed to get away.

She was flipped roughly to her back. She stared into the faces of her assailants. Black crept through their veins. A gray hue overtook their decaying features, features straight from a nightmare. Black teeth, black nails, black eyes. Hatred spilled from them, directed solely at her, as spittle flew out of hissing mouths and gnashing teeth.

Why did they hate her so much? She didn't understand.

One of them leaned forward, and Ro tried with all her might to press herself into the ground.

"Now that we have found you, huntress, we will not let you escape. You will die!"

They flew at her as one, black claws and deadened fingers outstretched, reaching for her face to tear her apart.

8

Ro's head cracked against the side of the wagon, and she woke with a gasp. The wagon jerked crazily as it settled to an abrupt halt. She bolted upright. Where was she? When had she fallen asleep?

Oh, all the saints above, that *dream*! She rubbed her arms, trying desperately to erase the images from her mind, but they continued to swirl around her memories and haunt her.

The wagon seat creaked, and heavy boots hit the earth with a *thump*, then pounded toward her.

She scrambled down the bed of the wagon to the back and jumped over the edge, landing with a jolt. Her wide eyes met those of the wagon master. He nodded past her, then started tying back the wagon's canvas walls.

Ro cautiously peeked behind her, then forgot everything else.

So much green. Everywhere. It filled her senses until she could almost taste it. Grass, shrubs, hedges, trees. The soft rustle of leaves danced in the wind. Sunlight streamed through branches bursting with life, warming her face. She was in a haven not known since the prince had left his people to fend off a curse they couldn't even begin to understand. Oh, the greenery!

And sunlight! Bright, blazing, yellow gloriousness.

Not the muggy fog that permeated her entire existence —since that day. The day the world had stopped, gray had invaded the sky, and black had overrun the green.

She barely heard his heavy boots circle the wagon to the other side.

Tears wanted to fill her eyes, but she couldn't find the strength to call them forth. She took a deep breath and just enjoyed the sweetness of it all.

A horse shifted, leather creaked, and Ro jerked back to her surroundings. The wagon still stood beside her, and she still didn't know where she was.

She edged around the wagon, afraid to touch it and awaken from the first lovely dream she'd had since Mère died. The ancient wagon driver, his back to Ro, stood talking to a goddess, a woman so lovely she couldn't be of this world.

Tall, stately, dressed in deep-red velvet, hair black as midnight, falling to her waist in rich, undulating silk. Her very presence filled the air around Ro and commanded her attention. Who was she?

Where were the Mesdemoiselles of the Mountain?

They were old, ugly, terrifying, and held all of France in their arthritic hands.

Ro stilled. The dream. She shook her head and laughed. She'd been so terrified to speak with them again, her dreams had made them into witches.

She chuckled at herself, crossed her arms, and leaned against the wagon, waiting for the wagon master to finish his conversation so they could continue on to the Mesdemoiselles of the Mountain.

As though the woman had heard her thoughts, her eyes left the wagon master's face and latched on to Ro—eyes dark and fathomless, skin, flawless. She smiled with blood-red lips and beckoned Ro forward. "Come, ma fille."

Ro straightened and took a hesitant step forward, once again overcome by the lush greenery behind the woman. A garden. A real one. Filled with vegetables. Beautiful, lush, glowing vegetables.

Ro's mouth dropped open, and her eyes shot to the woman in the clearing. "You grow all this food?"

The woman grinned, lovely, yet . . . not. "You could say that."

"But how—why—how?"

The woman winked at her. "Magic."

Ro shook her head. She needed to untie her tongue this instant. Well, what she really needed was Cosette. She always knew exactly what to say and in the loveliest way possible. Ro straightened and pulled back her shoulders. She would have to do.

She met the woman's eyes boldly. "May I see the Mesdemoiselles of the Mountain?"

The woman's smile crawled through Ro's belly and made everything vile come to life. Ro refused to squirm. The woman nodded, as regal as any courtier. "At your service, Mademoiselle."

"Y-you?"

The woman winked. "Oui. I'm the only Mademoiselle of this Mountain, in fact."

The woman's image wavered, and a hint of the pasty, frail creature that had visited her village peeked through. Yet there was something else Ro couldn't quite grasp . . .

At once Ro was back in her dream, being tortured by three witches. The woman before her, one of them.

She snapped back to reality, gasping for breath. "You're a witch?" she demanded, her voice more breathless than she would've liked.

The woman smiled, her beautiful visage wavering between bliss and all things hideous. "Oui."

"And you're the only one?" That couldn't be right. Ro had seen three. There were three of them. And they were haggard and ugly. Who was this woman? "What happened to the others?"

Her smile turned positively giddy, her voice filled with delight. "I killed them."

The witch's laugh sent shudders vibrating up and down Ro's spine. "You—you wouldn't."

Her eyes darted to the wagon master. He now unloaded the cart, not a change to his expression. He retrieved a small chest from under the wagon seat and carried it inside a house set behind the garden.

"Oh, but I did. Then I ate them."

Ro took a step back, her face twisting in revulsion. Any desire to ask anything of this woman shriveled up and died. She'd rather ask the huntsmen in her village.

And that wasn't going to happen.

The woman stalked toward her, the cadence of her words low, rumbling, exquisite, and Ro very much felt like prey. "You know how it is with sisters. Can't stand them, wish to be rid of them, then *poof*"—she stopped just in front of her and made an exploding motion with her hands—"it's done. No more troublesome, petty, nagging, grasping sisters. You know what I mean, don't you?"

The Mademoiselle's eyes bored into her very soul.

Ro hesitated as an unholy desire unfurled inside of her. The woman's words actually tempted her. It was what she wished for night and day—to be rid of her sisters.

All but one.

Her stomach clenched, and she hated herself. What she'd wished for and what this woman had done were but a breath away. Ro feared this is what she'd become if she let hatred lead her—the burning, broiling hatred that had consumed her since her life had spiraled out of control.

Ro shook her head furiously. "Never. I would never—"

No matter how many times she'd wished to be rid of them, she'd never kill them. Or eat them. What in all the realms?

"Oh? Never? Not any of your five sisters who refuse to work? Refuse to help? Those who pick on the youngest—"

Ro shuddered violently and threw her hands up, slamming her thoughts to emptiness.

"Oh. You can block me?"

I what?

"I see. It is no matter. I will learn her name soon enough. No mortal can withstand me." She flounced a few steps toward the wagon. "Fill it to the rim, Hamish! The townspeople are desperate for my goods." She smiled at Ro. "No matter where they come from."

Ro had to get out of here. Now.

She turned to run down the road they'd just traveled, but the wagon master was there, blocking her.

He nodded toward the house, wordlessly, right past the large burn pile he'd been heaving furniture into.

Ro didn't know what to do. So she made her way to the house, her heart beating wildly. What made her obey?

Her trembling knees and fear-wracked heart, that's what. Why oh why hadn't she stayed in her village?

The Mademoiselle of the Mountain fell in step behind her, and Ro's back crawled with the thought of that woman's gaze upon her.

She glanced back once. The woman smiled, a cunning, vicious thing, teeth stunningly white against too-red lips. Ro spun back around and marched forward, the wagon master close behind.

She passed someone in the garden, someone she hadn't seen before. Thin, scrawny, with a shock of vibrant orange hair, the lanky lad took a moment from his hoeing to stare at her, eyes the size of silver livres.

Help me, she mouthed.

Fear flashed on his face. He glanced behind her and ducked his head, working feverishly on his row.

Ro's heart sank even further. She should've known. She couldn't rely on anyone but herself.

Her eyes glinted as she got closer to the dwelling. She would escape, she would become a huntress on her own, without the witch's help, and Cosette would never want for anything ever again.

And she wouldn't give in to whatever the witch wanted, no matter what.

9

Ro stepped inside the dwelling and spun to face the door. The wagon master stood back, allowing the witch to enter, then closed the door.

His footsteps thudded away.

The Mademoiselle of the Mountain smiled at her, sending shivers all up and down Ro's spine, and moved to the wood-burning stove along one wall. She stirred something bubbling in a midsize cauldron on the stovetop.

Ro blinked. She thought witches belonged in stories, fairy tales, or legends, not real life.

"Now, what you've come to ask me and what you're going to ask me are two completely different things. So ask it."

Ro blanched. No way. Not ever. Not as long as she lived.

She crossed her arms and lifted her chin, offering the witch her haughtiest glare.

The witch chuckled, her back to Ro. "I can't do anything without your asking it, you know."

She poured the bubbling brew into two mugs and settled them on a tray, then filled a cup with real sugar and poured lovely, white, silky cream into a small service. Ro's mouth watered. The witch settled the tray on a table set between two overstuffed chairs and motioned for Ro to join her.

"Please sit."

Ro's boots padded over the deep-red area rug covering the ash-colored planks of the floor. Ro wanted to lose herself in the luxury of her surroundings, small though the cabin was, but instead stayed focused on her host.

Ro settled into the chair offered her and waited. She ignored the teacup. No way was she drinking it, sugar and cream notwithstanding. She wasn't about to be poisoned or have a spell placed on her somehow.

The witch nodded at her and took a sip from her cup. "Proceed."

"I'd rather leave, thank you very much."

"But you can't. Don't you listen to gossip, chérie?"

Ro's brows furrowed. What on earth was she talking about?

The witch's teeth gleamed in the dim light of the cabin's interior. "You should pay more attention. You've sought the Mesdemoiselles of the Mountain." Her smile stretched wider. "Well, the Mademoiselle of the Mountain, for quite some time now, actually."

Ro's stomach sickened. What in the realms had she been thinking, seeking a witch's help? She may not be on speaking terms with the Creator, but seeking the help of someone who so blatantly hated Him was crossing so many lines.

She was an idiot.

"In order for you to leave, you must ask what you came to ask and accept whatever help I give." She nodded toward the front window. "Or you have to stay and help me for the rest of your days, like that poor fellow." She shook her head and sighed. "It was such a simple thing I asked. Can you believe he didn't want to bring me his sister's still-beating heart?"

Ro gagged and clamped her hand over her mouth. The handful of radishes the wagon master had given her were going to stay down. They were.

The witch smiled, taking her time to lift the cup to her lips. "Ask away, my dear. I have no more need of a beating heart. Not yet, anyway. My face is still young enough to please me. Or would you rather stay?"

Her face what? Ro's jaw clenched. "I'm not staying, and I'm not asking anything of you. Not after what you've done."

The witch's smile grew impossibly bright. "Oh, but you will. Do you know how I know that?"

Ro shook her head. She didn't care. She just wanted out. But she was terrified of standing up to the witch, and she hated herself for it.

"Desperation has a certain stench to it."

"I'm not desperate."

"Non? You're here, aren't you?"

Ro's heart sank. She was. With shaking hands, all thoughts of being a huntress forgotten, she reached into her brother's jacket and withdrew the white rose, still as exquisite as the day Père had given it to her, even though she'd both crushed it and slept on it. It gave off a slight glow, lighting the cabin with warmth and a sense of peace.

The witch's smile froze, and Ro could've sworn fear flashed across her face, as swift and fleeting and violent as lightning.

"Where did you get that?" she whispered.

"My père traded me for it."

The witch's eyes stayed glued on the flower, though she made no move to take it. "And why do you offer it to me now?"

Ro had no idea. None. She just wanted out, to be rid of the blasted thing, to be away from this place.

"Ask me," the witch growled.

Ro jumped and stammered, "I-I wanted you to take it from me, I guess. I wanted to know if—if the promise holds. If I have to go." *But I'm not asking anything of you. Really!* The protest stuck in her throat.

The Mademoiselle nodded slowly. "All right. I will take it from you. In exchange, I give you your freedom, from here and the promise of which you cannot speak, the promise to the beast"—Ro's eyes flashed. How did she know that?—"food for your family as long as they all shall live"—which might not be very long if the witch had anything to do with it—"and your return to your père's graces."

Hope trickled into Ro for the first time since coming to this place. The witch could do that?

The Mademoiselle smiled, her carefree manner returning. "Of course I can do that, ma fille." She winked. "I might even throw in a touch of respect from your sisters."

Now she knew the witch was lying. That was impossible.

"Put the flower down."

Ro followed the witch's nod and set it on the tray that still held steaming mugs.

The witch took a full breath once she did so, and without moving, seemed to put as much distance between herself and the pulsating flower as possible.

"All I ask is one teensy tiny favor in return."

Ro stiffened. "And what is that?"

She leaned forward, eyes glowing with an unholy light. "The Fairy Queen's head."

"Her *what*?" First witches, now fairies? The beast, she accepted. Somehow. The curse, she'd lived with it for fifteen years. But this . . . this she couldn't handle. "What Fairy Queen?"

The Mademoiselle of the Mountain huffed. "You carry one of her flowers, stupid girl. You'll need it to gain entrance into her realm."

Ro just stared at her. She was insane. Completely, utterly insane.

The witch started muttering to herself, confirming it. "Of course not her heart—they wouldn't let me have that. It would disappear the moment you cut it out of her. But her head . . . now *that* they would not expect." Her smile grew, and her focus returned to Ro. "I want it on a platter."

"Never." Ro's voice erupted from her in a strangled whisper. She strengthened it. "Never." She didn't care whether this queen was real or not; she was not bringing the witch anyone's head. Ugh.

"Oh, but you will. You haven't the power to resist me, little one. Those who can are few and far between, especially once I place a compulsion spell on you."

"You won't. You can't. I won't let you." Ro had never felt this level of tangy, coppery fear before. It ate away at her insides, turning her into a quivering mess of cowardice.

"And the best part?" The witch smiled. "You won't remember any of this. And you'll wonder what beastly devil possessed you to do what I ask of you."

The witch's laughter rang through the cottage while Ro's heart shriveled and dropped past the floor.

Creator, help me!

The witch rose slowly, drawing out the moment, her smile letting Ro know how much she enjoyed this. She started muttering nonsensical words—Latin, Ro's brain told her past all the screaming it was doing—and a ball of light appeared in her hands, growing as she muttered.

She roughly turned her words to French. "I compel you! Do as I say, return with the Queen of the Fairies' head, and remember none of it."

She thrust her hands out at Ro, and the power with it.

Ro yelped and jumped to her feet. "Stop!"

The power wrapped around her, embracing her yet not

touching her, as if an invisible shield held it at bay, then shot back at the witch.

She screamed, her hands blazing with fire.

Thunder crackled outside and shook the house. Lightning flashed and lit every corner of the dark room. It wasn't as clean as it appeared.

A tingle started in Ro's scalp and slowly consumed her body. Buzzing filled her ears.

The witch plunged her hands into the mugs' bubbling brew, then froze, mouth open, eyes wide. She shut her mouth and fixed the worst glare Ro had ever seen on her. "Hamish!"

The door bounced open, the sharp noise covered by another crackle of thunder. The wagon master's composure was completely gone, panic enveloping every bit of him. "A storm! Inside the grounds. That's never happened be—"

"So you bring me a huntress, do you?" She bounded across the room, streaming liquid behind her that sizzled once it hit the smooth planks, wrapped her hand around Hamish's throat, and lifted him clean off the floor. "Do you have a death wish, old man?"

Ro stumbled back. "Stop! Put him down!"

The witch dropped him and spun to face her. "Careful with your words, girl. They have more power than you know."

Ro's eyes widened the same time as the witch's did, and the Mademoiselle clamped a blackened, blistering hand over her mouth.

"Why did I say that?" She pointed a finger at Ro.

Ro blinked. A finger that looked shriveled and, and *old* in the lightning flashes, not just burnt. The skin slowly knit back together and smoothed out.

"You're making me say that, aren't you? Aren't you?"

Three more bright flashes followed the first.

Ro shook her head. "I'm not. Honest."

"Get out. Get out of my house!" the woman shrieked.

Ro lunged for the rose and fled. She cursed herself. Why on earth had she grabbed it? She flew out the open door, bounded down the trail—nearly trampling the working boy who was running from the storm, right in her way—and flew past the wagon.

Just when she thought she was free, she slammed into something invisible, flew back, and hit the ground hard.

Ro sat up, rubbing her head. Thinking of the last time she'd hit her head. About three months ago. Saving Cosette. She blinked back tears. Would she ever see her sister again?

Laughter filled the air behind her. "Well, you aren't as powerful as I thought, ma chère."

Ro stumbled to her feet and faced her enemy.

"You apparently belong to me now." The woman's smile broadened as she stalked toward her, hands now completely whole, though her face wasn't as young as it had been. "But I can't have you around, burning me at whim, bringing storms into my haven. Fear not, little huntress. I will put you out of your misery, then you will never have to be unhappy again."

She raised her hands to the sky and uttered deep, dark words that filled Ro's soul with loathing and trembling.

Ro covered her ears, but it made no difference. The words snaked through her being and filled her with revulsion. Ro hunkered against the wagon and waited.

Nothing happened.

The witch paused, then repeated her strange-sounding words. She didn't raise her voice, but the timbre of her voice changed, going even lower.

Ro shuddered, tucking herself harder against the wagon wheel.

This time, panic lit the woman's eyes when nothing happened.

Ro frowned. What was she expecting to happen?

The woman started speaking again, but with greater urgency. The words began to churn in Ro's gut, physically painful, and she had to keep herself from writhing on the ground.

"Stop, stop, stop!" Ro cried in agony.

Thunder rattled the carriage, and a bolt of lightning zapped the ground next to the witch's feet. She flew back, landing on her side. Her head whipped around, and she stared at Ro, shock and hatred glimmering in her eyes.

Ro looked between the witch and roiling clouds above. She controlled the storm? But—how was that possible?

She stood to her feet, shaking, certain a random bolt of lightning would strike her next. She pointed a shaking finger at the witch.

She was going to provide for her sister, and no witch was going to stop her. And there was only one way to do that. Alive.

Ro shouted words that rose up in her being, coming from a place she didn't even know existed. "I command you in the name of the Creator to leave this place, never to return! You will not harm one more person! You will not curse one more soul! You will not cause anyone else to do terrible things, then forget why. You are *done*."

Lightning zapped around the witch, three strikes, three different places. She cried out and hunkered away from each one.

"Be gone, witch!"

The largest bolt of lightning Ro had ever seen lit up the ground where the witch had been standing. Ro stood there, mesmerized, not the least bit afraid. It arched and popped and hissed, just staying there.

Then it vanished. The storm faded.

And the witch was gone.

10

Ro sank to the ground. What just happened? She didn't believe in the Creator. Did she?

Yet the words were not her own. She knew she had to say them, just as she knew she had to breathe.

Without a thought.

Ro shook her head and staggered to her feet. Where the witch had been standing smoked, a burnt patch of grass the only sign someone had once stood there.

Ro gazed down at her shaking hands. How had she done that? Obliterated the witch with one swipe of her palm? Where had the magic come from?

Her hands shook even more violently.

Whooping penetrated her swirling thoughts, and she spun toward the noise. The wagon master, the quiet, stoic, never-made-a-sound wagon master danced behind her, cheering and throwing his hat into the air over and over.

"She's dead! By all the saints, you've done and killed that plague."

He broke into a jig that had the corner of Ro's mouth tilting upward. But only for a second.

"S'il vous plaît, don't tell anyone. I don't know how—"

"Don't tell anyone? You're dang-blasted off yer rocker if you think I'm going to keep this to myself. You killed that viper! Of course I'm going to tell everyone."

He took off running, heading for the path that would lead him out of the woods and down the mountain.

Ro darted after him and raised one hand, hoping to stop him. "Wait!"

He slammed into an invisible force and fell back, dust poofing where he landed. Ro jerked still, mouth open.

He looked at her, eyes wide. "You-you're the new Mademoiselle of the Mountain. You're a witch!"

She snorted. "Non, I'm not. Don't be ridiculous." She reached out a hand to help him up.

Fear filled his eyes, and he cowed away from her. "You've killed one terror, only to be the next. We'll never be free. Never!"

He curled into a ball, right there on the dirt road, and sobbed. Heat crawled up Ro's neck and set her face on fire. Now this was just embarrassing.

Ro rolled her eyes after the longest few seconds of her life. "Oh, for goodness sake." She crouched next to him and shook his shoulder. "Get up and knock it off. I'm no witch, and I have no intention of being a Mademoiselle of the Mountain. None. You have nothing to worry about."

He jerked away from her touch. "You don't get it, do you?" He nodded toward the invisible boundary. "No one leaves this place until they make a deal with the witch. The witch is dead, and you killed her. That makes you the new master of this place."

Ro stood, head reeling. What could she possibly say to that? But, if she were the new master of this place . . . Ideas exploded in her head, pelting her a thousand at a time.

What she could do! Her people wouldn't starve. Cosette wouldn't starve. Ro would never have to rely on anyone but herself ever again. She could learn to hunt. Here.

She grabbed the man's shoulder again. "Get up!"

He stood and faced her, a measure of dignity regained.

Ro forgot herself and grasped both of his shoulders, tightly. "Can you hunt?"

He nodded, eyes dead, face stoic, tear trails painting lines through the dirt on his face. "Oui, why?"

"Can you teach me?"

One eyebrow went up. "That is what you require of me?"

"What? Non, not require. I'm asking. Only asking. Will you teach me?"

"And once you learn, you will let me go? I'll be free?"

Ro scowled. What was it with this man's obsession that she owned him? "Since you won't believe me, oui, free, whatever. Will you?"

He looked resigned to his fate. "If that is what you require of me, then yes."

She nodded toward the wagon. "And will you still deliver the food?"

His quiet demeanor slipped over him like a mask. "Oui, Mademoiselle. And what of the boy?" He nodded behind her.

She glanced behind her. The redheaded lad stood behind her, hat in hand, trembling, dirt smudged across his cheek. He couldn't have been, what, more than fifteen?

"Oh." She faced him fully. "And what do you do?"

He wrung the hat in his hands. "Mostly tend the garden, draw water, start fires. Those sorts of things."

She nodded. "Right, then. Are you still willing to do that?"

His eyes sought the man behind her, and she glanced between the two.

The lad swallowed hard. "What I'd really like, Mademoiselle, is to go home."

"Oh. Of course. I understand."

His eyes lit. "So I can go?"

She nodded. "Of course." She met their eyes straight on. "You both can. But promise me you will not speak a word of what happened here."

The wagon master sniffed and turned away, jaw tight. He began loading the wagon with vegetables.

The boy ducked his head and walked forward, giving Ro a wide berth. As far as Ro was concerned, they were both being ridiculous.

Ro started to say something to the wagon master when the boy hit the invisible wall and flew back.

Ro stared, mouth open. "What on earth?"

The wagon master kept his back to her, but his voice was gruff, his tone hard. "It was as I told you. Only a witch can kill another witch. This cursed ground now belongs to you, and we are now your slaves instead of hers." His gaze pierced her. "Time will tell which of you is worse."

"Oh, for heaven's sake!" Ro stomped forward and pushed through the barrier. Not a tingle, not a zap, not a barrier. Not anymore. She spun around and put her hands on her hips. "I'm out. Now you try it." Neither male moved. "Come on! What are you waiting for? Surely if I'm out here, you can be as well?"

The wagon master moved forward and tapped the wall. It arched and popped and hissed. The boy didn't even try. Ro's heart dropped. It couldn't be.

"Mademoiselle, can you see the garden? The house?"

She glanced past him. "Of course. Why?"

His gaze was level. "Only the Mesdemoiselles could see through the enchantment."

Ro lifted her chin, refusing to believe him. "Oh, yeah? Then how can you find this place?"

"I am bound to go and return, as my master dictates."

Ro's shoulders slumped, and she trudged back to the

other side of the so-called "barrier" this absurd man couldn't seem to cross.

She rubbed her forehead. "Why can't you leave again?"

The wagon master shrugged. "We are the only two who have refused the witch's bargain, and she couldn't place a spell on us to do her bidding. We are cursed to remain in the witch's employ until one, the curse is broken, or two, the witches all die."

His direct gaze when he said it chilled Ro to the core. Great, now she had two curses to worry about instead of just one. And possibly a knife in the back.

She swallowed hard, then gave them both her best glare. "Let's get a few things straightened out from the beginning. One, I am not a witch. Two, I don't want either of you as slaves, and I will do everything within my power to break this stupid curse over you."

She raised her hand, though neither had moved to interrupt her. She lowered her hand. She'd have to get used to not being around siblings who constantly interrupted.

"Three, all I want is to feed my family and learn to hunt. That's it. That's why I came to see the Mesdemoiselles of the Mountain. I want to provide for myself, I want to break this curse over my country, and I want my people not to starve. Do we understand each other?"

The lad's eyes had brightened during her tirade, but the wagon master's had stayed dull and lifeless. Kind of like Père's. Her heart immediately went out to him and constricted painfully at the same time.

She implored him with a look. "I do not want to enslave you. I promise. If you help me, I will do everything within my power to set you free." She waved her hand to the path that led away from the cottage. "I would let you go right now if I could."

He didn't look convinced. "You'll need weapons."

Hope lit within her like a flame. "I have a crossbow in the wagon."

And why was this the first time she'd remembered it?

He nodded. "It's a start." He turned his back on her and concentrated on the wagon once more.

The boy was eyeing her, but he ducked his head as soon as she looked at him. He moved to go past her. She fell into step beside him, and neither said a word for a few paces.

Once they were closer to the garden—and farther away from the wagon master, Ro noted—the boy spoke in a low, fervent voice.

"Did you mean what you said? About letting us go?"

Ro snorted. "Of course! I don't want to keep anyone here."

The boy studied her. "That's good. If you stay strong, fight for what you believe in, maybe you can beat this. Power is a heady thing, once you've experienced it."

Ro frowned and met his gaze. They stopped and stared at each other. Ro realized with a jolt that the lad feared for her. He was afraid she'd give in to whatever power had seduced the witch.

She nodded. "Then I'll need your help, um—what was your name again?"

He grinned, a toothy but winsome thing. "Clement."

"Clement. I'll need your help, then. Think you can do that?"

He nodded.

She sighed and looked at the cottage. "Then let's get to it."

11

The door burst open. "What in the blazes is going on in here?" Hamish demanded.

Ro's head jerked up. Unfortunately, Clement was leaning over her, and her head crashed into his. "Ow!"

Clement grabbed his nose and sat down, hard.

"Oh, Clement, I am so sorry! Are you all right?"

He nodded and waved her back.

She glared at the wagon master. "Look what you made me do!"

Hamish rushed around the room, gathering armfuls of the gold and trinkets they'd collected from the chamber below the cottage. "Oh no, you don't. Put these things back right now!"

Ro frowned at him. "But how am I going to pay you both or bring France's wealth back if I put them away?" She waved her hand toward the piles of gold. "This belongs to my people, not me."

Hamish's eyes widened. "Are you crazy? I ain't touching cursed gold." He glanced down at his armful and flung it away. It clacked and bounced across the floor.

Ro moaned. "We just separated that."

Hamish pointed at Clement. "You, outside with your vegetables." Clement ran out the door, hand still over his nose. Hamish pointed at Ro next. "You. We need to talk."

He spun and stalked out the door. Ro followed, not knowing what else to do. Might as well get it over with.

Hamish spun to face her the moment they reached the back of the house. He shoved a calloused finger in her face. "You need to stop."

Ro crossed her arms. There were few things she hated more than bossy people. "Stop what?"

"Giving him hope."

She leaned forward, glare firmly in place. "I'd like to give both of you hope, only you won't let me."

He scratched his scraggly beard and paced before her, back and forth, back and forth. "Listen, let's say you're telling the truth."

"I am."

"And you really do want to free us and break this curse."

"I do."

He whirled on her and shouted in her face. "Then you don't touch blood money!"

"I—uh—what?"

He waved his arms. "Blood money! The gold. Don't touch it. Leave it alone."

Ro rubbed her hands down her face. "I'm sorry. I'm completely at a loss."

Hamish went back to pacing. "How do you think the witches acquired so much gold? Where do you think it came from?"

Ro raised an eyebrow. "Um, from the vegetables. What else?"

He shook his head furiously. Ro missed the laid-back guy from before.

"Non. Well, yes, but non. Blood money. Before France

needed food, her people needed curses broken, curses placed, and all manner of unseemly things done by the rich and the greedy."

Ro crossed her arms. She didn't have time for this. "Get to the point."

"Before they got in the business of farming, a very convenient profession during this era of history, I might add, the Mesdemoiselles of the Mountain were involved in many appalling practices. That gold is blood money, pure and simple."

Ro leaned forward, temper barely under control. "Let me make one thing very clear, Hamish—may I call you Hamish? Good. I don't care where the money came from; it belongs to the people of France. I don't care where the food came from; it belongs to the people of France. And I will do all within my power to make sure it gets back to where it belongs. Your only concern is to teach me to hunt so I can provide for myself. Are we clear?"

Hamish stared at her, jaw ticking. "Oui, Mademoiselle."

Ro nodded toward the wagon. "Keep filling it. My people are starving."

He nodded and moved toward the wagon without another word.

"Oh, and Hamish?"

He glanced back at her.

"Do not call me Mademoiselle here. My name is Ro."

He gave a curt nod and stomped away.

Ro turned back to her new house. It was purging time.

A bonfire lit the clear night sky. Orange danced off full leaves, and Ro drank in the sight. If only Cosette could see all the beauty here!

The burn pile had been cleared of furniture—to be

returned to the original owners, if possible—and now was full to bursting with books, scrolls, and dead animal parts.

Clement managed a whisper next to her. He'd been jumpy since she'd touched the first volume of witchcraft. "Aren't you scared?"

Ro snorted. "Non, why would I be?"

Clement nodded at the blazing flames. "Them spell books carry mighty curses. Ain't you scared one of them might come back on you fer burning them?"

Ro squared her jaw. She didn't expect him to understand; she just knew what needed to be done. "Not in the least."

"Well"—he glanced to either side—"don't you want to know how to break the curses?" At Ro's blank look, he continued. "Them books probably say how."

Ro leaned toward him and dropped her voice. "Do you really want me to become the next Mademoiselle of the Mountain?"

His eyes widened, and he shook his head.

"Then it's probably best I not read any spell books, oui?"

"Oui."

Ro shook her head with a smirk and poked one of the books deeper into the flame. As well as she knew her own name, she knew the moment she walked into the house that the place needed to be rid of filth. All of it.

And that included every spell book and dead animal part in the house. The herbs had other uses besides witchcraft, but everything else needed to go. And Hamish and Clement had watched her in wide-eyed wonder the entire time.

She glanced at her now-silent companions. "You can both go to bed."

"What about you?"

She nodded at the pile. "I'm not going to bed until only ash remains."

Clement folded his arms. "Then neither am I."

Hamish hunkered down on the other side of the fire and poked at another book.

Ro grinned. She just might win them over yet.

12

Ro jerked awake, a long stick jabbing her side. She grabbed the stick out of reflex and tugged. Hamish almost toppled over her. She rolled out of the way.

"What are you doing?" she hissed, crouched and ready to defend herself.

She glanced at a snoring Clement, his feet propped in front of the glowing embers, arms crossed and jacket clamped tightly around him.

"Teaching you to hunt, if you're up for it."

Ro raised her eyebrows. "Before it's even light?"

Hamish nodded. "Best time for it. Grab your crossbow and your bolts. Got anything else to wear?"

Ro glanced down at herself and shook her head.

"Then bring a blanket. It'll be cold."

Ro struggled to her feet, blinking the sleep away from her eyes. Energy surged through her. At last! She could be all Cosette needed and more.

She hurried into the cottage, downed a glass of water, freshly drawn from the well, then used the outhouse behind the cottage. She left the blanket where it lay. Pascal's jacket, worn though it was, would have to do.

In no time, she rushed to the wagon to retrieve her weapons and wait for Hamish. He approached and took the crossbow from her, settling it into a holster on his back. Without a word, he headed into the brush, away from the path that had led them to this place.

Ro followed. After a while, a thought occurred to her. "Hey! How are you able to leave?"

He shushed her, then said in a low voice, "Because I am fulfilling my promise to you."

Ro growled. His being unable to leave or not had nothing to do with her.

He shushed her again. "First rule of hunting, complete silence. Your prey shouldn't even hear your footsteps."

Ro immediately focused on every step she took and on the noises surrounding her. As she focused, the sound of her footsteps faded away. She somehow missed every twig and leaf underfoot. She could still hear Hamish's footsteps, however.

Hamish whirled around, frown firmly in place. "You still there?"

"Of course. Can't you see me?"

Hamish squinted, and Ro cocked her head. Hamish blinked. "Oh, well, stay close."

Hamish was very, very strange. And Ro had met her fill of strange people.

"Second rule: Be aware of your surroundings. Every flutter of a bird's wings. Every rustle of a blade of grass in the wind. Know where your prey is before it knows you're there. Stay alert." Hamish stopped. "Listen."

Ro stopped. Listened. A flitter of something there. A flutter of something else nearby. A leaf turning just so and brushing another. Heavy tread of a noiseless beast. Ro blinked.

She grasped blindly for Hamish's arm and found it. "There's something out there."

Hamish took several deep breaths and dislodged her hand. "Oui, I smell it. Let's get high."

After a few more steps, Hamish began climbing a tree. Ro followed him, her hands grasping each place his had, and she scaled the tree with ease.

Hamish turned once he'd made it to a level perch and reached out his hand. He jumped when he saw how close she was to him.

She offered an apologetic smile—unsure if he could even see it—and turned to peer into the dark woods. She listened to every noise surrounding her, every breath of wind caressing her face, and noticed something else.

"The air here—it is sweet. And it's not cold." She looked at Hamish. She could easily see him, though the moon didn't shine. "We're still on the witch's property, aren't we?"

"Yes, now be quiet."

"But what was that about—?"

"Shh!"

She settled back and listened, assessing and dismissing each sound as it came. There. The near-silent pad of heavy paws. She homed in on the sound, and her vision soon followed.

Her eyes widened, and she grabbed Hamish's arm. "A panther! Here? But how?"

He shook off her grasp. "Unhand me, girl! Yes, of course it's a panther, but"—he squinted at her—"how in the blazes do you know that?"

She pointed at the approaching creature. "It's right there. Fifty paces, coming this way. Black coat, gold eyes." She clutched at his sleeves. "Is it going to eat us?"

"Touch me again, and I will throw you from this tree, curse or no curse."

Ro snatched her hand back.

"Now, to answer your question, non, it's not going to eat us. Though how you can see the creature at this distance is beyond me. And how do I know it's not going to eat us?"

Hamish took Père's crossbow from his back and handed it to her. "Because you're going to shoot it."

Ro's eyes widened, and she stared between the crossbow and the man's face. The crazy, insane man, who could trade places this instant with Madame Savon.

"Me?" she squeaked. "I've never shot anything in my life! I only killed the wolf by accident, and with a knife, I might add. My family traps their food . . ."

"And you killed a witch with a bolt of lightning."

Ro nodded. "Which was an accident, too, by the way."

She tried to shove the crossbow back at him.

He kept it firmly in her grasp. "And now you will shoot the panther. Not on accident."

Ro reluctantly aimed the crossbow at the approaching creature. "Where did it even come from? Are panthers invading France now along with wolves?"

"Load it. That's right. Cock it back. Non, use your boot, girl. Pull it back with all your might till it clicks. There you go. Now aim."

Ro's trembling hands grasped the heavy weapon.

Hamish sighed. "Looks like we're going to have to work on building your strength, too."

Ro shot him a glare.

He must've felt, rather than seen, her gesture. He raised one hand in a calming motion, the other supporting the weapon. "Easy to do with good rest, proper nutrition, and hard work."

Ro sought out the creature. It gazed at her, just as she gazed at it.

Then it happened.

The creature's every feature lit up, blazing as if the sun shone on it full force, casting a glow on the branches around it. Slightly different than last time, but still unnatural.

Ro sucked in a breath. "Do you see that?"

"See what? I see nothing in this dark. I only know what I smell. What I hear. You're terrible at being quiet, you know."

"So are you," she shot back.

He shrugged. "So he hunts us as we hunt him. You see him?"

"I do." Her words came out breathless, full of awe.

She felt Hamish's unsettling gaze on her. "Now pull back the trigger, slowly, gently." She did. "Fix your eye on the target. Keep squeezing."

"You never told me where it came from."

"No talking. Deep breath. Now."

Ro released the bolt. It flew forward, swift, silent, deadly. It struck the beast, and a sound like a woman's scream pierced the air.

Ro's heart nearly leaped from her chest. "What was that?" she cried.

"Again! Again!"

Something heavy crashed through the woods.

Ro fumbled with a bolt, clumsily sliding it into place. She'd just wedged her boot in the strap when the creature reached their tree. She gasped and yanked back.

The bolt fell from its perch in the crossbow to the ground below. Claws outstretched, the panther jumped up the tree, hugging the trunk as it climbed, then paused.

Suddenly, it fell to the ground, dead, its unearthly glow snuffed out in an instant.

Ro stared between the beast and Hamish. "Did you do that?"

Hamish shook his head, trembling, knife in hand. "Non, you must've struck its heart. A near-perfect mark." His voice held awe, tinged with suspicion. "In the dead of night."

She stared at the panther, marveling at how the beast's light had snuffed out with its life force. She glared at

Hamish. "What is a panther doing here, and not in its wild jungles elsewhere?"

He shrugged and began his descent. "The witches kept all manner of beasts for their entertainment.

Ro felt sick. And she'd just killed a beautiful creature for hers.

As if sensing her thoughts, Hamish stopped and glared at her. "Creatures that, if they escape this cage they've been placed in, will tear your people to shreds."

Ro cocked her head. That was one way of looking at it.

Hamish dropped to the ground below. "Now help me with this thing. If you're going to kill something, then you're going to clean it and dispose of what you don't use, too."

Ro scrambled down beside him. They worked silently, Hamish showing her how to gut and skin it by an ever-so-slightly lightening sky.

She worked hard, though her arms grew heavy and weak from the rush of adrenaline leaving her.

A slight noise caught her attention, and she glanced up.

A panther, a second panther, smaller, lighter in color, yet no less deadly, flew through the air, right at Hamish. A line of crimson slashed across its neck from his knife and blood sprayed, but not before the thing toppled Hamish, raking him wide open. Hamish lay on the ground, mouth opening and closing, horror drenching his eyes as his blood drenched the ground.

The panther's mouth clamped over his face.

Ro gasped, and the creature was back in the air, flying toward them again, Hamish completely oblivious.

Without a thought, Ro grabbed his knife and lunged at the creature, slashing its throat wide open. Only this time, she wrapped her arms around it and fell sideways, away from Hamish.

They landed with a hard *thwack*, and the panther writhed for just a moment before lying still. Ro extracted herself from the panther's embrace and sat next to it, staring, shaking, and closer to sobbing than she cared to admit.

"Look at me."

Ro's head jerked up, and she stared into Hamish's concerned face. His perfectly fine, not-bleeding face.

She'd done it again. She'd seen something before it happened and had been able to stop it.

Hamish snuffed out his concerned look. She wasn't certain how many times he'd called her, but he must've said her name several times before she understood.

"Are you well, Mademoi—Ro?"

She nodded, teeth chattering.

He raised an eyebrow. "So you need me to teach you to hunt, do you?"

"This is my first time. I swear it."

"Uh-huh." He picked up his knife and eyed the smaller panther. "I'd forgotten about the female. I'm glad you were with me."

Ro didn't bother pointing out that he wouldn't be out here—in danger—if not for her.

"Well, let's clean this one too and get them back."

"We aren't going to eat them, are we?" Ro wrinkled her nose. She wasn't sure she could eat anything after that.

He just looked at her.

"Can't you take them to someone who needs them more than we do?"

He eyed her thoughtfully. "If that's what you want."

Ro rubbed her belly, the memory of being stuffed full the night before with all the food she could have hoped for and more warming her. It had been so long since she'd experienced such a glorious thing. "It is."

He stood. "We still need to carry them back with us."

Ro groaned and struggled to her feet.

Longest night of her life.

13

"You know, I've been thinking."

"Mm?" Ro didn't pay Clement much mind. He was a chatterbox once he'd decided Ro wasn't going to tear his heart out in his sleep. Ro shuddered. He had a gruesome mind, that one.

Of course, that was to be expected, living with whom he had.

She dug back into her butternut squash, tender and juicy from the fire, dripping with real, actual butter. Heaven itself didn't have better food than this.

"My cousin said a ghost's terrorizing their town. Ever since the curse and all. Well, I was thinking—think you can kill it too?"

Ro nearly choked. Hunting animals was one thing, but a ghost? Killing the witch had been an accident. Thank the Creator she only had to face the one, not three. How would she even begin to know what to do with a ghost?

"Um, I don't think it works that way . . ."

Clement continued, undeterred. "And goblins are eatin' what's left of the livestock in Vinsborough, though the huntsmen are trying to convince everyone it's just wolves.

Yet not one of them—the huntsmen or the wolves—will set foot near the town. Think you can rid them of the creatures?"

Ro glared at Clement. "Are you kidding me?"

"Ah." Apparently Hamish had decided to join the fun. "You banished the witch to the netherworld faster'n Clement here can skin a rabbit. I say you should go."

Ro turned the brunt of her scowl on Hamish. "Do you even hear yourself? Ghosts? Goblins? What's next, ghouls?"

He pointed at her, meat speared on the tip of his knife. She shuddered. That knife had been places. She'd never want to eat off it.

"You have a gift, young lady, and you say you want to use it for good. So do this." He muttered under his breath. "Though I ain't convinced you ain't a witch yerself."

"I heard that, Hamish. I'm sitting right here."

"The point is, you need to make a name for yourself. I've taught you all I know, and I barely even taught you that. The things you know and the things you can do are uncanny. It ain't natural."

Ro tore into her butternut squash, all desire for eating meat squelched by the many things she'd killed, as well as how much produce was available here. "So you've been telling me. For months."

He waved that knife around as if it were a flag. "You want to make a difference? You want to help?"

"What do you think I've been doing?"

"You want to get off your sorry bum and stop hiding in this little haven?"

Clement snickered.

She pointed her spoon at him, far less threatening than the knife. "Hey now. Nothing from you. You started all this, you know. And is that what you call all the work I've been doing around here? Sitting on my bum and hiding?"

He laughed and kept eating, thoroughly enjoying himself. At her expense.

Ro sighed. At least they were both comfortable with her now.

Hamish took to tearing into his meat, mouth full and wide open for all to see. Ro set her butternut squash to the side and waited for him to finish.

"The world is marching on out there, Ro. And it's leaving you behind."

Ro decided she was hungry and didn't care about Hamish's fireside manner. She had brothers, after all. She picked up her squash and dug in. Cinnamon apples would be next. Yum and yum.

"Gautier is picking up the pieces you've given the people of France, claiming them as his own doing."

Ro shrugged. She really didn't care. It was an ideal situation. She was slowly helping her people rebuild their lives, providing food, valuables, and funds in exchange for hard work, and she didn't need to have anything to do with them. It was paradise.

Hamish brought back news of her family's well-being after his many trips, and that was good enough for Ro. Who cared if someone else got the credit?

"Gautier—I've heard of him. Who is he again?"

Both Hamish and Clement stopped eating, staring at her with wide eyes. "Only the most powerful man in France!" burst from Clement's mouth.

"Oh?" She licked a golden stream of butter trying to escape down the husk of her squash.

Hamish glared at her. "You never pay attention to my stories, do you?"

Ro swallowed, a rush of heat creeping up her neck. "Of course I do."

It wasn't that she didn't pay attention; she only paid attention to the important parts. The parts about people eating, about their earning livres again—the parts about her family.

"Oui, the most important man in France," Hamish continued. "A man you should know."

Ro pointed her spoon at him, brandishing the thing like a weapon. "If you're thinking marriage, you can forget it. I'm not marrying anyone."

Hamish rolled his eyes, and Clement turned beet red.

"Saints preserve us. Of course I'm not suggesting matrimony. I'm suggesting you work for him. Make a name for yourself."

Ro shrugged, going back to her meal.

"I think he'd be ecstatic to meet the huntress who vanquished the Mesdemoiselles of the Mountain and instructed her lackey to bring him such magnificent game as she's been hunting."

Ro's head jerked up. "What?"

Hamish grinned, smug, proud of himself. The devil.

"You didn't."

"I did, and I'm not sorry."

The flame in the firepit gusted higher. "You will be."

He stared between the blaze and her. Now it was his turn to swallow. "Oh?"

She rolled her eyes. "That wasn't me, halfwit."

"Then explain it."

She growled, low in her throat. "It was just a breeze."

"It wasn't and you know it."

Ro shook her head, refusing to believe it. "I killed a wolf. By accident. I killed a witch. By accident."

"You killed those panthers—"

Her head whipped up. "Both by accident!"

"How?"

"Lucky shot and lucky guess."

"And all the game you've hunted since then?"

Ro opened her mouth, but nothing came out.

"The many other creatures you've killed? Perfectly?"

Ro whispered this time. "Accident. Had to be."

"Mon Dieu, I've never seen anyone hunt as you do. You have a gift, child."

"Then I'll use it. Here." She jabbed at her meal, not willing to admit how much she didn't want to leave this place.

Hamish shook his head and looked to Clement for support. Clement jumped and shook his head too.

Hamish nodded, satisfied. "Non. Wolves still prey on your people, as you won't stop calling them. The curse may not allow them to die of starvation, but it certainly doesn't repel wolf attacks."

Ro refused to answer.

"Ro. Look at me."

Ro lifted her eyes to meet his. She hated herself for it, but her eyes filled with tears.

"It is time for you to leave this place. To do what you were called to do. To break this curse."

"I am breaking it."

"Non, you are lessening its effects. Little by little. But the curse remains."

Ro's eyes drifted to the lush garden. "And if I leave this place? You said it was open to me, but the last time I left to hunt, I could barely find it. What if I can never enter this paradise again?"

Hamish shrugged. "You might not be able to. I don't know. But we will be right here, doing our tasks, until they are no longer necessary. Or until it's the right time for you to find us again."

Ro stared at the fire, tears dripping from her chin. "That's not fair to you. And how do you even know this?"

"How did you know to kill that panther?"

Ro didn't answer.

"In the same way, I know it's time for you to leave this place, and I know we will be fine."

Ro stared into the fire for a long time—they all did—until she tossed in the rest of her dinner and rolled herself in her blanket, settling before the fire. Dessert forgotten.

❧

Ro woke the next morning to hazy light, no fire, and a blackened landscape. She bolted upright, panic clawing at her throat.

The garden was gone, the cottage was gone, and all the greenery she had loved so very much—gone.

Ro cried out and untangled herself from her bedroll, running to where the garden had once been.

The stench of decay hit her nose with every footfall. She'd forgotten how much the curse made the land stink.

She stood in the middle of the nonexistent garden, mouth hanging open. Had it been another dream? Had she fallen asleep in the wagon? Had the wagon master dumped her here the first chance he got?

It was too much. She covered her face with her hands and sobbed. Oh, how she ached for the last months to be true! She'd been somebody important. She'd mattered.

She'd made a difference.

"Why are you crying?"

Ro choked back her tears and swiped her face, searching for the voice. "I'm not." She cleared her throat and tried to find her best glare.

"And do you make a habit of lying, Mademoiselle Rosette Jacqueline Reynard?"

Ro choked for real this time. "Who are you?"

A shimmering creature came into view—the most beautiful woman Ro had seen in her life—tall, lithe, graceful. Otherworldly.

Ro bowed on one knee. "Forgive me, Madame. I did not see you."

Knowing she should bow was as natural as breathing, though Ro couldn't have explained the knowledge to anyone who asked.

"Your manservant is right. It is time you leave this place and fight for your people."

Ro held in a snort. She'd like to hear the fairy call Hamish a manservant to his face. Wait, she was talking to a fairy? Not just any fairy—the Queen of the Fairies.

Now, how in the realms did she know that? And where were her wings? Didn't fairies have wings?

"Not unless we need them, and oui, I am the Queen of the Fairies. My charge is waiting to meet you. Quite desperately, I might add."

"Uh . . ." That was Ro. Miss Eloquent. Where was Cosette when she needed her?

"You will see your sister in time. Now, will you do as I ask? Will you leave this place and seek your fate?"

All Ro wanted to say was, "Non, I am quite happy here, merci beaucoup," but instead she found herself saying, "Yes, Madame. Right away."

Pleasure filled the beautiful, sparkling creature, a hidden light glimmering within, very much like her white rose. "Good. I will tell him to expect you and not to despair."

Ro frowned. Him? Did she mean Gautier? And what of the garden?

"It is hidden from your sight. For now." The queen held out her hand. "The flower, if you please."

Ro's hand trembled as she slipped the white rose from her pocket and held it out to the woman. The fairy gently lifted it from her fingers, and it melted into her hand like snow on a warm day.

"I accept your gift and offer my own in return." She leaned forward and kissed Ro's forehead.

Warmth flooded her, joy as she'd never felt, happiness, love, peace. Ro scrambled to her feet and jumped back, and the feelings faded.

"What—what do I—what was that?" Non, that wasn't right. "What do you want me to do?" Oui, that was what she wanted to ask. But still . . . "What did you do?" Ro clamped her mouth shut. Enough babbling, already!

"Go. All will become clear to you. The Creator be with you."

Ro bowed her head. "And with you, Madame."

The tall woman vanished, and once again Ro was assaulted by the stench of the land.

Well, this was just great. She'd made a promise to a powerful queen, and she had no idea what she'd just promised. Typical.

She shouldered her pack, checked her many weapons, and slipped her crossbow into the holster on her back. She glanced down at her lean, tanned, and muscular arms, then breathed out a sigh of relief.

Oh good. It hadn't all been a dream.

She glanced around her. "I'll be back, Hamish. Clement. Take care of the place for me. And go home if you can."

She headed straight for Gautier's château, the distance melting away at a glance, her path made clear. A gift from the queen? Perhaps.

She grinned. Wouldn't they be shocked to meet a person kissed by sunlight?

14

So Gautier had refused to see her. So what? It just meant Ro had to work that much harder to convince him she was who she said she was—that her reputation was truly her own.

Not that she cared. Well . . . apparently she did. Hence why she was dragging her latest kill before him.

Ro hefted the wolf pelt from her shoulders. It landed before the throne with a soft rush of fur and the clack of nails.

The man sitting there eyed it, then raised his eyes to meet hers. "You expect me to believe you killed this poor creature yourself? No help."

Ro lifted her chin. "Oui, Monsieur."

Everyone in the court laughed, including this Gautier she'd heard so much about.

The man's père had once been the king's steward, a man who'd tried and failed miserably to hold the kingdom together after the curse. Now Gautier had convinced the people he should rule in the king's—and his père's—stead.

Ro found it intriguing the man even remembered they had a king, and daunting that no one else remembered or cared about their missing rulers. Now this upstart was promising food, a future, and freedom from the curse.

Promises Ro very much wondered if he could keep.

Interest lit his eyes. She kept the light from her own. She had him.

He eyed the pelt. "And where is the meat?"

"I sold it in the village, then cured the coat, just as your instructions stated."

"By yourself."

His smile made her want to sprint across the room and scratch out his eyes. She took a deep, calming breath, determined to outwit her prey.

She refused to break eye contact. "By myself."

The rest of the court continued their heckling, but Gautier kept one fist over his still-smiling mouth, eyes considering. He lowered his hand.

"Bring me another. Treasurer, pay her."

The laughter silenced, and the treasurer spluttered, but soon she had a heavy pouch in her hands.

She nodded and slipped the coin purse within her leather jacket. "As you wish."

She turned and left, holding back her smile until she was outside the small château.

Soon her sister would have everything she wished for and more. And Ro could return to her home in the mountains, never to be bothered again.

❧

Ro stomped away from yet another village.

It didn't matter how many times things had gone right, she still couldn't figure out *how* she did it.

This time, she'd simply walked into the village, and the spirit terrorizing the people had left, shrieking the whole way, its trail of wispy, white smoke dissipating into nothing.

The people had cheered, thrown her a feast, paid her handsomely, and sent her on her way, scared out of their minds of her, no matter how much they praised her and smiled at her.

Ro didn't blame them. She had no idea how she worked either. She'd never again been able to conjure a storm, make a fire blaze, or see an event play out before it occurred. Every time, something different happened.

It was driving her crazy.

At least her prey still lit up in the night like it was daylight, but only when she was hunting.

She fingered the heavy pouch, clinking with gold coins.

Now that she received the same payment the Mesdemoiselles of the Mountain once received—though she tried to come up with creative ways to give it back to the townspeople—was hired by villagers all over France, and was paid handsomely by Gautier himself, she should soon have more than enough for Cosette.

But desperation spurred her on.

Would she earn it in time? Would her père accept that he no longer owed the castle's beast any of his daughters?

And how long until Père decided to send Cosette in Ro's stead? She was the youngest, after all.

An inkling of an idea had begun to form the last time she'd scoped out her family's refurbished home, and it had grown into a full-fledged mission.

Cosette needed to be far from her family, too. Far away from the curse. Far away from her lunatic père.

Somewhere she was safe, somewhere she could be the lady she yearned to be, somewhere . . . also far from Ro and her soiled reputation, in case anyone discovered who Ro's family was.

She almost had enough to send her away.

Just a few more jobs from Gautier, and she could do it.

She shook her head. Had she known she needed so

much to pay the priest and Madame LaChance for Cosette's safe passage, she would've never returned all the witches' gold. Though they needed it, Cosette needed it more. And Madame LaChance would not be bargained down in price.

Way to think it through, Ro, way to think it through . . .

She grabbed her horse's bridle, led him to a stump, and mounted the horse that was easily twenty hands high. Most people shied away from the massive beast, but Ro didn't mind. That meant it kept people away from her, too.

She nudged him from the village, wishing the entire way she could solve the mystery that was herself.

And keep Cosette safe, once and for all.

❧

Ro kept her head down as she hurried through the village, hoping her cloak's hood and the horse at her side would keep her fairly anonymous.

They didn't. She should've known better, especially with her giant of a horse and her vibrant-red cloak. Was any other hunter as conspicuous as she? Whispers followed her down the street.

"The huntress!"

"It's the huntress!"

"What's she doing here?"

"On a personal mission for Monsieur Gautier, no doubt."

"I wonder what she looks like? It's rumored no one has seen her face, not even Gautier himself."

Ro snorted at that one. She had a feeling the townsfolk would be highly disappointed to discover the mighty huntress was once their feisty little nobody.

Her horse stumbled to a halt, and she alongside him.

"Fairweather, what—? Oh."

Madame Savon stood before them, blocking their path,

and pointed one long, crooked finger at Ro. "Keep to this path, and it will claim you. You will *die*!"

Ro jerked back and hurried away, subconsciously and perhaps a little superstitiously taking another way to her family's home. Crazy old bat. Ro didn't come home often, but she needed to see her sister. She didn't know why; she just had to.

Her run-in with Madame Savon was unfortunate. She didn't want to be connected with her family. It was why she adopted a new surname.

She had to protect them at all costs. Especially her sister.

She gave her family's home a wide berth and headed straight for her treehouse. Her family was back in their country house. They couldn't yet afford to live in the city, but Ro had made them comfortable enough to ensure they could move into the opulent dwelling.

She sat in her treehouse, lit the lamp, and waited, watching the bustle of country life below.

Ah, they had a new serving maid. That made a cook, a butler, a footman, a stableman, and three maids. She watched them scurry about their daily tasks. They seemed to be working hard. Perhaps the family was in?

Cosette came in and out of view, and Ro's heart leaped. She leaned forward, peering through the wooden railing as Cosette flitted in and out of view in the different windows.

Ro had no hope Cosette would see her light until dusk had fallen, but how she ached to speak with her now. This very minute. To be welcomed into her old home with open arms and be treated like a sister again.

A wry grin touched her mouth. Even if that meant being picked on by her five pests. Cosette excluded, of course.

Her brothers weren't home. She'd already peeked into their places of apprenticeship. Pascal was studying to become a banker, and Claude, a silver worker. It'd only taken a small nudge to connect them with what they enjoyed doing. Their employers loved having such competent workers, and her brothers loved being away from their sisters.

And they would never know Ro had seen to it that they came highly recommended to the shop owners. And she'd never tell. Now a full smile touched her lips.

Her brothers. Hard workers. Who knew?

Now Cosette climbed the winding stairs to the upper floor. Ro held her breath and pressed her face against the slats. Could she possibly see her sister soon, not hours from now? But non, it would be hard to see the lamp in daylight, but Ro's heart refused to listen to her.

She so badly wanted to curl up with her sister and trade secrets and be normal again.

But her life would never be normal. Not since she'd chosen to be a huntress, and not since she'd overheard her sisters say their bad luck was her fault—because of the rose her père had taken from the Beast's garden—and their misfortunes had only reversed once she'd left.

Their misfortune had befallen them long before she'd asked for the rose, but her sisters didn't care.

And they were partly right. They'd had Père back—until he'd given her the rose.

She shook off the melancholy thoughts when Cosette turned her way, glanced toward the treehouse, and froze. Her face lit with joy, and she ran down the stairs.

Ro laughed and bounced. It was too good to be true!

Several excruciating minutes later, Cosette was scrambling up the ladder to the old tree fort, and Ro blew out the lantern.

Cosette tackled her in a hug. "Oh, my dearest Rosette!"

Ro laughed and hugged her back fiercely. "Hush, you! We don't want anyone to overhear."

She tugged up the rope ladder.

Cosette hushed her voice but set about squealing and bouncing in the most unladylike manner. "I wasn't expecting another visit so soon! What brings you? Not that I mind. Not in the least. Oh, I'm so happy to see you!"

Ro's smile stayed plastered on her face, but she didn't know how to answer that. "I can't say. I really can't. I've got another job"—Cosette's expression dimmed, but only for a moment, and she desperately tried to cover it—"and I had to see you. How are things?"

Ro's smile felt wooden. Knowing her sister disapproved, even the slightest, hurt more than she cared to admit. Everyone else in the world could disapprove if only her sister were on her side.

Ro slammed the trap door closed a little harder than she meant to, and Cosette jumped.

Ro offered an apologetic smile as Cosette launched into a monologue of every word and action of their five sisters and two brothers.

Neither mentioned Père, as it had been since the first time she'd visited, when he'd flown into a rage, denouncing her and not allowing her entrance. She'd never even been inside the updated version of her old house.

"So they like their apprenticeships?"

"Like them?" Cosette laughed. "You should see them strutting about. A banker. And a precious-metal worker."

She lifted her nose in the air and struck a snooty pose. Both girls dissolved into giggles.

It felt so good to laugh.

Cosette shook her head. "I think they're proud to be good at something. To work with their hands and take care of their family." A sly look entered her eyes. "Something tells me they didn't quite get us this house on their own, however."

Ro shrugged and winked. "Whatever would I possibly know about that?"

Cosette smiled, looking no less satisfied than a cat with a bowl full of crème.

"I thought so." Her eyes drifted over Ro's red cloak. "I see you still wear Mère's cloak. It suits you."

Ro reached for the strings. "You're welcome to—"

Cosette stopped her, covering Ro's hand with her own. "Don't you dare. It was a gift. Really. I want you to have it."

Ro smiled, and Cosette began a story about Reinette's latest mishap. The awkward girl loved to throw herself at any eligible bachelor and could never tell when the young man had a glaring lack of interest, lending many a tale to Cosette, and far too many giggles to Ro.

Finally, the sisters grew quiet, and worry flitted across Cosette's face.

Ro tensed. "What? What is it?"

"Nothing, I—"

"Cosette. You must tell me. The smallest thing could be of great import. I keep my association with all of you quiet for a reason."

Cosette took a deep breath. "You're not going to like it."

Ro's jaw hardened. "There isn't much I like in this world. Spit it out."

Cosette fiddled with her dress, creasing the fine fabric. "Père is . . . seeing someone."

Ro instantly felt lightheaded as all the blood drained from her face.

Cosette held her breath, watching Ro carefully. Ro tried to minimize her reaction for Cosette's sake, but she just couldn't manage it. Ro felt as if someone had delivered a right hook and left her reeling.

"Seeing . . . someone." She couldn't wrap her mind around it.

The details poured out of her sister's mouth. "She is a countess. Very wealthy from what I've heard. Oh, nothing grows in her gardens—she still has to rely on food from the new Mademoiselle of the Mountain, just like everyone else—"

Ro smirked. Yeah, Cosette—and the rest of the country—had no clue about the details surrounding the three witches. Or her. And she was going to keep it that way.

"But she didn't barter everything away, so she still has some standing in her community."

"Does Père . . . like . . . her?"

Cosette shrugged, not meeting her eyes. "He doesn't *not* like her."

"What on earth does that mean?"

Cosette looked at her then, misery etched in every feature. "I think he's thinking of her fortune, his daughters, and her daughters. Maybe a grasp at happiness?"

Ro could barely force the words past the burning in her throat. "Her . . . daughters? Has he forgotten Mère so soon?"

Cosette took both of Ro's hands into her own. "It's been almost fifteen years, dearest Rose. We mustn't begrudge him a chance at happiness."

Ro was suddenly glad she'd been kicked out. She'd never step foot in her père's home again.

"Cosette? Cosette!"

Both girls jumped. Ro would recognize that voice anywhere. Bernadette. Good *night* but the girl could screech.

"Oh no! I forgot!" Cosette scrambled for the exit hatch and ladder.

Desperation seized Ro. She still hadn't told Cosette what she came for. "Wait! Must you leave so soon?"

Cosette lifted the door and fed the ladder into the hole. "There is a soirée at Madame Chevyon's tonight. I must get ready now if we are to attend on time." She rolled her eyes, a very un-Cosette-like gesture. "Thanks to you, we now have to re-enter polite society and deal with suitors, parties, and everything else dreadful that comes with it."

"Oh, you love all that and you know it."

Cosette's grin was rather impish. "I do." She swung her legs over the edge.

"Wait! Please. I have something I need to tell you."

Cosette paused on the first step of the swinging rope. She clung to the edge. "Hurry. Or I fear discovery."

Ro leaned close. "I have another job—"

"Cosette! Don't make me come find you," Bernadette caterwauled.

Cosette dropped down one more step.

Ro hesitated. "I will send you a letter through one of our brothers. Obey every word, especially if Père remarries. Promise me."

"I promise." Cosette launched her petite frame at Ro, hanging on for one last desperate hug before she continued down the contrary rope.

Ro watched her go, then pulled up the rope and secured the hatch. Her heart broke into a million pieces as Cosette ran toward the house and the screeching Bernadette on the front steps. Bernadette brushed Cosette's skirts, looking as if she were scolding with every word she flung Cosette's way.

Ro groaned and propped her back against the rough wall. She still needed to talk to Cosette, but she had to set off for Gautier's tonight. He had a job for her—a rather lucrative one—and he wanted it kept secret.

A job for her only. Not for any of his trusted huntsmen, whom she often worked with, though she preferred to work alone.

The very thought gave her chills. She should've been flattered, but something was off.

She just felt like she needed to say goodbye to Cosette, to provide for Cosette, one final time.

And she had no idea why.

15

"I've found her."

Up until this point, Magic looked completely bored. She sat there twirling her hair, eyes staring off into the distance, seconds from severing their connection.

Now she bolted upright, fingers clenching the throne she was sitting in. The king's throne. Left vacant for many years. Gautier caught just a glimpse of the wreckage and decay behind her.

"What? Who?"

"The girl. The huntress. She can see the castle."

"What girl?" The woman's pale face matched her washed-out surroundings. Gautier held his smirk in check. She hadn't been that pale a few seconds ago.

"She's the best huntress I have. She's smarter, faster, and more tenacious than any of my other huntsmen. And get this. She doesn't only hunt wolves." Gautier's eyes sparkled.

If anything, the woman before him tensed further. "Get on with it. Explain what you mean."

He leaned forward and dropped his voice. She matched his posture, move for move. "There are reports that she does a little hunting on the side."

The woman's eyebrows rose, and the expression on her face clearly asked why she should care.

"Reports say—now this may just be gossip—but she rids small villages of ghosts, ghouls, and goblins."

He straightened and chuckled, adjusting the fur lining around his wrists. He needed to send his jacket to be combed and treated.

"A few of my contacts swear that at times, she is summoned instead of the priest."

The woman sat back and laughed. "Oh, Gautier, you're worse than a woman."

His attention snapped back to her, his expression frosty.

She continued, her practiced, bored look in place. "The only thing it takes to further gossip is to share it. You don't really believe any of that, do you?"

The outrage her words caused washed away, and a smile crept back onto Gautier's face. Nonchalant as she sounded, an underlying ripple of tension said she cared more than she let on.

Oh, yes. He'd found the huntress he'd been looking for.

He beamed. "Of course not."

She relaxed.

"Then again . . ."

Tension radiated from the woman. He winked.

"If she truly can see the castle as she claims—and perhaps enter it?—maybe we can hire her to take care of a little problem we both have, oui?"

"I see." Magic sat back, eyes hooded. "You've been planning this for quite some time, haven't you?"

Gautier smiled and bowed, neither confirming nor denying it. "Your concern is my concern."

Magic sat still, quiet, and contemplative for too long. Then her eyes began to gleam, erasing some of the sparkle from Gautier's. A hint of worry wafted through him.

This woman was not to be trusted—not in the least—but

he thought he'd found a solution to rid him of two troublesome problems at once.

One, the beast.

Two, Magic.

If the girl was as smart as she appeared. It would be so simple if only everything turned out according to plan.

"All right. Send her to me. I will ensure she enters, but it is up to you to make sure she hunts the right creature."

Gautier gave her a smug, self-satisfied smile. "I already have everything in place."

"Of course you do."

Her dry comment gave him immense satisfaction. Her image slowly faded from his mirror, replacing her image with his. He turned his face from side to side, admiring the strong jawline, the dark hair, the aristocratic nose.

That sister of hers—the huntress' sister—Cosette, was it?—would look lovely next to him. The only one of the bunch worth having.

She would make a fine queen once the prince was out of the way and he could be crowned king of France.

And if that cursed Fairy Queen hadn't made it impossible for him to be king otherwise, he'd already be crowned and on the throne.

His scowl interrupted his enjoyment of looking at himself. He could only be king once the beast was dead, and the beast would only die if Magic let him.

Magic was toying with them both.

He smoothed out his expression and smiled. Well, he'd force her hand. She was easily manipulated with just the right word. The right gesture.

He ran his tongue over his teeth, making sure they gleamed and not a morsel remained from his lunch. Oh, yes. The girl would kill the beast, work her skill on Magic, and he would get the beautiful, innocent little sister for his bride.

It was all working out according to plan.

His conversation with Magic replayed itself in his mind. She was so sure she would win, that Gautier was her puppet. She'd been stuck in her ivory tower too long.

Haughty, cold, yet with desperation shining in her eyes . . . and something else . . .

Gautier laughed. Oh, that was priceless. The sorceress thought she held him in her control? On the contrary, he was very much the one pulling the strings.

And he'd have it no other way.

THE END

THE HUNT FOR HANSEL AND GRETEL

Hansel et Gretel
"Hansel and Gretel"
—Jacob Grimm and Wilhelm Grimm—

The old woman had only pretended to be so kind; she was in reality a wicked witch, who lay in wait for children, and had only built the little house of bread in order to entice them there. When a child fell into her power, she killed it, cooked it, and ate it.

La vieille femme avait seulement fait semblant d'être si gentille ; elle était en réalité une méchante sorcière, qui attendait les enfants, et n'avait construit la petite maison de pain que pour les y attirer. Quand un enfant tombait en son pouvoir, elle le tuait, le cuisinait, et le mangeait.

1

"What do you mean two children are missing?" Ro snatched the missive out of Liam's hand.

He gave her a look that said he might fight her for the scrap, then visibly restrained himself from snatching it back.

He took a deep breath, something he did often around Ro, as if he were fighting for calm. "I didn't ask questions. Gautier said find them, so we find them."

Ro couldn't help the sour look she shot him. "You do realize questions are how we find out more about the job, right? We shouldn't go in blind."

Liam gritted his teeth. "We have all the info we need. The children were last seen with their father in the woods, now they're missing." He paused. "It's the third time it's happened."

Ro's eyes flew to his. That last part wasn't in their job description. "So you *did* ask questions! What else can you tell me?"

Now Liam's face was the sour one. "Just that the two other times they were found in their beds the next morning, and this time they weren't."

Ro was already gathering her gear from the small cell-like room Gautier provided for his best hunters. "We need to move before the trail gets cold."

"I know," Liam ground out.

Ro couldn't help flashing a grin—more like a baring of her teeth than a true smile—as she made sure she had everything she needed for the hunt.

Well. The rescue, this time.

She loved getting under Liam's skin more than anything else in this realm. He was so hard to rattle, and the man barely let any expression past his stoic face.

Except for around her.

As much as she wanted to keep picking at the walls he'd built around himself, she needed to know more. "Who's going with us? Gabin, Sacha, Hugo?"

Liam said nothing.

Ro looked up to find his jaw ticking, a wholly unpleasant look on his face.

"Wait." She straightened. "Just the two of us?"

His look could make thunder hesitate. "Just the two of us."

Ro's heart dropped, though she shrugged like it hadn't. "Then what are we waiting for?"

He swept his hand for her to proceed him out of the room—though he hadn't set foot inside. Ro swirled her red cape around her shoulders, grabbed her crossbow and several sheaves of bolts, and headed for the stables, not waiting to see if Liam followed.

2

Ro and Liam sat across from the woodsman, a big, burly, hairy man who curled his giant frame around his strong brew of café.

The red of his hair and beard reminded Ro of flames, and his lilting accent spoke of northern origins. He sat hunched on the other side of a well-made wooden table in his one-room cottage deep in the woods.

"Can you tell us what happened?" she asked gently.

Liam shot her a look, but Ro ignored it. Sure, she was usually gruff and spoke little, but these were missing *children* they were talking about here.

"I already told the constable. And the townsfolk, and that worthless Gautier. Why should I repeat it? My children have been missing three days—three days! Do you know how rare it is for anyone to be seen again after only *one*?"

Aldric the woodsman dropped his head, grabbed his hair in clenched fists like he might tear it out, and let out a choked sob.

The woman in the background, who stirred something on the cast-iron stove, wiped tears from her cheeks with her apron. Then she brought over mugs for Liam and Ro, setting them carefully before the hunters.

Her hands shook, and grief suffused her face.

Ro offered her a sympathetic glance and reached for her mug.

No, don't drink.

Ro went perfectly still—she hated that voice, but she couldn't deny it had helped her so many times—as Liam raised his mug to his lips. She touched his thigh, briefly and feather-light, and after making a show of raising it to his lips, Liam lowered it again without drinking.

The look of hunger on her companion's face matched her own, and she couldn't help but regret asking him to refrain.

A small furrow appeared between the woman's brows, and Ro realized she'd been watching them closely while trying to appear not to.

"What were their names?" Ro asked, to get the giant woodsman talking again.

"Hansel and Gretel. The lad is eight and the girl is but five. I lost their mother—"

At this, he darted a quick look at the woman at his side, but she turned away with a tight jaw and a loud sniff. The brave man finished anyway.

"—after Gretel's birth. Hélène has been a good mother to them since. They're smart kids, raised in these woods, but even I am losing hope."

"Can you tell us exactly what led to their disappearance?" Liam said in his low rumble of a voice.

The man sat up and detailed most of what they already knew. He was a woodsman, making his living by cutting down trees in the forest and then crafting them into something magnificent. Like this table. And most of the furniture in the one-room cabin with a divided loft for sleeping.

The curse had hit them just as hard as everyone else, and

although people still needed homes repaired and furniture built, fewer and fewer could afford it.

They lived so far away from civilization, the children and his wife often accompanied him, working together in the family business. They were barely surviving, just like everyone else in curse-ridden France.

He told them more than they'd known, too.

How each day, they'd packed their last meal, a crust of bread and a sip of milk for each, then went into the forest to work and hope they could survive long enough to scrape together just one more meal.

The first time the children had gone missing, the woodsman called the children as usual at the end of the day, then led the way out of the forest, heavy axe over his shoulder.

A furrow appeared over his brow as he said this, as if he wasn't quite sure of his words.

"Were the children with you when you came out of the woods?" Ro asked.

Aldric opened his mouth, then just sat there.

"Yes," the woman said. "I sent them off to play while we set the tree aside to be processed for the woodshop."

The man's expression cleared, and he nodded. "It's dangerous to move a log, in case it rolls or falls the wrong way, so they don't help with that part. But then they didn't come in for dinner."

A tale of the mad search, of wanting to ask for help from distant neighbors, and of his wife soothing that they were simply playing and would come in when they were ready, followed.

But they hadn't come home, not even after dark.

Aldric spread his hands. "And when we woke up the next morning, there they were, in their beds, sleeping as peacefully as little angels."

"But not this time," Liam said.

The woodsman's face went pale. "Not this time. Not for the past three nights."

Ro backtracked just a little. "When did you give up the search and decide to go to bed?"

Again, the man opened his mouth, but before he could answer—again, it looked as though he wasn't sure of himself—the wife jumped in. "It was dark, and we needed to save what firewood we could for cooking, not torches." She laid her hands on his broad shoulders. "It was just as I said—the little devils were playing tricks on us."

She said it like she was teasing, maybe referencing a joke between the two of them, and he covered one of her hands with his and gave a sad smile.

She squeezed his shoulders and went back to work.

While he was talking, the woman brought over a pair of decadent pastries, piled high with sugar-whipped cream, some kind of glazed fruit peeking out from under the cream and cradled in a flaky crust.

Ro's mouth watered, and by the look on Liam's face, he was seconds from shoving it in his mouth. The table was most likely in danger of being bitten into as well, Ro thought with a smirk, if Liam gave in to the ravenous hunger on his face.

Even working for Gautier, food was scarce and they got just what they needed to perform well, nothing more. And certainly nothing as delightful as this.

He didn't look at her, but she could feel the question pulsing from him. Could they eat it? Please?

Ro didn't reach for it, knowing she wouldn't be able to resist if she did. As it was, the smell of sugar and glazed apricots was enough to block out everything Aldric was saying.

He wasn't even paying attention to the food as he rambled.

Liam followed her lack of movement, keeping still,

though under the table she could just see his balled fists clutching the sides of his trousers to keep from reaching for them.

The woman hovered near the table this time, fingering her necklace—a slice of wood, it looked like, its life rings beautifully lacquered and standing out against the pale inner rings—as she once again tried to appear she wasn't inspecting their every move.

But Ro knew better. This time.

At the first break in the woodsman's words, Ro smiled at the woman, every inch of her aware of the food she hadn't touched or even seen since the curse fell. "You are too generous. Should you not save these for when the children come home? I'm sure they'll be hungry."

Hélène flicked a glance to her husband, who'd fallen silent but was still staring listlessly at the table's surface. "They were for the children. We'd found an apricot tree and have been hoarding a scoop of sugar—it was going to be our last meal." Her face crumpled. "We would've found a way, I just know it."

Ro hoped the smile she offered was kind, not reminiscent of a starving wolf. "Then please, by all means, save it for their safe return."

"Oh no." The woman shook her head adamantly. "I know you'll find them, I just know you will, but if this meager offering can help speed you on your way, help you find them that much faster, then I offer it and gladly."

Ro gave her a single nod. "Thank you for your generosity."

The woman turned away, dabbing at her eyes again with her apron, but Ro couldn't deny something else had leaped to her eyes—a gleam that looked a smidgeon like satisfaction.

Ro urged the woodsman to pick up where he'd left off.

He did, and for a while, what he said made sense. He

talked of what the children looked like, their favorite haunts —which he'd already searched—and where he had been cutting wood the three times they had disappeared.

Then he devolved into recrimination and self-reproach and everything he should have done differently.

Ro and Liam exchanged glances.

"Thank you for your time, Monsieur, Madame," Liam said. "We'd best be on our way."

The woman glanced at their untouched plates with something akin to panic in her eyes. "Wait!"

All three of their heads came up at her outburst.

She smiled sheepishly. "Please, refresh yourselves. Let it not be said you came to my table and went away again hungry."

The woodsman dropped his head and buried his face in his folded arms upon the table with a deep, heavy groan. Ro could feel his anguish through the solid wood of the table.

Liam stood, his features resolute. "And let it not be said we took food from your mouths when it was your last."

He strode toward the door, as if he stayed a moment longer, he would give in. Ro scrambled after him.

"But your payment!" the woman objected, waving at the food on the table, ignoring her grieving husband. "Let us at least pay you for your services with this meager offering. It is the least we can do."

Liam stopped, just outside the door, but didn't turn around.

Ro smiled at the woman, hoping it looked sincere. "You are too kind, but I must agree with Monsieur Liam. Our payment has been fulfilled, thanks to your agreement with Monsieur Gautier, and we'd best not tarry."

With that, Ro and Liam hurried to their horses, untied them, and prepared to mount.

"A moment, huntsman." Aldric followed them out, his

steps heavy, his head bowed. He held up a piece of paper. "Here's what they look like. To help your search."

Ro, closer than Liam, took the parchment and studied it. On it was a sketched garçon and fille, the boy and girl robust, laughing, and in full color, if younger than described. "Why, this is beautiful!"

She glanced up at the woodsman, surprised.

He nodded without looking at either of them. "Usually I take my little drawings with me, to show my customers what I can make, or to sketch what they want me to do. I haven't drawn much since—anyway, it is the most recent one I have of the children."

He turned and lumbered away without another word.

Liam leaned over and took his time with the picture, then nodded when he was done. Ro carefully folded the drawing and tucked it into one of her deep pockets while Liam mounted.

Just when Ro thought that might be the end of it, the housewife rushed out of the cabin, hands full.

"Wait!" The woman hurried after them. "For your journey." She gave them both a demure smile. "I hope you will forgive me, but I just can't take no for an answer."

In one hand, she held out clay mugs covered with wax paper and tied with string, then a folded wax paper–tent parcel of the treats she'd made with the other.

Ro smiled, thanked her, then carefully tucked them away in one of her travel bags, the one she used for jars and potions and medicinals and other things she didn't want near her food. She mounted Fairweather, and Liam led the way out of the clearing.

They followed the obvious path made from trees being dragged back to the peasants' cottage, making quick time.

Once they were well into the woods, Ro slowed Fairweather, dug into her bag, and tossed both drinks into the decayed undergrowth, pastries quickly following. She'd return the mugs when they brought the children back, alive and well.

Liam made a noise of protest.

"There was poison or a sleeping draft or something else nasty in them, Liam. I half expect we would've wandered the woods for a bit, maybe taken a nice long nap, then hopefully been on our way, none the wiser that we had a job to do. I'm not willing to take a chance on poison, are you?"

Liam made a choking noise. The man was eloquent with his grunts. "And you know this because . . ."

"Come on. That woman was far too obvious."

Liam stared at her, not budging his horse. Ro started to worry that if they waited there much longer, Liam would be on his hands and knees, licking every crumb of pastry he could find from the forest scrub.

She was fighting off such thoughts herself.

Ro shrugged. "The woodsman was fuzzy on so many details. The woman was insistent we eat or drink. This is the third time the children have been 'lost' in the woods. Either low-key poison or a sleeping draught of some kind, I'm sure of it."

Liam said nothing.

She glanced at him over her shoulder, then regretted it with the skepticism on his face. She said through gritted teeth, "Call it a hunch."

Liam stayed silent, disapproval coming off him in waves, and Ro urged her horse forward, doing her best to convince herself that she could trust her instincts—even if no one else did.

3

They combed the forest. The woodman's daily trail was easy enough to follow, as well as how he picked through the forest, finding the more mature trees that weren't completely rotten from the curse, cutting them down in a pattern that allowed for regrowth.

Whenever trees started to grow again.

The three sites in question sprouted deeper into the woods than the family's normal trek, one north, one east, and one west. The homestead was south of each lumber site.

At the first site, they spread out, marking where the children had played, gathered twigs, and rested, also noting where the wife had scavenged for food and the woodsman had cut down and dragged the tree behind his ox.

The footsteps were mostly faded after five days and a light rainfall, but between Ro with her magical eyesight that highlighted things of note and Liam with his eagle huntsman eyes that were just as good if not better than Ro's, they were able to piece together the family's time there well enough.

"Spread out," Liam said. "Only the woman and her husband went back this way. Find the children's path."

Liam worked his way around the site in a circular

pattern, and Ro went over to where the children had rested. If their stepmother had given them a sleeping potion, the children wouldn't have stirred when their parents left without them.

Sure enough, little footsteps led away from the place where two small bodies had nestled down for an afternoon rest, leading deeper into the woods. They glowed faintly golden to Ro, a slight indent in the blackened and dead undergrowth, just barely confirming what only she could see.

See? She wasn't crazy!

"Here!" Ro called.

Liam joined her, and they followed the footsteps deeper into the woods, Liam stopping, bending, and crumbling and smelling dirt and leaves between his fingers. Ro forged on ahead, trusting her eyesight. Soon she came upon an almost-indiscernible trail of small stones and pebbles.

"Liam, look!"

He bent and brushed his fingers over the pebbles that, although few and scattered, were unique to the trail and seemed to have been placed there.

Ro found little indents where some of the rocks had been dug up. Mouth in a firm line, Ro marched off the trail into the woods, and sure enough, after some searching, found more scattered stones.

Why, that witch! Had she tossed the stones into the forest so the children couldn't find their way home?

"What was that?" Liam asked from close by.

Ro jumped, her hands flying up in a defensive gesture. Liam eyed her mildly, but the subtle glint in his eye said he'd done it on purpose.

She forced herself to relax and answer as if nothing had happened. "Stones. Same ones from the trail. There." She pointed.

Liam dug around and found them. He grunted, which in

Liam language meant, "Good work." "These look like the pebbles in the rock garden to the side of the cottage."

He looked at her as if waiting for her assessment.

Ro blinked. "Um, oui, they do."

She started to sweat a little. Was he testing her? Again? Would he ever stop pestering her and just accept that she was a darn good huntress and worthy of being hired by Gautier, just as he was?

Not that she had noticed a rock garden anywhere near the cottage.

She tried to keep her face blank, but she was pretty sure she'd already given away that he'd surprised her. He eyed her like he could see right through her.

He lowered his head and went into teacher mode. "You must take in your surroundings, notice everything, retaining just enough to recall it in an instant if it becomes important later."

Ro gritted her teeth. "Why, merci beaucoup, O wise teacher."

He ignored her sarcasm and pointed. "This is the oldest trail, and it leads south, back to the woodsman's house."

"I know," she growled out.

"Most of the pebbles have been moved, likely by crows or kicked aside by the children placing the trail in the first place, but they have gone this way. This corroborates his story of the children making it home the first day." He stood and slapped his hands on his thighs, dusting them off. "Come on. Let's see if we can pick up the second trail."

Ro grumbled all the way back to their horses, wanting to slap the self-satisfied look off his face. Would he never stop treating her like some green huntress he was taking under his wing?

Gautier had hired *her* because she was *good* at what she did.

But she was *not* going to stick her tongue out at his

retreating back. Nope. Nuh-uh. Not gonna do it. No matter how satisfying it might feel.

It didn't matter how many times she'd proven herself; he'd still turn anything into a lesson of how she could've done it better and why. All while making her feel like she should've never left her hovel to make a life hunting wolves in Gautier's employ.

Well, she wouldn't have, had her father not given her in payment to a beast, then kicked her out the moment she refused to go. But this was the life she had chosen, and she wasn't giving up, no matter how miserable her fellow huntsman tried to make her.

Speaking of miserable . . . her mind drifted to the pastries left far behind, regret low and hot in her belly.

The pastries reminded her of the glitz and glam of high-crust Parisian life, decadent food in piles to be picked over and wasted because there would always be more, something she hadn't seen in an age. Maybe longer. If she'd known, she would've savored every bite. Thanked her Maker for every bite.

Not that she was speaking to Him right now.

They made their way to the second site, this one to the east, and they marked out a similar family routine. Probably what they did most days they went into the woods for their living.

"Why is Gautier concerning himself with this family again?" Ro asked as she searched for the children's resting place.

"I didn't ask."

And there's where Liam let the conversation die. Unless, of course, he felt the need to correct her over some other shortcoming. Ro rolled her eyes.

This site was just a bit harder to decipher. Though a day newer, it looked like more had been done to erase the passage of the family having been there.

Strange.

Ro frowned. "You think Gautier owed them a favor? Maybe bought furniture from them for his château or something?"

As much as she preferred complete silence herself, so many things about this particular quest didn't make sense. Gautier usually concerned himself with clearing the forests of ravenous wolves and making prestigious connections, not aiding peasant families.

Liam grunted. "You are more than welcome to ask him when we get back."

That would never happen, and he knew it.

"Here," Liam said. "I think."

Now Ro raised her eyebrows. Liam? Uncertain? This she had to see.

She hurried over to his side, and sure enough, he stood over what could have been the children's resting place.

But Ro wasn't certain either. She bent and traced feather-light grooves in the dirt. "Does it look more, I don't know, swept up to you?"

"Oui." Liam looked troubled. But that didn't stop him from issuing commands. "You go that way. I'll look over here. Be sure to go in circular patterns like I showed you."

Ro gave Liam her best glare, but Liam pretended not to see and started dutifully searching, though Ro could've sworn his eyes were twinkling.

"Insufferable huntsmen and their egos," Ro muttered.

"What was that, huntress?"

"Nothing," Ro shot back. He could just pay attention the first time if he didn't want to miss her insults.

After a longer search, Ro stepped on something sharp. She hissed and backed off, thankful she'd had boots made with thick soles.

She bent down and inspected what ended up being a pottery shard.

She whistled. If she would've stepped on that in her days of being a lady and wearing silk-thin slippers with soles made of soft calfskin, she would've sliced her foot wide open.

"What is it?" Liam asked from right over her shoulder.

Ro yelped, then smacked his chest. "Now I know you're doing that on purpose!"

His face remained suspiciously void of any expression whatsoever as he inspected the shard. He clapped her on the shoulder. "Good eye, huntress."

She didn't bother telling him she'd stepped on it. Goodness knew he'd just gloat and make her thank him for recommending the town bootmaker when she'd finally become a regular huntress for Gautier.

She glared at his back as he carefully inspected the rest of the area.

"Another," he said.

The second trail was much more scattered and had shards from what looked like a broken clay cup instead of stones, and once again, most of the trail had been picked at or dug up and thrown into the woods. Eventually, the trail led them south.

"You think the stepmother did this?" Ro questioned.

Liam grunted. "I had a stepmother, huntress. She was the best thing that ever happened to me."

Ro stopped walking even as Liam kept going.

Liam? Sharing something personal? With her?

She glanced all around her, and sure enough, the curse still gripped France in its clutches and pigs weren't flying, but maybe miracles did still happen.

She hurried to catch up. "I wish those kids had your experience."

Liam rounded on her so suddenly, she walked right into his broad chest. He set her back from him, his expression a thundercloud.

"I'm still not convinced they haven't. Huntress, can you be sure, completely certain she had something to do with this? Because all I saw was a kind, concerned woman caring for another woman's children, just as heartbroken as their father over losing them."

Ro gaped at him, just like a fish, and tried to come up with something non-stupid sounding.

Of course she wasn't sure! How could she say "It was this voice inside my head that's always right but I hate with every fiber of my being" without sounding like she'd completely lost her mind?

So she squinted at him instead. "You're still mad at me for throwing away your lunch, aren't you?"

Non-expressive Liam threw his hands out to the sides. "But of course I am! When was the last time you ate food like that? Non, when was the last time you *saw* food like that? And you just threw it away? I could just—"

Liam marched away and back again, looking like he was trying to calm himself.

Ro took a deep breath to keep from snapping at him. "Liam, I'm asking you to trust me. Non, I'm begging you to trust me. There was no portion of the treat untainted. I'm sure of it."

He opened his mouth to argue.

Ro cut him off, waving her own hands about. "Why would I lie to you about that? Didn't you say the most important thing to you in a fellow huntsman was trust? Well, trust goes both ways, ma peste! You can't expect me to blindly trust you without extending a little of that to me."

"I didn't eat any of it, did I?"

"Well, non, but—"

"Trust has to have a foundation to rest upon, huntress."

"Well, oui, but—"

"You've got to give me something to work with here.

You can't even tell me *how* you knew something was wrong with the food?"

"Oh, of all the stupid—" Ro took several deep breaths, closed her eyes, and counted to ten. Out loud. "Un, deux, trois . . ." Then she looked right at him and said softly, "I wanted to eat it too."

He seemed to deflate. Wow, he really did respond well to kindness, didn't he?

She needed to remember that.

Too bad her sister, Cosette, wasn't the one who'd taken up hunting and traveling the countryside with sweaty, stinky men and going days on end without bathing. Even her kind, sweet sister would've been grumpy at some of that, right?

Probably not.

She lightly touched his arm. "I'm sorry, Liam. I really am. I wouldn't have asked that of you if I wasn't convinced something was wrong."

He smoothed his close-cropped blond beard and eyed her. "How convinced."

Ro huffed and raised both hands, just shy of strangling him. "Well, I was completely convinced until you started questioning me!"

The skin around his eyes crinkled, but that was the only hint he was close to smiling. "If your convictions don't stand up under pressure, what good are they?"

Ro couldn't help her growl. "Maybe some of us like to keep our convictions to ourselves and let others believe whatever they want, no matter how wrong they are. Especially if such are to be torn apart each time they're brought up, as you so obviously relish to do."

Liam crossed his arms, settling in for the argument. "Maybe said convictions are too strong and can't be trusted if you can't talk about them without getting defensive. Maybe they should be reconsidered. Or I don't know, *discussed* with your fellow huntsman before acted upon?"

Dieu help her, it was all she could do not to strangle the insufferable man.

She glared at him. "And if you antagonize and dig at and make each person who tries to tell you something defensive, maybe they can't trust themselves to make what they *know* are good decisions."

He raised an eyebrow. "So you're saying you made a bad call?"

"What? Non, I said . . . argh! You are just so infuriating!"

Ro stomped off, Liam's chuckle chasing after her and doing its best to annoy her. This was why she preferred to hunt alone. Or have other huntsmen than just Liam in their party.

Then Liam was even more reserved and took on his self-imposed instructor role less. He also ignored her more, which was just fine by her.

He would've been right at home with all the snobs in Paris playing the gaming tables and insisting with subtle tones and snide remarks how ingenious they were and how every other person in the room was too stupid to live, but with enough flattery to make it seem like they were being complimentary.

But of course, Liam would do it without flattery and get himself mobbed.

Ro smirked at that.

"Let's call this one, huntress. I've found enough shards leading in the general direction of the cottage. Let's look for the third site. And stop pouting. You're scaring away our dinner."

Wordlessly, Ro followed him back, stomping less but fuming the whole way. She wasn't a petulant child, even if she was acting like one. She crossed her arms. She wasn't.

4

They rode north, following landmarks the woodsman had mentioned—Ro keeping an eye on the footsteps that glowed brighter than other sets—and Ro started to worry about time. They'd ridden far, searched far longer, and still had the third trail to find.

They needed to find or build a shelter before the clouded-over sun dipped and the temperature plummeted.

Fairweather's breath fogged in the air that always held a chill now, and she rubbed his coat. "Good boy. Thank you for all your hard work today."

Liam cocked his head.

"And not a word from you," she shot at his back before he could say anything.

He chuckled and raised one hand. "I was merely going to ask if you wanted to try to catch something or eat the . . . jerky . . . we brought."

Ro swallowed. It wasn't the best, no matter what Marceau insisted. Manna from heaven, her foot. More like tasteless, rock-hard, gummy scat scraped from the bottom of her boot that swelled in her mouth and was almost impossible to choke down.

But it was better than bark, so . . .

"As much as I'd rather eat anything else—anything—"

"Like perfectly made café and delectable, fluffy pastries straight from heaven?"

"Argh! I mean . . . I think we should eat what we have and hunt tomorrow if we have the time."

Without another word, though she could practically hear his self-satisfied smirking over the crunch of dead brush under their horses' hooves, Liam dug out his rations as Ro dug out hers.

Although he never said another word, she could feel him judging her as she chewed on the same piece for miles. The water from her waterskin only made it swell more.

She'd just gotten her first bite down as they came upon the third site.

Ro shuddered and wished she could scrape the flavor from her tongue. "This is the most recent, the one Gretel and Hansel never came home from?"

He nodded and slid from his horse, watering and then attaching a feed sack for him.

Ro tucked away the rest of her jerky and mirrored his movements.

Then Ro set herself to scrounging for clues, which were almost nonexistent at the third site. The glowing footsteps seemed to be the only thing left behind, and even those had been scratched at, brushed over, and attempted to be erased.

The problem was, the sun would be setting soon, and it always got darker faster in the woods than out. And although her eyesight highlighted things of note, it didn't always work, especially not when she wanted it to. They needed to find this third trail ASAP.

Only she couldn't find any pebbles or broken glass or pottery or anything.

Just under an hour later, the light started to change. Liam called, "Nothing?"

"Nothing," Ro confirmed. "Are you certain this is the third site? The one the children disappeared from?"

Liam scratched his beard. "It matches what the woodsman said close enough." He pointed at stumps where three smaller trees had been felled and dragged away. "If not for those . . . non. I'm not sure this is the site."

Ro grunted. If she'd suspected the last site had been tidied, now she was even more convinced. "Look at these brushstrokes. Here, here, and here. If I didn't know any better, I'd say someone went to a lot of trouble to erase footprints."

Liam came over and inspected the ground, then grunted.

High praise indeed.

Also, she needed to stop grunting. She was starting to sound too much like Liam.

He made his circle, inspecting every inch of the ground, smelling dirt occasionally, and brushing bent twigs or crushed undergrowth.

Ro scrutinized outside Liam's area, looking for a resting place, a trail of twigs or stones or pottery, but she was coming up with nothing.

And her eyesight apparently had decided it had had enough excitement for one day.

"Figures," she muttered.

"What was that, huntress?"

"I said it figures the most recent site would be the most void of clues."

"Keep looking. Clues want to be found. You just have to be ready for them."

Ro rolled her eyes. Sure they did.

But Liam was right about one thing. With how unreliable her gifting was, she did need to hone her other hunting skills for when her gifts failed her. Like now.

They were both hunched close to the ground, Ro behind a tree and Liam in some brush, when loud whistling met their ears. Ro instantly came alert, going just as still as Liam. Then the poor soul started to sing.

He really shouldn't have.

"Ohhh! A sailor's life, a pirate's life, that's all I want for me! To live with sea spray on my face and a bottle of rum-um in hand! Ohhh!"

Ro eased the crossbow off the holster on her back, while Liam did the same with his longbow. He needed a recurve. Save his elbow.

But that was the same argument for another time.

"Ohhh!" The oblivious stranger launched into another non-rhyming verse as Ro fitted a bolt in her crossbow and cocked it. Liam already had an arrow nocked and aimed, but not drawn. He counted off, and they shot to their feet as a dirty lad with bare feet and a pole over his shoulder burst into the clearing, singing for all he was worth. He was tall and lanky, and his bones sticking out at sharp angles could've poked anyone standing too close.

Both Liam and Ro aimed at the poor boy, and Ro almost felt sorry for him.

He fell right on his bum. "Whoa, whoa!" He held up the hand not clutching the pole. "You want my fish? Take 'em! I didn't want 'em anyway!"

He flung the pole into the clearing, and the fattest catch of fish Ro had ever seen in her life landed with a splat. Liam and Ro stared at it in awe for a moment, frozen, stomachs both verbally rejoicing at seeing something truly edible.

The lad started to scurry away.

"Hold it." Liam somehow tore his gaze away from the fish and stepped closer to the lad, bow pointed. Ro knew he wouldn't pull it back all the way until he was ready to shoot.

He was the fastest draw in Gautier's retinue, and most men knew not to test him.

This lad most likely knew none of that, and Ro sincerely hoped he wouldn't try anything.

"Where did you get that cap?"

Ro blinked. Cap? What cap? Then her eyes settled upon the lad's head. She'd been more distracted by the fish than she'd thought. It was red, in much better shape than the rest of him, but why was Liam worried about a hat?

The gangly lad tore it off his head and threw it at Liam's feet. "You want it? You can have that too! Just let me go, Monsieur. Oui?"

"Non," Liam said gruffly.

The boy started to shake.

"Mon Dieu. Liam, you're scaring him." Ro released the bolt, put away her crossbow, and took a few steps toward the boy, then stopped and pointed. "And where did you get that satchel?"

Heavily embroidered with flowers, it looked nothing like what a gangly young lad would wear. Then again, he was awfully sure of himself . . .

"This old thing?" The boy whipped it over his head and threw it at Ro's feet. "It's yours. Ain't nothing in it but fishing supplies, promise. But you want it? No arguments here!"

In a swift, sudden move that was all Liam, he put away his bow, hauled the boy to his feet by his threadbare collar, and pulled him close to his face.

"This cap and that satchel belong to a boy and girl who were lost in these woods three days ago. You wouldn't happen to know anything about that, would you?"

The boy's upper lip and hairline started to sweat, even in the cold. "Boy? Girl? Naw, I ain't seen nothing."

Though he was still obviously terrified out of his mind, defiance had entered his tone and eyes.

"Methinks he doth protest too much," Ro said in a sing-song voice.

Now Liam rolled his eyes. Maybe he was hunting too

often with her as well. "You shouldn't capture and beat up the Bard's sayings. They don't transfer well to French."

Ro's eyebrows shot up. Liam? Cultured? Who had he been before the curse?

Scratch that. She didn't want to know. No huntsman talked of his life before the curse, an unspoken rule between them, and she wasn't about to break that.

"Start talking, garçon. Now."

The boy did. "It's not enough you're taking my dinner and cap and satchel—you want my dignity too?"

Liam growled. "I'll take that and more if you don't start talking."

The lad started whimpering and pleading and begging for his life.

Ro frowned. What was he stalling for? She eyed the woods. It wouldn't take long for the sun to set and wolves to come out and steal their fish while they squabbled.

The boy's fish. Not their fish.

They might be acting like thugs, but they weren't. Not really.

"Look," Ro interrupted. "We don't have much time. Those kids' lives are in danger, and the longer it takes to find them, the bigger chance we won't. Help us. Please."

They were both looking at her, the boy with his mouth open, and Liam, with faint surprise in his eyes.

Ro shrugged. "We don't want your fish. We don't want your cap or your satchel—"

"They should go back to the boy and girl," Liam said.

"*But*"—Ro took a deep breath. What would Cosette do here?—"we do want to find them before it's too late. Help us? Please?"

The boy took them both in. "Ya mean, ye ain't robbers?"

Ro shook her head, though Liam looked like he still wanted the boy to think they were.

"Non," Ro said. "We've been hired to find them."

The lad yanked away from Liam's grip and brushed himself off, looking indignant. "Then you'd best leave me alone! I ain't playing your games. And you cain't have my fish. My cap and satchel neither!"

He frantically gathered his things and was just reaching for the pole when Liam stepped on it.

"I might not be a common thief—like you, apparently," Liam said.

The boy didn't deny it.

"But you're not leaving here until you tell us everything you know."

The lad stayed there frozen, for just a moment, before abandoning the pole and taking off running. Liam tackled him to the ground almost instantly, as if he'd been expecting it, and they crashed into the underbrush.

The lad didn't stand a chance.

The scrawny adolescent started yowling and protesting and calling Liam all sorts of names that in all honesty, Ro had heard him called before. By others he'd manhandled into giving him information.

Ro sighed. This was going to be a long night.

5

"I ain't saying a word. She'll kill me. She'll kill us all," the boy wailed.

Liam kept his glare firmly on the lad and raised the steaming-hot fish to his lips.

Ro lightly touched his thigh. "Liam, wait."

"Ro, I swear to Dieu if you say I can't eat this . . ."

"I wasn't—" Ro stopped and scowled hard at him. "Will you just let it go?"

"Never." He took a vicious bite of his fish and stared at her, chewing almost violently.

Ro rolled her eyes. Men. Specifically the grumpy, stubborn ones.

"As I was saying, before I was so *rudely* interrupted," Ro began.

Liam practically inhaled the second half of his fish, offering her a feral grin populated with flaky white meat in his teeth. It would serve him right if he choked on a fish bone right now and died.

"I think we should offer him sanctuary. If he is truly in danger of telling us what he knows."

Liam reached for a second fish—seriously, how was the

entirety of his mouth not melted skin right now?—and speared the lad with a firm look. "That would be up to Gautier, if the lad tells us truthfully what he knows and leads us to the children."

The young man waved a hand with a lightning-fast attitude switch. "All right, all right. Don't get yer panties in a twist. I'll tell ya what I know."

Liam scowled and Ro brightened, trying not to smile too hard while reaching for her own stick of fish.

Each was speared on a single twig and stacked above the flames in an elaborate pyramid structure. Once the boy and Liam had come to an understanding, the boy had busied himself first making the cook station, then moving the finished ones to the top to stay warm while sliding the next tier down to better cook.

"Start talking," Liam growled.

Ro dug into her fish, chewing with her mouth open and sucking air in and out to keep from scalding her tongue.

It was the best meal she'd eaten in her entire life.

Ro was stuffed. For the first time since she could remember.

She rubbed her satisfied belly and wasn't even embarrassed that it stuck out in a soft little mound past her open jerkin. Cosette would be horrified, of course, but Ro was too busy reveling in the feeling of being full.

They'd polished off the boy's entire catch, the boy's mouth going a kilomètre a minute. And spraying chunks of cooked fish as he talked.

Ro would've been disgusted had she not been busy stuffing her own face.

Now the bones were picked clean, the smell of a good meal saturated the air, and Ro was dangerously close to nodding off.

Unfortunately, robbers or wolves could set upon them at any moment, especially with the luscious smells their fire was leaking into the woods, and Ro would most likely just smile at them and die happy.

She jerked awake. Again.

Liam kept an eye on the boy, but he managed to give her a look, and Ro flushed in embarrassment. She was just warm and happy and full, n'est-ce pas? She wasn't a bad huntress for nodding off while danger was in their camp and most likely closing in.

All right, she was, but Liam could just keep his looks to himself. She needed a nap and she needed it now.

She settled in, determined to prove to him her exhausted self could stay awake on a full stomach. While sitting down. And warm in her red cape with the white-fur lining, a fire crackling its soothing sounds before her.

She snorted awake and opened gritty eyes to see Liam's hand on her thigh, his warmth soaking into her. She stared at it, wondering what it was doing there, how it had gotten there, and when would it leave?

"Repeat that," he demanded, then removed his hand.

Ro stared blearily at him, wondering what she'd said in her sleep to get him so riled.

The night seemed deeper, fuller somehow, and Ro wondered how much time had passed.

The boy's voice droned on in the background, but he was so full of false tales and boasting and useless information, Ro had gotten good at blocking him out in the short time she'd known him. And apparently good enough that she'd fallen asleep.

But then his words soaked into her brain.

"And so this witch, see, she likes kids. Lures them into the woods with bright colors and candy, things they ain't had in an age." He puffed out his chest. "'Cept me, o' course. I'm immune to her loverly charms, I am. Lets me fish in her ponds even, she does, just for shewing them kids her loverly home."

The boy slurped at Liam's favorite flask again, leaving crusted fish on the rim and weaving dangerously, even while sitting down. The boy was sloshed.

Ro's head whipped to Liam, but his eyes easily held hers, no regret in them.

"You got him drunk? He's just a boy!"

"He's a full-grown lad on his own," he said in his most patient of voices, the one that said no matter how riled she got, he would be the better man and keep this monotone if it killed him.

"Oh yeah? Then why can he barely keep his head up after a few slurps—which is just disgusting, by the way. Have you seen your flask? Never mind. You deserve it—when it doesn't even give you a buzz?"

He grinned wickedly. "Because I can handle what most others can't." Then he slapped the young man's back, nearly sending him headfirst into the flames. "Besides, it'll put some hair on his chest, and it's a thank-you for sharing his catch and his information."

The boy's caved-in chest looked as though it couldn't handle the strain of even a few hairs, and Ro scowled harder at Liam. "You know he's going to puke all that up, right? Waste a perfectly good meal that he *needs*? More than alcohol?"

Liam shrugged. "Bet he'll lead us right to the witch. Mission accomplished."

Ro spluttered, trying to figure out which insult to fling at him first.

"And then she eats them."

Their heads whipped around as one toward the boy.

"Repeat that," Liam said low, dangerously.

The boy shrugged, trying to get the flask to his mouth but not quite succeeding. "I says she cooks 'em, then she eats 'em, roast-pig style. Mmmm. Yummy." He started cackling, spilling the flask's contents all over the ground.

Ro and Liam looked at each other, eyes wide.

"We have to find those children. Right now," Liam said in his voice reserved for rivaling thunder. A low, rumbling throbbing that made the horses take note. And any self-preserving human in the vicinity.

Ro was already on her feet. "Show us this cabin. Right now."

The boy slumped over and threw up everywhere.

6

After a good dunking, two mugs of Liam's café that could strip paint from a wooden fencepost, and several hearty slaps to his face, the boy was perched upon Liam's horse, not able to do much more than hold on for his life and point the way.

There was a lot of groaning involved.

Ro and Liam raced their horses through the woods, a dangerous and foolish thing to do in the dark. A horse could break its legs. They could be thrown, knocked unconscious, speared by a branch, or worse. But neither of them slowed.

Their guide started flapping his arms and making stop motions. Liam pulled on his horse's reins.

"I cain't go no farther," he panted, his eyes wide with terror. "The witch—she lives right through there. Not far now. If she feels me step on her property when I ain't supposed to be here"—he shuddered—"let's just say it ain't gonna go well for none of us."

Before Ro or Liam could object, he flung himself off Liam's horse and fled deep into the woods. Ro and Liam exchanged glances, then slid to the ground.

"Coward," Ro muttered, half a mind to chase after the

gangly lad and offer *him* to the witch in exchange for the children.

"Be quiet, be still," Liam muttered to his horse, leaving the shortened reins dangling.

Ro repeated the mantra to her well-trained horse. The horses knew the stealth the hunters needed, but the huntsmen refused to tie their mounts in the wolf-infested forest in case the horses needed to flee.

They'd also been trained to soundly kick anyone who tried to take them.

Liam pulled his bow free while Ro checked her crossbow and made sure bolts were within easy reach, unencumbered by her red cloak.

Liam didn't even tease her about her addiction to her crossbow, just set off, clearly expecting her to follow.

Ro trailed Liam deeper into the woods, the rising sun beginning to illuminate the woods little by little. The trees opened before them, and they both sank into the rotting underbrush, Ro wrinkling her nose at the poof of stench thrown at them.

Liam didn't react, as unflappable as ever, as he took in the cottage before them.

It was brightly painted, built in the German style of white-washed walls and crisscrossed, dark-wood trim. However, it looked as though an artist had taken his brush to the rest of it.

Vibrant colors splashed all over the previously white walls, idyllic scenes of happy, dancing children, flowers, baby animals, and a kind, matronly, smiling old woman, and more, wrapping around the house like Ro's cloak.

And candy. Lots and lots of candy. Painted in every scene.

Ro was entranced in spite of herself.

Her mouth watered, and the remembered taste of sugar, potent and crisp and sweet on her tongue, nearly sent her to her feet to lick its walls. Or beg the owner for a treat.

The witch ate children, for heaven's sake! Yet her home filled Ro with happiness and drew her toward it as a fly toward an insect-devouring plant.

Ro was nothing more than prey to the woman within. And she needed to remember that.

Liam's voice pulled Ro out of her reverie. "If the lad is right, chances are the witch knows we're here. You go to the right, I'll go left, and we'll meet at the back." His eyes slid away from the predator's den long enough to burrow into Ro's soul. "Remember every detail."

Ro nodded her agreement, and they headed out.

Swinging in a wide arc around the witch's home before moving in close, they then crept up to the cabin's back wall, nodded at each other, then crossed paths, sliding just along the walls and peeking into each window.

The only visible door was on the front of the building, and all the curtains were drawn against the disappearing night.

Ro almost gasped when she realized the walls weren't merely painted with idyllic scenes—they were inlaid with sweet treats of all kinds, a mosaic of edible goodness.

Ro dared not touch it, in case it notify the witch within, but the walls were crafted to resemble iced gingerbread, the dark wooden planks carved like baker's chocolate, and the scenes painted on to look like something sugary and edible.

Hard candies and gooey caramels and soft pastries were set into the walls to give the artistry depth, and it was all Ro could do not to sink her teeth into the closest one.

How could children—especially starving children—bear to resist it?

Ro was along the side wall, peeking in the window, when she noticed the curtain had been caught, allowing a sliver of the scene within to shine through. The window pane, made of hard, melted sugar, if Ro's nose could be trusted, was just clear enough to see inside, though everything within was just slightly distorted.

A warm, golden glow from the fireplace bathed the interior, which seemed to be made from plain old wood, and an old shriveled woman rocked before it—but her eyes were on something else.

And maybe it was just the lad's chilling words at the forefront of her mind, but the woman looked . . . hungry. And she had a twig in her hand, squeezing it as someone else held it just out of sight.

Which was just odd.

Ro followed the woman's gaze, and something glinted golden in the firelight, something metal, something just out of sight.

Moving carefully, slowly, not allowing herself to make a sound, Ro twisted every which way, trying to see more.

She couldn't.

Ro finished her trek around the house, rounding the corner to find Liam's worried eyes on her, hidden just on the other side of the porch. Ro blinked. What was he worried about? Surely not her. Maybe the children?

The moment she came into view, his expression cleared, and he jerked his head.

Neatly skirting the porch, which would surely have creaking boards, even with the two windows and main door there just begging to be peeked in, she moved close to Liam and gave her report, repeating everything she'd been able to see.

He grunted.

A bit smug, she asked, "And you? What did you see?"

"Not a thing," he rumbled, turning away to run his eyes over the house.

Ro would have chortled had the need for silence not

been so dire. Even at moments like these, victory was sweet, sweet bliss.

"Did you touch anything?" he asked.

Ro sniffed, offended. "Of course not."

"On my count, we go in fast."

Ro nodded, not bothering to hide her cheeky grin, and he rolled his eyes as he led the way to the porch. They picked their way across it, testing and avoiding loud boards, both trying to see within the windows to no avail, then settled on either side of the door.

A croaking voice rose in frustration. "I don't understand why you ain't fatter, boy! I've been feeding you my best pickings for three days!"

A young, high voice seeped out under the door. "Maybe if you gave us those meat pies over there . . ."

"That's it. I've had enough of you both. I don't care how scrawny you are—I'm hungry!"

Something clanged, two children cried out in fear, and Ro's and Liam's eyes met. He held up three fingers, counted down, and grabbed the doorknob.

Pink light exploded all over the house, arcing through Liam's body as the flesh of his hand sizzled, and a loud thump sounded inside.

It happened so quickly, Ro could hardly track it.

"What was that—ahhhhh!"

The witch's ungodly shriek blasted out of the house, followed by another loud clang, her cry so loud and so shrill, Ro covered her ears. Liam hunched his shoulders against his ears, his body held to the door against his will.

The pink light vanished, and Liam curled around his smoking hand. Her sole focus on getting the children out, Ro aimed a well-placed kick next to the door handle, and the wood splintered with a satisfying spray of . . . gingerbread?

Wait, what? Ro leaned closer for just a split second. The house wasn't painted with candies and chocolates and gingerbreads—it was *made* from all those things. She'd assumed it was some trick, some overlay to cover a solid structure.

Ro's mouth watered, but she forced herself to focus on the scene within.

Two children, a young lad and a small girl, were holding closed a giant oven door as shrieks died out from within and the scent of charred flesh filled the cabin.

Ro honestly didn't know what to do. So she just stood there, crossbow aimed . . . at the stove.

The moment the old woman's cries ended, the children noticed Ro and jumped back, the boy shielding the girl with his body.

"We killed her, and we can kill you too!" the boy cried, his words defiant, but his chin trembling.

The girl hiccuped a sob from behind him.

A cage sat near the old woman's rocking chair, hung from the rafters and just big enough to hold several children, and fierce satisfaction swept through Ro that the witch was now roasting in the oven, also big enough to hold several children.

Ro would've gladly thrown the witch in herself.

She aimed at every corner inside the house, keeping her sights far away from the children. "Are there more?"

His brow wrinkled, and the boy eyed her for half a heartbeat before giving his head a single shake.

Ro quickly reholstered her crossbow and stayed at the door, giving the kids plenty of space. "Your father hired us to find you and bring you home. We're here to rescue you." Her eyes flitted across the cabin, then settled on the children. She allowed humor to peek through. "But it looks as though you're doing a fine job of that yourselves."

The girl grinned, instantly accepting her, but it took the

boy longer. He gave her a slow nod, and Ro stepped back, out of the house.

"Would you care to lead us back to your home?" She could easily find it, especially with Liam's help, but she wanted to give the lad a measure of control, something that had been wrested from him while held captive in the witch's lair.

He shook his head, and Ro's eyebrows rose. "Non?"

"Non, not yet," the boy clarified. He waved his hands to the mounds of food piled around the cabin, more food than Ro had seen since the curse fell. "We're taking this back to our father."

Defiance still filled his words, as if daring her to stop him or take it herself, and Ro kept her words gentle. "May we help you?"

He looked as if he didn't know what to say. Gretel tugged on his jacket, and he held up a staying hand. "What's my father's name?"

Ro smiled and gave it. "The woodsman Aldric. And your stepmother is Hélène, you are Hansel, and your sister there is Gretel. You are eight, she is five, and your father is very, very worried about you."

Gretel took a step forward, but Hansel shoved her back. "Prove it. Prove you are who you say you are. That you aren't *her* come back to take us someplace else to eat us."

Ro took out the sketch their father had made of them, and she held it out to the boy wordlessly.

He didn't come near her, but his eyes filled with tears at seeing one of his father's drawings.

"Hansel." His sister tugged on his jacket again. "I think we should go with her. I think we should go home. Besides, won't Father be glad to see all this food?" She offered him a hesitant smile.

The lad, with the eyes of someone much older, still

looked torn. "She could still be *her*. Come back. She could've taken one of Father's drawings."

Now Gretel's bottom lip trembled, and she looked up at Ro in fear.

"Who?" Ro whispered, bewildered, not sure how to salvage the situation. Wishing Liam would butt in as he always did.

Liam! Ro spun around. Her whole focus had been on the children and any further dangers within, assuming Liam had her back and was letting her take her time speaking with them.

She should've known better.

He was sprawled out on the porch, unconscious, as if he'd slumped over as she'd rushed past him.

"Liam!"

Ro knelt by his side, feeling for his pulse, and panic rushed through her that Gautier's best huntsman—second-best, when she was being contrary—might've died on her watch. On a hunt assigned to just the two of them.

No way would that look good.

"Liam, you had better be all right, or so help me . . ."

She felt more than saw the children come closer.

"Who is he?" Hansel demanded.

"The other huntsman your father hired to find you," Ro said absently, sagging in relief when her fingers finally found the right spot and a pulse thrummed under her fingers.

"There's never been another person with her before . . ." Gretel said in the background.

Had the lad with the fish not led them to the cabin? Perhaps they'd never seen him *with* the witch.

Ro ignored it, more concerned about Liam. Then she noticed his hand was clutched to his chest, his whole body curled around it. She frowned and tried to pull it away, noticing the angry red blisters curled around the back of his hand and trailing down his arm.

"What in the world?"

"She had wards up," the boy said matter-of-factly.

"Oh," Ro said eloquently. She didn't know exactly what that meant, but it clearly wasn't a good thing. "Will he be all right?"

"Of course I'll be all right," Liam muttered sourly. "Help me up."

Relief flowed through her, and Ro scowled to keep from throwing her arms around him in a relieved hug. "Well if you weren't sleeping on the job like a ninny, I wouldn't be all worried about you not having my back like you were supposed to."

He bared his teeth, the action more of pain than annoyance. "I aim to please."

Ro propped him up, and he heaved himself to his feet, still shielding his hand as his eyes settled on the children. "We need to get you kids back to your parents."

Gretel's wide eyes took in the hulking man, who surely looked like a huge, angry giant to the young girl, and Hansel looked torn between his earlier defiance and a newfound awe. "We're going to take the food back, mister."

"How about we get you kids home safely, then you can come back with your father for the food?"

Hansel shook his head, insistent. "Non, she said the house would disappear and move to a new place in the forest once she was done with us."

Speaking of . . . Ro's eyes flitted to the mounds of food, remembering a mention of meat pies. "Are you sure you want to eat anything here? You know, with her particular diet . . ."

She let the thought trail off and shrugged.

Gretel spoke up. "She only et children. She made all that other stuff to fatten us up, since we've been hungry for so long."

"That and eating people made her wards stronger," Hansel added.

Ro frowned. "How do you know all this?"

Hansel shrugged. "She liked to talk a lot. Said it was only worth talking to those who wouldn't be around to repeat what she'd said."

Once again, Ro found herself wishing she could shove the witch in the oven a second time. And possibly a third.

"Pack it up, quickly," Liam ground out. "We want to get you home before dark."

The kids scampered into the house, grabbing flour sacks and shoving in food as fast as they could, giving no thought to if pies should be mashed atop a roast or bread rolls crushed under fruit. They were just intent on snatching it all.

Ro turned to Liam. "Stop scaring them. You could be a little nicer, you know."

He grunted and trudged to the edge of the porch, his back to Ro. She rolled her eyes. Oh well. At least the kids were safe. They would soon learn they had far less to fear from a gruff huntsman than from what they had to fear before.

Liam whistled, and not long after, both horses came trotting into the small clearing in front of the house.

Ro leaned closer to inspect the wall.

"Don't eat that!" Hansel called out. "It'll put you to sleep, it will. Disorient you for days."

Ro grumbled to herself. She was just looking.

As soon as the children were ready, Ro helped carry food out of the house, and with no help from Liam whatsoever, tied the many bags to both horses. He mounted and waited for them, staring into the forest, an impatient look on his face.

She stuck out her tongue at his back, then turned for another load to find Gretel staring at her with wide eyes and parted mouth, as if Ro had just committed a crime. Ro flushed hotly, ducked her head, and hurried past the girl, duly chastised and hoping fervently Gretel wouldn't tell on her.

Liam would hold such a thing against her for the rest of her life. Though who knew if he would tease or tell all the other huntsmen or subject her to double a lifetime of glares.

Still a little miffed, and a lot mortified, she placed Hansel behind Liam on his horse, then pulled Gretel to sit in front of her. They rode out of the clearing, and as soon as they did, Ro glanced back in time to see the house merge into a swirl of colors and vanish.

Gretel saw it too, looked up at her and smiled—as if Ro's transgression had already been forgotten or forgiven—then fell into a deep sleep almost instantly.

Ro started to say something to Liam, then noticed he'd ridden ahead and was almost out of sight.

Grumbling, Ro urged Fairweather into a trot to catch up.

And sincerely contemplated sticking her tongue out at him once more.

7

Ro had to force Liam to stop twice, once to let the kids stretch their legs and visit the woods, and the second time, to eat something and take care of their horses.

Liam stayed reserved, gruff, and didn't help with either stop.

Ro managed to keep her grumbling to herself as she did everything her fellow huntsman normally did. Was he punishing her since he'd passed out and she'd witnessed it? And why wouldn't he let her see his hand?

Well if he wanted to be difficult, then so could she.

They made it back to the cottage with the setting sun at their backs, and Hansel almost broke his neck leaping off the horse and tearing for the cabin.

Ro caught the girl before she could fall headlong off Fairweather's massive height and lowered her gently to the ground.

She gave Ro the sweetest smile before tearing after her brother.

Ro's heart warmed, and she urged Fairweather closer to the cabin and slid from his back. Then she set about unloading the bags of food onto a table set idyllically in front of the house, one Ro hadn't paid attention to before, perfect for eating outdoors in beautiful weather.

She'd make sure to tell them to get all the bags inside before pests set upon them and emptied them in a heartbeat.

Or she'd ask Liam to do it.

Ro peeked over her shoulder to do this just as Liam turned his horse's head and started back into the woods. Ro stared after him in disbelief, then snapped Fairweather's reins straight down, harder than she meant to, to leave them dangling.

"Stay," she growled at her horse.

Fairweather bumped her with his massive head. No matter how grumpy she got, she was never short with her horse, the one thing she loved on this earth more than any other. And he knew it.

"Désolé," she mumbled. Then, "Stay. Please."

Fairweather gave her a look, then nonchalantly went scrounging for anything edible, and Ro marched toward the house with resolute steps. As far as she was concerned, their job wasn't done. If the stepmother was truly trying to lose the children in the woods, then they weren't safe yet.

Ro walked in on a touching scene, the burly woodsman sitting on the floor with his children, holding them close and not bothering to hide his tears.

Ro turned away, embarrassed.

"Non, come in, huntress! You are always welcome," the woodsman boomed.

"I didn't mean to intrude," Ro stammered, not sure where to look. "I simply wanted to make sure the children were safe."

"Thanks to you!" Aldric beamed at her.

Ro just nodded, accepting the thanks, though all she wanted to do was flee.

Aldric lumbered to his feet and rushed over to a chest

along the wall. He heaved open the lid and rummaged inside. "I must thank you, I must—"

Ro put out both hands, though he didn't see it, to forestall any such additional thanks. "No need, Monsieur. Gautier has taken care of—"

And he shoved a hand-carved wooden keepsake box into her hands, lid open.

Ro's words died on her lips. Within lay the loveliest set of hand axes she'd ever seen. "I couldn't possibly . . ."

She ran her finger along the ash-blond handles, the wood silky smooth under her touch.

"But where is your companion?" He strained to see past her and out the door, his eyes roving for Liam.

"Oh, um, he—well, we have to get back right away, so once the children were home . . ." Ro shrugged, hoping he would not be offended.

"No matter, no matter." He swung the lid closed and placed a smaller box atop hers. This one held a silver hunting knife, about the length of Ro's forearm, with a full-tang hilt sandwiched between two antler bones. The antlers curved off the handle, wicked sharp and just waiting for a reverse stab. It, too, was stunning. "This one is for the huntsman, with my everlasting thanks."

Ro tried to object, she really did, but the woodsman turned away, pulling his children back into his arms.

"We must tell your stepmother! Hélène? Hélène! Come! The children are home."

Hansel backed away from his father's embrace, and he started to shake, his fists clenched into tiny, angry knots.

"Why, Hansel lad, whatever is the matter?"

"She isn't here. She isn't coming back," Hansel said defiantly, though in a desperate way.

His father just looked confused, and Ro felt like the worst of intruders.

"I—I killed her. She isn't coming back."

A storm cloud began to gather on the woodsman's face. "You'd best begin explaining yourself, lad, and fast."

Hansel pulled something out of his pocket and dangled it before his father, a lacquered piece of wood on a chain, the rings eddying and swirling in an intricate, lovely pattern of a tree's age. A necklace Ro had seen before.

"I took this from the witch that tried to eat us."

His father's ruddy complexion went pale faster than anything Ro had ever seen, and he whispered, "I gave that to yer stepmother when we married . . ."

Ro stepped back, and the board under her foot creaked.

He turned that thunderstruck expression on Ro, and she froze. A storm of a new kind gathered on the kindly woodsman's face. "You'd best be going, huntress."

Her gaze darted to the children and back. "No harm will come to the children."

It wasn't a question; it was a statement. Yet she waited for an answer.

"None. Ye have my word."

She searched the children's faces, but they looked neither scared nor desperate, only a little sad—Gretel—or angry—Hansel.

She gave him a single nod and took another step back, toward the door. "The food. Outside. On the table. Pests . . ."

But no one was listening.

The burly man sank into the beautifully crafted chair at the table, burying his face in his hands. "Oh mein Gott, what have I done?"

Gretel put her arms around her father's bulky shoulders. "I'm so sorry, Papa."

That was good enough for Ro.

Ro turned and fled, only sparing the briefest parting glance for both children. Which she was pretty sure they hadn't seen anyway.

8

She caught up to Liam not far from where Ro had thrown out their pastries and café.

As much as she wanted to tear into him for leaving her to face the woodsman alone, Ro craned her neck, certain the food would have been devoured by woodland creatures by now.

But non, there it was. Two mud pies and a sludge of dirt—still in the shape of the pastries she'd tossed out. Her mouth popped open, and she swung her head to call Liam's attention to it, but then she caught the look on his face.

He was still in pain. A lot of pain.

He'd lied to her.

With great effort, he raised his head and their eyes met. His jaw tightened, and he got that obstinate "don't you dare say a word" look about him.

Worried, Ro urged Fairweather after him, wanting to ask him to stop but knowing he wouldn't listen.

In fact, Liam didn't stop until well past dark, dangerous for both them and their horses. Liam didn't ask her to, but Ro once again took over camp duties without complaint, wondering how best to bring up his wounded hand.

"Do you want me to—"

"Leave me to my tasks, and you worry about your own," he snapped, his voice like a whiplash.

Ro had already done most of his tasks, but she managed to keep her retort inside as he plunked down with his back to her, his eyes to the woods.

Still worried about Liam, Ro started to get out her bedroll, but that voice—that accursed, hated voice—said, *Your healing crème. Now.*

Ro froze. Liam had just bit her head off. No way would he let her touch him.

Now, the voice insisted.

Ro's heart pounded, and she almost didn't do it.

But not listening to that voice had dire consequences. Always.

And sometimes . . . sometimes . . . her gift did unexpected things. And the need to help Liam swelled within her so badly, she ached with it. It had to be her elusive powers coming into play, because she'd never ached to help Liam with anything. Ever.

She dug around in her medicinal pouch and came out with a healing crème, something Liam most likely had in his own saddlebag from Gautier's storerooms. Though Ro had mixed this one herself.

Hands shaking, she took a deep breath and made her way over to Liam. He looked decidedly grumpy, creases around his eyes speaking of considerable pain, and glared as she came toward him.

Ro almost scurried back to her side of the fire. But she made herself stay put, and she made herself open her mouth.

"I have something for you. For your burn." Her voice trembled, but she was too scared to care.

"I put something on it," he growled.

"Yes, but this is . . . special." At his raised brow, she

corrected, "Potent." When he didn't move, she said, "Please?"

His look thunderous, an attempt to hide the level of pain he was in, most likely, he held out his hand and turned his face away from the light.

Ro sank down next to him, the tremors in her body increasing with her doubt. What if it didn't work? What if she was wrong? What if she just caused him more pain and made him hate her more?

She unwound his hand, the covering sticking to his seeping, blistered skin, but he didn't move even one of his tightly wound muscles. But the tension radiating from him made Ro want to flee. She poured some water over the bandage, then eased it off the rest of the way.

The skin wasn't just blistered, it was melted. She could even see bone through it in places.

Fighting off a gag, not wanting to humiliate Liam any further, she kept her head down and smoothed a thick layer of crème over his hand.

He wavered—literally, actually swooned—but Ro held on to him, and he didn't fall over headfirst. He blinked his eyes rapidly, as if he were fighting for consciousness, and something wet glistened in his beard. Tears?

Ro's gaze dove to his hand as she pretended she hadn't seen a thing.

Now, hold it, the voice said.

Ro covered his hand with her own, a layer of crème between their skin, and spoke in her head. *O mighty Creator, if it please you, heal him.* Lightning fast, the thought followed, *Unlike you did for my mother.*

Soul-deep sorrow touched her and left, mixing with her own, and then warmth spread from her hands to Liam's. His eyes drooped, and he sagged, his full weight on Ro. She almost fell over, but she managed to ease him to the ground, wrap his hand in fresh bandages, and cover him with his travel blanket.

Then she settled in to keep watch until Liam was ready to wake.

❧

Liam awoke just as Ro was beginning to worry about nodding off herself, and without a word, Ro rolled over and went to sleep as Liam stood and stretched.

He allowed her a few hours before waking her. The sun was already high, and still without speaking, they set off for Gautier's small château.

Ro was close to nodding off by the time they reached it, and all she could think about was the small mattress upstairs she could call her own. When she was in town.

She almost hugged the guard who told them Gautier was away and would hear their report on the morrow.

They urged their horses into Gautier's stable. Ro's hand found the smooth boxes, the woodsman's gifts, as she was taking off her saddlebags.

"Oh! I almost forgot." She handed Liam's gift over the stall, not quite meeting his eyes. "This is for you. Thanks from the woodsman for finding his children."

Liam stood staring down at the contents of the box, no expression on his face, so Ro felt she had to explain.

"I—I tried to refuse, but he was most insistent. Besides, it was the loveliest dagger I'd ever seen, and quite useful for a hunt. He didn't give me much of a chance to refuse, so I didn't know what else to do but take them."

"We do not take gifts from peasants."

Ro raised an eyebrow.

"Our pay comes from Gautier. This is too close to bribery. And it steals from those who cannot afford to give.

These could have been bartered for food from the Mesdemoiselles of the Mountain."

Ro's jaw ticked, as it did every time the witches' names were brought up.

The Mesdemoiselles were no more. Ro had seen to that.

Guilt over accepting the beautifully crafted weapons tried to make an appearance, but Ro shoved it away. She would not be made to feel guilty for something she hadn't known was wrong. "Then you stick around long enough to refuse the gifts next time."

He tried to hand it back, but Ro's hands were busy, and she didn't even attempt to take it.

He paused. "Wait. Gifts?"

Ro swept her cape back and ran her hand along one of the hand axes tucked into her belt.

They were exquisite, balanced so well, and quite frankly, Ro didn't want to give them back.

His look turned to thunder. Thankfully Ro was immune. Or so she told herself. "You should not have taken those."

She shrugged and went back to unloading her saddlebags, then heaved the saddle over the wall, looped the reins on the nail tacked high on the wall, and started brushing down her horse.

"Gautier has said this?" she casually asked.

"Non, but—"

"And no one else under your charge accepts gifts?"

"If it were up to me—"

She interrupted with a level look. "When a gift comes from the heart, Liam, sometimes the only thing you can do is shut up and take it."

He snapped his mouth closed, and although Ro was terrible with people, hardly knew the right thing to say at the right moment, she had a momentary stroke of genius.

"Sometimes," she said softly, "it's just as hard for others to accept charity as it is for you. Just . . . let them. Not bribes, certainly, but a gift given in gratitude and joy, well, that can be a powerful thing. For both parties."

He looked down at the dagger still in the box and didn't say another word.

Ro doled out a careful measure of oats and water for her horse.

After seeing to Fairweather, Ro trudged out of the stables, weary, ready to find her room and sleep until dinnertime. Or maybe the next morning.

"Merci beaucoup."

The words were so low, she almost missed them. She peeked over her shoulder, and Liam nodded at her. The dagger was sheathed and tucked in his belt.

"For what you did . . . in the woods . . . merci."

He was eyeing her like she was one of the creatures they hunted. A bit in awe, a bit wary, and a lot interested in what she might be.

She needed to stop that right now.

Ro shrugged. "Don't thank me."

His brow scrunched.

Ro smirked. "I prayed."

And she left a bewildered Liam behind her, hoping she never, ever had to hunt one-on-one with the surly huntsman ever again.

THE END

THE LITTLE GIRL WHO WOULDN'T STOP DANCING

Les Chaussures Rouges
"The Red Shoes"
—Hans Christian Andersen—

"Dance shalt thou!" said he. "Dance in thy red shoes till thou art pale and cold! Till thy skin shrivels up and thou art a skeleton!"
"Mercy!" cried she, but . . . she must keep ever dancing.

« Danse, tu vas danser! dit-il. Danse dans tes chaussures rouges jusqu'à ce que tu sois pâle et froide ! Jusqu'à ce que ta peau se ratatine et que tu sois un squelette !
— Miséricorde ! s'écria-t-elle, mais . . . elle doit continuer à danser. »

1

"Paris?" Ro stared at Gautier, aghast. "You're sending us to *Paris*?"

The other huntsmen in the room went still, not daring to move or break the sudden tension.

Gautier leveled a cool look her way. "By all means, if this is too difficult for you, feel free to decline."

Ro snapped her mouth closed, half tempted to flee, but she remained silent.

Gautier went back to what he was saying. "My contact and his retinue have barricaded themselves at the Palais Garnier, the opera house, and I need you to get there as quickly as possible. They'll not hold out much longer."

But that's in the very heart of the city! Ro kept her protest firmly behind clamped-shut lips. But *Paris*? Only someone with a death wish went there.

Was Gautier truly foolish enough to kill off all his best huntsmen at once?

Ro's eyes traveled the room. Twenty of the strongest, scrappiest, and deadliest of the kingdom's huntsmen stood before Gautier's desk.

Twenty-one, if Ro counted herself.

It was rare that Gautier called in all his best huntsmen at once. If he wanted brute strength? Even the curse and lack of food hadn't diminished Victor's and Javier's hulking frames. Just honed them.

Basile, Hugo, and Nolan had possibly been bandits before the curse—and often sent lesser men scurrying away with one glance from any of the three scary men.

Sacha and Rayan had trained in the art of stealth and, probably, assassination. Axel and Lucian were brothers who spoke hardly a word but always came back with completed tasks and whispered rumors following them like bloodhounds.

Hector, Gustave, Milo, Gabin, Marceau, Sévère, Dieudonné, Honoré, Théo, Émeric—all huntsmen Ro had worked with in the past and knew to be competent.

And then there was Liam.

"With all due respect, Monsieur," said Liam respectfully, "Paris is more dangerous than any other city in all of France. Is the job truly worth it? May we have more details before we accept?"

As if any of them would decline. Ro was certain none of them would come back from this alive, and even she wouldn't dare decline.

Gautier fed them, clothed them, housed them, and made life in curse-ridden France slightly less unbearable. Plus the gold purse at the end of each hunting job was not too bad a reward, should any of them one day be able to spend it.

The only currency worth anything right now was goods, namely edible goods, not gold. It didn't stop her from sending each heavy gold purse to her family. Anonymously, of course.

She was pulled back into the conversation as Gautier shifted, breaking the steady stare he had turned Liam's way.

"You'll need to provide safe passage out of the city for

each of my trapped men," he said, his tone direct. Not to be argued with.

After a slight hesitation, Liam accepted it with a nod.

Ro didn't blame him. Gautier was not one to be crossed, and if he was trying to get important men out of the city—whoever they were—twenty huntsmen might not be enough.

Gautier spread a map over his desk. "Palais Garnier is here, and you'll be coming from this direction." He pointed north of the city. "Travel through this area, toward the city's center. I'm relying on you to get there as swiftly as possible."

Even Javier's usually bored expression was on the solemn side of things. "When do you need us back by?"

Gautier let the map furl and started tucking it away in a waterproof scroll tube. Rain would chase them all the way to Paris. He shrugged. "Whenever you complete your mission."

The stuffed animals on the wall could've come to life and started eating one of them, and Ro wouldn't have spared it half a glance. She stared at Gautier with wide eyes, heart sinking like a lead weight.

This was it. They knew too many of Gautier's secrets. He was offing them all.

Not that Ro could think of any particular secrets offhand . . .

Gautier smiled without taking in their expressions. "I expect you to come back when your mission is complete, of course, but swift action is of necessity to get there. But the mission itself is . . . delicate . . . and may take some time. I trust your judgment on how best to complete it."

He held out the tube to Liam. Liam took it with a solemn expression.

"Your mounts and gear have been readied for you, and I must insist you leave right away."

Basile, Hugo, and Nolan exchanged glances.

"And the payment for this particular hunt?" Basile asked.

Gautier said, "Double your usual fare, plus whatever gold you can carry out of the vault of kings." He smiled. "If you're skilled enough to make your way there and out again, of course."

Tension immediately shifted to excitement, to awe, to . . . greed.

Even Liam seemed not to be oblivious to its pull, but he steadied as soon as his eyes met Ro's. "Our horses will be set upon before we reach the city."

"True." Gautier shifted papers on his desk and unearthed a second map.

Ro craned her neck and saw three points on the map that had been zoomed in on and encased in a bubble with greater detail: a monastery with thick walls on the city's outskirts, the vault of kings in the royal Parisian palace, and the Palais Garnier or the grand opera house.

"You can set them free a few miles outside the city, or you can take them here, to this monastery, and lock them within until you return. Within reside a small order of monks that keep an eye on Paris and report their findings."

After pointing that out, he rolled this second map, encased it, and passed it to Ro.

Liam's jaw tightened at that, and Ro offered him a sweet smile, which he promptly ignored.

"They might not survive the night. Need I repeat my request for your immediate departure?" A strident tone had entered Gautier's voice.

Ro just barely held in a retort that it would take at least three days to reach the city, and if that was the case, why hadn't he sent them sooner, and also—just what was he *thinking*?

Without a word, his huntsmen filed from the room, all

heading to Gautier's stable. Ro followed, desperately wanting to shoot something.

Or run far away. That was likely the better option.

"Liam, Ro, not you."

Ro's skin crawled, but she forced a blank expression upon her face and turned back.

Gautier waited for the door to close behind the last person before looking at either of them. "There's more to this mission, I'm afraid."

Ro stopped herself from rolling her eyes. There always was, wasn't there? She took her cue from Liam and waited quietly, if not patiently.

"I need not emphasize the gravity of the situation to either of you, must I?"

Ro shook her head. "But what I don't understand —*Paris*. What job could possibly be so important? And if they can't get out of the city, how could we possibly do the same? Even with greater numbers, these wolves aren't afraid to attack in broad daylight, and they're *huge*. We'll be lucky to—"

Liam shot her a look, and Ro clamped her mouth shut.

Thank goodness. She hadn't meant for all that to come pouring out.

Gautier was quiet a long moment, his eyes on the scraggly wolf by the door. It was the only creature in the room fully stuffed—the rest had lost their heads to Gautier's walls.

The small creature with patchy fur was the first wolf Ro had killed. It was the wolf that had led her into this life and into Gautier's service—the one she'd killed to save her sister.

It still shook her a little to see it each time she came within Gautier's office. Why had he kept it?

Gautier spoke quietly. "I owe a debt to Monsieur André that can never be repaid, and for that, he has asked for my assistance—and my discretion." He shot a look at both Liam and Ro in turn, as if demanding their silence. "His daughter, Esmée, discovered a cursed object in the labyrinth under the opera house. Here, read his letter."

He handed the letter to Liam, and Ro crowded close to read it. Liam stiffened.

Boldly, Ro tilted his hand so she could better see it, then smirked at the little growl he let out.

Gautier did this all the time. Played favorites. And Ro worked hard to ignore it or smile and pretend she didn't care. Mostly she saved her smiles for Liam, since they annoyed him so much.

Getting on Liam's last nerve was one of her favorite things.

Her smirk was swept from her face by the contents of the letter.

The letter was pieced together from scraps of curled paper glued into some semblance of order, gaps of information liberally sprinkled throughout.

"Homing pigeons? From Paris?" Ro guessed.

"Oui," Gautier answered simply. "Read on, s'il vous plait."

Monsieur André's teenage daughter, Esmée, had found something dangerous in the vault, and it had taken her over completely. The man's heart cried out from the pages—he was afraid she hadn't long to live if it did not release its grip on her.

It might already be too late with how long it took the missive to reach them from Paris.

Ro searched for a date before Liam flipped the page, but she didn't see one.

The backside was more of the same, a plea for help, a rundown of their goods, and a reminder of how long they'd been holed up in Paris at Gautier's request.

Ro felt Liam's surprise at the same time her eyebrows

climbed her forehead. Gautier had been sending men to Paris? For how long?

It seemed whoever had sent this had flown message after message, hoping as many as possible would reach Gautier, each slip of paper containing slightly varying retellings of the same information.

It was rather well done.

The letter ended abruptly.

"What can you tell us about this cursed object?" Ro asked.

Gautier's ever-present smirk was notably absent. "Only that you must not touch it, and you must not put it on."

"And that object would be . . . what, exactly?" Ro persisted.

Gautier eyed her for too long a moment. "It would be better if you were shown."

Ro's jaw tightened. "It would be better if I had as much information as possible ahead of time in case additional preparation is necessary."

"Not in this case," Gautier said decisively.

Before Ro could protest further, Liam's steady voice cut in. "Why else have you asked us to stay behind, Monsieur Gautier?"

Gautier blew out a breath, his demeanor even more serious. "It's true that I don't send you into Paris lightly. If I thought you had a hope of making it without greater numbers, I wouldn't send you at all. I've asked you to stay because . . . you two are the only ones I trust to meet with Monsieur André. He has something of value for me, something he was asked to retrieve from the opera's labyrinth. It is *my* fault the girl was cursed."

Ro was startled by the growl that came out alongside the words, the flash of self-loathing Gautier had never before let them see.

As if he actually cared.

Gautier went on, somewhat hurriedly, as if he didn't want either of them to notice his slip of . . . humanity. "Everyone else is yours to do with as you will, tasked with getting you in and out of the city, but the success of this mission rests upon your shoulders alone."

"What of the object?" Liam persisted.

It was at that moment Ro realized she was still close to Liam—far too close—but she was afraid to move and break the spell of Gautier actually talking to them, giving them facts they desperately needed.

Liam seemed to realize the same thing, because he froze, going even more still than he already was, as if he were in a tree and prey within his sights.

Paper rustled, and Gautier held out a sketch of a dagger, intricately designed with blood-red rubies buried in its hilt. "This is your secondary mission. Monsieur André has searched long and hard for this dagger, in the opera house's underground labyrinth, and in the vault of the kings, but he is unclear in his letters whether he has found it. Nevertheless, I must have both tasks completed before you leave the city."

"Soldiers . . ." Ro started to say.

"Cannot know anything about this. Nor can lesser huntsmen. It is of the utmost secrecy."

Liam and Ro nodded as one, though Ro wanted to ask so many more questions.

"I'm trusting both of you to get as many huntsmen as possible out of Paris after the mission is over, of course, but I will need the two of you back no matter the cost."

Ro and Liam exchanged a flicker of a glance.

"So what you're saying is . . ." Liam sounded like he couldn't finish.

"What I'm saying is, no matter what it takes, no matter whom you must sacrifice, the two of you must come back with this dagger, alive."

2

Ro's horse was already saddled, her gear packed neatly and her red cape around her shoulders, but she went over it all again anyway.

She wouldn't leave such things to others. It could cost her her life.

Fairweather, safely in his stall, had his back to her, silently protesting her choosing one of Gautier's horses over him.

He'd already screamed at her and tried to bite her and kicked the stable wall until the stable boys went scurrying to find other tasks—outside—but she couldn't force the comfort he needed past her lips. She couldn't lose him too.

Fairweather would just have to be mad at her.

She swallowed, hard. Hopefully she'd be able to make it up to him.

Liam, a few rows down, was doing the same with his horse, also a different one than he usually rode. She was pretty sure he'd copied her, not the other way around.

She hoped.

Ro carefully kept her gaze away from his, Gautier's words ringing in her head as if he'd just said them.

"No matter whom you must sacrifice . . ."

That no-good, devious, rotting scum! That he was willing to sacrifice any of them was horrible enough, but how long would it take for him to say such things about her to his other huntsmen?

Her eyes strayed to Liam. Perhaps to her greatest rival?

Non! She jerked her focus back to her task. That was exactly what Gautier wanted. Them at each other's throats, doubting each other. And she wouldn't give it to him.

"It's been a while since we've been on a hunt together, eh?" Marceau said from right next to her.

Ro tensed all her muscles at once to keep from jumping and squeaking like a mouse.

She'd been teased for such things far too often already.

Gustave leaned against her horse, distinctly in her way. "Yeah, I haven't got to teach you my knife-throwing skills yet."

Hugo snorted. "Skills is overstating it."

"More like Ro needs to teach *you* a thing or two," Marceau put in.

Ro smiled and kept checking over her gear, the saddle, the reins—making sure everything was to her liking and secure for a long, hard, damp ride.

And keeping an eye on everything her fellow huntsmen got near or touched.

Besides, for all she knew, Gautier could have met with each huntsman separately, telling them all to off each other. She wasn't dying via broken neck by her saddle coming loose.

Her fellow huntsmen continued to heckle each other over their skills, or lack thereof, but Ro could feel the tension pulsing underneath.

No one went to Paris. Those who had stayed in the city were few and had been killed quickly. Anyone who tried to go in for a rescue hadn't come back out.

The wolves ruled that city, and they weren't giving up their dictatorship anytime soon.

Was Gautier done with them all? Had they done too much of his bidding, seen too many of his secrets, and now he was sending them to certain death?

And still, as they teased and tried to keep the tension light, the other huntsmen flicked covert glances at Liam and Ro, the question clear in their eyes. Why had Gautier kept them behind?

Ro could just strangle his smarmy little neck, setting them at odds before the hunt had even begun. When they needed to pull together, for this one more than any other.

"Riders, move out!" Liam called into the unspoken turmoil.

Ro mounted with the rest of them. They arrayed themselves into groups, then followed Liam toward certain doom.

3

The three-day journey passed quickly.

On the morning of the third day, Liam called a halt, dismounted, and said, "Gather round."

He unfurled the map and anchored it to a large flat rock with smaller stones.

They listened, coming in close, even if a few of them—notably Nolan, Hugo, and Basile—took their sweet time about it.

"Monsieur André needs us right away. We stable the horses—Basile, Nolan, Hugo—you'll take them to the monks to look after, then the rest of us will go into the city here."

Ro breathed a little easier. She watched her back around all of them, but especially around those three.

"That ain't where Gautier told us to go in," Victor put in helpfully.

Liam gave him a tight smile. "I'm going to get you in and out, all of you, alive. To do that, I need to change the plan a little."

He shouldn't have had to say it. But Gautier had placed

the seed, and now it was up to Liam to remove the festering doubt. As always.

Ro hung back, as she often did, a silent observer.

"If you're going to get into the city," Hugo said, the hardness in his eyes matched by his voice, "you're going to need all of us."

"We also need a way out," Liam said firmly. "And the monks keep tabs on the city. You will be in charge of getting us out when the time comes. I trust the three of you won't find the task of guarding our horses too difficult until then?"

Hugo mumbled that it wasn't, his look surly.

Ro almost smirked. Using Gautier's words against them now, was he?

"And what about our share in the vault of kings?" Nolan said in a quiet, dangerous voice.

Everyone went very still, waiting for Liam's response. A few nonchalantly rested their hands on their blades, matching Nolan's, Hugo's, and Basile's threatening movements.

It was rare—actually, Ro couldn't remember a time when they'd all worked together for a hunt. They were used to being the ones in charge, working alone, or in much smaller groups. They were used to making their own decisions.

It wouldn't take much to snap the tension and send them all into a brawl.

Ro swallowed hard.

Liam kept his voice level, his tone firm, and his posture unthreatening. "In order for this to work, we'll have to agree to split our shares."

Immediate protest came from all quarters.

Liam raised his hand until the grumbling less resembled an earthquake. "It's not what I would have preferred, either, but we need to escape the city with our lives. The treasure is secondary to that. Agreed?"

Liam didn't budge until he'd met their eyes and received an agreement from each huntsman there.

Ro couldn't help but note that he didn't seek her out. Not that he needed to. She wholeheartedly wanted to get out of there with her life. Forget the vault.

Not that any of them would.

"So what's the plan, chef?" Javier asked, calling him the French name for boss, just to remind everyone whom Gautier placed in charge. "Just run as fast as we can and hope they don't catch us?"

Liam's jaw tightened, and Ro almost laughed aloud. She didn't, of course—she didn't want to undermine his authority—but . . . "That's your plan? Really?"

The glare he sent her was blistering.

Ro crossed her arms and raised an eyebrow, as much to ward off the look as to demand an answer.

"We need to push hard for the center before the wolves corner us or hem us in," Liam insisted. "Speed is our best option."

Ro just looked at him. "Stealth is just as important."

Liam's jaw tightened further. "I know that."

"Not to mention we would wear out quickly and may not be ready for a fight when it came. It will take hours to reach the center, even running."

"What would you suggest?" Liam asked her pointedly, in a tight voice.

Ro shrugged. "I think we should create a distraction, several streets over from our intended entry point, with as much noise as possible, with as many of us as can be spared, and with as many weapons as possible, so the wolves focus their attack away from the palais."

Victor grinned. "I would be happy to make distraction."

Sasha nodded enthusiastically.

"The city is a big place . . ." Liam hedged.

Ro shrugged. "We can use the blockades already set up. Here, here, and here."

Ro tapped his map with her own map tube. The battle to win the city back from the wolves had been fierce, and its remnants lay scattered all over the city. Blockades, piled furniture, rubble from buildings—they could use it all to their advantage.

If they survived.

"We separate into three teams," Ro continued. "One team creates a distraction, the second sneaks past to create the next diversion, and the third relies on stealth to get past both. The second group will make enough noise to pull the wolves away from the first group, so they can sneak past us, and so on. And we'll, of course, kill as many as we can."

Appreciation rested in Marceau's eyes. "Then when each group kills their wolves, they can move on and help the next group. I like this plan."

Liam nodded, stroking his close-cropped beard thoughtfully. "That just might work."

Ro did not throw her hands up and shout in victory like she wanted to—each concession was hard-fought and hard-won with Liam—but a grin popped up without her meaning for it to. Hopefully Liam wouldn't see it and pronounce her plan the worst he'd ever heard.

On that thought, she carefully wiped all expression from her face and waited.

Liam glanced around the circle. "Are we agreed? Bon. Then we go in on foot."

The huntsmen gathered around to memorize blockades and entry points, as well as to plan for they would do if they were cornered. Then they gathered their gear and set off while Nolan, Hugo, and Basile led all twenty-one horses toward the monastery.

4

The first buildings they came to were the windmills surrounding the city. Used for grinding flour or crushing grapes for wine, among other things, the once-proud structures had fallen into disrepair.

Ro wouldn't have been surprised if they all needed to be torn down and rebuilt once habitation became possible in the once-great city.

The City of Lights in the distance had been abandoned right in the middle of a rebuild. Wooden structures were being replaced with stone, the former king and queen having commissioned an exquisite designer to bring their city into the modern era of their rule.

Ro knew, from her time living in the city before her family had lost everything, that the structures in the center of the city had been completed before the curse had fallen.

But here, on the outskirts, wooden structures still dominated. And desperately needed to be torn down. Before they caught fire and set the whole city ablaze.

With no one living there to fight it.

As they moved into the interior—if the wolves let them—Ro wasn't looking forward to seeing the half-built and abandoned projects that had once been the pride of the city.

Liam waved their group forward.

They'd broken into three groups: Since Liam and Ro needed to be in the stealthy group, surpassing the others for the Palais Garnier, they'd chosen Sacha and Rayan for their ability to become shadows, as well as Marceau and Gustave in case they needed additional muscle.

Victor and Javier each led a group of five. Both men were practically giants and had a good head on their shoulders for strategy and fighting. Ro wasn't too worried about them, especially since they would be off the streets, fighting from the buildings above as much as possible, but she couldn't help worrying a little.

Would they be enough for what was to come?

She kind of wanted Basile, Hugo, and Nolan back to strengthen their numbers. Maybe.

After checking over each windmill they passed for possible wolf dens—they didn't want to be attacked from behind, if they could prevent it—the three groups headed for the first structures of the city proper.

Ro, Liam, Sacha, Rayan, Gustave, and Marceau settled in to wait on the outskirts, while Victor's group dashed for the first blockade—and hopefully the buildings on either side of it—while Javier's company waited for the signal to move out.

It wasn't long until howls came from the first blockade. The howls spread into the city, the cry taken up and carried into the distance until it echoed around them and seemed to fill the city to bursting. A chill skittered down Ro's spine, and she could feel the small hairs rise at the back of her neck and down her arms.

There. Were. So. Many.

How would they ever escape the city alive?

Then came shouting, and not long after, bows twanging,

swords slashing, and outraged growls—the last from an onslaught of wolves.

Ro shuddered to hear it. The men with her were notably pale, fists clenched around weapons and shoulders strained against holding perfectly still.

The second group took off, bypassing the streets of the first conflict and heading to the next blockade.

This time, it seemed as if an eternity passed before more shouts came, much further away, and much softer from their position. Until a loud *boom* rocked the structures where they hid.

Ro's mouth dropped open. "Where on earth did they find working gunpowder?"

No one answered her—Liam and the others were already running at a low crouch. Ro scrambled to catch up, berating herself for letting herself get preoccupied.

They passed the first distraction, which was slowly growing quieter, and then the second, from a few streets over.

Shadows slithered past, but they all seemed intent upon the loud noises coming from the other groups, and none crossed Ro's path, thank goodness.

Liam scouted out a secure position to hole up, and they each crawled into what looked like a cold-food-storage pantry and pulled the door shut after them. Then they settled into the small—but not cramped—space, keeping their breathing shallow and not daring to move.

If any wolves had caught their scent or heard them racing to this position, they may already be compromised.

Ro strained to listen in the dark space, but the walls were thick. She could faintly hear the closest commotion, but she wouldn't know when the first group had passed them.

Unless . . .

First of all, she tried straining with her eyesight. But the thing her eyes sometimes did, lighting everything around her slightly, didn't happen. She held back a sigh.

Might mean they weren't in danger; might mean she just didn't work right.

She was pretty sure it was the second one.

Then she relaxed every muscle in her body, starting with her neck and moving down to her toes, then *listened*.

Her companions' breathing steadily grew louder, until it sounded like they were all panting from running a kilomètre. Her heart leaped in excitement, and the sound faded away.

Stifling a sigh, she forced herself to relax. She moved past the space she was in, straining for sounds from the other huntsmen.

The closest were still putting up a valiant fight. But try as she might, she couldn't hear anything from the first group.

Then, a brush of footsteps, stealing past where they were all hiding, two streets over as they'd agreed.

Ro couldn't hold back her gasp.

"What? What is it?" Liam said in a low voice, barely any sound to it.

But to her, it was as if he'd come up right next to her and bellowed in her ear. The sound was so sudden and startling, she jumped. She almost smacked him, then realized she wouldn't know which of them she'd hit in the darkness.

"The first group. They're passing us now," she whispered.

Then a silence followed that made Ro feel like an idiot. She could just hear them all thinking, "And how does the witch know that?"

She had to cover and fast. "Don't you hear them?" she asked innocently.

"I do not," Sacha said in a lightly accented voice, "but the wolves *can* hear us."

Ro snapped her mouth closed. Right.

A trickle of sweat made its way down Ro's back a veritable century later. Paris was stifling in the summer—or it had been, before the curse—and the closed space brought back memories.

She focused on them in order not to think of how close the walls were, or how many huntsmen were stuffed within: Boat rides. Splashing in the fountains or on the banks of the Seine. Suffering in the heat upstairs and being left out while her parents threw dinner party after dinner party.

Playing hide and seek in the Parisian townhouse, hiding in a closet very much like this one. Though the cook wouldn't have stood for their playing in her kitchen.

Rayan moved, pushing open the door a crack. Blessed light flooded the space, and Ro felt like she could breathe again.

And then the sounds came to her. A new distraction, the one behind them having fallen silent. How long until the wolves figured out what they were up to?

They moved as one without a word to each other, heading all the way across the city, to its very heart.

5

It had been going so well.

Then the wolves surrounded the building Victor's company was sheltering in, not allowing them to leave by any of the five streets touching it. Nothing Javier's group did pulled the wolves away, and Victor's group was out of arrows.

And the wolves had figured out there was a third group.

Howls chased them as Ro, Liam, Sacha, Rayan, Marceau, and Gustave ran for all they were worth.

They were only three streets away from the palais, but that would mean nothing if they were set upon.

The second group, led by Javier, merged with them. "Big pack coming this way. Even bigger pack holding the others at bay."

A howl punctuated his words.

Liam nodded and kept running. Ro focused on every pounding step, leaping over debris and skidding around street corners.

A sense of wrongness had followed Ro throughout the city, a sense Ro couldn't shake. Or talk herself out of.

Of course it was wrong! Wolves shouldn't be able to take over a city—drive people out.

But it was more than that.

Ro careened around another corner and came upon la Place de l'Opera, the square before the opera house.

And she nearly fell headlong over Liam's feet. He pulled her down beside him as he scoped out the best way across the square. Wolves roamed the edges of the open square, alert, hackles raised, sniffing refuse.

But Ro wasn't staring at them.

The place was bustling with people. People who strolled through the boulevard, eating at cafés, shopping, and flowing in and out of the Grand Hôtel.

The Grand Hôtel she *knew* lay in ruins, but to her eyesight looked as if it were gleaming with beauty and churning with life.

It took her a moment to realize what was wrong with the scene—it was like an image of what should be overlay the debris and crumbling architecture of what was.

And the wolves in the square took no note of the bustling people.

While she tried to blink away the ghostly images, the pack burst into the street behind Ro's crouched group.

"Go, go, go!" Javier called. "We'll make our way to the vault!"

The huntsmen veered in three directions.

Ro hardly noticed.

Liam grabbed Ro's arm—she normally hated when he did stuff like that, but this time she barely felt it—and he hauled her across the square, directly for the palais.

But she stumbled after him, wooden, unable to make herself run on her own. People walked around her, chatting, smiling, holding hands, wearing fashion she hadn't seen before—fashion that some hidden part of her told her would have advanced had the curse not fallen.

But they weren't there. They weren't real. How could they be?

Ro started to feel sick, dizzy. Like her world was collapsing around her.

"Ro? Huntress!" Liam's voice came from far away.

She didn't even realize she was falling till she slammed into the paving stones cheek first.

❧

She came to bouncing on Liam's shoulders as he tore across the town square. She hadn't been out long.

She raised her head to see wolves on their tail. Close. So, so close.

She double-tapped his shoulder, and like a choreographed move, he swung her as she jumped down, taking three strides to match his speed.

They tore for the Palais Garnier, wolves hot on their trail. Biting, snapping, snarling—yet Ro and Liam stayed just out of reach.

They hurdled up the steps three at a time, then Liam grabbed Ro and shoved her up on the fence surrounding the palais. She scampered up, and Liam vaulted after her.

The wolves hit the fence just as they reached the top, snapping, growling, then howling when Liam and Ro were too high to eat.

"The others . . ." Ro panted.

"We have to trust they'll find their way. Keep going."

Ro crouched on the fence, each step precarious. Plus the wolves kept hitting the iron spikes, rocking it underneath her. Ro held on tight.

Suddenly, the wolves took off in another direction.

"Quickly!" Liam called.

Ro was already moving. She sprinted down the rail, feet weaving in and out of spikes, as graceful as any dancer, to a window high on the wall, with a lattice leading up to it.

The only way to access it was from the top of the fence. By jumping.

Never one to fear heights, Ro crouched, gauged her jump, then pushed off.

The fence wobbled dangerously, but she had enough momentum to reach it. She dangled from the lattice, but it didn't feel like it could hold much weight. Clambering up as quickly as possible, she unlatched then fell inside the window, looking back out for Liam.

Half of the wolves were now *inside* the fence, jumping as high as they could and snapping at Liam, barely missing his sturdy boots.

The wolves on both sides took turns slamming into the fence. Liam held on with an iron grip, but even Ro could see it was difficult for him as his precarious perch rocked back and forth like a ship being tossed in the waves.

Ro rushed around the dim interior, but her eyes hadn't adjusted to the darkness. "Come on, come on, come *on*!"

She tripped on something.

The room suddenly flared to life, colors vibrant and objects glowing as if lit by a flame, and a rope made itself known to her, coiled under her feet.

She tied it to a heavy piece of furniture, then looped it through a hook overhead, something a plant or birdcage had likely hung from in days past, then called down to Liam. "Rope!"

He nodded gratefully, eyes on the predators trying to get to him.

She coiled it in several loops around her arm. Then she steadied her breathing and tossed it in a gentle loop over his shoulders. He let it fall over one arm, secured it to himself, then rocked a few times before launching himself at the lattice.

The force of his leap knocked the fence askew, and the wolves finished the job.

The fence went down.

Liam slammed into the stone wall. Ro pulled hard on the rope, lifting him up and away from the wolves, in case the lattice didn't hold.

The wolves landed on the fallen fence, which landed on their comrades on the other side. Trapped wolves yelped and whined in pain, then wriggled out from under it and took off.

The rest of the wolves turned their attention to Liam.

The hook in the ceiling loosened in a crumble of plaster. "Oh no, not now," Ro muttered. "Hold just a little longer."

"What was that, huntress?" Liam called from outside the window.

"Nothing. Just hurry!" She pulled hard on the rope, hoping he could sense her urgency. What was taking him so long? She was surprised that flimsy lattice had held *her*.

The rope slackened a bit, Ro pulled some more, the hook loosened further.

Ro grunted, holding on for all she was worth. He was *heavy*. "Come on, come on . . ."

Two things happened at once.

The lattice broke, and the hook came free of the ceiling.

The heavy chair came squealing across the floor, dragging Ro with it, and Ro's boots slid toward the window as Liam's bulk dragged her down.

"Non!" she cried out, leaning back as far as she could go.

Liam cried out in pain.

Suddenly, hands were there, holding Ro, grasping the rope, helping her pull.

Two men went to the window, leaning out and grabbing hold of Liam. As soon as they pulled him up far enough, Ro saw a wolf dangling off his calf, worrying the meat back and forth as if trying to tear it from his leg. Liam kicked at the creature for all he was worth. One of the men stabbed the wolf in the head, then Liam was inside, and the men were pulling the ropes off him.

Ro fell back, sitting hard on the floor, and the men took a moment to breathe, one immediately checking Liam's wound. Blood soaked his trousers, boot, and the floor under him.

Horrified, Ro instantly felt guilty, then angry, but mostly guilty. "What took you so long?" she demanded. "Why didn't you come up right away?"

Liam's glare could have broiled stone. "Really? After you drop me to be a tasty snack for the wolves?" His voice was low and husky, a little scratchy.

Ro raised her chin. "I wouldn't have dropped you if you'd gotten up here as fast as I did!"

The strangers in the room had grown quiet and still, except the one cutting away cloth to get to Liam's mutilated skin to rinse and wrap it.

Liam was quiet a moment, as if debating telling her. "You had one of the rope strands around my neck. I almost passed out."

That's when she noticed the angry red line around Liam's neck.

It felt like she'd been sucker punched.

Oh, Dieu. And she'd been pulling on that? And then he'd *dropped*?

She buried her face in her hands and groaned. "I could've killed you. Hung you." Her words escaped with a bit of a wail to them.

"Nearly did." Somehow, there was a hint of a smile in Liam's voice.

He was never going to let her forget this.

Once he was healed and no longer angry at her, that is.

"Mon Dieu, forgive me," she muttered.

One of the strangers cleared their throat. "I take it you're the huntsmen promised us by Gautier?"

Ro climbed to her feet. "Oui, Monsieur. I'm Ro. This is Liam."

"And it is . . . just the two of you?"

Worry swept her. "I sincerely hope not."

The man looked at Liam, questioning.

Ro quickly jumped in, not wanting Liam to talk more than necessary. "We arrived with greater numbers, but we are the only ones who made it to this point."

Most of the men uncovered their heads, crossed themselves, or looked to the ceiling.

It took Ro too many seconds to realize what they were doing. "Oh! Oh. Non. I mean, as far as we know, they aren't dead—we were separated."

The strangers looked at her pityingly, and Ro clamped her jaw tight. She refused to believe the huntsmen she'd hunted with and come to know in the past year and a half were all dead.

On a mission where Gautier had clearly stated he wouldn't blame them if that very thing happened.

"We just got separated," Ro insisted, not willing to let the point go.

Liam climbed to his feet with the medic's help, and Ro rushed over to help.

Liam waved her off. "May we see Monsieur André, s'il vous plait?"

"Right this way." One of the men led the way out into the hall, the others falling in around them in a cluster, weapons pointed out.

6

On high alert, Ro stayed close to Liam, partially in case he needed her help—not likely with the strong men on either side of him—and partially to assure herself he was going to be all right.

But Ro forgot all of that the moment they entered the main foyer.

It hadn't been maintained, that was easy to see, but even dust and cobwebs couldn't diminish the marble stairways, red-velvet accents, and gold everything else.

Literal gold, on every surface.

Her mouth fell open, and she just stood and stared.

"C'est magnifique," she whispered.

When Ro managed to pull herself away from soaking it in, Monsieur André's men were watching them with small smiles on their faces, weapons still out but pointed at the floor, shoulders relaxed.

"That's how we feel when we come this way, too," one of them said.

Liam grunted. "But the girl is more important. If we're done gawking, may we see her now?"

A few looked offended—a look Ro was used to seeing

directed at herself, not Liam—but most just looked surprised. The medic and the man who'd been speaking to them exchanged glances.

"Monsieur Gautier . . . told you?"

Liam nodded, a fine sheen of sweat on his brow. "Lead the way."

"After you've been seen to. I will get ointment." The medic hurried off with two of the men.

A few of the others helped Liam settle on the wide marble steps, and Ro sat next to him, staring up, up, up at all the gloriousness.

"Do you have any of your . . . special . . . ointment with you?" Liam asked in a low voice.

Ro glanced at him in surprise. She'd fully admitted prayer had healed him, not her, on one of their past hunts, and he was asking her to—what. Pray for him?

She dug around in her satchel to give herself a moment to decide what to do. Prayer was intensely personal for her, not something she enjoyed displaying around others, and it was one thing to do it in the middle of a forest with a nearly comatose companion versus in a quiet foyer with Liam and all these strangers nearby to witness it.

Besides, why Dieu would listen to her prayers while she was mad at Him and not speaking to Him entirely baffled her.

She came out with a small jar and met Liam's eyes. "It might not work."

"I'm willing to let you try it."

"Oh, you are now, are you?" Ro bit back her grumble and looked away from his twinkling eyes to focus on his leg.

The medic was going to be so mad if she pulled off his bandage, caused him pain for no reason, and ended up causing an infection to boot.

Will this even work? she asked nobody silently, refusing to acknowledge it as a prayer.

No response, but something outside of herself felt expectant, waiting. Someone other than Liam.

The others were mostly ignoring them, keeping watch as if wolves would burst in at any moment. Which they would if they could. Ro sincerely hoped they couldn't.

She knelt down next to Liam, tugged off his bandage, and met his eyes. "This will hurt."

"I wasn't expecting it to be a picnic."

She paused for just a moment, surprised, then went back to focusing on the wound. Liam? Making jokes? She must have strangled him just a little too long while he was climbing the building.

Not that she should be making light of that yet. Or ever.

She tugged off his bandage, slathered all the ointment she had with her over the length of his wound, and spoke low under her breath. "Mighty Creator, I pray you have mercy on this son of yours and heal him. Amèn."

"Amèn," Liam said in a low voice.

Warmth instantly swept from her hands into his calf, and the muscles under her fingers tightened and the skin smoothed over. She pulled her hand back the instant the warmth left her.

Then she wondered where to wipe the last of the ointment.

"You'd best wrap my leg before the medic gets back, huntress," Liam said in a nonchalant way, again where only she could hear him.

Ro wiped her hands on the bandage and had just finished wrapping his leg when footsteps echoed on the marble flooring.

"I hear you took all the excitement and left us with nothing!" boomed Javier.

Ro's head came up. Javier, Gustave, and Marceau were being ushered their way, from another direction deep in the opera house.

She jumped to her feet. "You're alive! The others?"

Javier stopped in front of them and folded his arms. "Sacha and Rayan took the others to help the rest of the huntsmen escape the wolves. They plan on heading to the" —he glanced at those he didn't know—"to a secure location if they are able to get free."

Which meant the vault of kings. Deep within the old palais.

Not far from their location, but not exactly close either.

Ro hoped they made it.

She nodded, and Javier turned to Liam, noting all the blood. "Are you well, chef?"

Liam stood. "Never better."

Gustave and Marceau, more demonstrative than many of the other huntsmen, leaned closer to get a better look. "Whoa, they sure took a bite out of you!" Gustave whistled.

"It looks worse than it is," Liam said. "We should see about the girl."

They both turned to Ro, eyeing her head to toe, and it took Ro a moment to realize they thought Liam was talking about her.

Her face reddened, but she didn't say anything. Liam could just explain himself. She wasn't going to be the one facing Gautier after ousting whatever his secret about the girl was.

The medic hurried over, bandages and small glass bottles clutched in his hands. "You should be sitting!"

Ro turned to Javier to get more information. This was Liam's fight now, and she wanted no part in it.

"Anyone wounded? Anyone . . . more than wounded?" She couldn't bring herself to say it.

Javier kept an eye on everything around them as he answered. "Axel was attacked when Victor's group tried to leave their building a back way, but they got the door closed and the rest of them were able to kill it."

Ro felt cold. “And Sacha and Rayan . . . ?”

“Were leading a perfectly healthy Milo and Hector away while we created a distraction the wolves couldn’t refuse,” Marceau said, watching Liam and the medic going back and forth. He grinned at Ro. “Fresh pigeon meat.”

The other men perked up at that, exchanging worried looks. That was when Ro remembered Gautier’s messages had come through carrier pigeons. Oops?

Hopefully they hadn’t gotten any of the trained ones.

Ro shuddered. She didn’t even want to know how they’d captured and butchered the pigeons. “I’m—glad?—you found something that worked. But we really should get moving . . .” She gave Liam a pointed look.

But he wasn’t even paying attention to her.

Somehow, the small medic had wrangled Liam back to the marble steps and had the bandage off, inspecting it with a pair of spectacles, one lens cracked. “I don’t believe it. I just don’t believe it.”

A small part of Ro started to panic. If the wrong person found out what she could sometimes do . . . if *Gautier* found out . . .

Liam caught her wide-eyed look and tried to wrap his leg once more. “Blood often hides the severity of a wound.”

“Oui, but—”

“And I really must insist we hurry. Gautier is not one to be kept waiting.”

He said this with just a hint of threat in his tone, and Monsieur André’s men stiffened.

The medic seemed to want to object more, but he set his jaw and began wrapping.

When he was done, Liam climbed to his feet and met the men’s eyes. “I mean no disrespect, but we were led to believe the matter is urgent. Please, let us be about our task.”

More exchanged glances, then the men started up the grand staircase.

The sound of weapons being drawn met Ro's ears, and she spun, hand going for her crossbow across her back.

Monsieur André's men were aiming weapons at Javier, Gustave, and Marceau, not allowing them onto the marble steps.

"What is the meaning of this?" Javier demanded, his thunderous look saying he was ready and willing to kill, but he *might* give them a chance to explain first.

"Huntsmen, lower your weapons," Liam said. "You, explain now."

That's when Ro realized they hadn't asked any of their names.

The first man who'd spoken had his hand on his sword, but he hadn't drawn it. "Our deepest pardons, Messieurs, but no one but the lead huntsman and the huntress are allowed past this point."

"Surely this is unnecessary," Ro insisted. "Gautier trusts his huntsmen implicitly." Not entirely true, but Ro found she wanted backup. "Surely they can only help."

She wasn't overly thrilled walking into a situation without information and with all these weapons surrounding her. They were here; why not use the huntsmen's expertise?

No one lowered their weapons.

Liam nodded. "I agree with the huntress's assessment. Besides, I do not appreciate my men being waylaid."

The man didn't budge. "It is a serious matter. They must remain below, off the stairs."

Gustave snorted and slammed his sword into its sheath, looking disgusted. "Might have been nice to let us know that *before* we risked life and limb getting in here instead of going with the rest."

The words were said to André's man, but they were directed at Liam.

Both men stiffened.

Ro rolled her eyes. They didn't have time for this. "Liam, please."

He shook himself out of the standoff. "They are sworn to secrecy. I must insist my men be allowed to help."

"And I must insist they stay behind."

Liam started to argue, but Ro jumped in. They needed to *move*. "S'il vous plaît, ask Monsieur André."

The soldier looked like he wasn't even going to consider it.

"If you want our help, I must insist." Softer, she said, "They can help."

His jaw tightened, but he finally released his sword and nodded at his men.

Marceau and Javier put their weapons away, then the rest of them did, too. Javier, Marceau, and Gustave moved up the stairs, flanking Ro and Liam.

She turned back to Liam and the other man. "Lead the way, Monsieur—?"

He bowed to her. "Laurent, Mademoiselle."

"Merci. Lead the way, Monsieur Laurent."

7

A disgruntled trio of huntsmen stomped up the stairs, but at last they were finally moving directly toward their goal.

Ro tried to focus on the task at hand instead of wanting to beat some good sense into Gautier. They'd made it to Palais Garnier. They were about to encounter a cursed object. And that was where their information ended.

A wash of cold swept over Ro as they neared the doors that led into the main opera hall. Whatever the cursed object was, it was dangerous. And powerful.

"Wait here, s'il vous plaît." Monsieur Laurent opened the door, and a faint wash of sound came out before he secured it behind him.

Ro was trying to place what it was when a merchant who looked as if he'd once been thickly padded, but now was deflated like a waterskin, burst through the doors.

"It is true! Gautier has sent us succor, praise all the saints and heavenly hosts above!" He pulled first Liam, then Ro, to him and abruptly kissed both cheeks. He spared barely a glance for the other three huntsmen.

Ro waited to wipe the spittle from her cheeks until he'd turned away.

"Monsieur André, the other men," Laurent began.

"Yes, yes, fine, fine. They can help." Monsieur André flapped his hand dismissively at the three huntsmen before beckoning urgently to Liam and Ro. "Please hurry. My daughter is right this way."

Ro had been expecting more of a fight.

Instead, he opened the door and ushered them deeper into the once-grand opera house.

As they stepped into the main room where all plays and operettas had once been performed, Ro and Liam stopped in their tracks.

The theater was grand, ornate, gilded in gold and enhanced with red velvet and satin everywhere, but that wasn't what held them captive.

There, on the stage, a young girl danced. And danced. And cried.

And left bloody footprints behind her with every step.

She flopped like a rag doll as her feet moved through the most beautiful, intricate, fast dance Ro had ever seen. It reminded her of the Spanish flamenco, only instead of sweeping Ro away as a beautiful dance always had in the past, this one left only horror in its wake.

"Please, do something! I am afraid she cannot . . . last . . . much longer."

The man broke down and sobbed, though it had a weariness to it that said he'd been crying long and often.

The huntsmen exchanged glances, then scattered, all moving toward the stage, down different aisles.

"How long ago did she start dancing?" Liam asked.

The heartbroken père tripped after them, almost as exhausted as the girl on the stage.

"Eight days ago. I started sending word to Gautier after

the first full day. I had heard one of his huntsmen had . . . experience . . . with cursed objects."

He looked at Ro with such hope, she had to turn away.

She went back to eyeing the red shoes. Vibrant, heeled, with red ribbons that held it to the foot, these dance shoes would make any Spanish dancer proud.

"Had she ever worn the shoes before then?" she asked.

"Non."

"Where did she get them?" Ro asked next.

"She found them when she was playing in the prima donna's dressing room. It's a labyrinth back there, all these rooms for changing and rehearsal and even sleeping quarters for the trainees. Used once upon a time, but no longer, of course."

"What happened when she found them?" Ro pressed.

"She put on the costume and the shoes and flounced right out here and started dancing. We cheered her on at first, of course, but then she wouldn't stop. She *couldn't* stop. And now I may lose my little flower—look at her. See how she fades. She how she *wilts*."

His voice broke off in despair.

Ro eyed the girl, forcing herself to be objective. To take in facts only. "How has she survived for eight whole days? She takes no rest?"

"Only when she falls asleep. Then the shoes sleep with her. But she is frightened and doesn't sleep well, or long, and soon the shoes take over and make her dance all over again."

"Food? Water?" Ro continued.

The man jerked his head. "We force them into her while she's sleeping. We've tried to hold her down, to tie her down, to force her off the stage—nothing works. The shoes are a demon!" He spat and crossed himself.

"She was playing alone when she found them?" Liam rejoined.

The child's père grew slightly defensive. "The opera is secure. There is no risk of wolves within. None." He frowned. "Well, unless you delve deep into the underground caverns." He jutted his chin forward. "But those have been sealed off."

They reached the stage.

Ro and Liam exchanged a glance. "She did not find them there? In the underground caverns?" Ro asked, just to clarify. That didn't exactly match the sparse information they'd received from Gautier.

"Non. Why?"

Liam and Ro nodded at each other, then Ro laid a hand on the père's arm. "We will do all we can to help her."

He snatched up her hand and placed tear- and snot-laden kisses upon it. "Oh, merci, Mademoiselle, merci! I cannot tell you how much that means to me. I will be forever in your debt."

Ro extracted her hand and moved onstage, wiping it on her trousers when he wasn't looking. The man really needed to keep his fluids to himself. Ugh.

Besides, his gratitude was misplaced until she succeeded.

With just a few hand signals, Ro motioned the huntsmen to surround the girl who was now watching them with fearful eyes as she stomped and snapped her fingers and twirled her flouncing skirts.

On Ro's signal, the huntsmen lunged as one.

The girl danced right out of their grasp.

They spent the next half hour trying to catch her, but she whirled and spun and evaded all hands. With a cry, the girl went limp.

For a heart-stopping moment, the girl's chest appeared not to move.

Her father rushed onto the stage and tilted her head back, gently drizzling water past her cracked lips. She didn't stir but to swallow.

Ro sprang onto the shoes, giving swift instructions. Two of the huntsmen tied the girl down.

"I'm telling you, it won't do any good," her père hissed. "She just snaps them like they're brittle strands of grass."

Liam carefully poured a sleeping liquid he kept for the most grievous of wounds onto a cloth and held it over the girl's nose. Her whole body relaxed, and she fell into a deep sleep.

Ro immediately set to work on the shoes. She cut at them with her blades. Her blades wouldn't penetrate the leather. The long knives wouldn't even nick them.

She tried to wedge her fingers between the girl's foot and her shoe, but it was as if they were a part of her skin.

The father tried to feed her a little bit of bread next.

Liam stayed his hand. "She is sleeping too deeply for that, Monsieur."

His chin wobbled. "But if she does not eat now, she might not have the strength to go on."

Ro tried to wrench the shoes from the girl's feet. She tried cutting off the sole. She grabbed hold of both shoes, called up her gift within, and delved deep, but no magic answered her summons.

No more than dousing Ro with a cold that penetrated her very bones.

The men took turns, Liam most of all. They all tried to get the shoes off, but they all failed.

Ro felt the shoes stirring. The girl let out a little whimper.

Liam looked at her in surprise. "I gave her a much stronger dose than that. She should be out for hours."

The father mournfully shook his head. "The magic is too strong. I do not understand it, but other than allowing her rest every few days, it will not bow to anything else." He spat the next words with bitterness. "Probably the demon shoes allow her rest only that they might toy with her longer."

He went back to trying to force bread past the girl's lips, but she turned her head away each time.

Then the girl's eyes popped open, and the shoes came fully awake.

Ro lunged forward and grasped the girl's ankles, her hands wrapping around the red ribbons. "I will do it. I will dance for her."

The shoes went quiet.

So did everyone else on the stage, but Ro was too focused on the shoes to care.

Even if Liam's gaze burned into her like a furnace and a growl escaped his throat.

Ro remembered the dance lessons at Madame Bavoir's. How she hugged the wall, self-conscious in her skintight dance clothing. How Cosette smiled prettily and won everyone's hearts with her sweetness and delicate features and perfectly executed pirouettes.

How Ro was awkward and gangly and too tall.

She'd just wanted to disappear.

But she'd watched the other girls in awe, wishing she could dance as they did, too shy to attempt more than basic motions, all wooden, all bringing derision from her classmates and a curled lip from her instructor.

How dancing in secret, when no one could watch her or correct her, proved that she *could* dance, just not for an audience. Not for a cruel audience, anyway.

How losing everything had made such things as dance classes frivolous.

How dancing had once been her dearest, most secret wish.

She felt the shoes perk up and focus on that secret wish, buried deep until just now.

"I will dance," she repeated firmly, not letting go of the shoes.

The shoes remained still, waited to see what she would do.

Slowly, taking only one hand off the girl's ankles at a time, Ro removed her boots, her wool socks, and her leather jerkin, leaving her red cape firmly in place, her long knives at her back, but making a show of putting her crossbow and other weapons aside.

The shoes still waited.

Ro waited.

The shoes did nothing.

Ro took a deep breath, let it out. She knew what the problem was.

Her cape. The shoes wouldn't touch her while she still wore her cape.

The deep-red fabric was the only thing left of her mère. She couldn't say what madness made her think so, but she felt safe, like she was protected, when she wore it.

She felt the shoes start to lose interest.

With a swift tug, she pulled her cape free, and it fluttered to the floor, leaving her in only her white underblouse and homespun breeches.

Ro felt naked without her gear.

Tentatively, the ribbons uncurled from around the girl's ankles and reached for Ro's.

"Huntress," Liam said, hand on the axe at his side.

She met his eyes. "Get the girl to safety. Then find a way to make me free."

"But our mission." He didn't elaborate.

She gave him a wobbly grin as the ribbons wound around her calves up to her knees, trailing ice-cold *wrongness* in their wake. "Then I trust you to make sure I can fulfill it."

The other huntsmen on the stage exchanged glances.

Liam gave her a solemn nod.

Suddenly releasing the girl, the shoes sprang for her feet.

Ro was ready. She gripped her long knives and stabbed them straight down, into the shoes.

The shoes passed through them like butter, mending themselves and suctioning to her feet with an audible *slurch*.

The shoes were now the most beautiful ballet slippers Ro had ever seen. Red satin with a deeper red stitching curving in elegant whorls and designs.

And they weren't just the ballet slippers she'd worn as a child. Non, these were pointe shoes, the coveted ballet shoe that all the other girls had fought hard to win, to be worthy of.

The ones Ro had only stared at with longing, knowing she would never be good enough.

The shoes seized on to that longing.

Ro gasped at the power that filled her. It wasn't welcoming. It wasn't warm. Its cold fist squeezed her heart and chilled her bones.

Dance, the shoes whispered, and Ro's feet hastened to comply.

8

Ro leaped to her feet and joined the dance, pouring her heart into it. Unlike the child, who had been forced to dance, Ro matched the shoes' expectations and exceeded them.

She may have never danced this way before another living soul—and she would've never chosen to do so before Liam, even under pain of death—but now she met everything the shoes told her to do and did more.

As a dancer is aware of the audience, so Ro noticed the awe, the admiration the shoes garnered, just enough to fuel her to go harder, faster.

The shoes rejoiced and lost themselves in her dance.

Ro danced for hours. All through the night and into the next day.

When she felt herself flagging, she thought of the little girl and how she shoes had forced her to dance for over a week, and Ro danced harder.

Her muscles may have been well trained for hunting, for stealth, for using weaponry of many kinds, but she hadn't used these particular muscles in such a way since she was a child.

When Ro needed to catch her breath, she eased the shoes into a series of slow, ethereal movements, like she was dancing underwater, which the shoes loved.

It may not have been the frenzied dance of before, but it was just as taxing.

Sweat poured off her.

Liam tried everything. To catch her. To get her to drink.

The shoes wouldn't let him anywhere near her.

Blisters formed and burst. Trails of clear liquid then blood began to follow her all over the stage, but she never once slipped and she never once stumbled.

Ro danced for two more days before she slumped to the floor. Just as she was losing consciousness, she felt Liam catch her, force water past her lips, then cover her nose and mouth with his cloth.

It was a strong odor, sweet and sickly, and Ro entered a dreamless slumber that she hoped she would wake from.

Days passed, her vision blurred, and Ro lost track of anything but how much she *hurt*.

Once again, Ro felt herself waking, slumped over on the floor, and despair filled her. Not again.

She didn't know how long the cycle had gone on—days, weeks, months, years—but she was now terrified to fall asleep, because it meant waking to excruciating pain.

Water dribbled past her lips, and she sucked at it weakly. Broth next, followed by bits of cheese and bread. Liam would make a wonderful nursemaid.

She was coming to slowly, too slowly, but she tried to stay in a restful state as long as possible.

Once the shoes were awake, she would have no rest until they tired and she dropped from exhaustion.

The one fact that penetrated her haze? The shoes seemed to need to recharge, to reset, every three days or so. There was a pattern to it. If only she could grasp what it was. What it meant.

But she was so tired. So very tired.

The shoes came awake at the same time Ro did, and her eyes flew open and met Liam's.

He cradled her in her mère's cape.

Clarity hit her for a split second. The wolves were attacking the opera house day and night. They wanted within, desperately.

Something was driving them into a frenzy.

"Wolves," was all she had time to say before it was gone. Nothing but the dance remained.

She flung off the cape and her entire body bowed off the floor, springing her upright from her ankles to her hands, which immediately went to first position above her head.

Her arms were so sore they were shaking.

If she let the dance drag her along, it wounded her, not caring whether she were a willing participant or not, and the only way Ro could see escaping this without broken bones or ruptured muscles or torn ligaments was to meet the dance head-on.

Which was getting harder and harder to do.

Ro did a series of pirouettes across the stage, then bounding leaps, then intricate footwork she'd only ever dreamed of being able to do.

But her body wasn't responding as well to her anymore. Her muscles were tearing, the ligaments close to collapse. She wasn't getting enough rest for her body to repair itself, to become stronger.

She was weakening.

She tried to speak to Liam again, to repeat whatever had been in her dream, whatever had come to her while cradled in her mère's cape, but her mouth wouldn't form words. Not unless the shoes wanted her to laugh or taunt or allowed her to cry. Not unless it served the dance.

Tears streamed down her face in wordless agony.

As far as she could tell from those around her, which truthfully wasn't much, her huntsmen were regarding her somberly, mournfully, respectfully, even as Liam gave the signal.

Then they tried to ensnare her, but she slipped past their fingers. They tried to tie her with ropes, but she just laughed and broke them like soap bubbles.

They tried to jump on her, to pile on her and drag her down, but they just fell around her as Ro danced in the midst of them all and leaped over them as if she had wings.

It was exhilarating in its own way, to know she couldn't be caught, that she could escape anything they did to capture her. Both the huntress and the shoes reveled in the feeling.

But even that was failing to buoy her spirits anymore, to give her strength to meet the dance. Ro's entire frame was drooping, and she wasn't meeting the moves so much as letting them drag her along.

She didn't know how much longer she could hold out.

A loud argument ensued, but the words were muffled in her ears, as if someone were covering them.

Liam tried to herd her off the stage, but the shoes wouldn't leave it. They were the opera house's prima donna, the belle of the ball, and they would not lose even a moment in the spotlight.

At last, at long last, as Ro wept from exhaustion and didn't know how she could possibly still be upright and still be this tired, Liam did as she'd asked.

He did what she hadn't even known she'd asked.

The room cleared, all except Liam, and he opened the door.

Snarling, yapping, howling entered Ro's world, and cold fear washed over her.

Only this time, it wasn't her own.

9

Ro welcomed the wolves. They would end this. This nightmare. But at the same time, Ro wept for her sister, whom she wouldn't be able to protect, for her family, whom she wouldn't be able to provide for any longer, and last of all, for herself.

This was not how she thought it would end.

She'd wanted to end France's curse. To watch those she loved lead a normal life once more. To find out what had happened to the prince.

Not only that, she'd wanted to grow old in a cabin deep in the woods, far away from others, with a rocking chair on the porch and perhaps someone clinking dishes together in the kitchen behind her. Perhaps a grandchild who came to visit her in her old age.

But the dream she didn't even know rested within—the one she'd never allowed herself to dare hope for, because she felt she didn't deserve it—was fleeting, and the wolves were suddenly there.

The pack snarled and snapped at the shoes that leaped and darted and tried to survive.

Tears streamed down her face, she couldn't help herself,

but this time, Ro raised her chin. These shoes would be torn from this stage. From her feet. They would never hurt anyone ever again.

And if it cost her life, so be it.

Hours later, Ro had to admit she was impressed. If these shoes ever wanted to go on a hunt of impossible odds with her, she'd be hard-pressed not to welcome them.

If they weren't murderous, raving, lunatic magical items, of course.

She twirled and spun and slipped past the wolves that had entered the opera house. Ro dearly hoped the others had escaped in time.

These wolves had overtaken the city, making it their own, not allowing humans to enter or leave.

Great hulking creatures, they snapped their teeth at her as their shaggy coats bristled, their shoulders easily coming to Ro's waist. And she was tall.

These beasts were bigger than any of the other wolves she'd hunted for Gautier.

She'd thought these massive gray wolves had been run out of Europe. Extinguished. No longer existed.

She wasn't sure if she were happy to be wrong or not, here and now, when she needed their help.

As far as she knew, there was nothing magical about them, but they were glutted on human flesh and were monstrous creatures confident in their prowess, with thick hides that resisted most weapons.

Even she had no desire to ever hunt one, and here she was. Dancing for them.

Her taunting laughter through her tears and her inability to be caught enraged the wolves further, and they renewed their efforts to tear the dancing slippers from her feet.

Or perhaps tear her feet off and eat them along with the shoes.

The longer she evaded them, the more she began to despair that she would ever be caught. Perhaps she could fall asleep?

As if sensing her thoughts, the shoes sent a bolt of energy through her, tightening its hold on her, bolstering her dancing to beyond frenzied.

Ro gasped for breath. "Please," she whispered.

The shoes were so focused on their survival, they didn't catch the whispered word in time, and Ro was able to let it escape.

The pack leader sat back on his haunches and studied her, then he circled round and round the stage, his head tilted, his ears straight up, his eyes calculating.

Ro met them as much as she was able, waiting for his move.

She would match it.

A smaller wolf behind her nipped at her heel, a distraction, and Ro focused on that with all her might. The shoes triumphed as they just barely slipped away from the sharp teeth, then Ro toppled.

The pack leader had made his move, and Ro was pinned.

Ro arched her back and screamed, trying to get out from under the wolf. He put his head on hers and held her to the floor.

He stunk, of wet fur and carcass and rancid teeth.

The wolf didn't move, allowing his pack to come in for the shoes.

They attacked, biting, tearing, snarling.

Ro had never been more terrified in her life. Bits of red cloth flew out in what looked like a bloody spray as the shoes were shredded from her feet.

Ro's screaming diminished with each shred torn away as the slippers' hold on her lessened. It burned, as if her skin were peeling off along with them, but not a tooth or claw delved into her skin.

Then the last piece came off, and the ribbons released her calves.

The giant, shaggy, smelly wolf on top of her lunged after the ribbons, catching them before they could slither away. As they tried to do.

Ro was in so much pain, she could barely fathom what was happening around her.

At that moment, red satin fluttered above her and overtook her field of vision as a heavy body slammed into her. She was too limp to even grunt.

But she caught his scent. Leather and fresh hay and bitter café.

Liam cradled her close and made sure her red cloak covered every inch of them as they lay mere mètres away from the most fearsome wolves in France as they tore the magical items to shreds and then gobbled them all up.

Ro curled herself into Liam's side and slept through the rest of the carnage.

10

Ro came to in a bed with a cool cloth on her forehead and her entire body screaming at her to go back to sleep and forget about waking up for a few thousand more years. Her feet burned as if they were consumed by fire.

She let out a weak groan.

Immediately her bed was surrounded by worried huntsmen.

"She's awake!"

"Can I help ye up, huntress?"

"She's in no shape to get up, you moron! Hows bout you ask her if you can get her anything."

"Oh. Can I get you anything?"

"Out."

Ro was having trouble following the voices, but this one she knew. Liam.

Amid mumbled well wishes and "We said a prayer for you" and "Get better soon" and other such kind comments, the rest of the huntsmen filtered out until it was just her and Liam and a matronly woman who stayed in the background.

Ro eyed Liam a moment before closing her eyes. "Was it as bad as I thought it was?" she asked weakly.

"Worse."

That brought a smile to her lips. "And the girl?"

"She will recover."

Tears filled her eyes, and Ro kept them clamped tightly shut so Liam wouldn't see. "Bon."

They slid onto her pillow anyway, letting Liam know she was nothing more than a weak girl who *cried* when things got tough. Not that she minded the tears. Just the audience.

"The huntsmen? Did they . . . Are they . . . ?" She didn't know how to ask.

"All lived, all escaped the city." A measure of teasing entered his voice. "You've got quite the share from the vault of kings, if I do say so myself."

Her eyes met his. "And the da—ah, I mean, and the item . . . thing?"

Liam briefly touched the pouch at his side.

A laugh burst out of Ro, one that said she couldn't believe it had all worked out—*nothing* worked out well for her—then she hiccuped a sob and covered her face, wishing Liam would just *go away*.

It took a hot moment, but she finally wrested her emotions under control. She took a deep breath and blew it out.

Liam waited patiently, carefully looking out the small window to give her time to compose herself, probably giving her a chance to ask more questions. But she was so tired. Just one more thing . . .

"And the wolves?"

Liam let out a big breath, and Ro peeked to see him rubbing the back of his neck.

"The opera house is lost. They refuse to leave it, and no matter what we do, we can't lure them out."

Ro tried to sit up. "You didn't try to *hunt* them, did you?"

She was trying to get out from under her covers, even if her arms didn't want to work, and Liam gently pushed her back down and held her there. With one finger. "Non, huntress."

He didn't remove his hand until she stopped struggling. Then he released her shoulder.

Ro lay there panting, exhausted from trying to *sit up*.

For heaven's sake. How long until she could attempt to leave Paris? If they were even still there.

"How did you know the wolves would go after the shoes?" he asked.

Ro thought about it, then frowned. "I . . . don't know. I don't even remember telling you that, but I guess I did, didn't I?"

He nodded confirmation.

She eyed him. "How did you know covering us both with my cape would work?"

He eased himself onto a little stool next to her bed, the matron in the background staying unobtrusive, giving them privacy while being present to chaperone.

Ro would've laughed if it didn't hurt so much. It had been so long since anyone had cared enough about her reputation to chaperone.

The way Liam sat on the stool was almost comical, as if he was afraid it would shatter under his weight at any moment.

Which was a fair concern with his bulk, Ro had to admit.

"One of the old wives' tales from my village said wolves couldn't see red. Besides, you wear it on every hunt. I thought there had to be something to that." He eyed her and waited, one eyebrow raised.

Ro smiled a little at that. "I wish. It was a gift from my mère, nothing more."

Although she'd heard the very same rumor. Especially about fey beasts.

Liam swallowed hard, looking a little pale. "Oh."

Ro couldn't help teasing him, just a little. "Thank goodness the wolves gorged themselves on the red shoes they couldn't see."

He gave her a sour look.

Ro laughed, then grabbed her side. "Ooh, not a good idea. Got any more of that sleeping potion? I could use a big whiff right about now."

He got up and bowed. "I will leave you to Madame's ministrations." And he left.

Ro scowled after him. He couldn't have at least given her a little of his sleeping draught?

Although the woman was gentle, Ro soon passed out on her own from the woman peeling back bandages, spreading ointment on her blistered and swollen feet, then wrapping them once more. It hurt too much.

Once Monsieur André's daughter was well enough to be moved, half of the huntsmen escorted Monsieur André and his men to Gautier, while the other half stayed at the monastery until Ro and the wounded huntsmen recovered.

Apparently they'd gotten out much the way they'd come, but this time, the wolves did nothing more than stalk them from a few streets over. And only a few of them at that, with most of them overrunning the opera house.

Ro didn't remember any of it.

But Ro *did* want to forget the last words of the woman who cared for her. She dabbed her eyes at the end of the tale and said, "That big strong handsome huntsman, carrying ye out of the city like you were precious cargo—I'd marry that one if I was you, Mademoiselle, and soon. Men such as he ain't likely to last long on the market."

Ro wanted to demand: *What market?* People were concerned about surviving, not flirting and courting and marrying—ugh.

She'd never been more thankful when she was finally deemed strong enough to depart—much sooner than any of them thought she would be.

That sometimes happened to her—something else about herself she couldn't explain.

Even if her feet still burned like fire, with no outward sign to explain away her pain.

Still, the monks wouldn't let them leave till the next morning, after being fed a tasteless and watery gruel. But they were soon on their way back to Gautier's.

And not soon enough.

11

Ro and Liam once again stood in front of Gautier's desk. They had made their report, and now awaited payment, which they would then distribute to the other huntsmen.

Gautier eyed them both in clear suspicion. Ro didn't know what he expected, but it clearly wasn't their success and each of the huntsmen escaping Paris with their lives—and their horses.

It was almost as if he were . . . disappointed.

Ro fought back her rage at his utter lack of humanity. Sometimes she couldn't control what she did when her emotions got the better of her, and slapping Gautier wasn't conducive to a long and healthy career . . . of any kind.

"Tell me again."

Ro made a frustrated sound in the back of her throat, but Liam calmly told him the same story he'd repeated four times now.

It was amazing how he almost did it word for word.

Losing the opera house had been a blow—it was one of the few remaining places in the city the wolves hadn't torn their way into. But at least the family had made it out safely.

After Monsieur André had given his report to Gautier, the monks were seeing them settled elsewhere.

And Liam had just opened the door at a whispered word from Ro. After making sure everyone else was heavily barricaded in another part of the opera house.

If he hadn't come back for her, Ro wouldn't be here right now.

Surely she could be patient through one more retelling of the facts, especially since she hadn't been present of mind for most of it.

When Liam fell silent once more, Gautier grudgingly got out enough pay for all of them and handed it to Ro. She couldn't help her swallow.

Her fellow huntsmen may have walked in awe around her, helping her with anything and everything after her sacrifice for the little girl, but it still felt so demeaning to dole out coins as if she were a lord and they her vassals.

It had been an expensive job, and from the sullen look on Gautier's face, he hadn't been expecting to pay out quite so much.

But he quickly covered it with his grin. "Well, I certainly hired the right huntsmen for the job, didn't I?" he said, just a bit too brightly. "I'll have to keep that in mind for . . . future jobs I may have for you."

Ro and Liam exchanged a glance. "May I ask why you did it?" Ro asked before losing her courage. "Why you risked your best huntsmen, not only for a trinket, but for a few opera singers?"

"People are a resource." Gautier smiled. "You never know when the beggar boy on the corner will find a goose that lays golden eggs and will bring them to you for trade."

His smile widened as if at a fond memory.

"And the dagger?" Ro persisted, feeling as though she probably shouldn't.

"That is not your concern," Gautier said sharply. Then

he softened his voice. "Though I am so very grateful for a job well done."

He gave them a simpering look before adjusting something on his desk.

Ro gave Liam a longsuffering look, and without a word, he gave Gautier a solemn nod and escorted her out.

"Merci," she breathed when they were far enough out of hearing.

He walked a few paces before saying anything. "You know, I tend to put the men's coin into smaller drawstring bags, then hand them out to each one privately."

Ro stopped. "Where can I find these drawstring bags?"

Liam nodded in the direction he was going. "With the steward's steward."

It was no secret Gautier, the king's steward, wanted to be king, had tried to crown himself king, even, but the people waited for their crown prince—or anyone from the royal line, really—who had disappeared fifteen years ago. With the curse.

Even if people looked confused or flustered when she tried to talk about him, as if they couldn't quite remember, Ro was holding out for him too.

She just had to find out what happened to him. She had to. She had to set him free.

Oui, she was breaking France's curse, by any means necessary.

"Huntress? Are you coming?"

Jolted out of her resolve, tucking it away for another day, Ro nodded. "Lead the way, Monsieur Liam."

12

Gautier finally allowed himself to look up, to let excitement trickle into his expression.

He hurried over to the door, listened at the latch, then opened it when his best huntsmen's footsteps and voices faded away.

The two guards standing across from his door—as they were instructed to do when he had meetings—stood at attention.

"No one gets in, no one disturbs me."

Both gave abrupt nods, then hurried over to stand in front of his door as he closed it.

He couldn't help it. Laughter bubbled up inside, and he gave voice to it, rubbing his hands together to get some warmth back in them.

His eyes homed in on the nondescript package on his desk, the one left there by Liam. Finally!

He rushed over and tore into it, not bothering to pretend for a room full of men who thought he was much older than he actually was.

He finally freed the dagger from its wrapping and held it aloft. The firelight glinted off rubies set in its pommel, its blade was silver perfection with undulating waves in the metal that only came from coveted Damascus steel, and Gautier laughed again in joy.

Finally! She would be pleased with him. She might show him the face of his mother—let him pretend she was alive a little longer . . .

Non! He was a man grown now, with responsibilities. And if he wanted to be worthy of this kingdom he so desperately wanted, he had to put away childish things like games, like pretending.

He needed to match his face, a much-older version of himself than his sixteen years.

He rushed over and pulled the hand mirror from his desk and looked into it, saying her name three times.

It wasn't long until *her* face appeared in the smooth glass.

He pulled back, lip curling.

Magic gave him a wan smile. "You could hide your reactions a little better, boy."

The enchantress had gray, stringy hair frizzing around her head like a demented halo, wrinkles all over her face, and wore a dress that looked a few centuries old. And maybe like it had started to decompose. Along with her.

She was much more tolerable when she wore his mother's face and at least *appeared* clean.

Gautier chose his words carefully. As she'd been teaching him. "Forgive me. You look . . . tired."

She waved her hand as if she didn't care, as if she wanted him to get on with it.

He held up the dagger eagerly. "We found your dag—"

"Where did you get that? Give it to me!" She reached out to him, but her hand bounced off the glass on her side.

Gautier smiled and wiggled it a little in taunt. "Ah, ah, ah! You have something I want, Madame. I would be happy to return your dagger, but first . . ." He held out his hand.

Magic sighed, rummaged around for something just out of sight, and held up a small bag. "You realize it might not work."

Rage flashed hot, and it was all he could do to hold it back. "You do realize I can leave you in that tower to rot, never contact you again?"

Magic grinned. "But you won't."

Non, he wouldn't, but he maintained his stony look. He was tired of being played by her like a puppet with strings wound tightly around his neck.

She sighed finally. "It took a lot out of me this time."

Gautier didn't care. She may have looked like she'd aged twenty years or so, but what was that to him? Nothing, not if it worked.

She held out the bag, close to the mirror.

"Can you at least guarantee some measure of success?" he asked in a cold voice.

Magic shrugged again. "It is strong. It is powerful. But until the beast is dead, people are not going to remember if you crown yourself king."

The unspoken "again" rattled the air between them, and Gautier's jaw tightened more.

That beast was always taking away what Gautier wanted. No matter; he wouldn't be able to much longer. Now that they had the dagger.

And the huntress.

Liam was good, was fantastic, even, but the huntress . . .

She improvised. Surprised him at every turn. Completed tasks only a magic user could do. Even if her manner was brusque and uncouth and unladylike. No matter—he cared only for her skill. She was exactly what he needed and—

Magic dropped her head, hummed a little, then held the drawstring bag up to the glass.

Gautier touched the mirror, and the little drawstring bag poked through. He took it from her and set it on his desk.

He would wait until she wasn't spying on him to go through whatever hell she'd put in her potion this time. They always hurt, and they always worked—but for a limited time.

She had better have made this one permanent.

Her eyes lit with eagerness, and she held out her hand. "Now, the dagger."

Gautier gave her a smile that wasn't. "First I shall measure the potion's success, then I shall contact you."

And if she'd just poisoned him, she'd never get the dagger. He'd see it done, hide it someplace shielded even from her, before he drank her latest attempt at making him king. Or rather, making the people remember that he had been crowned king—once more—every time they looked at him.

Shock widened her eyes, and she stared at him with her mouth open.

He allowed a low, tightly controlled chuckle. "I'd think about how you speak to your king in the future, Madame, if I were you."

And he ended the magical connection.

But not before her shriek of rage penetrated his eardrums for a split second.

He rubbed an ear and put away the mirror, locking it in its hidden drawer. Then opened the drawstring bag.

He cautiously sniffed its contents, then snorted in disgust. Ugh! Had she simply filled a bag with rat droppings and called it a potion? He wouldn't put it past the witch.

Still, he heated water and made himself dark, thick, potent tea. The worst she'd given him yet.

He choked it down, then spent a few hours vomiting and using the chamber pot and lying on his floor in a cold sweat, alternating between shivering and burning up.

At once, the reactions eased. He sat up, got shakily to his

feet, and washed. Then he put on new clothes—those of a kingly nature—and opened his door.

The guards looked at him, blinked at different times, then fell to their knees, heads bowed. "Your Majesty! Forgive us—we didn't know you were within."

His exulting smile froze on his face. Did they see him, or—?

He gritted his teeth. Non, surely the witch wouldn't have given him Beau Alexandre Trêve's face. Surely the witch wouldn't have been that cruel.

Gautier nodded for the guards to rise—he seriously needed to train them to be better at their job—and to escort him down the corridor.

As he passed the ancient mirror in the hall, he gave a quick, furtive glance. But as always when he was under a spell, his face was a blur, and he couldn't know what he looked like.

No matter, he was king! He'd focus on that.

Now for a full day of courtiers and petitioners to bow and scrape and make absolute and utter fools of themselves while calling him "Your Majesty."

Hopefully it lasted longer than two days this time.

THE END

SOME GHOSTS FROM THE PAST REALLY ARE DEAD

L'Arbre des Fées
or
"The Fairy Tree"

It was a bitter day for us, that day that Père Fronte held the function under the tree and banished the fairies. We could not wear mourning that any could have noticed, it would not have been allowed; so we had to be content with some poor small rag of black tied upon our garments where it made no show; but in our hearts we wore mourning, big and noble and occupying all the room, for our hearts were ours; they could not get at them to prevent that.
The great tree—l'Arbre Fée de Bourlemont was its beautiful name—was never afterward quite as much to us as it had been before, but it was always dear.

—Mark Twain's *Personal Recollections of Joan of Arc*, "The Fairy Tree of Domremy"

1

Ro warmed her hands by the fire in the town square.

The village she'd stopped at was small, but it provided a warm fire for travelers as well as a passably edible gruel, and the owners of the inn didn't ask questions.

Exactly how she liked it.

She'd been slowly making her way back to Gautier's château after a rather simple job, one she'd completed in nearly half the time she'd allowed for it, but she just couldn't make herself move any faster.

Working for such a monster as Gautier was weighing heavier and heavier upon her these days.

And the worst part? She couldn't *prove* he was all she thought he was and more.

Sure, he rubbed her the wrong way, but what the people saw, the front Gautier put out for everyone, including Ro, was a kind and caring steward, overseeing the nation during the curse until its rightful rulers could return to power.

He was fair. He paid well for the wolves his huntsmen brought him. Dieu, he was the reason France's wolf problem was getting better—he wasn't allowing the creatures to hunt his people. Mobilizing his huntsmen force had been an act of sheer genius.

The people loved him for it. And Ro had to grudgingly admit he was doing a good job.

But Ro hated being in his presence. Something about him made her skin crawl. And every once in a while he let something slip that said he wasn't who he claimed to be, that he had plans in motion Ro couldn't even begin to guess.

So, non, she was not looking forward to returning, even to receive payment for her latest kill.

One so secretive and unbelievable, if surprisingly easy—she'd tell no one she'd found the otherworldly creature gorged on human flesh and fast asleep—she'd made her kill, hidden the body, and only extracted the teeth and claws as Gautier had requested. They were stuffed safely in the secret compartment of her saddlebag, awaiting payment. A hefty payment.

But even that thought couldn't force her feet to move.

So she huddled around this fire with other travelers, when she could be on her way, one step closer to getting Cosette out of France and away to Madame LaChance's boarding school.

It was the only thing driving her these days. Just not today.

"You there. Girl."

Ro's head came up. Everyone was staring at her, expectant, as if she'd missed the words several times over.

Her eyes rested on the old woman trying to get her attention. "Oui, Grandmère?" she said, using the term of respect for an older woman.

"I would speak with you. Come. I would speak with you." The gnarled hand waved Ro to follow.

Ro sighed and looked back to the fire. It was a cold, blustery evening. Not enjoyable, and not an evening to step away from a good fire.

But her inborn manners coaxed her after the woman. Still, Ro was cautious, one hand on the long knife at her side.

It wouldn't be the first time a bandit had used an elderly person or a child to try to rob her.

The old woman stopped several feet from the other travelers, just out of the light. "You the huntress everyone can't gossip about fast enough?"

"I"—Ro blinked, not sure how to respond to that—"think so?"

"You either are or ye ain't. Which is it?"

"Um, I am. Oui. Yes." Ro snapped her mouth closed.

The woman eyed her up and down. "Huh. Well, that'll do, I reckon. You for hire?"

"I—" Ro's mind scrambled for an answer. Gautier wouldn't expect her back for a week or so yet. She often took jobs on the side, mainly so her only income source wouldn't be from Gautier, but also to pay the outrageous sum Père Guise had quoted to get Cosette out of France and to Madame LaChance in Angleterre.

But did she want to take on another job right now? She wasn't sure she was in the right headspace for it.

"Ain't too bright, are ya?"

Ro flushed and stammered out a response. "I am expected back soon. I'm not sure if I can take on another job, Madame. Who's asking, and why?"

The old woman whistled. "Madame, eh? Look at you with all the fancy talk." She jerked a thumb over her shoulder. "I be looking to hire ya. For my children."

Ro followed the woman's thumb to the town's inn, a dilapidated if somber affair. It didn't look like much.

"Not that inn. The one in the next town over. The one no one will stay at. My daughter and her husband runs and owns it, but there be too many strange things going on to make others want to stay for more than a meal." She snorted. "And this town be getting all the profits from my children's misfortune. Sad, sad, sad." The old woman shook her head with the words.

Ro eyed her shabby clothing. "I don't work for free. How much does the job pay?"

The old grandmère snorted in disgust. "They said you didn't come cheap. Don't you worry none now, huntress. We've saved enough for yer services that even *you* won't turn up yer nose at us humble folk."

Ro highly doubted that. The woman wasn't being straightforward about anything—the problem, the price: the two most important aspects of her job—and she was too tired to haggle.

Ro nodded at the fire. "If you care to explain the problem in detail, and name the exact price you are willing to pay, that's where I'll be. For the next hour, anyway."

She started to move away, but the woman jumped toward her and grabbed Ro's arm, hanging on with the grip of a mule.

"Don't go. Name yer price, huntress. What'll it take to hire ye?"

All right, then. Ro named an outrageous sum that she highly doubted the woman had—a sum Ro would most likely feel guilty over taking later—but she'd take it. For Cosette.

Cosette was the entire reason Ro had become a huntress in the first place. Now wasn't the time to be turning down jobs just because she didn't feel like it.

The old woman didn't bat an eye. "That sounds fair enough. Sure."

Ro raised an eyebrow, making sure her doubt clearly peeked through. "And the problem?"

The woman worried her lip, glancing around to be sure they were still alone-ish. "You wouldn't believe me, even if I told you straight out."

Ro removed herself from the woman's grip and crossed her arms. "I suggest you tell me the full situation before I lose interest and move on."

"D'accord, lookie here." She drew herself up and looked as dignified as a hunched old person in rags could make herself. "You can laugh at me, you can make fun of me all you like, but you cain't laugh at my babes, got it? They deal with enough from the others. They ain't dealing with it from you too."

Her glare was comical, though Ro was certain she was trying to be fierce.

Ro nodded solemnly. She knew what it was like not to be believed. One night a year, she still moved into position, deep in the woods, to see a castle shimmer into view in the moonlight and stay there the whole night through.

Exactly where the king's summer palace used to be.

No one else saw it, no one else believed her, and no matter what she did, she couldn't find a way to get inside.

If the only gift she could give this woman and her children was her belief, the gift of not allowing derision to peek through, then she would do her best.

"Tell me."

The woman looked around nervously. "The inn seems to be—and there is evidence to back this up, mind you—haunted."

The woman stared at Ro. Ro stared back. Neither said a word.

"You ain't walking away yet."

Ro gave a single nod. "What haunts it?"

The woman's mouth hung open. "What do you mean, what haunts it? Ain't there just one thing?"

Ro considered. How to answer without sounding like a madwoman? She finally settled on: "Not always."

Sometimes simplest was best. Especially since she took to stammering when she got flustered.

The old woman grunted. "You believe me, then? Non, scratch that. Don't answer me that. You will come?"

"I will come."

The woman whooped, startling everyone at the fire, and took off into the forest. She called over her shoulder, "The next town over, ya hear? Due west. I cain't wait to tell everyone!"

And then she was gone.

Ro sighed, looked back to the fire and its cheery warmth, and went to saddle Fairweather, housed at the local stable. It was rare he had a warm stall and hay while they were out, and he was in bliss.

Of course, Ro had also been looking forward to bedding down in the warm hay next to him, wrapped in her red cloak, instead of on the always-cold ground outside as she normally did.

That would just have to wait.

Wouldn't he be thrilled they were setting out tonight after all?

2

Still mounted on Fairweather's back, Ro stared up at the inn. It looked so much nicer than the other inn; she could tell the family had tried to keep it in repair.

This one had a stable attached to it, firm, sturdy, and without gaps in the walls. She'd much rather spend the night here.

"See, boy?" she said as she slid off his back and gathered up the reins. "It's better than that other place."

Stony silence met her words.

Ro sighed. "Well, it will be. You'll see. Just wait till you have a warm stall and fresh hay. Then you'll thank me."

Fairweather snorted, right into her hair, blowing out loose strands from her braid. Uncanny sense of humor, that one.

"You'll see," she muttered again and pulled him forward.

The walls of the inn looked as if they'd been treated against decay. The sheen from the oil made the wood lustrous, but it would be terrible if it caught fire.

Yet although lamps were lit, a welcoming beacon in the gloom, the sounds of patrons dining, or even quietly conducting their business, were notably absent.

Ro led Fairweather around the building in a loop, then up to the front door and left the short reins dangling. She slung her saddlebag over her shoulder. "Stay."

She never tied him up, and she'd taught him to defend himself against wolves and those who would steal him. Still, this late at night, she'd feel better if he were in the stable and away from the wolves.

Ro went to the front door and pushed it open, staying where she could keep an eye on her horse.

An argument abruptly halted, and a woman, a man, and the old woman she'd spoken with earlier stared at her in fright.

The old woman huffed. "It just be the huntress I told you about. Come in, come in!"

The younger woman hurried over. "Our deepest apologies for your trouble, Mademoiselle LeFèvre. You are welcome to stay the night, but we don't need anyth—"

"Hogwash!" the old woman nearly shouted. "Will yer pride leave ye with nothing? It ain't like the curse is bad enough! You going to add destitution to no customers?"

"Grandmère, be reasonable . . ." the man started, in a tone that said he knew his words would be worth nothing, but he was obligated to try.

"I am being reasonable. You be reasonable!" she retorted.

Ro inched back a step, wanting to be anywhere else. Anywhere.

At least Gautier was a known element.

"I's gots gold, if that be your concern," the woman said proudly to her children. "And I already paid her, so you'd best be accepting her help."

Actually, she hadn't been paid. And Fairweather had been outside too long. "My horse . . ."

The man jumped up and rushed toward her. "I'll stable it!" And he was gone before Ro could thank him.

"But, Marc!" the younger woman called. He did not answer. She looked to Ro apologetically. "I'll show you to your room, Mademoiselle."

"Actually, dinner would be lovely . . ."

"But of course." The woman hurried into the back room, still looking flustered, and soon pots were banging noisily.

Ro lifted an eyebrow. "I've been paid, have I?"

The old woman waved a hand. "Only way I could get them to accept yer being here."

"The only way to get *me* to stay is to pay me. Now."

She'd learned the hard way that most people didn't actually have what they said they did. Or were begrudging of payment once the job had been done and their problems erased.

The old woman jutted out her chin. "Run the ghosts out, *then* you get my gold."

"I knew it. There is no gold, is there? I bid you adieu." Ro turned to leave.

"Wait!"

Ro didn't. She kept walking.

She did *not* look forward to taking her horse out of another warm stable. Fairweather was going to bite her. And she wouldn't even blame him.

The woman fumbled behind her, then the heavy sound of gold coins rattled. "It be right here!"

Ro paused. Then she looked at the woman and held out her hand.

The old woman bit her lip. "How do I know you won't just take it and leave?"

"How do I know you will give it to me once my task is complete?"

The two women stared at each other, neither budging.

Ro sighed. "Half now, half when the job is done?"

The old woman's rheumy eyes lit up. "You would do that?"

"Just this once, oui."

She rushed forward and filled Ro's hands with gold. Ro carefully bit one. The soft give let her know it wasn't some other metal coated with gold leaf, and then she dropped a coin atop another. It was just the right sound.

Ro made them disappear, using sleight of hand to store the gold elsewhere than where the woman would assume she put them.

People who were reluctant to part with their gold often tried to get it back.

"Oh, merci, huntress, merci!"

The woman clasped her hands together and looked so much like a child, innocent and happy, that Ro once again felt guilty for thinking such thoughts about her.

"Now come back inside before my daughter finds out you tried to leave."

Ro was hauled into the inn just as the door to the kitchen swung open.

The old woman tried to look innocent again, but pretending just didn't work for her. The young innkeeper eyed them both suspiciously.

Even still, the younger woman hurried over with her tray laden with a mug, a sickly looking baguette, and a watery vegetable stew. "It's been a while since the Mesdemoiselles of the Mountain's wagon came through, but the vegetables are still edible, and the stew is hardy."

"I'm sure it is wonderful, merci beaucoup," Ro said, taking a seat that allowed a view of the whole establishment. She wasn't going to ask what kind of flour the baguette was made from, or what was in the stew. Sometimes it was better not knowing.

As Ro ate, it wasn't long until villagers began to trickle in, most ordering café, watered-down red wine, or the more potent drinks Ro tended to stay away from.

Several nodded at her or stared openly, but most

pretended to ignore her while keeping a close eye on her every movement.

And also looking nervously around the inn, flinching at every sudden or overly loud sound.

Ro ate every bite, not certain when she'd get another meal, and was pretty certain the baguette was made out of acorn flour. Not the worst she'd had.

The vegetables were wilted but edible, and her watered-down red wine mild enough to give to a baby. Not that she ever would.

The minute her meal was gone, her dishes were made to disappear, and the owners and the old woman stood at her table, watching her nervously.

"Is there anything I can get you?" the younger woman asked, her voice shaking a little.

"Oui, please sit." Ro indicated the bench across from her. "I have questions."

The three moved as one and sat on the same bench, watching her intently.

"In order for this to work, I need you to give me as much information as you possibly can."

The three nodded solemnly.

"What has been happening?"

The younger woman blew out a breath. "Where to begin? Patrons have run out of the inn in the middle of the night, saying the inn is cursed, that they'd rather take their chances with the wolves than remain another moment under our roof, that we should just cut our losses and start over. But my inn isn't cursed!"

Ro raised a calming hand. "What did they say was happening?"

The three looked at each other. "Clothing and shoes moved in the middle of the night. Fire on the curtains and bedspreads that doesn't leave a mark. Water, or worse, pouring down the walls." The innkeeper swallowed hard. "Flying . . . objects . . . flung at a person's head."

"Have any of you experienced this yourselves?"

The husband started nodding enthusiastically even as his wife straightened and lifted her chin. "It's just a trick of the imagination, is all. If you ignore it, it goes away."

Marc rubbed his head and muttered, "If ye ignore it, ye gets hit in the head."

The old woman rolled her eyes. "My daughter, the only person in the whole of France without a superstitious bone in her body."

Ro held back her smile. She didn't want to offend the innkeeper. "How long has this been going on?"

"Months," the female innkeeper said simply, with a shrug.

"Years, more like," the grandmère muttered.

"Probably somewhere between those two," the man said timidly, earning twin glares from both women.

"And what do you suspect is causing it?" Ro asked.

The three glanced at each other. But it was the old woman who answered. "There be rumors that before the curse fell, a man and his wife lived here."

"In another house," the husband added quickly.

The old woman nodded. "In another house. They both died in their sleep when it caught fire."

"Our inn is not built on the remains of another home!" the innkeeper burst out. "There was nothing here when we built. And we are not being haunted by ghosts!"

She jumped to her feet and moved away to see to other patrons' needs, dabbing at her eyes with her apron.

Ro almost called her back, and briefly considered following her, but she knew what it was like to need a moment to oneself. She would speak to her alone later.

The old mère watched her daughter go with sadness in her eyes. "The curse has been hard on my daughter. O' course, it's been hard on everyone, but on her most of all." She turned a firm gaze on Ro. "She may be in denial, but the fact remains that we have a problem, whatever it may be, and no one will stay here."

The husband spoke quietly. "We haven't had this many people within our doors for months."

Ro eyed the room once more. Everyone indeed looked skittish, but Ro was a novelty, and she was used to this kind of attention. The townspeople weren't going to miss out.

Once the woman looked composed enough to talk, Ro waved her over while speaking to the two who remained at her table. "May I speak to her alone?"

The husband and the innkeeper's mother got up and left, one eagerly, and the other, dragging her steps.

The innkeeper took a moment more to compose herself, then reluctantly sat at the table, looking as if she had been wrung out—for a long time.

Ro leaned forward and captured her attention. "In order for this to work, I need your cooperation, Madame. Are you willing to let me help you?"

The woman shot her a disgruntled, distrusting look and didn't say anything.

"Why do you not wish to believe your house may have been built upon another? One that perhaps had a tragic end?"

The woman looked away, obstinate, jaw firm, until finally, she deflated and tears filled her eyes. "The house—it belonged to my dearest and oldest friend. The inn was built before I realized . . ." Suddenly, she leaned forward and grasped Ro's hands. "You must understand, the fire changed the surrounding area drastically, as did the curse. If I had known, if I had realized, I would have *never*—"

Then she started to cry, great, heaving sobs, and Ro couldn't get another word out of her.

But she kept Ro's hand.

Out of her element, Ro squeezed and let her keep it. "She does not blame you, Madame."

"B-but, if she d-did . . . it was m-my f-fault!" the woman practically wailed.

Ro didn't do so well with emotion. She looked around for help, but the husband was nowhere to be seen, the patrons were watching with interest, and the old woman watched her with a look that said, "Fix it. This is what I'm paying you for."

Ro gritted her teeth and plunged on. "How was it your fault?"

"She—I—we—" The woman stared at Ro as if she didn't know where to begin.

Ro didn't blame her. She was regretting taking on this particular job. So many uncomfortable emotions. "What if you started from the beginning?"

The whole story came pouring out like water, and the innkeeper's mother kept a wide circle of empty tables around them, ensuring nosy patrons stayed away from their conversation.

A quarrel, a new bride leaving with her new husband to make a life elsewhere, harsh words between friends, then moving back after the curse fell only to find she could never make it right—and may have in fact made it worse. May have in fact started the fire before she left. Everyone said so.

Not to her face, of course.

But it had happened the night she'd left, after their quarrel, and then she'd unintentionally built an inn on the very site.

And it had been tearing her up inside, even though she'd acted as if it hadn't.

Ro stood once there was more crying than telling. "Show me to my room, s'il vous plaît."

The woman stared up at her, mouth parted, nose red,

and tears glistening in her eyes and on her cheeks. "You—you still wish to stay?"

Ro gave her half a smile. "I know something about regrets and should-haves and things not being exactly as they seem."

"Oh, merci!" The woman flew at her, gave Ro a hug she decidedly did not want, and rushed up the stairs ahead of her, candle held aloft.

Ro resolutely followed, ignoring the curious stares that followed in her wake.

❧

After inspecting every inch of the room she was shown, Ro stood in the middle of a simple room, alone finally, curtains and bedclothes worn but clean. The mattress was well stuffed, if a bit musty smelling.

She waited till the noises faded away downstairs and the innkeepers went to bed, then prowled around the inn, looking for clues, until she had a pretty good idea of what she was dealing with.

But she wouldn't be sure until it showed itself.

Ro settled on her bed, clothes on, bedclothes under her, and resolved to wait until the spirit—or whatever it was—showed up.

Without falling asleep.

3

Ro jerked awake, half of her face sore, a loud crash ringing in her ears.

The water basin lay shattered on the floor next to her, and her cheekbone throbbed.

Every instinct screamed at her to jump up, to fight, to run, to do something, but Ro stayed firmly planted where she was, hands folded over her stomach in apparent disinterest.

Ro spoke to the room at large when nothing else happened. "That all you got?"

There was an expectant pause.

Then blood started to run down the wall opposite the window.

Ro raised an eyebrow. "D'accord, I'll admit that's impressive."

The blood froze where it was before gushing down from the ceiling and globbing all over the floor. It started to pile up.

Suddenly, fire jumped from the fireplace and licked up the bedspread toward Ro and then up the curtains, flickering in a mad dance.

Ro held her hands out to it. "Not even warm."

Everything froze, even the flickering flames, and then the room flared into a raging inferno. Like someone was throwing a tantrum.

Ro sighed and rolled off the bed and onto her feet.

Even though no heat could be felt, still, strands of her hair moved in a current of wind, rising in a halo around her head from her long braid.

"Arrête. Stop," Ro said.

Everything snuffed out. No blood, no fire, nothing.

A decided feeling of someone being miffed filled the air.

"Do you really want to keep doing this to these nice people? People who haven't run you out or treated you poorly? Do you really want to torture the innkeeper into thinking her best friend is still hanging around her inn, haunting her for a crime she didn't commit?"

Ro had been getting hints of emotions, but now shame washed over her.

Not her shame. Someone else's.

"Show yourself," Ro commanded.

A fey creature, about the length of her arm from her elbow to her fingertips, resolved in midair, hands clasped behind its back and head dropped forward.

It was slender, reminding Ro of a blade of grass, yet its substance filled the space. In turns solid and see-through, it was made up of transparent pastel colors that subtly shifted from one to another.

Spiky hair, jagged little clothes that undulated in an unseen current, pointy little hands and feet—Ro couldn't tell if it were male or female, but that hardly seemed to matter.

A sprite. She'd never seen one before, but it matched the description in one of her fairy stories perfectly.

It didn't scuff its foot, but the motion would have fit its dejected air.

Ro huffed out a breath, more to cover her awe and hold

on to her pretended air of sternness than from any real feeling of exasperation. She so rarely got to meet non-evil fey. And according to lore, sprites were merely mischievous, not of the eating-humans variety.

"Are you even supposed to be here?"

The creature shook its head with a long face.

"Can you get back home?"

Once again, the sprite shook its head.

"So . . . while you're here, wouldn't you rather help the nice innkeepers instead of running off all their customers?"

The thing tilted its head as if considering.

"Or would you rather I try to help you find your home?"

The sprite lit up, literally, with what looked like blue and orange flames curling up its body, as it flitted excitedly around Ro's head.

Ro tried to smile, but a yawn cut her off mid-grin. She eyed the bed. "Think I could get some sleep first?"

It chattered in a language Ro couldn't hear, its lips moving but no sound issuing forth, then it tugged on Ro's cape, pulling her toward the door.

Ro sighed. "Figures."

The creature winked out of sight, and a whorl of air flitted downstairs. Ro rounded the corner to find all three innkeepers staring anxiously up the stairs.

"We heard noises—are you all right, Mademoiselle?" the innkeeper asked.

Ro gave the woman a tired smile. "I think I might have discovered your problem."

"Really?" The woman's eyes widened. "And what would that be?"

The thing whooshed back upstairs and gave Ro's braid a hard yank—where the others couldn't see. Ro winced and rubbed the back of her head.

"I'll let you know when I know for certain."

She felt disapproval coming from the little being in waves.

"If I can," she said carefully.

At that, the sprite zipped away—no one else reacted, so apparently Ro was the only one who could feel it—and she made her way down after it.

"But, huntress, where are you going?" the bewildered innkeeper asked as Ro made her way toward the door.

"Out," Ro said simply, opening the door for the sprite and waiting to follow it out.

It flew straight for outside, slammed into seemingly nothing, and fell back on the floor, rubbing and shaking its head.

"Huh," Ro said, eyeing the creature, then the door.

"What is it? What do you see?" the innkeeper asked in a fearful voice.

Ro plastered a smile on her face. "Go to bed, s'il vous plaît. I need to work alone."

They took their sweet time, just as reluctant as Ro would have been had the same been asked of her, but she didn't take her eyes off them until they had left her and the little sprite in peace.

Her eyes found the little creature's the moment they were gone. "Trapped, I take it?"

The thing mournfully nodded.

"Same with the other doors? Windows?"

It nodded again.

Ro investigated every door and window, looking for something out of the ordinary.

Nothing stood out to her.

She tried to open one of the small windows above the door, but it was stuck fast. She rattled it, just a little, and a fine powder rained down, getting on her hair and cloak, but thankfully not in her eyes.

The sprite zipped far away from her, up into the corner of the ceiling.

Ro hardly noticed.

Clearly the window just needed a little forcing. Enough dust had accumulated on top of it, though that was somewhat surprising with how clean they kept the rest of their inn.

As she was rattling another window, this one closer to the ground, trying to get it open, dust still falling in a fine mist, footsteps rushed her.

"What are you doing? Get away from there!"

Ro had her hand axes out and her back to the wall before the old woman reached her. Once she realized who it was, she jerked the weapons out of the way, but the old woman stumbled and nearly impaled herself on them anyway.

Ro eased back and said cautiously, "Grandmère?"

The old woman hauled over a chair and began inspecting the top of the casement. "You could've doomed us all, girl!"

Ro wasn't exactly sure what to make of that, so she put away her axes and waited for the old woman to explain. And pretended not to notice the innkeeper and her husband peeking into the main part of the inn.

Without answering, the old woman heaved herself off the chair, toddled into the kitchen, and returned with a mortar and pestle and a scoop of what looked like sugar. She carefully added some and ground it to a fine powder.

Then she took it over to each window Ro had touched and carefully shook the powder on the thin strip of wood above each window and door. "Trying to add even more spirits to haunt the inn, are ye? Some good you are."

Ro's eyes widened. "You mean—sugar keeps spirits out?"

"Salt, girl. Salt. What have ye, half a brain?" The old

woman muttered more insults under her breath, though Ro could clearly hear them.

Ro rolled her eyes. "So you're saying something's been haunting the inn for years, and you've been keeping it trapped inside by applying powdered salt to every window and door?"

She honestly had never heard of something like that, but she was most definitely going to keep it in mind for later.

The old woman froze. "What?" she said in a harsh whisper, absolute horror in her voice.

Ro moved a step closer and attempted to speak gently. "If it's as you say, if salt truly keeps things out, do you think it might keep something in?"

She looked stricken, as if Ro had slapped her across the face, then laughed at her, then doused her in a well for good measure.

Ro felt sorry for her. "Can you remove some of the powder, s'il vous plaît?"

"And let in all the other spirits that haunt the forest at night?" the woman snapped. But her eyes darted around the inn, indecisive, looking panicked, maybe fearful.

Ro gently laid a hand on her arm. "Just one. The front door. I'll stand right there and guard it for you."

The old woman blinked back tears, and Ro helped her off the chair and over to the front door.

"Do you mean I've been . . . causing my children all these problems? For all these years?" she asked in a broken voice.

Ro took a moment to answer. She wasn't good at saying the right thing, and she didn't want the old woman to feel worse. She wanted to get this right.

"Sometimes," Ro said carefully, "you do the best you can, and you seek help when it isn't working. Sometimes, asking for help can be the hardest thing in the world—but it just might be the very thing to turn the situation for the better."

The old woman sniffled and patted Ro's arm. "You're good people, ye are, huntress. Merci."

Ro smiled and started to climb up in the woman's place, but she stopped Ro with a sharp, "You ain't the protectress of this place, I am. I have to do it."

Ro paused, took a deep breath, then traded places with the old woman.

It took a rather long moment for the woman to work up the courage, but then she closed her eyes and swiped her finger through the powdery dust.

Ro glanced up at the sprite, still as far away from the salt as possible, but it shook its head.

Ro looked back at the old woman to find her staring at the same spot, a frown on her face.

"Do you see it?" Ro asked, hoping someone else could.

"Nooooo," the old woman said suspiciously.

"Of course not." Ro sighed. "I think it all needs to be gone."

The old woman looked mutinous, so Ro firmed her tone. "Just swipe it all off, s'il vous plaît. You can put some back once it leaves."

She turned away angrily, but she did as Ro asked. She kicked up a fine powder, which stung Ro's eyes and made her sneeze, but the sprite wouldn't come anywhere near it.

Ro sighed and spoke to it, not caring that the old woman would hear. She was tired and wanted her bed. "Can't you at least try to leave?"

The little creature looked just as fearful as the old woman, but after a moment, it jumped into the air and dove toward the door in a spiral.

Once it hit the cloud, it let out a soundless shriek, which Ro couldn't hear, but she could most definitely see its pain and hear what sounded like sizzling skin. And the cloud slowed its progress. With another soundless shout, the creature pushed through the cloud with a mighty effort and out the other side.

Ro stared after it in shock, a part of her wondering how the creature could have survived that. She shook herself and hurried after it.

"Are you all right?" she demanded the moment she was outside, but she didn't see it anywhere.

The dead grass rustled not far from the inn, and Ro rushed toward it. Sure enough, the sprite was upside down in the dried-up greenery, and Ro wasn't sure whether to try to help it or touch it or leave it there or what.

"What can I do to help?"

It slowly climbed to its feet, and raw, angry-red burns and blisters covered every inch of its visible skin, its clothing blackened and crispy looking. Ro winced on its behalf.

But then the blue and orange flames rose in a swirl around the creature's body, and the burns lessened.

The sprite let out a silent whoop, spun in a circle, and zipped into the forest. After a moment of indecision, Ro followed it, a half-smile on her face.

4

Ro tromped through the freezing wood, following the dim fairy light zipping all over the place, not willing to risk Fairweather to a broken leg or a hunting wolf or a fey circle.

If she were going to be trapped in any way, perhaps in retribution, she hoped the innkeepers gave her horse a good life—and weren't forced to eat him if they ran out of food.

Ro's jaw tensed. Oui, that just meant she had to come back from this—whatever this was.

The sprite led Ro not far from the house and flitted around a particular tree. Ro watched it, uncertain of what exactly to do.

"Is that your home? Is there anything I can do to help?" she asked.

The thing flew at her hand, grabbed it, and before Ro knew what was happening, placed it on the tree.

"What are you—ouch!" Ro tried to yank her hand away, but the sprite held her there with hardly any effort at all.

The tree started to glow both blue and orange in a swirling pattern, both freezing and burning to the touch. Waves of hot and cold washed over Ro, and sweat dripped from her brow while gooseflesh prickled all over her arms and scalp.

She'd never experienced anything like it.

She kept trying to pull away, but the sprite held her firmly in place, not allowing her hand to move.

Ro gritted her teeth, the feelings so intense they hurt like a burning ache deep inside, and suddenly, it looked like the stars came crashing down to earth. But out of the tree.

Floating motes of warm yellow light drifted all around her, in a lazy slow spin, radiating from the tree and Ro. The sprite released her.

She tried to pull back, but now Ro *couldn't* pull her hand from the tree, almost as if her hand had been glued there. At least the burning-cold sensations had snuffed out.

The motes drifted in slow motion, and the sprite zipped excitedly through them all, hovering in so many different directions at once, Ro could hardly track it.

But she still couldn't move.

Trying not to panic, she tugged harder and harder, just wanting to get *away*.

The sprite came up to her, wrapped its arms around her neck in what Ro hoped was a hug and not the beginnings of a fey strangulation, then zipped right toward the tree where her hand was stuck.

Right before he crashed into the tree, he was sucked inside of it, and the glowing motes cascaded in falling stars right into the tree's center.

For a moment, just a moment, Ro glimpsed another world beyond—one she couldn't even begin to describe, if pressed. Full of blinding light and soft beauty and deep woods teeming with life and things flitting through the air.

Many of them converged upon the new arrival, and this time, Ro could hear tiny voices crowing in delight. Her new friend gestured wildly her way, and they all turned and looked at her, just as the last of the falling stars were sucked into the tree.

And then all was dark once more.

The tree released her, and she fell back on the forest floor, stunned.

It took far too many moments for everything Ro had just seen to fade enough from her mind for her to function, but eventually, Ro sat up.

She held out her hand, inspecting it as best she could in the void left by fairy lights. It tingled, but it didn't feel like she'd been burned or frostbitten, both things she'd been concerned about with how intense the sensations were.

A wolf howled in the distance, and Ro was instantly on her feet. She grabbed her crossbow off her back, loaded it, and aimed toward the sound. When it didn't come any closer, she hurried toward the inn.

She could inspect her hand once she was safely indoors.

5

"Well?" the old woman demanded the moment she stepped inside. "What was it? Is it gone? Are all our troubles over?"

Her words were brusque, but her eyes still looked haunted.

She hadn't felt it before, but now Ro could tell a bubble of pressure, like the air was compressed all around her, permeated the inn. The old woman had apparently wasted no time erecting whatever barrier the salt provided.

"Well, surely not *all* our troubles," the innkeeper said, biting her lip. "France's curse isn't lifted, after all."

Another task Ro was determined to see through to its completion. But sleep first.

Ro gave them both a tired smile. "I believe you'll have no more trouble, but might I spend the night to be certain?"

"By all means!" the innkeeper exclaimed. "But—"

Ro raised her hand to stop the questions on the woman's tongue and in her eyes. "I'll answer what I can in the morning."

But they weren't listening to her. They were staring in her hand in horror.

Ro flipped it over, and there, in the center of her palm, an orange and blue swirl glowed faintly, pulsing with color, fading with every heartbeat.

A glow that apparently wasn't visible in the dark.

"Huh," Ro said.

But the others weren't looking at the peculiarity in awe, like Ro was. They were looking at her in fear. And they'd had plenty of that around here lately.

Ro didn't want to add to it.

She made her way toward the stairs, and the innkeeper and her mother stayed as far away from Ro as possible.

6

The next day, Ro slept far past morning, enjoying the luxury of a clean bed, four walls, and the washbasin someone had replaced while she was out being stuck to a fairy tree.

She stumbled downstairs in time for the noon meal.

Which happened to be a feast in her honor—all the surrounding towns invited and stuffing the inn full and spilling outside to more tables laden with country fare.

From the looks of things, they'd ravaged the Mesdemoiselles' food wagons.

Before Ro knew what was happening, the old woman cried out, "Three cheers for the huntress, who has driven away the foul spirit haunting this inn and cleansed the air within to allow a place of refuge for our weary guests once more!"

The room erupted in cheers, and Ro could only blink.

They urged her down the stairs the rest of the way, ushered her around to greet their guests, then settled the best of their food before her.

Ro didn't know what to say—what to do—so she

enjoyed a meal that rivaled most, stuffing her face so she wouldn't be expected to talk.

True, she hadn't been visited by another nighttime visitor—not that she'd expected to be—and she hadn't been disturbed by anything else, but she hardly felt she'd done anything worth celebrating.

She didn't know how her magic worked, how she could sense the little creature, or what part she'd played in ushering the little being home. Or even how the salt barrier worked and why.

But at least the innkeeper and her family were happy.

And most importantly, Ro's hand had stopped glowing.

Ro breathed out a relieved sigh. She couldn't even begin to imagine how she'd explain that to Gautier. Or her fellow huntsmen. She shuddered.

Or Liam.

Not that she'd be opposed to wearing gloves for the rest of her life, but still. She'd have to watch and make sure it didn't pop up at inappropriate times.

The innkeepers served her quietly, their mouths smiling, but their eyes watched her like she would morph into a giant ogre and gobble them up at any moment.

She mostly ignored the curious townspeople who trickled in and out of the inn throughout the whole meal, never going too far and intently watching her every move.

At least she'd learned the effectiveness of a quiet nod from Liam.

"Well? Is it gone or isn't it?" the old woman demanded in a quiet hiss when Ro had taken her last bite.

She pushed back her bowl, and the innkeeper took it but just held it, going nowhere.

Ro wiped her mouth and chose her words carefully. "You had a guest in your inn, one that was trapped here but truly meant you no harm."

The innkeeper's husband rubbed his head. "Tell that to my noggin."

Ro cracked a half smile and kept her voice low. "I helped . . . it . . . return home last night, so I shouldn't think it will bother you again."

At least, she thought that's what had happened.

She had no idea what she'd truly done or how, but she was going with her instincts on this one.

"And it weren't no . . . ghost?" the innkeeper's mère asked.

Ro shook her head. "It wasn't a ghost." She turned a resolute expression upon the innkeeper. "You were right. No one is haunting this inn. The spirit of your friend is at peace."

Relief flooded the innkeeper's face, and tears pricked at her eyes. Ro gave her a smile, which was returned with a wobbly one.

"But it ain't gonna bother us no more?" the old woman persisted. "And what was it already?"

Ro gave them all a smile and stood, swinging her saddlebags over her shoulder. "I don't believe it wanted me to say what it was, but oui, I am fairly confident it will bother you no more." She paused. "But keep those salt barriers up, just in case, and contact me if you start having problems again."

The three exchanged glances. The man shrugged. "She did stay the whole night through without being run out to kingdom come."

The old woman grinned at her daughter. "Told ye it was a good idea."

The innkeeper rolled her eyes and muttered, "There'll be no living with her now."

Ignoring her, the old woman pulled a heavy coin purse out of her deep pocket. "I suppose you'll be wanting the rest of yer payment."

Ro never knew what madness possessed her, but she found the words "Keep it" coming out of her mouth before she could stop them. "Put it into getting this inn back on its feet."

And then she turned and left before the stunned innkeepers could find anything to say—and before her brain had the good sense to snatch the heavy purse out of the old woman's hands.

"Oh, merci, merci!" followed her out to the stables.

She quickly saddled Fairweather and rode away before there could be more thanks. Though they seemed to be following her, not only to see her off, but perhaps also to make sure she didn't come back?

But that didn't bother her for long.

Her mind was filled with swirling colors and her role in making them appear and the glittering world beyond and what it could possibly mean.

If only she knew where to find the answers to all the questions piling upon her faster than she knew what to do with them.

But she was forced to admit one thing to herself as she rode away.

It wasn't too terrible of a diversion after all.

THE END

GAUTIER'S NEW CLOTHES

Les Nouveaux Vêtements de l'Empereur
"The Emperor's New Clothes"
—Hans Christian Andersen—

So the two pretended weavers set up two looms, and affected to work very busily, though in reality they did nothing at all. They asked for the most delicate silk and the purest gold thread; put both into their own knapsacks; and then continued their pretended work at the empty looms until late at night.

Alors les deux tisserands prétendus ont installé deux métiers à tisser, et affectés à travailler très occupé, bien qu'en réalité ils n'aient rien fait du tout. Ils demandaient la soie la plus délicate et le fil d'or le plus pur ; mettre les deux dans leurs propres sacs à dos ; puis ont continué leur prétendu travail sur les métiers vides jusque tard dans la nuit.

1

Ro trudged to Gautier's château, dragging her feet more in the manner of a petulant child than a huntress returning at the conclusion of another successful task.

She didn't want to see Gautier.

She wanted to turn right around and be on to her next hunt. Any hunt far away from here.

But she didn't have another hunt to escape to, so here she was.

The guards at the many entrances let her pass with no more than a nod from each. Although Ro had never made a habit of stopping and speaking to any of them—usually she hurried past to deposit her latest wolf carcass or pelt, snatch up her payment, and rush off for the next hunt—she wished she'd made more of an effort to get to know the soldiers.

Mostly to delay her further.

But she wouldn't even begin to know what to say, then or now.

So she crept by at a snail's pace and all too soon was standing outside Gautier's receiving room. After having been redirected from his private office, where they usually met. But it still hadn't taken more than a few minutes of her time. She sighed.

She didn't even want to see Gautier, much less receive her next assignment in front of an audience.

Hoping she wouldn't be noticed, she slipped into the room and crept along the back wall, hiding behind some potted fruit trees—from the Mesdemoiselles of the Mountain's gardens, no doubt. The guards in this room eyed her but said nothing.

They knew she was a personal favorite of Gautier's, unfortunately.

Two tall, lanky men were currently peddling who knew what to Gautier, and curious despite herself, Ro moved aside a leafy branch to better see their wares.

Gautier's eyes met hers in that instant.

"Ah, huntress, there you are!" boomed his voice.

Ro flinched. Darn it.

He waved both hands at her. "Join me. You have to see this. Come!"

Her neck feeling a million degrees on fire, Ro slinked up to the dais, careful not to make eye contact with the many courtiers straining their necks to capture every moment of the new drama about to unfold, whatever it may be.

"Regardez. Isn't this the loveliest cloth you've ever laid your eyes upon?"

His wording sprang to mind her physically laying her eyeballs upon the cloth, and she choked on an inappropriate laugh. She cleared her throat to cover the half-gurgle that escaped and bent closer to appear to be inspecting it.

Her brothers would appreciate her quirky humor, but Gautier most certainly would not. As she knew from experience.

But as so often happened when she was on the spot or uncomfortable, it took a moment for her brain to tell her what she was seeing.

She gasped belatedly.

There, wrapped in bolts and held in a streaming cascade down the men's outstretched arms, was the loveliest, shimmering, glittery fabric Ro had ever seen. And in the most vibrant colors, too.

Turquoise, a pink that made her eyes ache, deep-citron yellow, such as when lemons ripened past the point of light yellow to a deep golden glow, and more.

She'd never seen anything like it.

"Where did they come from?" Ro asked, and, without realizing it, stretched out a hand to let her fingers glide over fabric that surely would be softer than silk.

The nearest man deftly kept it out of her reach.

Stung, Ro withdrew her hand and remembered where she was—with half the realm watching her.

Also, she hadn't taken the time to wash up after her journey as she usually did, and if she sullied this costly fabric, she had a hunch she'd be working for Gautier for the next year . . . for free.

Also unfortunate because she'd just been looking for excuses to prolong this meeting, and she could've made washing up last at least half an hour. Maybe included a bath and a change of clothes.

Then this peddler of cloth wouldn't be peering down his long nose at her and judging her quite so very much. Perhaps.

Still, she wanted to slink to the nearest potted plant, use it to shelter her while escaping out the exit, then ride Fairweather so far and so fast that every person present forgot who she was.

She was just turning away to make some kind of escape when Gautier threaded her arm through his and took her on a tour of the bolts of fabric piled in great mounds in the center of the room.

Ro was careful not to touch any of them.

He prattled on, possibly giving her time to compose herself—more possibly not noticing she needed that time—until one phrase caught on her mind like a nail catching on fabric.

"Fit for a king, eh?"

She looked at him then, and he looked back, expectant, as if waiting for her to make some kind of connection.

"You want this . . . for the crown prince?" she guessed. "When he comes back?"

Because the king and queen had been lost at sea, right before the curse fell. Leaving the crown prince as the next royal to take the throne—unless another in the royal line could be found to rule in the meantime.

In fact, Gautier was acting as regent, ruling in the king's stead, as he was the steward of the kingdom, ready to give it back once the crown prince was found.

Or so he'd led everyone to believe.

His face shuttered, and he sighed, releasing her hand with a condescending pat. He turned to the men and continued as if she wasn't there.

But he'd left her even farther from escape than before.

"You were saying?" he prompted them. Before the man could once again wax eloquent about the cloth draped over his arms, Gautier interrupted. "Never mind that one. You have special cloth from the Realm of the Fey, n'est-ce pas?"

The men exchanged startled glances.

The man who'd been speaking, the one who'd kept the cloth from Ro's dusty fingers, took on a soothing, cajoling tone. "I believe you are mistaken, votre Majesté."

Ro jolted as if struck by an arrow. How dare he call Gautier king!

She'd taken a step forward when her brain caught up to her temper and warned she'd be better served taking in the scene instead of starting a brawl. For once she listened to the rational part of herself that rarely took precedence.

Besides, Gautier would surely correct the peddler.

He did not.

Just smiled as if the words were his due.

Ro's mouth popped open as the man continued speaking.

"We said our cloth comes from a far distant land, one of exotic spices and a swarthy-skinned people, one with thousands of tales of djinn and robbers and treasure beyond imagining—"

"Yes, yes," Gautier interrupted, "that's all well and good. But come now, let us speak plainly. You were overheard at our fair tavern speaking of a fabric from the Realm of the Fey, one fit for a king—*only* for a king. Why else do you think you are here? Show me at once, or be off with you."

Gautier started to turn away.

Ro stared among each person, wanting to shout at them all, hardly knowing what she'd say. What was all this nonsense about being king? Surely he wasn't . . . *giving up* on the crown prince?

Ro's heart stuttered in fear.

The two men scrambled to keep his attention. "We meant no offense."

"Surely you must know how valuable such a cloth would be."

"Only for a king, oui."

"We rarely show it."

"Only to those worthy . . ."

"Enough!" Gautier's voice echoed in the chamber, and his cold gaze made the two men grow paler than their ruddy complexions could handle, giving them a greenish hue. "I shall not waste my time further. Good day, Messieurs." He turned to Ro. "You have a report for me, oui?"

Before Ro could even begin to respond, the lead peddler snapped his fingers, and a host of servants converged on their piles of fabric and carted them away, clearing the room in an instant.

With great fanfare, four tall men with bulging muscles, hard scowls, and the same swarthy complexion of which they'd just been speaking marched into the room, armor clanking. A heavy, chained chest was carried on poles between them, and with a well-practiced move, they placed the chest precisely before Gautier and stepped back, removing the poles and holding them like staves.

Ro widened her stance in case they started wielding them like weapons.

For a moment, she thought they might leave—as did Gautier, if the quick glance he threw them could be counted upon—but they remained as if planted, guarding the chest.

"You must understand, Monsieur," wheedled the first merchant, "we do not show this cloth to just anyone. Most do not even know of its existence."

"You see," continued the second, "it has a . . . peculiarity . . . due to its special origin. That being of the fey, if you know what I mean."

"Oui, and due to its fickle nature, we only bring it out upon rare occasions."

"The last to see it was the Spanish king, I reckon."

Ro's head came around at that.

"And you know how many years ago that has been," the first hastened to amend.

Ro forced herself to relax, especially now knowing they were paying as much attention to her as she was to them. But it didn't *seem* like they'd meant that they'd shown it to the Spanish king before the curse fell—more like it had been recent, and they were covering a slip.

One thing was certain: Ro would be wise to keep an eye on everything these two said or did.

"Yes, yes, go on," Gautier urged impatiently.

"You see," the first peddler said, stepping close and pitching his voice as if sharing a confidence—though his voice easily reached the far corners of the room, "the fey created this cloth to weed out any usurpers to the throne, when the question came up in Angleterre."

"That's England to them," added the other man.

The first had a look of extreme patience on his face. "That only matters in England, dimwit," he said under his breath. Then, louder, "The only person who can wear the cloth is someone worthy of the throne."

Gautier nodded, trying to seem regal, but even Ro could see he was seconds from strangling the man for still speaking instead of opening the chest.

"And the only person who can see it"—the merchant swept his gaze about the room, making sure every person was hanging on his every word, and that every eye was glued to him—"is the person worthy of his post." His eyes settled on Ro last. "Or *her* post."

Many people in the room stiffened, but Ro shot him a frosty glare. She was becoming less amused by these two by the second.

And judging by the look on Gautier's face, a whole new host of concerns had descended upon him and frozen him to his spot.

With a flourish, the man accepted a key from a servant who slipped to his side and away hastily, and started unlocking the many silver chains wrapped around the chest. They fell away to a soft susurrus of sound, as gentle as rain, as quiet as a whisper.

Ro's eyes widened. Most definitely fey made.

The last chain came undone, and the servant was back, removing the key with all haste.

But Ro's attention wasn't on the servant, nor anyone else's.

The lid opened, and Ro almost imagined a slight glow came from within. The first peddler pulled on a pair of white gloves, and with great fanfare, lifted a silver bolt from the cavernous chest and held it aloft for all to see.

An empty bolt.

With no fabric on it whatsoever.

The room had been quiet before, but now it went still. Absolutely, positively still. As if no one dared to breathe.

"As you can see," the peddler stage-whispered quietly, reverently, "this cloth is the loveliest you will ever lay eyes upon. There is none like it to compare, not even in the Realm of the Fey. In fact, the fey ensured only the worthy can even see it so that the king will only surround himself with those competent enough to serve him. Isn't it just . . . wonderful?"

He paused, the look of raptured awe on his face extremely convincing.

To everyone except Ro.

After hesitant agreement from all sides, a timid voice came from the crowd. "And no one can wear it . . . but royals?"

Gautier swallowed noticeably.

"Exactly," the merchant said. "A demonstration." His eyes darted to the crowd. "You there. Come here."

A man's wife shoved him, and he reluctantly shuffled forward, looking decidedly uncomfortable.

"Now, although this fabric is costly—dear enough that only kings can afford it—allow me to show you how inadvisable it is for the wrong person to attempt to wear it."

After shoving the bolt into his partner's hands, who seemed to stagger under its weight, the peddler flourished an enormous pair of scissors, comically so, and pretended to unroll and snip the barest sliver of cloth, by his meticulous pantomime of measuring out the fabric.

Ro looked between him and the crowd and Gautier several times. They weren't seriously buying this, were they?

Next, he took out a needle and an empty thread spool,

made a few looping stitches, and patted and smoothed out the invisible cloth several times.

He held it up for the man's inspection. "Just enough for a cravat, non?"

The man looked to his wife, and she made a desperate shooing motion. He wilted. "Non. I mean! Oui. Of course. Perfect for a cravat."

The man clamped his lips closed, and sweat appeared at his hairline.

Ro crossed her arms, not even trying to hold back her scowl.

"You are not of the royal bloodline, oui?" the merchant asked.

"Oui. I mean! Non. Of course not." The man's shoulders were hunching around his ears, and Ro was starting to feel sorry for him.

Her scowl deepened. But she'd never stoop to lying about invisible cloth just to keep up appearances.

"Observe." With a flourish, the man tied a precise knot around the man's neck and stepped back, one hand in the air, the other clamped around the man's arm. He paraded the man about the room, and unintelligible murmurs of admiration followed them. "Ah-ha, but see here? See how the cloth melts away?"

"Like butter, it is," said the second peddler. "Melting butter."

A hitch in the first man's step was the only indication he was ready to strangle his partner, but he also raised his voice to drown out anything the other man might say. "Look closely. See how it fades? And there, oh my, there! It is now gone."

He spun on his audience, and after but a heartbeat, effusive astonishment rose from all sides, then a pall fell over the courtiers like that at a funeral.

Now Gautier's forehead was sprouting its own fair share of moisture.

"For our second demonstration—"

Ro couldn't help it—her burst of laughter echoed in the chamber. They couldn't be serious. She choked it back, but not fast enough. All eyes were upon her.

"Well we can certainly see who isn't worthy of her position," the peddler said darkly, his partner still holding the empty fabric holder out to Gautier.

Ro's mirth died a sudden death. Imposters these two may be, but her reputation was everything.

If she didn't have that, she wouldn't get more jobs from Gautier. If she didn't get more jobs from Gautier, she couldn't provide for her family. If she couldn't provide for her family, she wouldn't be able to pay to get Cosette out of France.

And she'd never get the one job she'd worked so many years toward being trusted for: to kill the beast who was holding the prince prisoner.

She didn't know how to get within the château's walls. Not without Gautier.

She met Gautier's eyes, and he had the same panicked look on his face.

He, apparently, didn't want to lose his favorite huntress either.

"Imbecile. That's because you're blocking her. Step aside." To Ro he said, "Now, isn't that much better? Isn't the cloth just lovely?"

His eyes commanded her to parrot his words.

Immediate revulsion hit Ro. She hated to lie, and she especially hated being coerced into anything that went against her beliefs. But all eyes were upon her, and her future balanced on this very moment, and she just wanted all the staring to *stop*.

And then the worst thought of all hit her: What if she

was incompetent? She didn't know how she worked. How she did what she did. She fumbled through every hunting job, relying on instinct, skill with her crossbow, and sheer perseverance.

There was no one to train her, no one to ask questions of, no one to explain how creatures were sneaking in from the Realm of the Fey and how she was able to stop them.

She was alone.

If anything, the thought made her angrier. Incompetent or not, she was *going* to get Cosette out of France, she was *going* to kill the beast, she was *going* to rescue the prince, and she was *going* to break the curse, no matter the cost to herself.

Her eyes traveled the room for one face. Surely Liam would back her. Tell her she wasn't crazy. That these men were the ones in the wrong.

But her fellow huntsman was nowhere to be seen.

"Huntress? I am waiting," Gautier said imperiously.

She gritted her teeth, and she instantly knew how that poor courtier felt. And determined never to make another vow she couldn't keep. To never cast such quick and ready judgment until she'd been in the same situation.

"Much. Lovely," Ro muttered, more growling the words than saying them.

"There. You see? She is fine. Now, is that the only color? Or . . ." Gautier's voice trailed off as if he wasn't sure how to continue.

"But, votre Majesté, why would you even *need* another color?"

"Is not this one enough?"

"See how it shimmers, the colors cascading from one to the next. See how it *glows*, even . . ."

Gautier rested his chin on his fist, his scowl apparently a valiant effort to look like he was deeply pondering their words. Or the cloth. Or something.

But he nodded along with them, and Ro's heart sank that he wasn't going to call these liars out for what they were.

Charlatans. Swindlers. The worst of humanity.

Ro couldn't stand it.

"You don't really think—" Ro began.

"Hush, you," Gautier all but snapped. "Go on," he said in a much kinder voice to the two Messieurs, though he was still having trouble controlling his scowl. "You were saying something about a second demonstration?"

"But of course!" With a flourish, the first peddler waved Gautier forward. "For our second demonstration, stand right here, s'il vous plaît."

With as much dignity as he could muster, Gautier moved to where the man indicated. Though he took his time about it, whether from trepidation or dislike of being told what to do, Ro didn't know or care.

She was close to leaving him on his own until these two were done with him.

With the same exaggerated movements, the man cut, sewed, and tied a cravat around Gautier's neck, then stepped back.

Both men had rapt looks of awe on their faces, and the first clasped his hands under his chin. "Magnifique."

"Truly," the second echoed.

Ro scowled and glanced at Gautier's neck. And did a double take. There, just barely seen, shimmered a cravat. One that hadn't been there before. One that, though it looked as if it could melt away at any second, was ethereal and lovely and regal and very much non-transparent.

And it wasn't disappearing.

"See how it isn't fading?" cried the first.

"Best-looking cravat I ever did see!" crooned the second. "Truly fit for a king!"

Slowly, as if he were being led to the gallows, Gautier

met Ro's gaze, and she could only stare in astonishment. What did it mean that she could only partially see it?

But Gautier looked about ready to faint, and she had to give him some kind of encouragement.

At her slow nod, and quite possibly the look of astonishment on her face, confidence flowed back into Gautier in spades, and he puffed out his chest and walked up the dais to the throne he used to hear petitioners' complaints. And to pay Ro for her hunts, before she'd been permitted in his inner circle.

Ro couldn't stop staring at the bit of cloth just barely visible, opaque enough that Gautier's skin could not be seen through the cloth, even if the fabric itself was hard to see.

And neither could the courtiers stop staring, from the sounds of things. All were muttering in awe and delight—and a fair amount of relief.

But something nagged at the back of Ro's mind. She'd seen something like that before . . . but where . . . ?

Gautier preened and smoothed out his vest and breeches and fluffed the lace at his sleeves. "How long until I can have a suit of clothing made, one fit for a king? One for my own coronation?"

Ro felt as if she'd been sucker-punched. All this time, all the misgivings she'd felt about him—he'd been setting himself up as king in the prince's stead.

No wonder he hadn't yet seen fit to help her find a way into the hidden château to free the prince.

Now, to find out if it was from malice or if he was truly doing what he thought was best for the country. Maybe he didn't know how to get in, and he'd been misleading her this whole time? Either way, she had some digging to do.

Ro stepped back and crossed her arms, having missed most of what the peddlers had been saying while her entire world was changing.

She still didn't trust these two.

Gautier didn't want to hear from her? Fine. She'd watch from the edges and be ready to run them off and clean up whatever consequences came of their deceit when it was time for her to do her job.

"Get on with it," Gautier interrupted, both Ro's thoughts and the peddlers' words. "Can you or can you not make a suit of clothing worthy for a king in time for my coronation? You are not the only seamsters I can hire to accomplish the task."

They exchanged another glance and went back to whatever they'd been saying. "You cannot rush art, votre Majesté," the first man said. "This cloth is so expensive and rare, and will only hold thread also from the Realm of the Fey, that we can only achieve perfection if we do not rush. Remember, it is only gifted to those who are worthy to rule, of which we've already established you are."

"Most worthy," the other parroted with a little giggle.

Ro started to say something, but Gautier held up a hand and stopped her. "How *long*—"

"A month . . ."

"Maybe two . . ."

"At the very least."

They both leaned forward and eyed Gautier expectantly.

He puffed out a breath. "Very well."

A flurry of celebration and plans being made aloud by the two peddlers followed.

"We must have a place to work. A place for multiple fittings."

"A big space!"

"With lots of light. Lots of windows."

"Lots of windows for lots of light!"

"And we shall, of course, discuss payment before we begin . . ."

Gautier interrupted. "But no more than a month! I do

not wish to wait even that long to give my people what they have been waiting so long for."

Ro was beginning to suspect the *people* weren't the ones who'd been waiting so long for Gautier to be crowned . . .

The first peddler bowed. "But of course, votre Majesté. That will, of course, cost more, but I am certain we can accomplish the task in that time."

The second one giggled again.

Ro eyed him, but his sole focus was on Gautier—as was the other's, as she'd been effectively shut down and dismissed—and she took in his gleaming eyes and the way he rubbed his hands together.

Oh yes, Gautier was about to be taken in, and Ro was going to enjoy every minute.

She'd already tried to warn him, after all.

2

Later, Ro was angrily brushing down Fairweather, half debating leaving and not coming back. For a month. Maybe two. After this whole coronation debacle was over and done with.

Of course, if the people accepted Gautier as king, she was signing her own death warrant if she didn't show her support.

But if the crown prince came back and found out she'd backed another king, she might be executed for treason . . .

The whole thing made her head pound.

Not only that, after the peddlers had been shown to the best room in the château, they'd ushered Gautier inside, and the tall one had shut the door in her face with an imperious look. She could get nowhere near Gautier after that.

She hadn't even been paid yet.

Straw rustled behind her, and Ro spoke in a low, growly voice. "What did you think of that little demonstration back there?"

One of her fellow huntsmen whistled. "How does she *do* that?"

"Magic. Gotta be."

Ro's head whipped around at that, but Marceau just winked at her.

Gabin cackled, and Hector shook his head. Axel and Lucien stayed in the background, as they usually did, but Ro didn't sense more than these five in the stables with her.

All the others must be out on assignment.

"What can I do for you fine Messieurs?" Ro asked as she went back to brushing out her horse. Even though he didn't need it.

Her hands just needed to be busy, and she craved his massive height, gentle presence, and quiet warmth. Fairweather just stood there, allowing himself to be pampered, munching on a rare serving of oats.

"Well now, that's the question, isn't it?" Marceau said.

Ro kept brushing. She knew him well enough to know he'd eventually get around to what he'd come to say, whether she were involved in the conversation or not.

"We was wondering if you'd talk to Gautier about those two," Hector blurted. "Get his permission to run 'em off, maybe."

"Or even run 'em off without his express permission," Gabin added.

Ro kept quiet.

"Someone should at least try to get him to see reason." Although Marceau's voice still had a lighthearted lilt to it, there was now an edge of steel that hadn't been there before. "Someone close to him."

Hopefully his ire was directed at the situation, not her.

Ro huffed a laugh. "I'm the last person who should help with these kinds of things. You do realize I have no tact, right?"

"Me, I ain't got no problem being stupid," Marceau said around a piece of straw in his mouth. "It's my employer being made to look stupid that bugs me. Makes me itchy, ye ken?"

After a pause of tense, loaded silence, in which Ro kept brushing, as if pondering their words—which she was—Gabin cleared his throat and crowed, "Don't matter none as long as he pays!"

The three huntsmen howled with loud and exaggerated laughter, while Axel and Lucien looked on without a sound or a hitch to their expressions.

She wasn't sure what to make of those two.

But she did know she wanted the same thing as the other three huntsmen.

Ro huffed a sigh. "Fine. I'll look into it." She jabbed a finger at the huntsmen pestering her. "But no promises I'll accomplish anything. He's already dismissed my concerns multiple times."

At that, Axel and Lucian moved deeper into the stables, saddled their horses, and rode away, not a smidgeon of expression to show what they thought of the conversation.

They may have been satisfied with what she'd said, confident she had it well in hand, or were immediately setting off to find Liam to rescue them all from Ro's attempts at diplomacy.

She was betting on that last one.

And in her heart of hearts, so deep she'd never admit it to another living soul, she wanted Liam's help. Craved it, even.

He would know what to do.

Or at the very least, Gautier might actually listen to him.

But she'd rather be stretched out on the Anglais's barbaric rack than admit that aloud to anyone. Ever.

Then again . . . if she had help and didn't use it . . . and something happened to Gautier . . . or the kingdom . . .

She turned to the three huntsmen still in the stable with her. "Any of you know how I can get a message to Liam?"

Marceau frowned. "Perhaps . . ."

"Bon," she said. "Anyone up for a little adventure? Together?"

"Teaming up?" Marceau tapped his forehead twice and pointed at her. "I like it."

She shrugged. "I need your help as much as you need mine."

"I'm in," Hector said quickly.

"Me too," Gabin added.

"Well, now." His movements slow, methodical, as if he were giving Ro's words the greatest of thought, Marceau crossed his arms and said, "The mighty huntress asking for help from us poor subordinates? Who've been around longer than she has, I might add?"

Ro rolled her eyes. "You want to look into these guys or not?"

"I want to take the message to Liam. Then, oui. I most definitely want to help."

Ro set down the horse brush and started outlining her plans. "Here's what I need from each one of you."

3

Gabin had ridden south to see what he could find of the peddler's other customers. If there were any.

Hector had volunteered to track down Ro's contact who sold handwritten fairy stories to children, often in exchange for leaving their work to listen to her read around the town well or at their own kitchen table.

Ro couldn't even begin to describe how much she admired the woman and her business practices—but Ro had threatened Hector within an inch of his life if he in any way damaged her relationship with the woman. Ro was perfectly capable of messing things up on her own, thank you very much.

Marceau was off with a missive to Liam.

And Ro was currently babysitting their utter *infant* of a future king.

"Not that way! The fabric must sweep across my chest. *Sweep*. As in the manner of the old kings. And watch where you put that needle!"

Ro wasn't sure how she managed to hold back each of her eye rolls, but she was already exhausted from the effort.

Had it only been a week since the simpering peddlers

had waltzed into their lives? And did she really have to wait three more to be rid of them?

She silently urged her fellow huntsmen to hurry along their tasks, wishing she'd been brave enough to seek Liam herself. She should've let Marceau babysit the infantile king becoming much too big for his breeches.

"I don't *care* if you have to work all through the night. It must be ready in time for my coronation!"

Ro yawned and tried not to nod off in the corner. She needed to be alert. Look as if she were taking her self-proclaimed role as bodyguard quite seriously.

Though she was protecting Gautier against the peddlers, not assassins, as she'd insisted.

After the impromptu meeting in the barn, Ro had planted herself outside of Gautier's quarters, and the next time he'd tried to leave, informed him that now he'd made his intentions of becoming king known, she was to protect him against assassination attempts until other huntsmen returned and they could implement a rotating schedule.

It was the only thing she could think of to get him to take her seriously.

And it had worked.

Anytime he was not within his quarters, Ro was stuck to him like paste, and she highly regretted ever attempting to be clever.

She could hardly take him in small doses, let alone all waking hours.

And still she prowled the perimeter at night, keeping an eye on the seamsters' room from her perch in the forest, in which they seemed to be measuring, snipping, cutting, and sewing all hours of the night and day.

Ro was exhausted already. And it had only been a week.

She jerked awake as the peddler's wheedling voice cut into her nodding off.

"Votre Majesté. S'il vous plaît. We must take your

measurements exactly. Each piece must be fitted to you as we make it, and we must take care with each individual stitch until the suit of clothing is complete. We are hurrying as much as we dare."

"Well hurry a little faster," Gautier groused.

Week two went along in much the same manner as week one.

Then week three came along, and Ro vowed never to complain about any hunt that took her far away from Gautier and the simpering fools that made up his court. Whether in deep snow, drizzling rain, or blistering heat, she'd take the worst nature could throw at her over this.

Then came discussions of matching decorations on his frock coat, shoes that must be made to match as well, of course, and a train that would sweep behind him on the way to the coronation.

A train that would "take twenty men to carry behind you!"

Gautier's eyes shone with each addition to making his ensemble more kingly.

Even Ro was amazed at the amount of gold making its way into the peddler's hands, and yet she choked as they named what the train would cost.

Gautier ignored her, as he always did.

"But of course, that is for the length of such a train. If you cannot afford it . . ." The peddler's voice trailed off. "We could always shorten it. Two could hold it up? Four, perhaps?"

"Of course I can afford it!" Gautier snapped, then went back to preening in front of the mirror. The shimmering cloth they shoved his limbs into and out of multiple times a day had resolved into a gray crushed silk that not only looked costly, but was rather striking on his figure. And he was enjoying every minute of it. "I just don't know if I want to."

The peddler gasped. "Do not . . . *want* to, votre Majesté?"

Gautier nodded absentmindedly, as if the words were careless. "The gold spent on this alone would be better served feeding my people."

Ro, who'd been lounging disgustedly against the wall, shot upright, her gaze intently upon Gautier's face.

Gautier pretended not to notice, but his chest swelled slightly, and he met the peddler's gaze. "And if I am to be the best king for the job, therein should lie my focus."

The peddler's mouth hung open for a stunned moment, and Gautier risked a glance at Ro.

For the first time in her entire life, she was proud of him. Glad to be serving him. And would gladly call him king.

Though that could quite possibly be her delirium talking.

A smile lit his eyes, briefly, one that said Ro communicated clearly what she felt without any words, before the peddler cut in and gobbled up his attention once more.

"*Of course* your attention must be on feeding the people!" the peddler said in a desperate way. "And how better to do that? By proving once and for all that you are *meant* to be on the throne. You are absolutely right!"

Ro's newfound respect was quickly snuffed out as the peddler wheedled and cajoled and found out Gautier's unarmored spots and where best to tug on his pride.

Gautier so badly wanted whatever this man was selling —and it wasn't clothing—that he was soon agreeing to every additional thing suggested.

But on just the one outfit.

It would enhance the ceremony to crown him king, of course. The people would understand such an expense, and it would better help *him* help *them*.

Ro's scowl was back, but no matter how much she tried

to catch his eye, no matter how many disgusted mutterings she made, Gautier ignored her.

The peddler speared her with a frosty glare. "I do believe the terms of our agreement were that if you cannot keep your growling to yourself, you cannot be in here at all? I do believe there are *dogs* better behaved than yourself."

Ro shoved her back against the wall once more, arms folded, boot propped up behind her, and refused to budge. She would *not* rise to that bait.

She knew a few dogs—wolves—that would happily tear their throats out as well, but was she being uncivilized and saying so? Non. She was behaving.

But only until Liam got back.

All she wanted to do was stalk out in disgust, perhaps find a few wolves who would lie at her feet and do her growling for her, but she'd promised Marceau she'd watch Gautier whenever these vipers were present, and Liam wasn't here to help her.

Dieu, how she wished Liam were here.

It wasn't exactly a prayer, but if the Creator wanted to take it as such and help Marceau find Liam—as well as urge Liam home from whatever hunt he was currently on—she wouldn't object.

She could use some help here.

Before she went mad and did something she would regret. Maybe.

If she loosed wolves on these men, could anyone truly blame her?

4

"Please, Monsieur," Ro practically begged, "Liam will be back any day now. As well as the rest of your huntsmen. Can we not wait for the coronation until your most important citizens can attend?"

Ro stood before Gautier, not kneeling, as many of the others were doing, and held her breath. He looked ready to cave to any excuse to postpone, but the peddler, standing at his right hand, took up his defense.

"His most important citizens *are* here! What do a few huntsmen matter? They can swear their allegiance whenever they return." He turned to Gautier. "The suit will be finished this very night as you sleep. You must reveal it to your people tomorrow morning. You must continue with the coronation as planned!"

Gautier looked between the two of them and then the rest of his courtiers, who were hanging on to his every word, and not for the first time, Ro thought he looked years younger than he appeared to be. As if a scared little boy were hiding inside, unsure of which way to turn.

"Surely you can wait a few days more," Ro said, leaving the *peddler* who was acting like a *counselor* out of the conversation entirely. "You trust Liam's judgment. Surely you want him by your side as you take this most important of next steps."

A part of her hoped he would stop this madness entirely.

"A common huntsman!" burst out of the peddler's mouth. "When our fey-made cloth has already proclaimed there is no one else in the land better fit to rule? Why, I—"

Movement at the far corner of the room caught Ro's eyes, and she blocked the rest of the peddler's irate words. She'd been verbally sparring with him for four weeks now, engaging as little as possible—except when she couldn't help it—and she didn't care if she never heard another spoken word of his.

There, hidden among the courtiers, were a dusty Hector and Gabin, trying to catch her eye without being intrusive.

"My mistake," Ro interrupted. Ignoring the peddler completely, she sketched a light bow in Gautier's direction and met his eyes with a bold, firm look. "I think your coronation should continue as planned tomorrow. Without delay. Excusez-moi."

Without another bow, she hurried from the room and down to the stables.

Most of the other huntsmen were back, except Axel and Lucian, and except Marceau and Liam.

"Well?" she demanded, the moment Gabin and Hector joined her.

"What was that? Encouraging him to go forward with the coronation?" Gabin demanded.

"Yeah, I thought you were going to *stop* it," Hector said.

Ro looked between the two thoughtfully. Whether they'd meant to or not, their words spoke more to how they felt about forgetting the crown prince than they probably realized.

And as much as Ro agreed, their words—and whatever

response she gave—were perched upon dangerous waters. Waters she wasn't quite certain how to navigate.

She finally settled upon saying, "You saw what I've been dealing with for the past month. Neither would have listened to anything I said. At least my agreement put him off-kilter enough that he might listen to me next time, oui?"

At their bewildered looked, Ro realized she was prattling, most likely thankful to have a listening audience for once. She quickly moved on.

"Have you any news for me?"

"A few odd tales," Gabin said. "They've definitely been seen in other parts of France."

"And the storyteller wanted me to give you this." Hector held out a package held together with twine, and Ro took it greedily. It gave, as if something soft lay within.

Finally, answers.

"So . . . shall we stop it?" Gabin asked, shattering the silence. "The coronation?"

Ro jumped as his voice boomed in the small space they all occupied.

Each huntsman who could get away had crammed themselves into the small back room for a security meeting Ro had called in Liam's absence.

They'd each told their tales, Ro had perused the package's contents, and then they'd fallen into silence. Which hadn't been broken in quite some time.

Ro sat up from her slouched position upon a bale of hay and stretched out her neck.

"Non. We should let it continue as Gautier wishes." At their half-uttered protests, Ro held up a hand. "I have a plan, promise. The information you brought back, and this"

—she held up the opened package—"is more helpful than you could possibly know."

They waited expectantly for her to continue.

She grinned, fiercely. "Tomorrow we shall patrol the crowds, make sure Gautier is as safe as we can possibly make him. Here's what you'll be looking for, and what you need to do once you find it."

Before she could delve deep into her plan, Hector's quiet voice intruded. "But . . . the coronation?"

In it held all the unspoken worry each of the huntsmen harbored in their hearts, including Ro.

She struggled to find the right words. "Something tells me the coronation part of the evening will take care of itself." She waved off an interruption. "Something I can't explain, not really. But a part of me has this sense of déjà vu, as if the coronation has taken place—multiple times—and as if, well, we don't have to worry about that right now. Later, but not now."

Ro fully expected to be ridiculed for her words, but the men nodded along, as if they couldn't argue, or her words sounded right, or perhaps it was just that they trusted her judgment.

She could only hope.

"Now, if there are no more objections?" Ro raised an eyebrow and waited.

At their acquiescence, Ro laid her plans bare.

The portion she was sharing with them, anyway.

5

As Gautier paraded around in naught but the slenderest pair of undergarments, a pair of shorts that in all honesty should have been much looser and much thicker, through the small town of Champagne from end to end on the way to his "crowning ceremony" at the chapel, Ro circled the crowd.

Every courtier, villager, milkmaid, errand boy, and peasant from the surrounding area—as well as many who had been able to make the journey from farther away—were present, waving scraps of cloth as flags and forcing cheer into every cry.

Gautier's beautiful suit of clothing had melted off about halfway to the chapel, but Gautier still kept his chin stubbornly raised. The others in the coronation march acted as if nothing were amiss, and the twenty men holding up the train kept their elbows locked, arms held out, eyes staring straight ahead.

Ro had the huntsmen patrolling or keeping watch from the trees all along the thoroughfare, spaced too far apart for her liking, but they knew what to look for, and they knew to contact her immediately if they found it.

Liam still wasn't back, and she was half mad at him for not being here and half relieved he wouldn't see their employer in such a ridiculous state.

But that was a scolding for another time.

Not that she'd chew Liam out over this—he'd just gloat and forever bring up the fact that she'd needed him and hadn't been able to handle this on her own. Insufferable man.

Right now she needed to focus on finding those two peddlers.

Sure, they'd given every appearance of having moved on this morning, but something told her they'd stick around for this humiliation—the culmination of all their efforts.

It was on her third circuit that snickering came from a few trees overlooking the thoroughfare. Ro kept a steady pace, then doubled back when she was out of sight.

There, in the trees, were the two peddlers, clinging to branches and crying with laughter as Gautier paraded before the whole of the town in nothing but his skivvies.

They were doing a good job keeping their voices below the roaring of the crowd—who were making an impressive effort to pretend all was normal, all was well, all was . . . not horribly wrong.

Using every skill she possessed as a huntress, Ro did what she needed to do, then climbed the tree they were both hiding in, every footfall silent, easing herself up without a sound, counting on their laughter and the tears in their eyes to shield her as long as possible.

She made it behind them without incident, then carefully looped the nearly invisible rope she'd been sent around each ankle, making sure it didn't touch their skin.

The storyteller had better not have been lying.

Now to test the effectiveness of the rope.

"Enjoying ourselves, are we?" Ro said casually.

Both men gasped and tried to escape down opposite sides of the tree.

They were pulled up short as the rope pulled taut and ensnared them both. One man fell, then the other, and they both dangled upside down from the tree, stopping short from bashing their heads into the ground.

Ro couldn't have possibly planned it better.

She eased herself out of the tree, careful not to touch the rope that was strung up as a web in the trees behind, the only way the peddler woman instructed it would work.

Otherwise, the fey could escape the fey-made strands. The same material she'd sworn she'd seen before, long ago, from this woman.

She loved it when everything lined up just right.

Ro stood before them and propped his fists on her hips.

"Well now, I seem to have caught two treacherous flies in my web. Care to explain why Monsieur Dubois is no longer wearing the suit of clothing you made him?"

"You can't tie us up like this! We are tailors to the king!"

"Yeah, and we won't stand for it, neither!"

"And, and—it burns! It burns!"

As Ro watched, both men seemed to lengthen, their forms thinning out, their ears turning pointy, and a wash of color started from their necks and overtook their faces, one lavender, and the other, pastel green.

Whatever Ro had been about to say was thrown to the ether as she watched them with wide eyes.

She had, after all, suspected they were a form of trickster fey—it was why she'd requested the fey-made rope, after all, something that could only be used to ensnare the fey, if used properly—but seeing it with her own eyes stole all her words.

They seemed to realize what she was seeing at the same time.

They ripped human-skin-colored gloves from their hands, then a flood of desperate words overtook her.

"We meant no harm."

"Only wanted to have a bit of fun."

"What would you have done if you were trapped in a human realm with nowhere to go?"

"Please, you can't let them see us!"

"They'll chop off our heads."

"Boil us in oil."

"Do all manner of things we can't come back from."

Ro highly doubted either chopping off heads or boiling in oil would work, merely because the fey would never give away what would actually harm them—just what people had tried.

"We'll never do it again."

"Ever again."

"Please let us go!"

Ro held up a hand to stop the flood that was becoming overwhelming. "I will let you go"—both creatures went perfectly still—"if you will agree to never again play a trick on another human, not as long as you are in my realm, the human realm, not as long as you are trapped here. Or if you come back after you are . . . untrapped!" she hastened to add, trying to remember all the things she had to do to worm a favorable bargain out of the fey.

They could not lie, but they could misdirect. They could stay away for her lifetime, which would be nothing more than a few moments of time for them, then come right back for more tricks. If there were any holes in her words whatsoever, they would find them and exploit them.

"You cannot trick another human in my realm, ever," she repeated, desperately hoping she was covering everything most important.

"Aw, man!"

"That's not fair!"

"Not another human? Ever?"

"Ever," Ro said firmly. "And you will return the gold you stole from Monsieur Gautier. His—our—*my* people need it."

"We stole nothing!"

Ro raised an eyebrow. "Is he wearing the clothes you made him?"

"Well . . . he was!" blurted the second fey.

Ro tilted her head, curious despite herself. "What happened to them, anyway?"

"Wouldn't you like to know?" he continued obstinately.

"You're right. It isn't important," Ro said, though she still dearly wanted to know. "Do you agree to my terms?"

The fey masquerading as the second peddler crossed his arms and jutted out his pointy chin. "It ain't fair, and I ain't agreeing to nothing."

The first fey, the one with a speck more intelligence, bit his lip and looked between Ro and his companion.

Ro just shrugged and pulled a small bag from her pocket. "Very well."

She uncinched it and pulled a small handful of white powder from within and let a few strands sift from her fingers. Then she started swooping it in a wide circle around them.

Thank Dieu for her last job, when she'd found out about salt's effects on the fey.

It was moments like these, precious few, when she thought the Creator truly was leading her, working all things out for good.

Then she remembered her mère, how she should still be here, and she slammed shut such thoughts. Enough thinking, just doing.

Both started howling at once and raising the biggest fuss.

Ro raised both eyebrows and waited.

"We knew it! We knew you was one of them!" the second howled.

"You can't do this to us!" cried the first. "We'll agree to it! To anything! Just let us go!"

But Ro had homed in on those words. "One of them? Who? What do you mean?"

But nothing else she said or did would draw more information out of them about whatever she was, even the threat of more salt.

"We can't tell you—promise! We can't even speak the words on this side. You have to believe we're telling the truth!"

Both were weeping by now, and Ro was starting to feel terrible. Oui, Gautier would be terribly embarrassed, but the gold would be returned, the miscreants would not strike again, and Ro wasn't here to torture anyone.

Even the evil creatures she fought met swift, sudden deaths. And these two lads did not deserve this, if salt truly was so painful to them.

She put the bag away. "You have my deepest apologies. It was not my intent to harm you. Only to stop you. But I must have your promise if I am to let you go."

Both still seemed hesitant, then Ro remembered something else. Another legend about the fey.

"What about an exchange? You tell me what happened to the clothes, return the gold, and apologize to Gautier, and I let you go immediately after?"

"No deal, sister," the shorter one said, arms still crossed.

"Very well. I shall take you to Gautier for punishment."

Ignoring their howls of protest, Ro tied another length of rope around their wrists, cut them out of the tree, and left the makeshift web behind.

She would need to get someone over here to guard it, even if they couldn't see it. It was far enough back from where people usually walked, but if anyone accidentally went through it and disturbed the web, the two miscreants would be off in a flash.

"I thought you said you'd let us go!" wailed the first, sounding incredibly young.

Ro gave him a sharp look. "I always keep my word. Keep yours, return the gold, and promise to leave forever, and I will let you go instantly."

The lavender fey went quiet, but the pastel green one was sniffling and glowering in turns.

"Agreed?" Ro pressed.

"Agreed," said the first, after a moment. He nudged his friend, and the second finally said, "Fine. Agreed."

Ro relaxed and smiled. "Well. Very well, then. Looks like I won't need these anymore."

She untied the rope, put it away, and clamped down on both of their shoulders. "Let's go make this right, shall we?"

6

She'd just spotted the guard she was looking for when the worst happened.

"But Maman, he's naked!" cried a child in the crowd, his sweet voice pitched just right to carry above the noise.

The crowd went dead silent, flags hanging frozen, mouths parted, eyes wide.

The poor mother's voice carried just as well, hushed as it was. "Yes, he is—oh dear—I mean, that may very well be, but—I mean! You shouldn't say such things . . ."

"But Maman," the child wailed as he was being dragged away, "you always said to tell the truth!"

Ro couldn't help it. She barked a laugh.

Just as her eyes met Liam's furious ones.

She wanted to clamp a hand over her mouth, but both hands were currently occupied with dragging the two miscreants behind her.

As if she'd just released an unspoken pressure on the crowd, a titter started here, a loud guffaw over there, and it wasn't seconds until the entire crowd was roaring with laughter.

A few daring souls even pointed at Gautier.

The two supposed peddlers looked at each other and snickered.

After darting a peek at Gautier to be sure he wasn't glaring at her for starting the cascading laughter, she lifted her chin and marched to the captain of the guard at Liam's side.

"Monsieur, these are the two men Monsieur Dubois will be looking for. I highly suggest you chain them in iron and see that they are held securely until he can speak with them?"

Both peddlers whimpered, but Ro was done playing nice. She just wanted this over with, and once they were cooperative, she would see to their release.

Besides, iron was rumored to hold the fey just as well, perhaps better, than the fey-made rope, and without the complicated web design, too. It just hadn't been silent enough for her purposes earlier.

The guard jumped forward, his neck bright red, either from embarrassment on Gautier's behalf or from his efforts at holding back his own laughter, and said, "Oui, Mademoiselle. Right away, Mademoiselle."

"Huntress will do," she said, her neck pricking from Liam's heated stare.

As soon as the guard latched on to the prisoners, Ro dodged Liam and marched away. The moment a building blocked his glare, she darted across the road and deep into the forest on the opposite side from where she'd caught the troublemakers.

And she didn't stop until the crowds could no longer be heard. She paused, looked around, crawled into a withered grove, and laughed until she couldn't breathe.

7

Ro had to stop several times on the way back to get a hold of herself, but she eventually made it to Gautier's château as the day was at its end.

She came back to an uproar.

Gautier was demanding the person be found who had started the laughter, and Ro almost lost it once more. She was certain he'd recognize her laugh if she did, so she choked it down, even though it almost suffocated her.

She felt eyes on her, and with a sigh, turned to find Liam standing across the room.

The scowl hadn't left his face, and his arms were crossed as he stared steadily at her. *Tell him. Now,* the look on his face demanded.

Ro lifted her chin and turned away. Liam may very well hold her life in his hands, but she wasn't about to get herself into trouble.

"Monsieur Gautier, if I may have a word?"

Her voice echoed in the smaller chamber, and all fluttering ceased.

"Thank Dieu," Gautier said, rushing toward her. He

took both her hands in his. "We assumed the worst when those two escaped and you couldn't be found."

Ro withdrew her hands and stepped back, all mirth vanishing without a trace. "Escaped? When? How? Were they not bound in iron? I shall take a contingent right away . . ."

Gautier was already shaking his head. "It's no use. No traces of their passage could be found to track them, and their gaol was left tight and closed up, as if no one had ever been inside."

"But . . . they were clamped in irons, oui? As I requested?" she persisted.

Gautier frowned. "With rope, I believe. But does it matter? The fact is they are gone, and I cannot believe my guards' incompetence." He shot them another glare.

Ro couldn't believe it. They shouldn't have been able to escape, not until they'd kept their word. The fey were bound by their word.

"And the gold?" she demanded.

Gautier threw his hands wide. "In a massive pile before my throne! Along with this stupid note."

He thrust it at her, and she snatched it from him. It only read, *Sorry*. Ro choked back laughter once more, not daring the slightest noise that resembled mirth.

Why, the tricksters. They *had* fulfilled their bargains. And they wouldn't be back. Unless she'd missed something in the bargaining process.

Gautier went on. "I didn't even get to my coronation ceremony after I was hustled away from that ridiculous crowd and their stupid laughter!"

Ro blinked at him. "Coronation? What coronation ceremony? For the crown prince?"

He blinked at her. She blinked back at him.

It was dead silent in the room.

"You mean . . . you don't remember?" Gautier sounded like he was being strangled.

Ro wasn't quite sure what he was talking about, and from the looks of things, neither did anyone else.

Back to important matters, then. "You said they left no trace of having escaped?"

Even if they'd kept their side of the bargain, she'd love to know how they'd managed it.

Gautier dropped his head into his hands and groaned.

"None," came Liam's deep baritone. "It was as if they'd never been jailed at all."

"But they were! I swear it," said the captain of Gautier's guard. "Put them in there myself."

Ro started to ask why she hadn't been informed sooner, when she might have had a chance of going after them, then straightened. Because she'd been crying with laughter in the forest, neglecting her duty.

Gautier seemed to rally as the discussion moved on without him, as he usually did when there was tension to be exploited, and he answered as if she'd asked it anyway.

"Ah, well. You may look, of course, but if Monsieur Liam couldn't find anything, I'm not sure you could either." Gautier swept a hand toward Liam, then stared at Ro expectantly.

"You're right," Ro said.

"Well if you feel so strongly about it, of course you can search for signs yourself . . . wait. I'm . . . right?" Gautier stared at her, bewildered.

He was always pitting them against each other, and normally, Ro rose to the occasion, unable to stand his insults. But, unfortunately, she'd come to the same conclusion.

"What was that, huntress?" Liam's glare didn't go away, but it somewhat . . . lessened.

Ro gritted her teeth. He'd heard her. She wasn't about to repeat herself.

She focused solely on Gautier, who still seemed a little dazed. It had been a trying day, after all, and now his huntress was agreeing with him.

Ro kept her smirk off her face.

Because it would most likely lead to more laughter.

"There *was* cloth on that spool, Monsieur, but it was meant to shimmer and appear insubstantial until sewn together, then solidify for a few short hours before disappearing entirely."

Gautier's entire face reddened and paled in turn as he relived his humiliation.

Ro cut in before he could work himself into a lather. "And I believe I know how they are missing as well."

"You do?" Gautier asked. "Tell me. Right now. S'il vous plaît."

That fact that he'd said please did more to reveal his frenzied state than anything else. He never said please.

"You happened to play host to two trickster fairies, Monsieur. The cloth was real enough, meant to make those who barely saw it question themselves, and as it disappeared, doubt themselves."

See? She was learning tact. She said "them" instead of "you."

"And once they returned the gold, and apologized, they should never again be able to return and trick my—your—*our* people."

Liam looked impressed, and Ro tried not to let it go to her head.

Who was she kidding? She was totally going to let it go to her head. Later.

"But, but . . . if they were fairies, maybe the cloth really *was* meant for kings, and maybe I really *wasn't* meant to rule, and maybe I'm *not* fit for my position—"

Ro cut him off. "Non."

"Non?"

"Non. It was trickster cloth. Nothing more. Meant to give them a good laugh at the wearer's expense."

At least, she was fairly certain.

And look at her, encouraging him when all she really wanted was the crown prince back.

Gautier was shaken, even Ro could see that, and often nuances of expression flew right past her. "But how do you *know*?" he practically wailed.

"Because you pay me to know these things."

With that, she turned and left.

She needed to find Fairweather and head out on the trail so she could laugh as much as her heart desired.

She'd come back in a week or two, after things had settled and Liam had hopefully forgotten all about her role in Gautier's humiliation.

Though she was most likely hoping for too much.

As soon as she was far enough from the château, she laughed until she was spent. And even then, she giggled herself to sleep under the stars.

She'd ask for payment from Gautier another time.

THE END

THE LEGEND OF THE GREAT WHITE WOLF

Le Petit Chaperon Rouge
or
"Little Red Riding Hood"
—Charles Perrault—

And, saying these words, this wicked Wolf fell upon poor Little Red Riding Hood, and ate her all up.

Et, en disant ces mots, ce méchant Loup se jeta sur le pauvre Petit Chaperon Rouge, et la dévora tout entier.

1

Ro bent over the tracks, smelling then crumbling the dirt grasped in her fingers. Dry. Barely any scent at all. And she hadn't been able to find any more prints past this set.

The trail had gone cold.

All because Gautier had sat on his info instead of giving it to her right away. Instead of sending her on her way when she still had a hope of catching the foul beast.

With angry steps, she swung herself up on Fairweather's back and urged her mount on.

He whickered at her, and Ro took deep breaths to calm her racing heart.

"You're right, Fairweather. All will be well. We'll get him."

Of course, who knew what the animal actually said; but he did seem to sense her moods and comfort her—or at least calm her when her temper was getting the best of her.

There was nothing for it. She would have to keep pushing till she picked up something more than weeks-old prints. Partial prints. And then . . . no more prints.

The stories had sent her north. They said the beast was

massive. That it would explode out of the snow, bigger than a horse, then drag away livestock, horses, and even small children.

She wished she knew the size of the beast, how much of the wild tales were fact versus fiction. All she knew was that she hunted a wolf, its coat as white as the deep snow it hid in.

A wolf that seemed to know how to walk lightly, to stay away from mud, to stick to clumps of grass and other places that hid tracks well—to confound those who hunted it.

And still she was only getting partial prints, which disappeared the moment the tracks led into the area of the country that got the most snow.

North it was. To find the village that had hired her in the first place.

Shivering, Ro entered the tavern to a blast of heat.

Her small town of Champagne, though always cold as the seasons had frozen into one solid winter when the curse fell, only received a light dusting of snow. This town was practically buried.

That and the bone-deep chill seemed to reach into Ro's soul and try to freeze the life out of her.

Not to mention the mounds of snow she and her horse had had to trudge through to get this far north. She was wet, cold, starving, and in need of a great deal of sleep.

She made straight for the fireplace, putting her back to it and taking in the room.

And the people who were terrified of going outside, at any time of day.

Conversation that had gone completely silent as she'd entered now resumed, but it remained hushed as people stole fervent glances her way while trying not to make eye contact.

The villagers were shabbily dressed, just like the rest of France, but Ro could tell these people were trying—their clothes, though threadbare, were layered, faded from multiple washings, and clean.

Unlike many of the other villagers she'd come across in her hunts.

But fear permeated the room like a visible guest sitting in the corner, judging them with cold eyes, urging them to dwell on the worst scenarios.

Dusk was falling outside. Fairweather had been more than happy to be stabled, brushed down, and fed. They'd barely made it before the heavy outer gates—an impressive wooden wall of sharpened pikes built around the village—had swung shut and been bolted fast.

These people were terrified of the beast that haunted the outer walls.

"May I get you anything, miss?" called the barkeep from across the room.

Ro tried to keep her teeth from chattering, she really did, but they rattled out her discomfort anyway. "Anything that will warm me right down to my toes." At the smattering of laughter, she amended, "While not impairing my judgment."

The barkeep's hand changed direction, and he soon brought her a steaming mug, filled to the brim with spiced liquid that smelled of apples.

Her eyebrows climbed her forehead. "Apples?"

He smiled, his chest puffing out a bit in pride. "Our apple grove still produces, though the fruit be old and sparse and a bit wrinkly." At Ro's surprised look, he amended, "Though it struggles as much as the rest of us."

At muttering behind him—whether from his telling a

stranger what had to be a closely guarded secret, or perhaps something else Ro wasn't aware of—his brow lowered.

"I assume you've come to rid us of the foul beast that won't let us anywhere near our provisions?"

Ro was busy burning her lips on the too-hot liquid. She sucked in a breath, then blew on it to be able to drink it faster. "That is my intention, oui."

He stuck out his hand. "Monsieur Rousseau, mayor of Beaufort."

Ro wouldn't exactly call this a beautiful fortress, but she knew enough not to blurt that out and make enemies right away.

That seemed to happen when she was too gruff or too short or froze when she didn't know how to respond. The enemies would come, or at the very least, those she offended.

Especially once she met with her contact on the morrow, the town's priest.

Best to find out what she needed to know and be on her way as quickly as possible.

"Ro LeFèvre, huntress for Monsieur Gautier Dubois." She nodded, but she didn't move from her position by the fire, nor did she take his hand.

Without seeming offended, he pulled his hand back and smiled. "Praise the good Lord up in His heaven! Gautier finally answered our many letters. Which one finally got through to him? What changed his mind? Never mind, that's not important. What do you plan to do about the foul beast that makes leaving our fortress all but impossible?"

A woman called from across the room, "Give her some breathing room, Henri!"

He flushed a little, but said good-naturedly, "And that is Madame Bodin, our town matron and altogether busybody."

"I can hear you, you know, ye old sauerkraut."

Ro hid a smile behind her mug.

He introduced many other patrons, all of whose names flew right out of Ro's head, as they always did, and soon she had a gathering of townspeople surrounding her, all eager to hear what she planned to do about the wolf.

So she asked questions, sipped her cooling cider, which did in fact warm her to her toes, and listened to wild tales and gossip.

As exciting as her arrival had been for the townspeople, she could hear the terror underlying their words.

Villagers who'd braved hunting the beast themselves had been sprung upon, knocked off their mounts, and dragged deep into the woods, never to be seen again. Horses left to themselves, even for a moment, were soon screaming as one of their number disappeared.

They hushed as they spoke of one family, not present, whose little girl had been taken.

They'd never found her body.

Ro's knuckles turned white around her mug, and she took deep breaths to keep the buzzing sound of rage out of her head and to keep from dragging Fairweather from his warm stable to hunt the beast this very night.

She needed information first. To know what they'd done already. What had worked and what obviously hadn't.

As uncomfortable as she was around other people, she needed to know what they did.

They were close to France's border—the coast and La Manche, or the English Channel, just on the other side—so a few wild theories were that the beast dragged the victims through the impenetrable mist that kept them trapped, created by the curse, then kept coming back for more because they were such easy pickings.

And the size of the beast kept growing. First, it was the size of the village's largest hound. Then a horse. Then the mayor's house.

Ro hid another smile behind her mug.

She honestly wasn't sure if she were relieved at being warm, or if the open honesty and kindness of those welcoming her put her in a good mood, or if perhaps the cider had a bit more alcoholic content than she normally drank. But she was enjoying herself *much* more than she usually did with townspeople before a hunt.

They seemed like warm, caring, open people who desperately cared about each other and the lives they'd built here.

Ro was so used to working with disillusioned people looking out for themselves, she felt herself relax as conversation swirled around her, only asking leading questions when things seemed to be going too far off into the forest.

"I seen him," one young man said. "We was hunting him, and we turned our backs on our horses for but a moment, only a moment, I swear, and then all the horses raised a racket, screaming and whinnying and crying and the like. I spun round just in time to see the beast burst from a snowbank, so well hidden we'd walked right past him, clamp its massive jaws round me own filly, and drag her off into the forest. We runned after him, screaming and shooting our arrows and throwing the spears we'd made, and he just backed right up, lifted me horse in its teeth, and bounded away, carrying the horse like it be nothing. Our weapons did nothing but bounce right off him."

The listeners nodded and murmured, whether in agreement or from having heard the tale before, Ro wasn't sure.

"Did anyone else see the creature? See him carry off the horse?" she asked.

The young man exchanged glances with several other men present. "Well, you sees, once it started kicking up snow, it was hard to see anything more."

"But we heard the horse screaming, and we never found it," put in another man helpfully.

Ro smiled in a way she hoped appeared that she wasn't doubting the story, though she was. "That is most helpful, merci."

He didn't seem like he'd taken offense, and the tales resumed, now including ones she'd already heard as she made her way north, to one of the many ports that used to send off ships to Angleterre, or England, but now couldn't be reached through the thick fog.

Ro had only heard of it, never seen it, and she had to admit she was excited to see the border that kept France's citizens trapped within their own country.

If she could find a way to penetrate it, as Père Guise and Madame LaChance had done . . .

It would open so many possibilities.

But she'd worry about that later, when she got there.

As the embers were dying, the mayor-barkeep-innkeeper offered her his best room, and she gratefully escaped the villagers for a few hours of sleep.

Tomorrow, she'd hunt the great white wolf.

2

Ro came downstairs as the sun would've peeked over the horizon, had the endless clouds let any through. Her internal clock was very much used to sleeping outside, but she wasn't about to do that here. If she could help it.

She wasn't a morning person by any means, but she wanted as much daylight as possible to hunt the creature.

There was such a crowd waiting for her, all hunched over a hearty breakfast of some kind of gruel that smelled of apples—or perhaps the apple smell came from the ale mugs each person nursed, though Ro couldn't imagine anyone drinking spirits this early—that Ro half wondered if they'd spent the night where they sat.

A balding man in rough brown robes rose from his place and smiled at her. "Bonjour, huntress! Did you rest well?"

Ro grunted at him and made her way to an empty spot at the bar for her own breakfast.

The mayor-innkeeper-tavern owner gave it to her with a sympathetic smile, and Ro hunched over and dug in.

It wasn't bad. Not at all.

The cracked grains tasted of dried apple, and the mug

was a heady cider that she was once used to having in the fall, not mid-spring, as it was supposed to be right now.

As it would have been, if not for the curse.

"I trust your journey was no hardship?"

Ro paused from shoveling in food to glance at the priest, who was now at her elbow. She wanted whoever had moved to give the priest his or her seat to come take it back.

Someone who wouldn't talk to her this early, preferably.

He gave her an understanding smile. "Though any journey this far north must be a hardship, n'est-ce pas?"

Ro grunted an affirmative and turned back to her bowl, hunching over it to protect what little of her eating time she had left.

"We are more grateful to Monsieur Gautier than we can say for sending you."

"Though it took him long enough," muttered the barkeep.

The priest gave him a gentle smile. "All in God's timing, my friend."

Someone, a woman, grunted behind her. "If it was God's timin', that little girl wouldn't be dead."

Ro stiffened, the priest flinched, and the barkeep nodded.

Ro swallowed her bite and said in a scratchy voice, "Gautier receives many letters, many pleas for help. I didn't know about the little girl, the severity of the situation, or I would've been here sooner. Je suis désolé."

Not that an apology could ever make up for it.

Gautier *should* have sent her sooner. Much sooner.

Madame Bodin continued. "You're not hunting in that, are ye?"

Ro looked down at her hunting gear, what she normally wore, and glanced up with a frown.

The older woman sniffed. "You'll freeze solid. Stop by

my shop before ye depart, and I'll fix you up with some furs."

Ro swallowed. She had enough funds stuffed away for food, lodging—but furs.

She'd just sent another payment to Madame LaChance through the priest that hated her, Père Guise, so Madame LaChance would take Cosette through the barrier, free her from this curse and their père, who would surely send her to the beast in Ro's stead if she didn't take preemptive action.

The priest always took an exorbitant payment, and Ro was certain not even a fraction reached Madame LaChance in Angleterre—or any of it, if the priest lied about having a way through the barrier, even if he did bring her fine parchment with exquisite penmanship from Madame LaChance and small tokens of life outside the curse.

Ro had to get Cosette out. By any means necessary.

And paying for furs . . . would not only wipe away most of what she had left, but would also make it take that much longer to get Cosette out to the boarding school. To freedom, to warm air and sunshine, to a life different than any of them experienced now.

At her brief hesitation, the look on her face, Madame Bodin waved a skeletal hand. "It is, of course, part of your fee for hunting the creature."

Ro deflated a little and muttered a "merci beaucoup" to her gruel, embarrassed that she'd been so transparent.

The older woman sniffed. "Think nothing of it."

"I'd hoped to speak with you before your departure," the priest continued. "I may have something you'd be very interested to read."

Someone called in good humor, "If you're trying to proselytize her before she hunts the wolf, you may want to give her a chance to finish her meal first."

A few people chuckled good-naturedly, including the

priest, and Ro attempted to crack a smile while focusing solely on her food.

She dearly wished she had the words to ask these people to leave her alone until her eyes could stay open of themselves.

The mayor was filling her bowl again almost before she knew it, and she stared at him with raised brows, amazed at the amount of food this town had if they could offer so much.

Or should she feel guilty for taking what they couldn't spare?

The man just smiled and motioned for her to finish.

It was difficult—her stomach had most definitely shrunk from the conservative meals she scrounged when she could—but she didn't stop till the bowl rested empty.

She waved off any more, hoping she wasn't taking food from someone else's mouth, and turned to the père rattling on at her side like a hissing teakettle.

She'd been dreading this conversation.

"Pardon?"

He paused, looking slightly startled, as if he didn't know which of his many words to repeat.

Ro attempted a self-deprecating smile, but it was early, and she was trying very hard not to resent his cheerfulness. "I must be on my way. Is there anything in particular you wished to discuss with me? I must hurry."

The slight man sprang to his feet—Ro tried dearly not to resent him more—and gestured to the door. "Might I show you something in my church, huntress? I have the highest hopes it might pertain to your hunt."

Ro nodded. "If you agree to point out your blacksmith, I will spare a minute for you."

He positively beamed. "Bon, merci."

Ro looked at the barkeep, raising her voice to ensure she

was heard by all. "I leave straight after. And I need to be shown the site of the last attack, s'il vous plaît."

Why bother hunting for it when she could be taken right to it?

There were instant protests from all sides, but the mayor nodded and set his jaw. Ro sincerely hoped that meant he would fight for her, not try to keep anyone from going with her outside the safety of their wall.

She stood and followed the père out, grateful for an escape from such noise so early.

Although, if he was going to lead her in prayer, she was in danger of nodding off.

Real worry replaced her relief of seconds before. She already had one priest upset with her—she didn't want a second eyeing her with dark looks every time they happened to meet.

The père took her across the town square and into his church's small library. "I was in prayers all the night through for your hunt, but I could not get away from the thought that I may have just what you need."

Ro's eyes lit with interest as soon as three shelves of books came into view. Three whole shelves!

Of course, it was nothing compared to the libraries she'd once browsed in Paris—that her family had once *owned*—but the tomes were well cared for, and Ro found herself incredibly grateful there was at least one other person in the whole of France who hadn't resorted to burning books for warmth.

Ro would've rather frozen solid.

He gently ran his finger down the line of books, on the hunt for a particular title.

"The feeling persisted, so I am certain it is from the Lord. Ah-ha! Here it is."

Ro went still. Many things were done in Dieu's name that in fact had nothing to do with Him, and she was wary of such proclamations.

Ro's mère had been adamant her children learn Latin so they could read Scripture for themselves—and thus know if their spiritual leaders shared what was truly within—but it was just one more thing Père Guise held against her.

That and her trousers. And hunting ability. And general disdain for liars, charlatans, and swindlers.

Such as Père Guise.

Mère would've hated how jaded Ro had become of the priests and religion she'd loved so dearly when she was still alive, but Ro had found, more often than not, it had kept her from being taken in by smooth words and a corrupt heart.

She would have to be cautious of anything this man said.

And then he handed her a book of fairy stories. She looked between it and him.

He smiled at the look on her face. "I've only heard tale of such a creature in the children's story, 'The Wolf King.' Page two eighty-one."

Ro fumbled to flip to the page, face burning.

She'd honestly thought he might have something useful for her. Spiritual proclamations aside.

She quickly scanned the first page, then went back and carefully read each word. And studied each illumination.

And completely forgot about the priest in the room with her.

3

The Wolf King

There once was a king who roamed this realm, and many others besides, in the form of a wolf.

Although his lands were vast and his wealth unaccountable, he was lonely, for he ruled no one but himself.

His most treasured item was his cloak, given to him by his greatest opponent, who'd once ruled his realm before he did. By it, he would clasp it to his shoulders, and he would transform into a wolf, one of great size, fur the color of midnight, eyes as golden as the setting sun.

By it he could enter and leave the world of men at whim, for none could see the terrible creature he was underneath.

Once, when he was roaming the land of tangled thickets and wide-open expanses where the wind cut through like a blade, he came upon a fair maiden, fierce of face and wild of hair, bravely fending off a pack of wolves that sought to claim her.

With a roar, he sprang upon them, and those he did not kill fled in terror.

He turned to the girl, but she was already fleeing into

the brambles, her wild, fiery hair and plaid kirtle caught in the thicket and ripping as she tried to tear herself free.

The branches were sticky with blood.

He could not speak in his wolf form, so he reached up, tore his cloak from his shoulders, and bellowed. "Hold, fair maiden! Fare thee well?"

She turned, caught sight of him, and swooned in a dead faint.

(Ro scoffed. Anyone brave enough to fend off a pack of wolves wouldn't swoon so easily—she'd almost be willing to bet a few precious livres on it. Not that she ever would. Not with her père's ghastly betting habits.)

He sighed. He knew his height, wild antlers for horns, blue-gray skin, and swirling whorls etched into his skin frightened most mortals, especially those of the fairer sex. But he couldn't leave her helpless for the wolves to find upon their return.

So he strode through the thorns and tangled branches, which curled away from him at his passing, gathered her in his arms, and strode toward where her scent led him.

The smell of blood was thick on the air, but as he left the clearing behind, the scent of blood stayed with them. Her blood.

He lay her gently on the ground, saw the severity of her wounds, and used old magic, older than the fey, to close wounds and speed healing.

He waited till her breathing grew strong to gather her in his arms once more.

"You—you helped me. You didn't kill me."

He smiled, his bared, pointed teeth fearsome to behold. He'd known the moment she awakened, but as she lay very still and tried not to let him know it, he let her pretend a little longer. The screaming, the trying to get away from him, would come soon enough.

"Aye. 'Tis a mortal wound they gave you, but fear not. 'Tis healed."

"Thank ye," she said quietly. After a moment, she said. "Can ye put me down now? I can walk."

He settled her gently to her feet, then stepped back, awaiting her reaction.

She gazed about her. "How do ye know where I live?"

He wondered how much to tell her. "Your scent led me here."

"Oh." She looked uncertain for a moment, then put her shoulders back and lifted her chin. "Might I offer you food, shelter, and drink in my father's home? We haven't much, but it's warm, and it's clean."

"You want to do this?" he asked carefully.

A deep red stained her cheeks. "I owe ye a life debt."

"Aye. That you do. And you think this will repay it?"

Now her eyes flashed fire. "Of course not. 'Tis Christian charity I offer you, nothing more. I'll accept my fate thereafter."

(Ro didn't care for the damsel-in-distress, helpless, "I'll accept my fate blindly" type, but she had to admit this story was holding her rather captive.)

"Aye. I'll accept your hospitality. And I thank ye."

The family welcomed him warmly after hearing of her brave rescue, and the hearth was warm, the mead welcoming, and the bed comfortable, but he sat next to it all the night through, in no need of sleep, and awaited the dawn.

When it came, the girl's father met him outside his door. "We did not speak of it last night, but I fear the time has come. Might we have a private word?"

The Wolf King followed him into the empty dining room, where he asked plainly, "And what do you require in exchange for my daughter's life this past night?"

"For her to become my bride."

At which the wife and the girl's brothers, who had been

hiding behind the door, burst into the room and raised a ruckus, demanding that it couldn't be so. They would not let it be so.

The Wolf King mildly watched their fuss, waiting for it to be over.

He had spoken. No amount of pleading, bargaining, or offering absolutely anything else—for the daughter was well beloved—would sway the Wolf King's mind.

He had never seen one of the humans fight as bravely as the girl had against certain death, and her blood was sweet to him, unlike most other humans. He wanted her at his side, to bear his lineage.

(Ro snorted. She would've had more than a few things to say to *that*, were she in the girl's place.)

The father's pleading was interrupted by a firm, "I will go."

"Ah, daughter, do not say so! Shall I never see you again?"

She read the answer in the Wolf King's eyes. "You would not have seen me again after this past night, da, if not for this . . . man. My rescuer."

The Wolf King's eyebrows rose. She did not call him a monster, as he was used to being called.

"I will be safe, and I will be cared for. What more could you want for me?"

A smile found its way to the Wolf King's face. She almost said it to him like a challenge, as if it were not so, she would make it so, and accept nothing less. He inclined his head to her in agreement, and congratulated himself that he had chosen well.

Once his offspring challenged him for his throne, and killed him for it, she would continue on for the short while her human lifespan allowed her in his realm, only a thousand years or so, then his spawn would be free to hunt for his own bride.

As it was for every Wolf King since the beginning of time.

He stood, effectively cutting off her father's protests, and expanded the space within the room to hold his height, though it would look the same to the mortal's eyes.

"I will give you a fortnight to say your goodbyes."

She bowed her head. "As you wish, my laird."

(Ro skipped ahead a little, scanning the text faster to find out what the père had meant for her to read.)

After a fortnight full of the family pleading with the girl not to go, the Wolf King claimed his bride, much to the lamenting of the family, but their short lifespans were but a breath, and too soon they were forgotten from the earth.

But the bride with the wild red hair, whom he called his Jade, fiercely loved traveling among the many realms, seeing lands and creatures she'd never dreamed existed, and even better, came to fiercely love him as well.

Until one day, he lost her.

Lulled into a deep sleep by a mischievous trickster who'd sworn revenge for one slight or another—all such lesser beings were beneath his notice—he awoke to find the ground beside him cold and his wife gone.

His howls shook the worlds, caused great cracks in the deep and the mountains to tremble, and he put back on his cloak for the first time since he'd rescued her, desperate to find her, and ran through all the realms, stirring up whirlpools and waterspouts and shaking the earth with his thunderous footfalls.

But he never found her.

He roams the realms still, often stealing into this one, to see if his stolen bride has been returned, and you can often feel his anger in a burst of thunder or the tremble deep in the earth or the spout of fire he spews into the sky at his greatest rage.

And once a year, he gathers the spirits of the greatest

hunters from each realm, the fiercest animals, and the fellest of beasts to join him in his hunt for his wife.

You can feel his passing at the time of the harvest, when the winds howl and you feel the brush of a foul breath against your cheek and the hairs raise on the back of your neck for no apparent reason. The master seeks his mistress.

Beware, for the Wolf King is on the hunt, and he will accept any and all to roam to and fro upon the earth, to find that which was stolen from him.

Do not find yourself in his path, or you will be stolen, just as she was, but never returned.

Close and lock your doors, be in bed before nightfall, and do not go outdoors when the air turns crisp and leaves fall from the trees.

Or you will find yourself a part of the Wild Hunt.

4

Ro sat back, bleary-eyed and deep in the world of the author's making.

Was the père implying he thought the creature she hunted could be this Wolf King? Perhaps some awful fey creature that hunted for revenge, not sustenance?

It would certainly match many of the clues the creature left behind.

But surely not every word of the story could be true. Men had made up tales for centuries to explain away the world's most puzzling phenomena, and who would have met the Wolf King to be able to tell his story, anyway?

It was nothing more than fiction.

Which was more disappointing than she cared to admit.

For a moment there, she felt herself a part of the wild hunt, wished to know what it was like, to seek prey that had eluded the greatest of hunters for centuries. But non, it was all nonsense, a story to keep the young from roaming the woods at night and being carried off by a wolf. Or some other predator.

But she would keep it in mind, just in case.

She wasn't sure when the père had left her alone in his

library, or when she'd moved to his little desk, hunched over the tome as she poured over each word, but the sun was slanting differently now, and she hadn't even been to see the blacksmith yet.

The priest somehow sensed when she was done and gently knocked on the open door. "Was any of it useful?"

Ro stood, leaving the book open on his desk. "I'm not sure, honestly. It has . . . given me much to think of."

He nodded and carefully put the book away before leading her toward the door. As they walked into the main sanctuary, small but meticulously clean, he genuflected, crossed himself, and kissed his fingers.

Ro quickly bobbed to copy him, unable to remember the last time she'd set foot in a sanctuary. Her work kept her away from such things.

As it had since her mère died.

Then he said, "Huntress, might I ask of you a favor?"

She paused in the echoey chamber and gave him a wary look.

"I'm about to sit with the family who lost their little girl to the foul creature. Might you come with me? Before you depart?"

Ro froze, knowing the look on her face must reflect the panic beating wildly in her heart.

His smile for her was gentle. "It might offer them comfort to hear of your efforts from your own lips."

Ro could only nod, not knowing what else to do. She was terrible with people. Especially grieving people. She could never think of a single thing to say.

He smiled at her brightly, retrieved a basket full of prepared food items and more, and led the way out into the day and in another direction from the tavern.

Ro couldn't help feeling as though she were being led to the gallows.

She wasn't good with people. She just wasn't.

She was brisk, abrupt. Always said the wrong thing.

People didn't turn to her for comfort. Just to kill things. Just to get rid of their problems.

Even with the deep cold outside, she felt too warm, a little sweaty. And she hoped they couldn't tell her hands were shaking through her thick leather gloves.

She was determined to keep her mouth shut, no matter what.

❧

Ro stood at the back of the room, feeling like the worst of intruders as the priest introduced her and comforted the family.

The father stared at a wall, not acknowledging their entrance. The mother was beside herself that the child must be found, that there was still hope, ranting her frustration at nothing being done, that a bloody, torn shoe meant nothing, then swinging to wailing and sobbing that her little girl, her angel, was gone, while a cluster of young children watched with wide eyes and pale faces.

The priest offered what comfort he could with his soothing words, passing out treats to the children, all while putting food away in the cupboards, checking their supplies, urging the mother to keep her hands busy, to provide for her family.

Nothing he said caught the father's attention.

When the priest brought attention to Ro once more, the mother's eyes swung to her as if seeing her there for the first time. "Find her. Find what that creature did with my Maggie."

Ro nodded solemnly, though she had little hope of finding anything, it had been so long ago. The horse was the most recent kill—she would have to follow that trail first.

At the woman's words, her husband slowly lifted his

head, taking Ro in from the top of her dark hair, down the length of her red cloak, to the tips of her sturdy boots.

Ro tried not to squirm.

His perusal wasn't disrespectful, but she would've loved to know what he was thinking. Especially since this was the first time he'd taken note of . . . anything.

Then the woman ran to a hidden place in her kitchen and pulled out a small stash of coins. She tried to shove her meager coins in the priest's hands. "For my girl. In purgatory."

He gently closed her hands around the coins. "Keep them. Your family needs them more than I, and I shall not stop praying for her soul. But perhaps you can come to the church and light a candle? We have so missed your fellowship."

Ro stared at him with mouth open. Who was this kind person? Père Guise would've snatched the coins with a sorrowful look, saying he would pray for her soul, but there wasn't much he could do with such a meager offering.

Her brain almost couldn't handle that he was handing the coins *back*.

The woman turned on her next, desperation in her eyes. "Then you take them! Anything for you to wipe that foul creature off the face of the earth."

"Madame, I assure you, I have already been paid," Ro said stiffly, unable to make the words sound natural. Kind. If only Cosette were here to do it for her. "The priest is right: keep them. I will do all in my power to keep this wolf from hurting anyone else, I promise you."

The woman seemed to wilt at that—though in relief, if Ro were reading her correctly, and not in feeling powerless to do anything, though surely she was feeling that too—and Ro hoped she'd said the right thing.

From the priest's kind smile, she might have?

Though surely he would upbraid her the moment they were alone.

Though Père Guise preferred to do it with an audience.

After a few more murmured comforts, as well as praying with the family, the priest led the way outside and to the blacksmith.

Ro quickly concluded her business there, but from the position of the light, it would be smarter to put her effort into finding anyone willing to accompany her and set out with them the next day, at first light.

Today, she would have to turn back for the fortress far too soon. She wouldn't make it to the barrier before dusk.

They were almost to the tavern when the priest spoke again. "If I may be so bold to ask, huntress, which diocese do you hail from?"

She eyed him. "From childhood, when I lived in Paris, or currently?"

He smiled at her. "Any of them, though currently, perhaps."

Too late she answered where her family lived, before correcting to where she stayed in between hunts, at Gautier's château.

"Ah. Père Guise?"

Ro gave him such a sour look, he laughed aloud. He sobered before they reached the door and looked at her solemnly. "I hope you will not judge the whole church on . . . past experiences."

She took a deep breath. "Do not fear for my soul, Père. Although the Creator has no use for me, my mère loved Him dearly. I have yet her words in my heart."

Because she did not need a sermon right now. She needed to finish her tasks and retire early.

She wasn't about to get into how abandoned she felt after her mère's death, how she felt He could have saved her . . . but didn't.

"I see. But they have to be your beliefs, don't they?"

Ro blinked at him, but there was no judgment on his face, no cruelty.

"I can't help but feel you are . . . unsettled. If it would help, I would be honored to hear your confession before your excursion."

He made no move to open the door, calmly awaiting her response.

Her jaw tightened. Ah. Père Guise had put him up to this. To get information from her she would never share on her own. She'd trusted him once, but no more. Never again.

Was there nowhere the hateful old priest's arm didn't reach?

"Non, merci. I am fine. And I must be on my way."

Another smile, just as kind, just as false, as the rest. "But of course, huntress. I am here if you ever have need of me."

Ro pulled open the door a little harder than necessary. "That won't be necessary, I assure you."

And she was inside before she could hear any response.

Now to find a few villagers willing to accompany her.

5

It took a lot of convincing, but Ro managed to get several of the burliest villagers to show her where they'd last seen the wolf.

The little girl's father was one of them. He'd shown up at the tavern as they were leaving, not saying a word, but bringing his own mount and accompanying them into the forest.

Although Ro had no hope of finding the beast from her death, the kill that had most likely prompted a response from Gautier—though he had said nothing to her about the girl's death—she was thankful to have him along. To give him something to do about his daughter's end.

No amount of convincing could get the young man who'd seen the creature to leave the fortress walls.

Ro hated to go without him, but he didn't care about appearing a coward. He cared about being safe, about not being eaten, about going nowhere near the beast ever again.

She couldn't blame him, though she dearly wished she could convince him otherwise.

With how much Ro and Fairweather had struggled through the deep snow to reach the fort, it was heavily debated whether they would take their horses or wear snowshoes.

It had never snowed so much in this area before the curse, but with so much cold, what would have been rainfall dumped centimètres upon centimètres upon the area, making their horses wade through chest-high drifts and snowshoes a necessity instead of a rarity.

The men insisted the horses could run faster than they could, so of course they should be ridden to the site.

Ro sighed but followed their lead.

They were right, of course.

What she wouldn't give for a team of dogs and a sled.

When she brought this up, they said they only had the one sled, and it was all they could do to keep the few dogs they did have alive. Most had gone feral and run off into the woods when there wasn't enough food.

So they'd put all their efforts into keeping their horses and themselves alive.

It made sense, though Ro still had so many questions. Especially about the apple orchard. But first, the hunt.

They traveled deep into the forest, along a line of traps, before reaching the spot.

Now draped in heavy furs, thanks to Madame Bodin, Ro wrestled on the snowshoes and got down on the snow, digging around where they thought the creature had hidden, right behind where they'd left the horses.

Of course, the recent snowfall had wiped everything clean, so Ro had to comb the entire area for broken branches. It seemed as though the wolf wove its way through the forest, mindful of the trees.

A chill swept over Ro at the thought, and not just from the deep winter.

Wishing one more time for the young man who could do more than guess where the wolf had last been, Ro noted the area was slightly depressed, though it could just be the slope of a hill under all that snow.

"Which direction did the wolf drag the horse?"

The men pointed in several different directions, and changed their minds several times, before deciding based on where the line of traps were.

"That way. We think," said one of them.

Ro managed to turn her back on them before rolling her eyes—a feat she was sure Cosette would be proud of her for—then struck out into the forest.

Any bent twigs would have bounced back by now, but perhaps . . . there.

Ro rushed forward, bending low to examine the branch. It had been snapped neatly. Although, it wasn't hard to break the dry and brittle dead trees, so anything could have done it.

"Do you venture back this far?" she asked.

At no answer, she turned to find the men huddled where she'd left them. This time, she rolled her eyes without turning away first, not caring who saw.

"Do you have any lines back this far? Do you come this way?" she called, louder.

The men looked at each other and shook their heads.

"Do you . . . oh for heaven's sake." Ro waddled her way over to them, snowshoes awkward, but at least she wasn't down to her shoulders in the snow. "Do you have any reason to go that way? The orchard, perhaps?"

"Non, our lines go this way, and our orchard is sheltered on the opposite side of our village. We have no reason to venture so deep into the woods."

Ro nodded. "Then I shall be off. Return to the village. I'll be back when I have a wolf pelt to drag behind me."

That's when Ro noticed Fairweather was shivering, looking downright miserable.

"Oh, you poor thing," Ro said without thinking.

Fairweather gave her such a pathetic look, Ro had to smother a laugh.

She'd forgotten he appreciated pity about as much as she did.

Who said her horse wasn't all personality?

The men exchanged glances. "If you're willing, Mademoiselle, perhaps you can rest in our town tonight and set out fresh in the morning?"

Ro shook her head. "I might have a trail. I need to follow it now. I've wasted too much time as it is."

They exchanged glances, and it took a moment for one of them to be brave enough to speak. Ro waited impatiently.

"Then, perhaps we can take your horse back? This isn't weather to keep your beast out in. Any beast."

Except a wolf sporting lots of fur. Ro eyed what she'd packed on Fairweather, wondering if she could carry it all.

Of course, it wasn't the first time someone had tried to separate her from her horse.

Mostly to try to eat him.

"Your horse will be stabled and well taken care of until you return. I give you my word," said the man Ro still didn't know the name of.

She was terrible with names.

"Even I wouldn't keep my horse out in such weather," the man continued. "Will you be back before dusk?"

Ro eyed the sky. "Perhaps. But most likely not. I will follow the trail where it leads."

"Then please. Allow us to take your horse back with us."

Ro eyed their horses, then hers. Just then, he gave a pathetic shudder, dropped his head as if to nose for something edible, and stopped just before he touched the cold snow.

He truly did look miserable.

The last thing she wanted was for him to get sick.

And their horses had thick winter coats, and although few, they did appear to be well taken care of.

As long as they didn't try to keep him from her when she returned, she couldn't leave him in a better place. For now.

And she was wasting daylight.

With a sigh, she retrieved her satchel, removed her extra bolts from her saddlebags, and handed the reins to the stranger.

"I will come for him, and he'd best be in as good shape as when I left."

The man nodded solemnly, and Ro struck out before she could second-guess herself. He was right, of course he was, but it was still painful to leave her hunting companion behind.

But from his lack of protest as the men led him away, he didn't mind one bit.

Traitor.

6

Farther in, Ro found more broken branches.

And farther still, she found the kill site.

Snow had covered a great deal, but from the red smeared on the trees, and the amount of blood peeking through the snow, she soon found the carcass.

The animal had suffered.

And had not been eaten. Only toyed with. Ripped apart. Made to suffer a long and painful death.

Ro sat back, taking in the scene, little clues presenting themselves to her, telling the tale of what had occurred here. Remembering the stories she'd heard, about livestock, horses, and children being taken without a trace.

The creature was not hunting for food, but for sport.

If the pattern held, he'd made them all suffer.

Ro felt sick.

The ground under the snow had been churned up, yet she couldn't get any prints. Just chaos.

This wasn't how wolves hunted.

They'd gotten braver, more desperate, since the curse fell, true, but they tended to ravish whatever they took.

Eating it down to the bone, gnawing at the bones, even, to get to every little bit of nutrition.

Wolves didn't leave good meat behind. Repeatedly.

She didn't know what she hunted, but this was no wolf.

❧

After scrutinizing the kill site, Ro struck out again and again from its epicenter, seeking where the monster could have gone next.

Once again, the creature was covering its tracks, walking lightly, careful not to brush brittle twigs, leaving no trace of its passage. That he'd left.

The thought sent a chill skittering through Ro. There were quite a few snowbanks it could be hidden within.

Until, finally, Ro found a tuft of white fur stuck to a bramble, a bush that would have held luscious blackberries in only a few more months. Had the curse not fallen.

And then another, on the other side.

Ro plucked off a clump, sniffed it, and gagged at the strong musk.

Not like other wolves—this one smelled of death, rotting meat, and a strong odor Ro couldn't identify. But it was fresher than anything else Ro had found of the wolf yet.

It wasn't enough of a trajectory—Ro would've preferred a few more, plus the creature could pivot to a new course at any time, especially as the trees made walking in a straight line impossible—but she carefully set off in the direction the two clumps pointed, searching for even more clues.

Her mind spun with what she knew.

Little children were being dragged off and eaten. The smallest, the weakest. Those who couldn't flee or get away.

Ro never felt guilty about hunting. She was never cruel, never let her quarry suffer, and only killed animals for sustenance or creatures who hunted humans.

She was also careful never to waste what they gave her.

But this was different.

This wolf killed in the cruelest way possible, making its prey suffer. Toying with it. Drawing out its agony until its prey died and the wolf lost interest.

It also left most of its prey behind, not hunting to eat, but for the pure joy of the kill.

It wasn't natural.

Its tracks were massive. Ro was certain she'd never seen anything so large.

The dire wolves of the north had gone into legend, hunted to extinction well before her time.

But Ro didn't know what else to call it.

Survivors, of which there were few, said they saw nothing, heard nothing. That it rose up out of the snow, leaving a massive crater behind, that it was all confusion and spraying snow and screaming and droplets of scarlet upon white.

She carefully skirted every mound of snow, wondering if she were walking past it like so many others. But then she'd find a hair or two on a branch, the tip of a branch broken off, or a deep well where it appeared a paw may have breached a pocket below the snow, and the snowfall wasn't enough to obscure it.

That's what she told herself, anyway. There were so few clues.

And then she reached the barrier.

Here snow barely dusted the ground, as if the barrier itself kept the heaviest snowfall away, and Ro could again walk without snowshoes.

She tore them off and tied them to her pack as quickly as possible, not wanting to be hunched over if the creature attacked.

Prints were everywhere, as if something large had come through multiple times. But few were full paw prints.

And then she came upon one by itself, and she stared down at it in disbelief.

Every piece of evidence said it was humongous, but to see it for herself—Ro could barely wrap her mind around it.

Ro held out her long, slender hand, comparing.

Her hand looked like a child's. The beast's paw print, the size of a bear's. Perhaps larger.

Ro tracked it north, to the borders of her kingdom, where it paced along the impenetrable barrier, unable to get out.

Ro's jaw tightened. She wouldn't let it get out. She wouldn't let it harm anyone else.

Not in her kingdom, not without.

It was the first time in her life she'd ever been thankful for the barrier.

The solid white mist roiled inches from her face, but when she put her hand against it, it was as solid as any wall. And carried a bone-deep chill.

She followed it up, up, up.

White mist poured off the top of it into her kingdom, darkening the sky and making the sun—which should have been bringing them a warm, beautiful spring right now—struggle to make itself known.

She'd known the endless winter was unnatural, that the endless cold was so much harder to bear because of its length, but it was so much worse seeing its cause with her own eyes.

Knowing their land could not survive being cut off from its source of warmth for so long.

Oui, she was breaking her kingdom's curse, by any means necessary.

But first, she was ridding it of one foul beast, then the other—the one she suspected was responsible for the curse in the first place.

She placed her hand alongside the track one more time.

If she wouldn't have known she hunted a wolf, if she wouldn't have intimately known the intricacies of a wolf's paw, she would've thought she hunted a bear.

Or some other creature of impossible size.

For once, she was thankful she'd left Fairweather with the villagers. She wasn't willing to lose him to this thing, whatever it was.

Several times, the hairs on the back of her neck would rise, and she would pause, seeking what watched her with all her senses, but rien. Nothing.

But she couldn't help thinking of the story she'd just read.

She could imagine a creature hovering over her, hidden in the trees, just waiting to snatch her up, his foul breath the wind that swept across her neck.

She didn't like it one bit.

Following the tracks along the border, she came to a place where the creature seemed to pace back and forth multiple times, as well as rise on its back legs and, she assumed, paw at the barrier.

Perhaps it thought it had found a way through? A weak place?

Or perhaps it was becoming desperate.

And Ro was running out of daylight. She needed to make camp.

She made her way back to a place she'd noted on the way in, a clearing in the middle of a copse of trees that would shelter from the wind and the deepest snow, not too close to the barrier, and began her preparations.

She had to survive this night and continue her hunt in the morning.

7

Ro had cleared all brush away—using it for her fire, piling it and other twigs she'd gathered into heaps all over the clearing—and currently bent over roaring flames, feeding branches to it, a monstrous shadow of herself thrown onto the trees behind her.

It was much warmer here, with the massive fire, with the shelter of the trees, with her warm furs and red cloak. But the trees were too close for her liking.

Any creature who hunted her could get much closer than she preferred, especially since it was so large and could leap so far.

But she had to be warm if she were to spend the night outside.

She eyed the piles of brush and branches she'd gathered to keep her warm all through the night. It may have looked like a lot, but it might not last. She sincerely hoped she wouldn't be forced to gather more in the dark, her main goal in gathering so much before the sun set.

She carefully scanned the trees at intervals, looking for any hint of the wolf she suspected stalked her.

Suddenly, without warning, the trees exploded at her back, spraying her with a cloud of snow and debris.

Cloak already wrapped tight around her, Ro rolled right through the fire and on out of the clearing, spinning to close the circle with a fistful of salt the moment she was outside of it.

Something barreled into an invisible wall right in front of her face and fell back.

Ro slowly uncurled from her crouched position, long knives in her hands, ready to fight.

Her furs smoked, even though her cloak didn't, but she'd rolled through quickly enough not to burn herself or her clothes.

Just one more protection her mère's red cloak gave her.

A deep-throated, ungodly howl shook the trees, and the creature ran round and round the clearing, churning up snow and flinging itself at the barrier she'd made again and again.

Ro put her back to a tree—in case there were more, or even if a normal wolf tried to take a bite out of her—and waited for the creature to calm.

The only things she could tell were that the creature was massive, and that he blended in with the snow perfectly. Now to get a good look at him.

After far too many minutes, the creature settled right in front of her, face pressed to the barrier, long snout pointed straight down, eyes focused on her with an intent that made Ro desperate for the barrier to hold.

She'd gotten the idea while looking at the curse-made barrier that kept everyone trapped within France.

While that barrier could hold everyone, fey or human or animal, the fey especially were susceptible to circle magic. Ro was beyond lucky that not only was the creature fey, but since she'd made the circle out of a ring of salt buried under the snow, no branches had fallen across it as she rolled out.

Or that the creature hadn't sensed it as it stalked her.

And that it had burst through the clearing exactly where she'd wanted it to—why she'd kept her back to one section of the trees while scanning the rest.

So many things could have gone wrong.

So many things could still go wrong.

But she'd made a guess, a rather good one at that, based on the knowledge she had, and she couldn't help the relief that streamed through her. She was almost shaking with it.

Now, what to do with the creature now that she'd trapped it?

First, its eyes became visible, a steady red that peered right at her, inches from her face. Then his snout, his lolling pink tongue as he panted and bared his teeth at her in turn.

He was not happy at being caught.

Then his shoulders came into view, and Ro realized he bent over to bring his face level to hers. While she was standing.

She tried not to react, she really did, but she nearly fainted when she better saw the size of him. For once, the stories hadn't been exaggerated. Had a dire wolf survived and grown to an even greater size than ever reported? Or had a myth truly stepped out of legend and was attacking anything it came across?

Her reaction seemed to please the creature immensely.

She had to clear her throat twice to get words to come out of her mouth. "Am I speaking with the Wolf King?"

She felt positively ridiculous saying the words, but she couldn't get away from the story. She felt it needed to be said. And she felt like a complete moron doing so.

At her words, the doggy grin slid off his face, and he snarled and threw himself at the barrier again and again, snapping his massive jaws inches from her face, as if he wanted nothing more than to tear her head from her shoulders.

That either meant . . . he hated the Wolf King, used to be the Wolf King and was now nothing more than a raving beast, or her voice had reminded him just how much he wanted to eat her.

Ro sighed. That's what she got for putting so much stock into a fairy tale.

Emboldened, she spoke further. "Whoever you are, whatever you are, you are harming my people, toying with the weak and the helpless. And it must stop. *I* am going to stop you."

She honestly had no idea if it could understand her, but it most certainly did not like her voice. Its attempts to get at her increased.

"If you don't leave, if you don't go back to wherever you came from, you *won't* like what happens next, I can promise you that. So it's your choice. Leave, go back to wherever you came from, or I will end you here, now."

Not that any of the creatures had ever responded positively to her ultimatums, but she always gave them.

Everyone deserved a chance to make a better choice. To stop hurting people.

She sighed when the creature showed no signs of letting up, of acknowledging her words.

Most fairy creatures she hunted were merely beastlike, showing little to no intelligence, and she honestly hadn't expected anything different with this one, but she'd hoped.

She always hoped she could send one of the creatures back to the fey realm where it belonged instead of ending its existence.

But that apparently wasn't going to be the case with this one.

Along with fey magic responding to circles and salt, the fey usually couldn't stand fire, or so had been Ro's experience.

According to some legends, some of the fey wielded ice, and some had other forms of magic, but usually not fire.

Usually they fled from fire. It was one of their weaknesses.

As she distracted the wolf with her words, the fire in the center of the clearing burned brighter and brighter, melting the snow in an ever-widening circle, feeding on itself as if it had a life of its own.

Once again, Ro didn't understand how she worked, how she knew what to do, how she did the things she did—just that she needed to take salt with her this day, then she needed to make a circle, then she needed the fire to consume the beast from within the circle.

She hadn't the strength, or the tools, to fight it as she did most other beasts she hunted.

She had to do it differently this time.

Part of her was still concentrating on increasing the fire's size, making it leap and jump from the center to each pile of sticks she'd gathered and lumped around different places in the clearing. To fill every section of the clearing with fire except for the one Ro stood in front of now.

Suddenly, the wolf's tail caught fire, and he yelped and whipped around to bite at what hurt him.

When he saw the size of the fire, that it was growing, that it was spreading, and that he was in one of the few places without any flame, he hunched his head and shoulders and started growling. Then he threw back his head and howled.

Ro clamped her hands over her ears at the sheer volume, the pitch, of its howls. It felt as if her bones were rattling, as if covering her ears did nothing.

Though the knife handles she held most likely didn't help.

The fire dimmed a little.

Resisting the pain, she held out her long knives once

more, that way she kept her hands held toward the fire without his noticing she did so, and made herself keep them there.

Not that the creature noticed anything she was doing in his panic.

He howled and jumped and tried to keep out of the flame, yelping each time the fire got too close.

The heat had to be unbearable by now, although Ro couldn't feel any heat outside the circle, and she tried very hard not to feel guilty.

But the creature had hunted children. Had made them suffer, had killed for sport and to cause pain, and she was going to make sure this beast could never prey on her people again.

She gritted her teeth and coaxed the fire higher still.

There were times her job sickened her. Few and far between, but this was one of them.

A quick death would've been preferable. Although it'd hurt others, although it hadn't cared about any of the children it hurt, Ro still didn't want to make it suffer.

Stop it, oui. But suffer? Non.

It smashed itself against the wall of Ro's barrier, its coat going flat and curving with the invisible wall, and lifted its snout and howled again and again and again, changing its pitch and cadence.

Ro had crafted the circle in such a way that the walls curved up and in, coming together in what amounted to a knot of magic over the fire.

In other words, the wolf couldn't climb out.

Ro started gripping the knives harder, sweat beading on her forehead and slipping down the middle of her back, even though it was beyond freezing outside the circle, with no warmth to be had. It was taking monumental effort to keep the fire growing.

Thank goodness the circle only needed to be closed once and not messed with again.

She couldn't have done both at the same time.

Suddenly, the snow started to churn on the other side of the circle, whipping up as if a gale-force wind were picking up snow and throwing it—in just one spot.

The fire dimmed without Ro's permission, but she couldn't look away.

What was happening? Was the wolf doing that? Something else? Another wolf, perhaps? Was *she* doing it? Surely not.

She might have had a terrible time figuring out how her magic worked, how she did the things she did, but she also was pretty aware when she was making something happen or some other creature was.

The wolf howled more desperately, even as Ro had a harder time keeping the fire going—especially since it was burning up the fuel so quickly.

Then the snow stopped churning, the wolf stopped making any noise, instead cowering with its head between its paws, belly flat to the ground, and Ro's fire dimmed to a small, steady blaze on each of the brush piles.

The fine hairs all over Ro's body stood on end at once, as if an electric current filled the air, and she froze, not daring to make a sound or move a muscle.

She had night blindness—she'd been facing the fire too long—but she strained to see past where all the snow had been kicked up.

She was probably just making it up, but the woods seemed almost . . . denser . . . than they had mere moments before. Darker. Fuller.

Her eyes traveled up, up, up to the tops of the trees, and she tilted her chin up just slightly to stare at the very tips of the branches.

And froze when glowing golden eyes stared back.

Glowing as bright as if a furnace or a setting sun writhed within.

Two tufts of fur seemed to spring past two pointed ears poking just out of the treetops, but that could've been Ro's imagination. It could've also been an owl. Or some other creature up in the tree, peering down at them.

It could've been her eyes playing tricks on her, the ears and tufts of fur no more than branches and just a few dead leaves scraggling off them.

But she didn't think so.

The white wolf stayed still. Ro stayed still. Neither dared to move.

Flaming orange eyes took in the scene, skipping over Ro in her red cloak, and settling on the white wolf cowering within the circle.

Then a deep rumbling shook the trees surrounding Ro and the ground she stood upon, and she staggered under its roiling.

The white wolf whined and crawled on its belly toward the sound, rolling over onto its back and showing its belly and throat as the rumbling persisted.

The deep vibrations cut off.

Then a giant clawed hand reached out of the trees, grabbed the top of the magic circle, which resembled a monstrous transparent onion the moment he touched it, and pinched the magic in its clawed, black-haired fingers.

Then the creature yanked straight up.

The entire magic circle unraveled and fell to the forest's floor like a performance tent losing all its structure at once.

The wolf shot to its feet and tried to leap away from whatever that thing was, but, unfortunately, that meant it leaped straight toward Ro.

Ro was too stunned to scream, too scared to flee, and it all happened so fast, too frozen to react.

Praise the Creator, her indecision did not cost her life . . . this time.

Just as the white wolf sprang at her, the thing grabbed it from behind and whipped it to face him, the wolf dangling over the firepit.

Its voice went deeper, the growls felt inside Ro's chest as if it rattled her heart.

The white wolf whined and pawed at the air and tried to get away, but the creature held firm.

It appeared the two creatures were having a conversation. Ro couldn't tell what they said, not even a little, but it seemed the tree-sized one demanded answers, and the bear-sized one merely gave excuses. If her instincts could be trusted.

Whatever was happening, the towering creature didn't like what the wolf was whining about—or just didn't like the wolf—and it threw the white wolf right at the tree Ro was standing in front of.

With a yelp, the wolf crashed into it, and a massive crack rent the air as Ro rolled away and came up standing just as the wolf rolled to the base of the tree and lay still.

She hunched into her red cloak, making sure it covered every part of her but her eyes, as one of the many rumors of the fey said they couldn't see red.

And her cloak had protected her more than once.

Whether from the love of her mother, or some other magical property the cloak possessed, Ro didn't know, but she wasn't going to start discounting it now.

The giant hand came into view again, held over the fire —as if fire didn't bother it one bit—and pointed at the wolf as if in command.

Ro stared between the white wolf and the unseen creature, terrified, wondering which was the bigger threat.

The yellow-orange eyes seemed to sweep the area once more—once again skipping over Ro entirely—before the snow started churning again. Then the snow stopped swirling, and Ro couldn't feel anything watching her, as if a great well of terror were suddenly sucked away, and the void rang with its absence.

She searched the trees for a few precious seconds, making sure no golden eyes revealed themselves, but both those and the tufts of ear fur were nowhere to be seen.

And that part of the forest didn't feel so dark and deep and dreadful anymore.

Ro reluctantly turned her gaze to the wounded creature lying on its side, panting, flecks of red foam on its jowls.

No matter that the creature in the trees couldn't see her —if there truly had been a creature, that was—this one most definitely *could*, and it had just been furious with her for trapping it.

Should she spring upon it now? While it was wounded? Drive her knives into its throat and take it out while it least suspected an attack?

Or had whatever that thing had been taught it a lesson? Told it to stop killing? Or was that just wishful thinking?

Why couldn't the creature have taken this foul beast with it? It would've solved all her problems. Not that life tended to work out that way.

Ro hesitated too long.

Rolling to its feet, the white wolf lowered its head and growled, its fur sticking up on end in a ruff around its neck and shoulders and chest, then darted into the trees—straight for the village.

With a gasp, Ro dropped her knives, pulled her crossbow off her back, loaded it, cocked, and hurled a single bolt after the creature before it was lost to the trees.

She missed.

Ro stared after it with mouth parted, horror growing, dread churning in her belly.

It was heading straight for the village, to attack the people she'd just sworn to protect.

And Ro had a feeling their defenses wouldn't do a blasted thing against the enraged beast.

What had she done?

8

Ro took just enough time to retrieve her weapons, dump snow on the dwindling fire before it reached the dead trees, and tie on her snowshoes before hurtling herself after the wolf.

It felt like she'd spent a lifetime on meaningless tasks, but she didn't want to set the forest ablaze while chasing after the wolf.

Especially with the barrier being unraveled so easily by . . . whatever that was.

Not long in, she found droplets of blood, and her heart leaped. Had she actually hit it with the bolt? Or had it been wounded when the wolf was thrown into the tree? Or by the claws that grasped it?

It didn't matter. Only that it had in fact been wounded.

Farther into the woods still, she found tracks closer together, then . . . in a wavering pattern, as if the wolf were slowing, then staggering.

Hope once again leaped to her chest and spurred her on.

She wished she could throw the snowshoes aside and run even faster, but then she'd just sink to her waist in snow and not reach the village in time.

She hurried after the wolf as quickly as she could.

Then, the best tracking sign yet—the wolf had flopped over for a short time before heaving itself to its feet and going after the village once more.

Ro could certainly hope the wolf fell over dead from its wounds before it reached the village, but no one could be that lucky.

Least of all her.

She heard shouts before she came upon torchlight flickering atop fortress walls. Men were shouting, waving torches, and driving the creature back as best they could with long pikes as the wolf sprang at them, over and over.

All were fighting to defend their homes.

Ro finally reached the area around the fortress they kept clear of trees, brush, and piled snow, and she ripped the snowshoes off her feet. She had to get closer to make sure her shot went true, especially in this deep darkness.

As if responding to her thought, everything lightened on the field, even though the cloud cover was dense and the moon nowhere to be seen. Ro could make out the wolf snarling and snapping and leaping up at the wall, testing for a weak spot.

She crept forward, careful not to make any sound, careful not to alert the wolf to her presence. She needed to get close enough for a kill shot. She needed to stay downwind. She needed to end this now.

She also made sure not to look at the torches.

Though her eyesight was bringing down the glare while lightening the field.

"Where're those arrows the huntress had us make? Get 'em up here!" bellowed one of the men.

Ro took a deep breath. They should've already been in place. Then she settled on her stomach, aimed her crossbow just behind the creature's jaw, where it would pierce straight through and up into its skull, and let a bolt fly.

The wolf turned just then, and the bolt slammed into its hide. The bristly snow-white coat shivered, and a bloom of red seeped out. The wolf spun toward where it had come from, searching the darkness, growling.

Ro kept herself flat on the ground and didn't move a muscle.

The men kept yelling and poking at it, and the wolf turned back and snapped at the person who'd dared try to stab it.

The man was leaning over just a little too far. The wolf leaped up, sliding neatly past the length of the weapon, grabbed the man by his neck, and hauled him over the edge.

He was dead before he reached the ground.

Ro cursed and jumped to her feet, already reloading. Its speed was incredible. Even following its lead, sweeping her weapon after it to find the perfect shot—or at least one that would incapacitate it—the way it leaped and snapped and whirled in new directions was making a kill shot almost impossible.

And she was outside the wall, where if she missed again, and the men were unable to distract it, she'd be dead before she could reload.

"Here they be—the arrows!"

"Fire, fire!" shouted someone, voice high-pitched.

There was too much clatter as the men fumbled the iron weapons Ro commissioned the metalsmith to make, thick, sturdy arrows for their rustic longbows.

Regular arrows wouldn't pierce its hide.

She only had a few iron bolts herself. She had to make each one count.

Ro set her jaw. She would have to get in close. She would have to use her long knives, leap on its back, and sever its spinal cord.

While running through a hail of deadly arrows.

She instantly tamped down any thoughts or feelings of fear, not allowing them a place in her wildly beating heart.

If she must fall to pieces over facing this incredibly huge beast, it would be *after* she'd defeated him. Or the villagers had. If they could get past their panic.

Apparently the wolf preferred to pick them off one by one while they were outside the walls, and being attacked in the middle of the night was more than they could handle.

Especially since the wolf kept using its paws to bounce off the wall straight up, its head clearing the top of the fortress with each bounce, teeth inches from tearing the next man down.

Ro needed to act fast.

But they needed to fire the blasted arrows!

After too long a moment, the first whizzed past the wolf, and where it slid past the fur smoked and sizzled—Ro could even hear it from her spot across the field, just outside the tree line—and the wolf yelped and danced sideways, retreating a few paces to investigate his wound and the arrow plunged deep into the ground.

As soon as he scented the iron, he snorted and leaped back as if burned, then turned furious eyes upon the fortress.

His growls went deeper, and he rushed the men, attacking with greater vigor, his leaps higher.

"Fire, fire!" men shouted.

Ro sprang to her feet, let the bolt fly as arrows rained down—the wolf couldn't tell he was being attacked from behind with projectiles falling all around it—but it leaped and twisted and stayed out of the path of each burning arrow in a dance that was impressive, to say the least.

Ro threw her crossbow over her back, its strap keeping it there, pulled her long knives, and bolted for the creature.

The moment she reached where arrows were raining down, each iron arrow lit up in a golden glow, a swirl behind it to show its passage, and a thin line of blazing gold in front of it to show where it would land.

Ro dodged and leaped and rolled and avoided each one in her own dance of survival.

She had just enough time to hope they would pace themselves, that they wouldn't fling all the arrows the blacksmith had been able to make in the short time since she'd commissioned them at the wolf, that they actually aimed a few that struck home.

The wolf fell back to the ground after one of its leaps and prepared to springboard to the top again.

Ro leaped, one foot off its hindquarters, the other off its spine, and straddled its neck. It twisted under her, and she brought her knives down into its neck even as it thrashed and started to fall back, to pin her under its weight.

"Hold yer fire! It's the huntress!" someone called from above.

"Keep shooting, keep shooting!" she called back, voice hoarse from disuse, fear, and pounding adrenaline.

After a pause, arrows continued to rain down, and Ro had time for one more stab before the creature was near the ground and she had to roll away.

The creature pivoted and came up on its feet, just out of range of the arrows, crouched and ready to spring at her.

As with the bolt that had pierced its hindquarters, apparently no more destructive than a bee sting to a human, red seeped out along its neck, slowly growing, as if a mild wound, nothing more. She hadn't stabbed where she'd meant to.

Ro gripped her knives tighter, prepared to use them.

What would it take to kill this creature?

"What do we do?" someone atop the wall shouted.

Ro spoke low, hoping her voice wouldn't drive the wolf into a frenzy as it had before.

"When it comes into range, shoot it. And keep shooting. And for the love of the saints, get someone who can aim?"

There was an uncomfortable silence, then someone blurted, "But we cain't see nothing in the dark!"

Ro gritted her teeth as the wolf circled her, as she slowly pivoted to face it, to stay centered so she could lunge in any direction. She'd forgotten her eyesight made hunting in the middle of the night possible. That others didn't have . . . whatever afflicted her.

"Then wait till its head breaches the wall." *Obviously,* she didn't say.

The men waited breathlessly, not making a sound, as Ro waited for the wolf to make its move. When her back was to the fortress, she took a slow step back, then another.

She retreated, just like prey did.

The wolf liked that.

Growing bolder, it pranced forward, tongue lolling in a doggy grin, one that promised it would soon be eating her face off.

Then its power gathered in its hindquarters, and it started to leap toward her.

Too quickly for her mind to comprehend, the wolf sprang into the air, Ro wrapped her arms around its massive neck, driving her knives into the soft parts on either side, but they weren't long enough. She didn't have time to slice through its throat.

It didn't work.

And the wolf crunched down on her face. Her entire head fit in its mouth.

And then nothing. Blackness.

Ro blinked, and the wolf was just beginning its spring at her, all over again.

So she dropped her knives, swept up one of the iron arrows, and slid under the leap, driving the weapon up and into its brain through the bottom of its jaw.

The wolf continued its leap forward, Ro cleared its mass underneath it, and the wolf crashed to the ground. And lay still.

Ro scrambled to her feet, hands empty of weapons, and grabbed up two more arrows, just in case.

What if it hadn't worked? She didn't think it likely, but she wasn't going to underestimate the creature.

"What's going on? I don't hear anything. Did it eat her?"

"Non, I think she killed it!" called someone from one of the few areas that no longer had a torch lighting up that section.

"Huntress? Are you there? Do you . . . live?"

"Hold your fire, s'il vous plaît," she called, not wanting to rouse the wolf with her voice, but she also didn't want to be skewered by a rogue arrow while she checked the wolf for life signs.

Sounds of relief came from the fortress, and someone else called, "Did you do it? Is the beast dead?"

"I'll let you know in a moment," she muttered under her breath, then louder, "Unclear."

She crept closer, keeping her footfalls light, her breathing shallow, trying to keep her heart from pounding right out of her chest.

She kicked the wolf with her boot, but he was too heavy to roll over in the usual method.

So Ro crept toward his face, arrows out and in front of her, ready to jump forward and stab if need be.

It stared, eyes glassy, iron arrow poking out the top of its head, smoking and burning anything it touched, even after death.

The relief that swept through Ro had her staggering, and she couldn't make her voice work to tell them the good news, to call that it was safe to come out—well, safer than it had been.

There could be more, and regular wolves still hunted

nearby. They would come flooding back to this area once the musk from this fey creature faded and stopped scaring them off.

But for now, the townspeople were safe.

And that's all that mattered to Ro.

Bending forward, Ro rubbed a tuft of its fur between her fingertips. It would make a fine cloak, especially were her hunts to bring her this far north again.

She would wear it to hunt and kill the beast in the prince's summer château.

THE END

HIS BEARD IS BLUE?

La Barbe Bleue
"Blue Beard"
—Charles Perrault—

"You must die, madam," said he, "and that presently."
"Since I must die," she answered, looking up at him with eyes all bathed in tears, "grant me a little time to say my prayers."
"I grant you," replied Blue Beard, "ten minutes, and not a second more."

« Vous devez mourir, madame, dit-il, et cela maintenant.
— Puisque je dois mourir, répondit-elle en levant les yeux vers lui avec des yeux tout baignés de larmes, accorde-moi un peu de temps pour dire mes prières.
— Je vous l'accorde, répondit Barbe Bleue, dix minutes, et pas une seconde de plus. »

1

Now

Ro paced, hardly knowing what to do with herself.

This was it. Gautier was trusting her with a job she'd been angling for since she'd brought him her first wolf.

He was sending her to the château. The one no one could see but her.

He'd apparently known how to get in all along—and tonight he was finally going to tell her.

She'd already been to see Cosette, to say her goodbyes. Something had told her she needed to. And not that annoying voice she wasn't speaking to. An instinct, something dark and sinister and what felt like death breathing down her neck.

The other huntsmen were away, including Liam, and Ro couldn't help but think that was intentional.

But now she was impatiently waiting for Gautier to be done with his festivities.

Or, at least, to leave them long enough to give her the details she needed to succeed.

She had no plans after this hunt. She was going to enter the château, kill the beast, and end this wretched curse once and for all.

And if she didn't live through it, so be it.

How had she come so far? Going from groveling to be trusted for the best hunts to being the only one trusted for the mission she wanted more than anything.

She would have to face her biggest fear and biggest wish, all at once.

But threatening her sister was beyond the pale.

She should have skewered him then and there for the insult, but frankly, she needed him. She needed his information, his expertise, to get her inside the château in order to kill the beast that had harmed the prince.

Was Prince Beau Alexandre Trêve even still alive?

She was going to find out.

Gautier made her wait for hours.

And unfortunately, all she had were memories to keep her company.

Specifically, of her first official hunt for Gautier, the hunt that had led to this very moment, the hunt that was for something more than a wolf pelt—a monster who wore the face of a man.

She pulled out a sheaf of papers, trimmed a pen, and opened an inkwell.

If all she had were memories to keep her company, she might as well write them down.

2

Then

Ro took a deep breath and let it out slowly. Finally. She'd hunted enough wolves for Gautier, and now he was trusting her for a big job. Something he normally sent his other huntsmen out for. The experienced ones.

Ro squelched the urge to squeal and perform a happy dance right there in the château square. Cosette might have let her get away with such nonsense, but it would seriously damage Ro's stoic huntress persona.

Besides, the other huntsmen around the fire in Gautier's courtyard were already eyeing her. She'd always walked past them, a dead wolf draped over her shoulders, but this was the first time she'd joined them.

One handed her a small lump of wood, and Ro took it automatically. She stared between it and the huntsman. With a gap-toothed grin, he held up the small raven he was whittling into being.

Ro nodded gratefully and set to work shaping the piece of wood in her hands.

The distraction worked . . . for a little while. The stubborn thing refused to shape itself into anything other than a mangled lump, and Ro was growing frustrated.

How in the realms did so many of these huntsmen do this for so long? It was maddening.

Plus, her hands were shaking. Not ideal while wielding a knife.

"Ah, there she is."

Ro came to attention at the sound of Gautier's voice, shoving her knife away.

"What have we there?" He was looking at her hands.

Ro followed his gaze to the hacked-at wood. "Nothing."

She tossed it right into the fire and crossed her arms, feeling the need to shield herself.

Then she uncrossed them and straightened her back when she realized she was hunched over and looked unsure and defensive. She needed to look confident, strong. Even if she was just pretending.

"Ah," Gautier said. "I see. Monsieur Liam, this is the huntress we spoke of. Mademoiselle Ro . . . ?"

"LeFèvre," Ro said hastily. She wasn't sure why she'd given her mère's maiden name the first time she'd brought him a wolf, but it brought comfort, reminded her why she was doing this, and ensured she'd most likely answer to it. Oui, it was a good choice. "But just Ro is fine."

That's when Ro's freaked-out brain noticed the tall man at Gautier's side. Strong physique, dusky blond hair, and warm brown eyes, which lit with interest. "But of course. The huntress who has brought us so many wolves. Good work, Mademoiselle."

Ro inclined her head regally, in a move Cosette did so well but Ro was pretty sure she'd mangled as badly as the wooden carving, and said nothing. She was too afraid she'd vomit all over Gautier's shoes.

"I thought she would be perfect for the matter we

discussed," Gautier said to the huntsman at his side, though the others at the fire had grown quiet and were listening as well.

Liam nodded. "I agree."

Ro didn't know how she felt about being discussed like this, in front of her and only somewhat including her, but then she decided she was just grateful she wasn't expected to talk.

"Very well. Please take her and the huntsmen of your choosing to meet with your contacts, then set out on your task posthaste."

The men around the fire straightened, hope leaping to their eyes, posture changing from relaxed to charged.

Liam nodded, all business. "Marceau, Gustave, with me."

A few of the men deflated, but more still casually went back to whatever they were doing. Two men immediately strode for the stables, as if leaving before Liam—or Gautier, perhaps?—could change his mind.

Liam's eyes found Ro. "Mademoiselle, if you will come with me, I shall endeavor to do my best to teach you all you need to know for a successful hunt." He seemed to catch himself. "Well, for the kinds of creatures you will be hunting now."

It was said gallantly, but it rankled. As if Ro were a wee babe, just learning to walk and being patronized that she would make it across the room—one day.

No matter that the comparison fit more aptly than Ro cared to admit.

She clenched her fists, but Liam was already on his way to the stables as well.

"Oh, was I not clear? She's leading the hunt," Gautier corrected, and Liam spun back to study Ro from the crown of her head to the tips of her boots.

She quickly relaxed her hands.

"Monsieur, with all due respect . . ." he began.

"My word on the matter is final." Gautier walked away, turning back briefly to say, "I will be expecting a full report, however?"

Which made Ro break out into a cold sweat.

Liam jerked his chin, and Gautier grinned, resuming the trek to his small château.

As Liam's hooded eyes continued to take Ro's measure, it was all she could do not to flee into the forest. Her? Lead a hunt? She may have been adept at hunting wolves on her own, but leading a hunt was so far out of her purview, she couldn't even begin to express how bad of an idea this was.

Was this what she could expect from Gautier? Throwing her into a task without her being ready for it?

She had a feeling she would find out.

If she lasted through her first hunt for otherworldly creatures.

Pretending a confidence she certainly didn't feel, Ro strode past Liam and into the stables, hoping it looked less like fleeing than it felt, and readied Fairweather as quickly as she could with shaking hands.

The two other huntsmen—Marceau and Gustave, was it?—leaned on her stall door, watching her every movement. "A brand-spanking-new huntress." One of them whistled. "What a day this is turning out to be."

"And she's to lead our hunt, no less!" the other put in.

Liam entered the stables quietly and crossed his arms, watching them.

"Gotta say," Gustave or Marceau said happily, "this hunt has quite possibly become my favorite."

Liam made no move to stop the flow of words making Ro more and more uncomfortable.

When she couldn't ignore him a second longer, she lifted her eyes from her saddlebag and met Liam's eyes across her horse.

Although his face gave nothing away, she could almost read his thoughts. Why her? Why had Gautier chosen her, a green huntress, and the only female, to lead on her very first hunt? Instead of more experienced, reliable men?

Well she didn't know the answer to any of those questions either.

She gave Liam a long look, not backing down.

"You heard Gautier," Ro surprised herself by saying. Her voice crackled with authority she didn't know she possessed. Though the emotion she was feeling could only be described as sheer terror. "Let's set out so we can be back again with our report."

No one moved.

"Now," she said simply and quite firmly, and led Fairweather out into the courtyard.

Ro peeked over her shoulder, mostly shielded by her horse.

After a moment, the men moved to ready their own horses, though Ro didn't miss the looks they gave each other.

Why her? Was she ready? And with her brusque manner, would she end up being a useless tyrant and no good at all?

All right, the last one was simply Ro's fears rearing their ugly heads, but Liam especially looked less than pleased to have his hunt stolen out from under him.

Although he didn't look happy about it, at least he moved to saddle his horse with the rest. Thank Dieu.

And Ro dropped Fairweather's reins and stumbled off to discreetly empty her stomach behind an unsuspecting bush.

3

Ro tried to pick her gaping jaw off the table, but she was quite certain she wasn't succeeding.

Two gentlemen sat across from her—handsome, oozing charm and a *je ne sais quoi* that came from being professionals in their respective fields, former dragoon and musketeer—and spun such a wild tale, even Ro had trouble believing them.

She sneaked another glance at Liam, Gustave, and Marceau.

They hadn't batted an eye.

Liam met her wide-eyed gaze, read her features in an instant, and took on an amused look. Ro cleared her expression, her gaze shooting back to Gautier's clients, trying to pretend a calm she wasn't feeling.

"And you immediately went to try to see your sister?" Gustave prompted, when one of the men, Henrique, wiped his face in despair.

"Of course we tried to see her!" the other, Alistair, said. "But we couldn't step foot on the property, no matter how hard we tried."

Ro blinked. That sounded rather like the château she could see one night a year . . .

"Peace," Liam said calmly.

The younger brother, Henrique the musketeer, whipped his hands away from his face. "How can you say that? It's not your sister being held by a monster!"

Liam took in the raised words without the slightest shift in temperament. "Why don't you tell us one more time, from the beginning."

Ro stared at him in amazement. If it were her being shouted at, whether by distraught brothers or not, she'd already have the dragoon pinned and be sword fighting the musketeer.

Not that she was particularly good at sword fighting.

But that was beside the point.

"We already told you," annunciated Henrique through gritted teeth. "Our younger sister met and married a man while we were away. His beard is as blue as my brother's uniform—"

All the huntsmen at the table spared a glance for the deep-blue coat, though to Ro, that was the hardest detail to believe.

"—but other than that, our sister was quite obsessed with marrying him, what with his good fortune and sizable estate, even in this cursed land, and would not wait for our leave to marry. Or for us to return for the nuptials."

Alistair the dragoon spoke up next. "He seemed amiable enough, but when we went back to our regiments, we met a man searching desperately for his sister. She had married a man with a blue beard, and he had never seen her—or her new husband—again."

The younger brother finished the tale with a quiet voice. "He had gone quite mad searching for her. He fears . . . he fears . . . that she no longer lives."

"And if our sister married the same man . . ."

Quiet settled between them, and Ro just . . . sat there.

This was not what she'd been expecting for her first official hunt for Gautier.

"And his name?" Liam asked quietly.

"Monsieur de la Tour," Alistair supplied in the same somber tone.

The silence had barely had a moment to settle when Henrique brought his fist crashing down upon the table. "Gautier must send for her right now! While she yet lives!"

Ro jumped, then tried to sink into the chair. Even though Gautier had given her this hunt, she was certain she was more than disqualified. Rescue someone a dragoon and musketeer couldn't? What had she gotten herself into?

Liam stood, Gustave and Marceau seconds behind, and Ro scrambled to her feet.

"Despair not. Gautier is sending us to look for your sister this very day. We will search for her posthaste."

Liam didn't usually talk like that. Ro eyed him. Was he trying to sound impressive for the dragoon and musketeer? The last vestiges of the former king's regime? Or for her, the newly minted huntress that Gautier had trusted with this job . . . for some reason?

Either way, she hoped he returned to his normal self right away. This stuffy and stilted Liam was making her ill at ease.

All right, everything was making her ill at ease.

Hunting alone, that she could do. This? Well, she needed to figure out how to pretend, and fast, to be trusted with more jobs in the future. To be trusted with *the* job.

The brothers exchanged glances, then jumped to their feet. "And we're coming with you."

Liam stood straighter, using his height to intimidate.

It was working. On Ro alone.

"That was not the agreement with Gautier, Messieurs.

Leave us to our task, and we will hasten to return—with your sister."

Both men got obstinate looks on their faces, and Ro was fleetingly reminded of her own brothers. How she missed them.

"Our agreement with Gautier be hanged! We are both trained men, Monsieur Liam. We will not be in your way, we can ride just as hard as the rest of your men"—Alistair stuttered and glanced at Ro, then went back to ignoring her, as the brothers had done after the initial introduction—"and we will assist in any way we can."

"Besides," Henrique argued, "we can lead you directly to the country home he took our sister to."

Ro hung back while the three argued—Liam insisting they stay behind, the brothers insisting that wasn't going to happen—until they all marched out of the meeting place to mount their rides, the brothers triumphant and Liam disgruntled.

Ro smirked a little, not surprised the brothers had won, and wondered if her brothers would have done the same for her.

They both had been gentlemen of leisure before the curse, and rather lazy after it. Most of the gentry learned some form of swordplay, but had her brothers been forced into the military, had they been made to work when they didn't have to, she wondered how like these two they might have turned out.

But the curse had fallen before they'd had the chance.

Liam caught her smirk and directed a glare her way that seemed to blast through her like a gale.

Ro blinked, bewildered why he was directing his ire toward her, then took a moment to recall why she'd been smirking in the first place. Oh. Um, oops?

"Move out!" he called in a thunderous voice, not

breaking their gaze until he wheeled his horse about and took off down the country road.

She rolled her eyes heavenward the moment he tore away. Great. Her first hunt, and she'd offended the lead huntsman.

Even though she was supposed to be the lead huntsman. Er, huntress.

She urged her horse after the retreating huntsmen and soldiers. "Come on, Fairweather," she said. "Let's go see how I can make this worse."

4

Ro stomped up the curving, crushed-shell drive lined with trees, cursing Liam with every step.

She would smirk at him every day for the rest of her life, laugh at him outright, even, and she would enjoy it.

This plan was insane.

But mostly she was mad at herself for going along with it. For not offering an alternative.

The outfit she was stuffed in was ridiculous. The bonnet was frilly and cut off most of her vision, except for what was directly in front of her, and the flouncy dress hampered her movement.

She had half a mind to rip it all away, but then she wouldn't get even half a word in with the man inside.

She lugged a basket with her, full of jars and preserves and vegetables, all from the closest farmhouse's pantry. She wondered if she'd have to use it for protection, though she'd much rather have her weapons.

Not a single knife in her boot.

"Anything can be used as a weapon. Anything can be used as a weapon," she muttered to herself so she wouldn't forget.

It took everything she had not to look back at the men hidden deep within the woods, using the dragoon's spyglass to keep an eye on her.

If only she'd been assertive and insisted on *her* plan, instead of going along with this travesty. Not that she had a plan, but still.

The next time she was put in charge of a hunt, she was going to actually take charge.

Ro stepped onto the creaky porch and settled her nerves with a deep breath.

She could do this. Her sisters flirted. The village girls flirted. Bon, even her mère had flirted, making everyone who met her fall in love.

Surely Ro could copy them, pretend to flirt, for just a little while? She was French, for heaven's sake. Flirting was in her blood!

Or so others had told her with annoying regularity. Usually accompanied by "Why can't you smile prettily, like Cosette?" or "Stop scowling so hard. Your face will stick like that."

With those pesky words circling her mind, she had to concentrate even harder on wiping the scowl from her face.

She raised her hand to knock, and the door opened. Ro blinked, startled.

A man with the bluest of beards stood there, looking just as startled. "Pardon! I . . . was not expecting you. May I help you, Mademoiselle?"

She couldn't stop staring at his beard. She thought she'd been prepared, but it was so full, so monstrous, so very . . . blue.

She shoved away her shock with effort and took in the rest of him.

He was tall. And broad. Muscular. And very, very handsome, in spite of the blue monstrosity upon his face. His shirt was a fine cut, modest, but it did nothing to hide his perfect physique or his tapered torso and strong legs.

Uh, his trousers on his legs. That covered his legs. Ro's thoughts stuttered all over themselves.

And Ro was staring.

He waited with an outer calm of patience, but a turbulent undercurrent briefly touched Ro's awareness.

It jolted her back to her mission.

"Oh! Pardon, Monsieur. I have heard of your recent loss and have come to offer my comfort." Heat rushed to her face. "I mean, my basket. I have come to offer my basket. Of food. Here."

She held it out, blushing hotly. He didn't take it.

"We have all the food we need, surely, but perhaps . . ." His impatience seemed to fade as he took her in from head to toe.

Ro's face grew warmer, especially once his eyes returned to her face and she saw appreciation there.

It was as the woman's brothers had said. He was enamored with a pretty face and modest, humble clothing and countenance. Which was just weird.

Not that she considered her own face to be anything remarkable. But they'd certainly fussed over her long enough at the neighboring farmhouse.

"You are too kind, Mademoiselle," he said in an intimate, rumbling voice that almost had Ro sighing aloud.

Wait, sighing? Since when did she sigh over any man?

According to the gossip she'd been forced to endure at the closest farmhouse, Monsieur de la Tour was a recent widower, which had sent the brothers into a near panic. Only Liam's calm reasoning had kept them from fruitlessly trying to get back on the property, and possibly alerting him to their presence. They had guessed—and been right—that Ro would be able to walk onto the property, and the most recent Madame de la Tour's brothers had begged Ro to investigate immediately.

Ro wasn't interested in flirting with someone who may have murdered his wife. Wives, plural, possibly.

That got her back on track.

She dropped her gaze and fluttered her eyelashes. "It is nothing."

"It's more than nothing."

He came close. So close, Ro could feel his warmth. She almost backed up a step, but she found she didn't want to. His presence was . . . intoxicating. He dropped his voice to a sultry purr, and Ro's knees went weak.

"To give of your time, to comfort one in their time of distress? It is not nothing. It is a touch of the divine, Mademoiselle."

He reached up and trailed his finger down her cheek.

Ro slapped his hand away, then gasped a heartbeat after meeting his startled eyes.

"Oh . . . pardon. You . . . surprised me, that's all. I'm not used to being . . . touched."

She gave off an airy laugh and twirled her skirts a little, as her sisters Yvette and Nicolette liked to do when they flirted. Ro thought it looked addled, but how was she to know what was attractive?

This was *not* what she'd expected to be doing while leading her first hunt.

Thank goodness he was handsome, or she probably would've just scowled at him the whole time and been booted off the property immediately.

She tried to think of something appropriate to say.

"Here I came to comfort you, and you're comforting me." She giggled and hated herself for it.

His smile eased back into place. He glanced behind him. "I would invite you in, to share the contents of your basket with me, Mademoiselle, but you have no chaperone . . ."

He left the words hanging, as if giving her room to refute them, as if giving her room to walk right into his den anyway.

Ro felt a measure of disgust that she covered with another bat of her eyes. *Don't mind if I do.* "Why, you are just so thoughtful! I won't be but a moment, then I'll be on my way."

She brushed past him and into the house, setting her basket on the dining room table. She categorized everything in a hot second. Well-made furniture, painted white. Minimal decorating, three exits. One leading out of the kitchen, one that perhaps led to a master bedroom, and of course the door at her back.

A staircase off the entryway led upstairs.

Her eyes riveted on a sprig of wildflowers in a jar of water on the table.

Flowers. Real, live flowers. In France.

The pastels against drab green were so beautiful, tears came to her eyes. How had he gotten something to grow? Had it come from the Mesdemoiselles of the Mountain's garden? But they grew only food, did they not?

He came up close behind her and spoke in a deep, sultry voice. "Find something you like?"

Innuendo dripped from his words, and Ro didn't like how close he was. She forced her muscles to relax, to stay loose in case she needed to move quickly, and let off another brainless laugh.

"Ooh, wildflowers. So pretty. I haven't seen them in an age."

"Then they're yours." He kissed her neck.

Ro jumped and spun away, putting the table between them.

His hand, perfectly formed and kissed by the sun, flew to his chest. "Mademoiselle, forgive me. But you looked so enchanting just then. My grief got away from me, and I—

didn't realize what I was doing. Forgive me. I miss my wife so, you must understand."

Tears came to his eyes, grief transforming his features into a perfect replica of remorse, and he dropped his head.

Ro rolled her eyes. She didn't care how good-looking he was. If he tried to kiss her again, she'd punch him.

At least her brain had gotten past his gorgeousness to take in the ick factor.

And his beard was just so darn *blue*. How?

Ro forced herself to walk close enough to touch his arm lightly, a chair still between them. "No harm done, Monsieur. All is forgiven."

How on earth could she get away from him long enough to explore the house? Would he leave soon so she could come back? Maybe sneak in?

Something fell over upstairs, and they both stared at the ceiling at the same time.

"Forgive me, but may I ask you to return another time?" He swept a dazzling smile over her face and down. "With your chaperone, of course. I would love to get to know you better."

Eyes up here, you cretin. Ro smiled sweetly. "Why, I couldn't imagine anything lovelier." Then she made herself look worried. "I do hope everything is all right."

She flicked a glance at the ceiling.

His smile looked rather wooden. "Perfectly. I like to paint, and it seems my easel has fallen over. I hope you understand my concern to go rescue it."

He steered her toward the door.

And then a methodical pounding, like someone kicking the wall or perhaps hitting it, began.

Ro tilted her head. "So. She's still alive."

She punched him right in the face, right past his stunned expression, and he toppled straight back, felled like a tree.

"Yes!" She'd punched exactly how her brothers had

taught her, and it had actually worked. But she didn't know how long she had.

She hiked her skirts past her boots and trousers and took the stairs two at a time.

"Bonjour? Madame de la Tour?" Ro called through the first door she came to. "Henrietta?"

Scraping and muffled noises came from behind it, and Ro rattled the doorknob and searched the frame for a key.

"Stand back!" Ro called, then lifted her boot and kicked straight forward.

The door rattled on its hinges but didn't budge. She kicked a few more times, but it was well made. And reinforced.

Flustered, she looked around for something she could use, then laughed. Of course! The hinges. She reached under her skirts for the knife tucked in her boot.

She'd worked off two and was reaching for the third when the noises on the other side of the door turned frantic.

Ro put her ear to the door. She could only make out "basement" and possibly "brothers."

"Désolé, but I cannot understand you. Don't worry! I'll have you out soon."

She started to wedge the last pin out of the hinge with her knife, but strong hands grasped her shoulders and threw her straight down the stairs. Her knife went flying.

Ro cried out and tumbled all the way down, curling her body to protect her head, then came up on her feet at the bottom. Dazed, she stumbled against the wall and used it to hold herself upright.

She tore the bonnet from her head so she'd have no more blind spots. Stupid thing.

Then she wedged her fingers into the slightly torn neckline of her gown and ripped, all the way down, exposing her hunting leathers and red cape, which unfurled behind her like a flag.

She'd never seen a hunt without it, nor would she ever.

"Why are the prettiest ones conniving, scheming wenches?" The gorgeous man with the unsightly blue beard seethed, his expression ugly as he came down the stairs after her, one predatory step at a time. He eyed her clothing with distaste. "Can't have you off telling stories, now can I? I guess two brides will do just as well as one."

Ro's comeback was drawn up short. "Two . . . brides?"

"Can't have you leaving this world without being a bride. Where would the justice be in that?"

"That is most definitely not happening."

He just smiled in response.

Ro had been too flustered to notice before, but his accent was decidedly not French.

Italian? Greek? It was too faint to tell.

Then a thought struck, not her own. It was too *ancient* to tell.

Not important right now.

At that moment, he sprang for her. Ro lunged for the table, spilled wildflowers everywhere, and cracked the jar over his head.

He didn't topple this time.

Non, his hands connected around her throat and immediately began applying pressure. "Now you'll just have to go to sleep for a little while so that I can make myself free to marry you. Then we'll have a little talk. And a little honeymoon."

Ick. Gross. Disgusting. No way. Never happening.

He'd die first.

Ro struggled, but he pushed forward, squeezing harder. So she toppled backward with his momentum, getting her feet up under him just right and sending him flying over her head. She gasped for breath the moment his hands came free and rolled away, putting her back to the wall.

Ro flicked a glance out the window, hoping she'd soon

have support. Seriously, did they not hear all the crashing going on in here? Weren't they supposed to be watching and close by to help?

She saw something blue coming at her in the reflection and ducked his swing just in time.

"They won't be coming to help ye, lass. No one comes onto my property. *You* shouldn't have gotten through."

"Lucky me," Ro muttered.

He bore down, settling into a fighter's stance, punching with one fist, then the other.

Ro tried not to panic.

He was massive, the power behind each swing enough to make her sweat.

If even *one* of those punches landed . . .

She threw everything she had into dodging, evading. Escaping.

They rounded the kitchen table, then she ducked around the doorframe just as he swung. Wood splintered, jagged chips went flying, and he didn't even lose momentum.

Ro's foot caught on a rug. She gasped and went down, hard.

He grinned and dove for her.

She rolled away just in time and came up to her feet.

And thankfully, somehow, her cape stayed just out of his reach.

With his size, her only hope was to be quicker. As tall as she was, she couldn't tuck herself into small spaces, but she was slender and wiry and fit, while he was huge and bulky and muscle-bound.

It wasn't much of an advantage, but it was one.

And once it was gone, she was dead.

So she danced. Twirling, jumping back, feinting one way then dodging another direction. Keeping her muscles coiled tight, her tells to a minimum, working hard not to give anything away.

Just like Liam had shown her, dang it. While they were waiting for the farmwife to finish her clothing for this task.

Where was the bossy brute, anyway?

It was more a flitting feeling than an actual thought, wishing for Liam, as she poured herself into staying alive.

After a trip down the hallway, leaving massive fist-size holes in the walls and a cracked support beam, they were back in the kitchen.

Ro flung every chair his way, which he simply snatched up and threw straight down, smashing each one to kindling. As if in a show of strength he didn't want her to forget.

As if she *could* forget.

The table, wedged perfectly into the elongated space, was the last whole piece of furniture in their wake.

Ro whipped the covering off the basket and hurled jar after jar at him. He just raised one arm at a time, letting the glass shatter on his massive forearms. Food dripped down his arms, a few glass pieces cut him—Ro nearly got distracted when his blood came out blue, too—but he let her empty the basket before jumping toward her in a quick, darting fashion.

She squeaked and heaved the table over in front of him, its top blocking his way. He laughed and started kicking it. It didn't take long for the well-made wood to splinter.

But she'd distracted him, just as she wanted to.

Her hand closed around her goal.

The table shattered, and he lunged for her.

Just as she brought the iron skillet down upon his head.

5

She'd timed it perfectly. He was out cold. For real this time.

She hoped.

She snatched the key from his waistcoat, jumped over his prostrate form, and dashed for the stairs.

The door was hanging just a bit, open slightly from where she'd taken out the two pins.

She immediately started to unlock the door.

"No!" a woman's voice called from within. "Do not unlock it!"

Ro froze. At least she could hear the woman through the crack this time. "Whyever not?"

"If anyone tries to unlock the door but him, the room will burst into flames, and I'll be burned alive. Please! Don't unlock it."

Ro recoiled from the door. She eyed the pins. "Might I still take the pins out?"

"I—I don't know. I got it open a little . . ." The woman's voice faltered. Then she demanded, "Where is my husband?"

Ro heaved the frying pan in her hand, as if showing the

woman, though she couldn't see it through the door. "Frying pan to the head."

She was rather proud of herself for that one.

The woman barked a surprised laugh. "Huh. Not bad." Before Ro could thank her, the woman rushed on. "You simply must go to the basement. They're more important than me!"

"Madame, your brothers would certainly disagree."

"My brothers? They're here?" She choked on a sob. "You can delay no longer. My husband will be awake soon. He . . . heals . . . faster than a mortal. Please, they will rescue me. You must hurry!"

"But—"

"*Go*. Now! Before he wakes."

Ro eyed the final pin, checked the stairs, then rushed forward and heaved it out of the hinge before she could talk herself out of it.

"Is the room on fire, Madame?"

"What? No, I—"

"Bon. The hinge is out, the iron skillet in front of the door. Free yourself if you can, I will—"

"Go to the basement! *Now*."

Ro jumped and rushed down the stairs, half-wondering why she was listening to the woman who sounded half-mad instead of freeing her from her captivity.

The man with the blue beard—for heaven's sake, she was just calling him Bluebeard from now on, because why not? —still lay where she felled him.

She quickly searched and found twine in the kitchen, which she wrapped around and around his wrists and ankles so firmly, his limbs were in danger of blackening and falling off. They were already starting to purple.

She didn't care. She just hoped Liam and the rest got here in time to help her.

Not that she expected anyone to help her. Ever. But it would be really nice if her backup showed up as they said they would.

Pounding started from upstairs, like the woman had taken her words to heart and was trying to escape in earnest.

Ro fumbled with the door at her back. She'd just take a quick peek, find out what she was up against, and go for help.

Though she was quite certain she was going about things in the wrong order.

But this was her first sanctioned hunt, she was leading it, and she needed to get this right.

Ro stumbled down the stairs into the pitch-black basement, belatedly wishing she'd brought some kind of lamp. Or kept the iron skillet.

The light from the open door didn't penetrate past the stairwell.

The floor was sticky, tacky, and tried to suction her boots to its surface.

She followed the wall with her fingers, searching blindly with the other hand for a lamp or torch or anything to light her way. She ran right into a small table, and everything on its surface rattled. Something cold splashed onto her right boot.

She found a little box of matches, half soaked, and felt around until she found an oil lamp. Cold metal somethings were strewn all over the table, and she nicked herself and sucked in a harsh breath, which sounded too loud in the quiet space.

Then a match flared in the darkness, and she used its short life to set the wick aflame.

Small metal blades of all shapes and sizes were meticulously laid out all over the table's surface—well, those Ro hadn't jostled, anyway—as well as some rather . . . imaginative . . . instruments.

Ro couldn't begin to guess what they were for. Was Monsieur de la Tour a surgeon of some kind?

A basin was filled with dark liquid, which she'd spilled. She leaned forward and sniffed gently, in case it was something that could incapacitate her, but it was metallic, cloying, somewhat familiar, but had no effect on her.

Once she'd replaced the glass to protect the flame, she lifted the lamp high to see why Bluebeard's wife was so desperate for her to go into the basement.

And hoped she wouldn't be trapped in here.

Something dark covered the floor's entire surface, with dark water lines on the walls that looked like it'd been higher, much higher, at some point.

Pale white dresses were everywhere, filling a basement that had to be absolutely humongous, as if on the wirework mannequins that dressmakers in Paris used to display their wares.

But these mannequins were no wirework.

She moved closer.

It looked as if the dresses hung on perfectly made marble statues, and although she'd certainly seen better-made wigs in Paris, all powdered white or gray or blue, or the more fashionable green or pink or yellow, these wigs were natural-colored, if still elaborate.

The mannequins, made of a grayish marble with faint lines of blue, were in many reposes all over the room: conversing, holding up teacups, seated at tables, reading, and a few in the corner even looked to be dancing, arms linked, skirts held in one hand, smiles wide, skipping to some lively tune.

All had streaks of moisture down their cheeks, as if the

basement were too humid, and water had collected under their eyes and run down.

They were fascinating.

Ro leaned close to one of the statues, seated at a table, teacup in hand, laughing at what her companion was saying. Ro reached out and touched a cheek.

Although it looked like marble, the cheek indented with her finger and felt just like . . . frigid skin. A bead of water slid down it, moistening Ro's finger as she pulled away.

Suddenly, the eyes shifted and looked right at her.

Ro screamed and dropped the lamp, heading for the stairs at a dead sprint. The lamp shattered and went out, plunging her into darkness.

The light at the top of the stairs darkened, and Ro looked up to find Monsieur de la Tour blocking her path. Snapped twine lay around his ankles, dangled off his hands.

"I see you've found my secret. Don't feel too badly—none of the others could resist sneaking around, feeding their curiosity, either. But I'm afraid I can't let you leave."

Fear held Ro frozen at the bottom of the stairs, one foot on the first step.

She didn't know what to do. She didn't know what to do!

She didn't want to be leading her first hunt. She wanted to fade into the background, learn all she could for when she faced the beast. She didn't want any of this! All she wanted was for things to go back to normal, for the curse to end.

She didn't want to be here!

Her heart pounded, her ears roared, and it was all she could do not to give in to her fear. She had to stay calm. She had to *think*.

He eyed her up and down. "My brides all wear their wedding dresses, bleached to take the sinful colors out of them, but you're not my wife, are you?" He eyed her cape.

"That cape becomes you. I think you'll do nicely in red. And you'll remember the sin of curiosity all your days."

Before Ro could move, act, or even decide what to do, the man tore at his beard. Most of it came off into his hand, leaving bloody patches all over his honey-toned skin.

Then he blew blue powder down the stairs and right in her face.

Ro gasped and tried to run, but she couldn't move.

No matter how hard she tried.

She was frozen, just like all the other statues.

6

The loathsome man pounded down the stairs, his heavy frame making every step creak and sag, and he picked Ro up and leaned her against the wall.

Her foot remained in the air, her arms out to each side, as if still reaching for a banister that wasn't there, and her frozen gaze stared at the ceiling she couldn't see in the blackness.

Only her clothing moved, her cape hanging behind her, sticking to whatever was all over the floor.

He rummaged around until he found another light, then he went about the room, lighting sconces on the walls, illuminating the entire space in a warm, golden glow.

Ro could only see the spatter of something dark on the ceiling. Something brown and old and . . . everywhere.

She just couldn't make out what it was.

The man moved furniture about for a while, and Ro could make out the soft swish of clothing here and there, but she couldn't turn her head, roll her eyeballs, nothing, to see what he was doing. Her eyes started to burn, but she could do nothing to relieve them.

After an eternity, he picked her up once more and heaved her across the room.

Her skin crawled at his touch, which she could most definitely feel through her clothing, but he carried her facing the wall, so she still didn't know what was going on.

Then he suddenly set her upright, facing the rest of the room.

"Ta-da! What do you think of my beauties, my sinful dear?"

Ro could only stare in horror. Literally. The scenes she'd witnessed earlier had been rearranged, the tea party she'd dared to touch moved deeper into the room, and the other scenes moved back and out, to be better seen.

But the worst part?

All the furniture he'd been moving, all the space he'd made, was now set up for a new scene.

A picnic basket lay on a checkered blanket. Her basket. Her checkered cloth she'd used to cover its contents. Chopped wood lay nearby, an axe buried deep in a stump. A stuffed deer stood across from the little picnic, frozen as if startled.

It was just out of Ro's peripheral, so she wasn't sure if its eyes were moving or if it were truly stuffed.

A bow made of exquisite redwood and a quiver full of matching arrows were propped up nearby, as if awaiting . . . something. Or someone.

As if awaiting her.

"A hunting scene for my huntress. Isn't it just lovely?" He moved so she could see the hunger in his eyes, the wolfish look on his face as he leered at her. "But not as lovely as you'll look as the star of my puppets, my dear."

Ro's heart shriveled up and every part of her recoiled, though she could make no outward sign. She'd never been so scared in all her life.

Because there was nothing she could do to stop him.

"Now, let's get you prepped."

He started humming cheerfully, rearranging things on the table, or so it sounded to Ro, moving more furniture, and finally turning Ro to face the wall.

It too was splattered with brown flecks Ro couldn't identify, though in much more abundance than the ceiling.

She could just see Bluebeard out of her peripheral.

The man seated himself in a tall chair that made him level with her height, then stared down into the basin. "Well this is spoilt." He tossed it out of Ro's line of sight, and it splashed onto the floor. "No matter." He gave her a bright smile. "There's more where that came from."

Then he settled the basin below her arm, pulled out a spool of blue thread, and started to sew.

Tears rolled down Ro's face as her mind screamed in blinding terror, her body unable to let any agony out except through tears.

He used no disinfectant, no pain relief, nothing to numb the bone needle as he pulled it in and out, in and out of her skin.

Threads of blue lined the fingers she could see, by her cheek, each finger delicately stitched to look as if stretching a bow string back, the other hand still as it had been, motionless, as if resting on a banister.

Blood ran out of the wounds into the basin, only stopping once the skin had turned gray and cold. Complete paralysis had followed the blue thread all over her upper body.

She somehow knew those limbs would never move again, no matter how much she wished it, no matter how much she tried.

She couldn't pass out, she couldn't sleep, and she

couldn't die, though at some point in her torture, she wished for all three.

She had been embalmed. Alive.

He'd been working for hours, covering almost every inch of her upper body with blue thread, holding the cloth out of the way until the blood stopped seeping.

Then he'd settle the clothes around her, gently, modestly, arranging them just so.

And as he did, Ro could only watch in horror as his beard regrew, little by little, until it was even more full than it had been.

Ro was in too much pain to wonder what had happened to Madame de la Tour, to her brothers, to the huntsmen, to Liam.

Her entire world was pain, stitches, and those loathsome fingers upon her skin.

A deep agony settled into where she was sewn, a bone-deep ache that wouldn't go away. Somehow, it began to hurt more than the trail of fire being stitched into her skin.

7

Just when Ro couldn't take it anymore, when she was past that, even, her hand twitched. She glanced down, her eyes the only thing she'd been able to move as the hours wore on, and sure enough, her fingers curled just slightly.

Hope filled her for the first time, but she tried not to let it show. Desperately hoped Monsieur de la Tour wouldn't choose that moment to look into her eyes.

But no, he was still concentrating on his work, something along the side of her body that blocked her hand from his sight.

She had to use this advantage before he stitched her other arm straight out, as if she were holding a bow, something he'd been more than happy to tell her was coming.

She peered down the length of her arm again, still held out like it was resting on a banister, and her eyes riveted on the axe handle.

Her hand was so close. If she could just inch her fingers closer. Get her arm to move. Her shoulder to rotate. Her body needed enough torque to twist around and bury it in his—

His chair groaned as he leaned toward his little table, fingering another instrument that looked like it was only made for torture. Or butchering.

Come on, come on, come on! she chanted in her head.

Whatever magic in his beard was still in her system, but it seemed to be lessening. Could she get it to wear off? Sooner?

She could only take shallow breaths—because her chest couldn't move—but she took the deepest breath she could manage, held it, and concentrated.

It wasn't long until her brain was screaming for oxygen, but she could feel it. She could feel the blue magic pulsing through her blood, circling her entire body, holding her captive.

The stitches she could do nothing about. They were firm, unrelenting.

But the magic from his beard . . .

She pushed. Hard. And it flared up, pushing back.

She sucked in a breath, then a few more quickly, and her sense of the magic faded.

So she held her breath again, and this time, as the blue dust flooded through her arm on its circuit of her body, she tugged at it gently, pulled it away from her blood and muscles little by little, bit by bit, until she could feel it lessen.

As she pulled on the strands, separating them, a few granules of blue sheared off. The moment they were no longer connected to the whole, they burned up, into nothing. Ro gently pulled away as many as she dared, weakening his hold on her further.

Her muscles were fatigued from being held in one position for so long, but she forced them to stay still, to keep the same pose without trembling, using the magic left in her system to her advantage.

And then her moment came.

She cut off the magic to pile up in her limbs where the stitches already were, clearing it from the rest of her system.

He started to turn back around, a wicked-looking saw in hand. "Well, my dear. It looks like one of your fingers doesn't want to cooperate. We'll just remove it, shall we, to get it to look just right?"

Ro grasped the axe with one hand and swung with all her might, just barely torquing her hip and her foot to give it as much power as possible.

The axe cut through his neck like butter.

The last thing she saw of him was the surprised look on his face as his head went flying from his body in a spray of blue blood. Then his body toppled out of sight.

She'd killed enough animals to know it wasn't supposed to work that way, but she didn't question it. She was just glad he couldn't hurt anyone else.

Too weak to hold it any longer, she gasped as the axe slipped from her fingers.

The crash of the weapon on the floor was accompanied by a door slamming open upstairs, footsteps pounding down the creaky main stairs, the front door being flung open.

Ro's barricades started to fall. The blue magic was piling up in her system. Too much for her to handle.

As if sensing it, Bluebeard's power flared up, for merely a second, and washed through her system in a gentle cascade, a humming shushing of sound.

Ro, once again, couldn't move. Though this time, the magic was lessened, leaving her limbs stiff instead of rigid. Ro's eyes drooped, and she hoped she'd stay awake long enough for whoever that was to get down here and help her.

The basement door crashed open, and light footsteps rushed down the stairs and straight toward Ro.

Soon cool fingers were on her face, lifting her eyelids and checking her body for injuries.

"Ma chère! Are you all right?" A lovely woman came

into view, though it was hard for Ro to focus on her. "Here, let's get you out of those stitches."

She kicked the bloody axe out of the way, and without another word, the woman sat where the man had been and began removing each stitch, one at a time, with a little hook she took from the tray.

The pain was just as agonizing—perhaps even more so—but it wasn't long until the rest of Ro started to droop, no longer held in place by the stitches . . . by Bluebeard's magic . . . as the blue dust clung to the stitches and was pulled out along with them.

The men crashed down the stairs not long after, but Ro couldn't make herself open her eyes and look at them to see their reactions. She hurt too much.

But their pause and stunned silence spoke volumes.

As well as Liam's, "If his head weren't removed from his body, I would be doing that very thing right now."

The other men murmured their agreement, and Ro decided she liked these huntsmen very much.

8

As Ro regained feeling, the woman would feed her bits of bread or sips of a too-sweet lemonade, before returning to her bloody work.

Well, it would have been bloody. Had Ro not lost so much blood already.

But with each bite, with each sip, she felt that much more restored. And as the threads came out, so did a smidgeon of color return to her skin.

By the time the woman was finished, a fine sheen of sweat rested on her brow. She dabbed at it as Liam and Henrique lowered Ro to the little checkered blanket and wrapped her in her red cloak.

"Rest there, dear one. You are safe."

And the last thing Ro saw as she started to nod off was the woman, Madame de la Tour, move on to the next mannequin of flesh and begin her laborious work, one stitch at a time.

By the time Ro woke, Liam, Gustave, Marceau, and the woman's brothers, Alistair and Henrique, were bustling around the room, carrying women upstairs as Madame de la Tour finished with them.

Ro quietly observed as she woke up by degrees, every inch of her body aching, every part of her soul hurting.

She'd never had control of her body wrested from her before. Someone just do what they liked with her, without her consent, without her permission.

She didn't like it.

"Huntress."

She met Liam's eyes briefly, then looked away. He helped her sit up, then gave her a clay mug filled with something warm and aromatic.

"She said to drink this."

So she drank it. As it flooded through her, it brought warmth, it brought relief—it made her feel more like herself again.

But the soul-deep pain didn't go away.

"Can I get you—do you need anything? Anything else?"

Ro just shook her head, not meeting his eyes.

"She said some of these women have been here for hundreds of years." Liam grunted, the sound full of disgust. "It's hard to take it in."

When Ro didn't say anything, he went on.

"She's having a harder time reviving those who have been here longest, but she said with rest and nourishment and care, they may yet recover."

Ro nodded, still steadfastly looking away. She may have been the one to end Bluebeard, to make it possible for Madame de la Tour to escape and the men to access the house, but she felt she had failed, as a huntress, as a fighter, failed at protecting herself, and she just couldn't look at him right now.

Liam briefly rested one heavy hand on her shoulder—

Ro stiffened—then after a moment or two, he moved away, back into the room, to see to the others Madame de la Tour had just unstitched.

And Ro sat there and felt sorry for herself.

Ro slept on and off, until Madame de la Tour made her get up and start helping.

Or Henrietta, as she insisted on being called.

Ro didn't want to—she didn't want to do anything, really—but Henrietta was right. The more she moved, the more she helped others, the more she felt like herself.

Henrietta told Ro her story as she spoon-fed the women in makeshift beds all over the house, then had Ro help her wipe them down, shift them on the pallets, and tuck clean sheets around them.

The neighboring farmwife had been busy sewing garments and sheets ever since she'd found out what had happened. Pieces of what had happened, anyway.

All she knew—all anyone else would know—was that the monster kept his old wives locked in his basement so that he could marry new wives.

It was enough to rally the small community to their aid.

Ro had no idea how long she'd been sleeping, but it was apparently long enough for Madame de la Tour to unstitch seventy-six wives.

Tending them all twice a day was not only a lot of work, it was also doing a lot to pull Ro out of herself, and she was grateful.

Henrietta kept talking, and Ro made herself pay attention.

"He made the basement sound so foreboding. He gave me the keys to everything else and said I could go anywhere but the basement. I did everything I could think of to distract myself, but I just couldn't get it out of my head.

"Despite my reservations about marrying him, he had thus far been a good, kind husband—but he looked so cruel when forbidding me, I just had to know what could alter him so.

"You know what I saw. The floor was so covered in blood, it washed up over my slippers, and the women . . ." Her voice broke with grief. "So many women, everywhere, all with marriage bands on their fingers. Marriage bands exactly like mine."

She fingered the thin band of metal, misshapen from being hammered out unevenly, something she still hadn't taken off yet.

"I took my shoes off and hid them, but the blood was enchanted. It left footprints everywhere upstairs, from my stockings, from my feet, and no matter what I did, I couldn't clean it out. So I stopped trying and focused on my escape."

Ro gasped. "The stuff . . . all over the floor . . . is *blood*?"

Henrietta's gaze was instantly full of sympathy. "Oh, you poor girl. Did you not see? Or did you wish to deny it as I did?"

Ro couldn't answer. She'd known. Known. But she'd kept telling herself she had no idea what the liquid splattered and pooled everywhere was.

Even when it was running down her own arms.

"It didn't smell . . . right," she said feebly, realizing it was a thin excuse.

Even as she'd frantically scrubbed out her cape, even as the water had changed color, even as she'd had to burn her light-colored blouse due to the stains, she'd still denied what it was.

Henrietta patted her arm most gently, which still throbbed from having the stitches removed. "Don't you worry, my dear. I'm quite certain it had something to do with the enchantment."

Or it was too horrible for Ro's mind to process.

Still, Ro didn't disagree. It was a perfectly reasonable excuse, and she was more than glad to have it.

Henrietta studied her face. "You know, this will make you stronger, if you let it."

Ro raised agony-filled eyes to hers, and all she wanted to do was slap her. How *dare* she say something so unfeeling!

She hadn't been through the stitches, not like the other girls. She couldn't possibly understand how Ro was feeling. How much it hurt. How much Ro just wanted to . . . give up.

"Ah, I see. This pain is too much for you right now, isn't it? No matter. I will help you. You see, I was . . . studying . . . before my mother made me marry this man. I will help . . . ease your pain."

Then Madame de la Tour rested her fingertips on Ro's forehead, and before Ro could wonder why the woman's brothers thought she had married Bluebeard readily and willingly, Ro slumped over in a deep sleep, but she could still hear Henrietta's every word, not that she would remember them later.

"Now let's see if I can remember," Henrietta mused. "Touch the memory, but not the threads around it."

She concentrated wholly on rooting around in Ro's mind, tugging out the streams of energy of the worst of what had happened to her at her husband's hand, tugging and delving around without Ro's consent or knowledge.

"Don't you worry, ma chère. We'll have you right as rain in no time."

What Ro didn't know, couldn't know, was that this would make it much easier for others to touch, to twist, to influence her memories in the future.

All while she slept on, unaware.

9

Ro woke the next morning feeling deeply satisfied, as if she'd slept well after strenuous physical excursion, like a run or a hunt.

She stretched, bathed, dressed, and skipped lightly down the stairs to find breakfast.

The door to the basement had been walled off, but Ro didn't wonder at it. In fact, she hardly glanced at it.

There was a hearty spread for the men—made by the men, Ro found out as she was digging in—and the one thing she noticed was the wrapped body near the new wall in the kitchen, as well as a basket with some kind of blue hair peeking out of it.

Henrietta came downstairs just as Ro was finishing her meal, and one of her brothers asked her what she wanted done with the body.

A part of Ro knew who it was, knew that she'd been the one to separate his head from his body, but it was a distant memory, one that didn't bother her much.

Madame de la Tour looked at the body and separated head dispassionately. "Burn the body, bury the head. As deep as you can dig, in the darkest part of the forest you can find. His beard can't be destroyed, and should someone find it, someone with darkness in their heart, then they'll take on the mantle of the blue beard, and the killing will start again."

The men in the room recoiled from the man's head as one.

Ro tilted her head. That didn't sound right. "Killing?"

Henrietta gave her a small smile. "This isn't the first time this creature has been unleashed upon the earth. Rumors of women taken, killed, bodies found years later, abound for a reason. But this reiteration liked to keep his trophies." Her voice turned quiet and sad. "It's the only reason so many survived."

Ro knew she should feel sadness for the twenty-five or so who hadn't made it, in spite of Henrietta's careful ministrations, but it was more she *knew* she should instead of actually feeling anything at all.

Ro shrugged and went back to eating. She didn't stop to ponder why the words didn't affect her more.

Henrietta's eyes traveled over the men, taking in their subtle movement away from Bluebeard's body. "Don't worry. If you dig the hole, I will bury the head. Let me get my trousseau de mariage so it can be locked within."

Ro had never seen someone look so determined—so resolute—before. It was as if righteous fury had overtaken Madame de la Tour, and she wasn't letting anyone else fall to Bluebeard's curse as long as there was breath in her body.

Admirable, but again, Ro thought it more than felt it.

The brothers exchanged heartbroken glances, and Ro could tell they mourned for all their sister had been through.

Their sister marched up the stairs, soon returning with a small chest she easily carried in two hands.

Ro's mouth fell open. "That's your hope chest?" she said without thinking.

Her sisters had trousseaux that rivaled the size of their

beds once Ro had read them the common practice of the ancient Egyptians.

Aristocratic French girls had no need for hope chests, not with their dowries, but Ro's older sisters had seized upon the idea with joy, filling each one to the brim with things they "just had to" take into their new marriages, if they could one day find anyone willing to marry them.

It was much more common for peasant Mesdemoiselles to pack things away for when she started her own home, but Ro had never seen one so small.

The young woman offered Ro a tired smile. "I didn't want to marry, but my mother insisted upon it, to save our family." She frowned at the box. "There was something about him I didn't like, but he made himself so pleasurable, so kind, that I doubted myself."

She stood lost in her thoughts.

Her brothers exchanged glances, a frown on one of their faces, a wrinkle on the other's forehead, as Liam, Gustave, and Marceau moved forward to take up the rolled-up body and carry it outside.

Ro waited till all five men were outside and she'd finished her meal to say, "May I ask what's in it?"

"Of course." Henrietta's smile was brighter this time, as if throwing off the weight of her thoughts. She opened it and pulled out a pair of dainty lace gloves, a hand-sized book, and a thin gold chain with a cross dangling off it. "My grandmère, a lacemaker, made me these gloves before she passed. My père gave me his Bible as he lay dying. And my mother gave me this necklace, the only jewelry she had, as I was leaving for my new home."

She looked around the kitchen distastefully, then sadly looked back at the cross.

"I was angry at her for making me leave, but I should never have taken it off."

Ro shifted uncomfortably, not sure what to say to comfort her.

Thankfully, not long after, the men came tromping back in, the smell of woodsmoke following them and fresh dirt on their boots. "'Tis done," Liam rumbled in the quiet space.

The girl put her treasures on the table. "Bon. Now, we'll put the head in this."

The men all looked at the head, obviously trying to figure out how to pick it up without touching it, when the girl reached down, moved the covering, and plucked it up by its hair. She shoved it into the box, slammed the lid, and raised her eyes to the gaping men. "Shall we?"

They followed her out, but Ro went back for a second helping. She couldn't remember the last time she'd been this hungry, but she was starved, and there was plenty of food.

A flash of blue caught her eye as she was returning to the table.

There, on the rim of the basket, a clump of blue hair had survived, probably ripped out when his latest wife had removed his head.

Without thinking, Ro reached down and plucked it up, staring at the blue strands in awe. First of all, the color was the richness of the summer sky. Second, the strands seemed to glimmer when held up to the light.

Third, if what Henrietta said was true, she probably didn't want this lying about when the men came back.

Ro started to move her hand away when the blue strands seemed to melt straight into her fingertips. She stared at it a moment, on the verge of panicking, when the memory of it just . . . slipped away.

Ro picked up her fork and shoveled in another bite of food.

That dragoon could cook like no other.

10

The dragoon and musketeer left to fetch Madame de la Tour's mère as soon as they were convinced their sister was truly safe. And after Liam agreed the huntsmen wouldn't go anywhere till they got back.

Ro didn't miss the tightening of the girl's jaw, or how she looked as though she dearly wanted to object.

Ro suggested burning the house, and all the memories alongside it, but Henrietta decided to keep it. It was a beautiful house, large and simple, and she didn't want it to go to waste.

She shrugged and said simply, "We need someplace to live."

Plus, the pantry was stuffed full, there was enough room for the wives, many of whom were from centuries past and had no family to even attempt to find, and Liam and the huntsmen had walled off the basement so none of the women would ever have to see it again.

"Someone needs to be there for them. Someone who understands."

"And your mère?" Ro asked.

The woman's jaw tightened. "She is welcome, of course,

but with the understanding that I am a woman grown, and my decisions are my own."

Ro nodded, not saying anything further. Her mère had been kind, softspoken, always seeing to others' needs before her own; she couldn't imagine having a mother who bowled her over and forced her to do everything she wanted.

Ro wouldn't have handled that well.

Still, and maybe this was just her recovering from the heavy dose of magic she'd taken in, but she ached that Henrietta's only response to her brothers fetching her mère was to build up walls around her heart.

Like Ro had to do with her père.

As the days wore on, Ro's mind settled into a state of remembering what had happened while remaining distant from how she felt about this particular hunt.

Which was just fine by her.

Not soon enough, the brothers were back, and Liam was ready to depart.

Ro tied her crossbow on her horse, preparing to leave with the other huntsmen.

"That was very well done."

Ro did not jump and shriek at the voice at her elbow, and she was rather proud of herself for turning a cool, level look Liam's way.

Liam gave her a single nod. "That man deserved what he got."

"Oui." Ro swung herself up on her horse. "He certainly did."

"You were hurt on my watch," he said abruptly, out of nowhere. "And for that I must apologize."

Ro smirked, though it was humorless. "Technically, I was hurt on *my* watch."

He slid a disgruntled look her way. "I should have protected you."

Ro raised an eyebrow. "When? While you were trapped

outside the boundaries of the man's homestead? Non, I'm a professional and a huntress. I should have protected myself."

"But I sent you into that danger."

"Technically, Gautier did."

His jaw tightened. "Once we got here, I mean."

Ro nodded. "Oui, but you couldn't have gone into the danger with me, even if you'd wanted to. Besides, you came in as soon as you were able."

His expression didn't shift, and Ro sighed.

"I accepted the consequences when I accepted the job from Gautier."

"But I was supposed to look out for you."

Ro scowled. "It isn't your job to look out for me."

"But the fact remains—I should have."

Ro gritted her teeth. "I disagree."

"But—"

"It was *my* hunt. *I* was in charge. And I did what I had to do."

She turned Fairweather's head and rode off.

How he was able to turn an apology into an argument she'd never know.

As she urged Fairweather down the path, toward Gautier to see if he were true to his word and would offer a heavy purse to her for something other than a wolf pelt, she tried to push Liam and this hunt's events from her mind.

She hoped she'd never have to kill another man in her life.

A monster, oui. A beast, certainly. That Bluebeard was a fey creature, an immortal being, according to his wife, hardly helped. He wore the face of a man.

And her stomach twisted every time she thought of it.

Although he deserved it, although it was the only course Ro had seen to save the other women's lives—and her own

—his head sailing from his body with one swipe of her axe replayed itself over and over in her mind.

Though with considerably less horror than Ro should have felt.

Just thinking about it made her fingers tingle, and she accidentally dropped her reins. She fumbled for them before Liam could see and add that to his report.

Odd. For a moment there, she didn't have any feeling in her fingertips.

But the sensation quickly passed.

Unfortunately, the memory of Bluebeard's glassy eyes stared at her for the entire ride, keeping Ro company, and Ro found herself wondering if she could truly do that to the beast when his time came.

11

Now

Ro paused in her writing. Of *course* she could do that to the beast, especially with two years' experience in her quiver.

The creature had captured and quite possibly killed the prince. It had plunged her kingdom into this curse . . . somehow . . . and Ro was going to do everything in her power to break it.

It was nothing more than a monster, just like Bluebeard.

And it deserved the same fate.

She scanned the pages, this nagging feeling tugging at her that she was forgetting some detail, but she brushed it off without realizing she'd done so.

What had she been thinking, scribbling down her first hunt? Now her mind was right back to where she'd started, filled with longing to begin what was quite possibly her final hunt.

Ro started to chew on the end of her pen only to get a mouthful of quill feather.

Gautier chose this exact moment to fling open the door and stride in.

Ro leaped to her feet, shoved the papers into the fire—ink still wet and smearing everywhere—and stood at attention, trying to pretend she hadn't just stuck her quill in her mouth.

Gautier eyed her a moment, then the flames, before his ever-present grin blossomed on his face. "Are you ready for your greatest hunt since this scraggly thing?"

He rested his arm on the head of the fully stuffed wolf forever posed springing at every person who walked through his door.

Her first kill.

When she'd been trying to save Cosette's life.

Just as she was trying to do now, but this time, from this bigger worse wolf before her.

She lifted her chin. "I am ready."

"Parfait." Gautier flung himself behind his desk, propped up his boots, and inspected his teeth in a spoon he dug out of the mess. "I guarantee you've never hunted anything quite this monstrous before."

Non, that would be when she'd hunted the Great White Wolf, the closest she'd ever been to being terrified out of her mind.

But if she could make a pelt out of that great creature, then she could certainly do the same to the beast.

Still furious with him for threatening her sister, for pushing her in such a way she could never forgive him for, she stayed aloof and stared at the wall over his head.

"Your orders for me, Monsieur?"

"Come now. Has it truly come to this? We have worked so long and so well together these many years."

Ro allowed her gaze to drift down the wall, and she speared him with her deepest, frostiest glare. "That was before you threatened my sister."

The monster dared to smile at that. Smile!

Ro returned her gaze above his head before she leaped across the desk and pinned *his* hide to the wall.

Then she'd never get into the château.

She must only remain calm until she got into the château. Then she could take her fury out on the creature, then she would be back.

Gautier would answer for his threats.

He waved a hand dismissively. "Come now, that was only to motivate you. To let you know how much is at stake."

"My people's freedom is enough to motivate me. There was never any need to get personal." At his opening mouth, she said, "Enough of this. I must leave in order to be in position on time. What are my instructions?"

"Oh my darling huntress. How I have waited for this day. This night. This moment!"

As have I, Ro did not say aloud as he started speaking. She clung to every instruction, every step of what she'd waited so very long to hear.

The moment he was done, she spun on her heel, sparing a quick glance to make sure her story was fully ash, then marched upstairs and started preparing.

This was it. Her one chance.

And then she'd be back. For him.

THE END

Ro's story continues in
Kill the Beast
Book One of the Beast Hunters.
Available Now from L2L2 Publishing.

REVIEWS

Did you enjoy this book? Please leave a review!
It helps our authors more than you can possibly know.
Thank you so much!

~The L2L2 Publishing Team

THE LOST SLIPPER

COSETTE'S STORY

Did you know there's a story *missing* from this book?

Gasp!

The Lost Slipper was originally the seventh fairy tale, told entirely from Cosette's point of view.

Set between *Beast Hunter* and the next book in the series, *Kill the Beast*, this (now) novella takes two beloved fairy tales, twists them together, and unravels into a fractured new addition to the Beast Hunters series.

But this story is no longer in the book you hold in your hands.

Instead, this 5k short story blossomed into a 50k novella, based on some wonderful feedback, and had to be moved into its own book. Or this tome of shattered fairy tales would be even more monstrous!

So if you want the missing story, all you have to do is sign up for my newsletter—the ebook is completely free for anyone who wants my exclusive updates. (But you can also find the paperback at your fave bookseller.)

Enjoy!

Cosette dreams of her life becoming the perfect fairy tale—until her wishes come true. Can her fairy godmère take it back?

Every day is the same for Cosette. Get up, clean, make breakfast, and meet her stepmère's and stepsisters' every demand.

That is, until an encounter with a fairy of the forest—or is she a witch?—and an invitation to a fête in honor of Monsieur Gautier promises Cosette's life is about to become the beautiful fairy tale of her dreams.

Or so the story should go.

Except her fairy godmère demands a high price for her help, one Cosette isn't willing to pay. Her stepsisters are as afraid of their mère as Cosette is. Can she truly leave them to their fate? And the handsome Monsieur Gautier hides a dreadful secret, one she's desperate to know—if only she can get close enough.

Cosette is faced with a choice: Should she feign ignorance and accept her happily ever after? Or dig deeper to find what may be lurking beneath?

If you like fairy tales turned upside down, and lovely young ladies learning to stand up for themselves and for others, then this "Cinderella" and "Diamonds and Toads" reimagining is the book for you.

Get it now at: **bit.ly/lostslipper**

"*The Lost Slipper* is a retelling of two fairy tales that could have easily been enough to carry the story on their own, but the addition of 'Diamonds and Toads' to the Cinderella narrative brilliantly escalates the tension and increases our poor heroine's suffering. A thrilling, emotional tale for anyone who ever thought, 'Cinderella had it too easy.'"

—C.O. Bonham, author of *Runaway Lyrics*

"*The Lost Slipper* is a short but satisfying read about grace and kindness when beset with cruelty, creatively combining two beloved fairy tales into a new, complex fable."

—H.L. Burke, award-winning and bestselling author of over twenty eclectic fantasy novels

"As someone who enjoys every Cinderella iteration I've ever come across, *The Lost Slipper* blends my favorite familiar elements of the story with unique twists—such as who the Fairy Godmother really is and the behavior of the stepsisters. With allusions that bring to mind *Ever After*, *Ella Enchanted*, and *Into the Woods*, readers will enjoy how Harper weaves this story and will be left wanting more!"

—Alicia Grumley, poet, Cinderella aficionado, and cohostess of Diversity Is Lit Book Club

ACKNOWLEDGMENTS

First of all, I praise and thank my Lord Jesus Christ for His lovely gift of storytelling. I am in awe of all the beautiful stories out there, and I am humbled to be a small part of it. To think *You* created *me* to be a *writer*!

And to you, dear reader. Thank you for taking a chance on my book. Your time is precious, and I am so happy you spent some of it on me. I hope you enjoyed yourself!

To my lovely beta readers for *Beast Hunter*: Jebraun, Laura, Kara, Tim, Sarah, Barbie, Dominique, Josh, Savannah, Alex, and Nicole. I am eternally grateful for you and your encouraging comments!

Lindsay A. Franklin, editor extraordinaire: You get me, my voice, and my heart for my stories, and I adore your edits. Thank you for taking time for this author!

Laura Hollingsworth. For one of the most gorgeous hardback covers I have seen in my entire life. Thank you for bringing Ro to life! I cannot wait to see the rest.

Sara Helwe, who created my paperback covers. I love them so very much, thank you! You have been with me from the beginning, and I cannot wait to finish this series with you. Thank you for all you have done for me!

To each of the illustrators who created such beautiful art that I was able to include in this special hardback edition: I am in awe of you and your creativity. Thank you so much for bringing such lovely art to life!

To each of the classic fairy-tale authors who penned such beloved stories that continue to live on in my world. Gabrielle-Suzanne Barbot de Villeneuve, Charles Perrault, Hans Christian Andersen, Jacob and Wilhelm Grimm, Madame d'Aulnoy, and many, many more.

Your stories have captured my imagination, and I have absolutely loved exploring their depths and variances in these pages, as well as the rest of this series.

And to every other reader and author who loves fairy tales as much as I do—thank you for reading, writing, and devouring fairy tales so much so that it has become such a popular genre, with so many new options of fairy tales to read. I am in heaven.

And to my Ben, who supports my writing and my business, and to my Blaze, Maverick, and Gwenivere: I love you so much I can hardly stand it.

With all my heart,

Michele

ABOUT THE AUTHOR

Michele Israel Harper spends her days as an acquisitions editor for L2L2 Publishing and her nights spinning her own tales. Sleep? Sometimes . . .

She has her master's degree in publishing, is slightly obsessed with all things French—including Jeanne d'Arc and *La Belle et la Bête*—and loves curling up with a good book more than just about anything else.

Author of ten published novels (and more on the way), Michele prays her involvement in writing, editing, and publishing will touch many lives in the years to come.

Visit MicheleIsraelHarper.com to keep in touch or to learn more about her!

About the Author

Michele loves to hear from her readers! Follow her on social media, check out her website, or drop her a line to let her know what you thought of Beast Hunter and Other Fairy Tales. *Happy reading!*

www.MicheleIsraelHarper.com
Facebook: @MicheleIsraelHarper
Twitter: @MicheleIHarper
Instagram: @Michele_Israel_Harper

Be sure to sign up for her newsletter for bookish news and a free copy of *The Lost Slipper*!

MicheleIsraelHarper.com/My-Newsletter

More from L2L2 Publishing

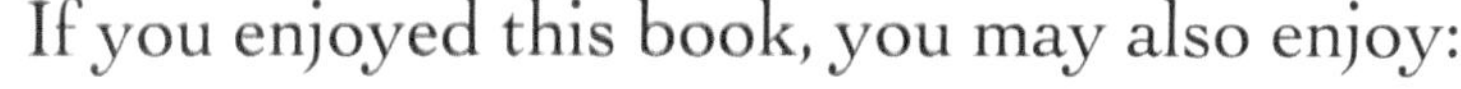

If you enjoyed this book, you may also enjoy:

Ro remembers the castle before. Before the gates closed. Before silence overtook the kingdom. Before the castle disappeared. Now it shimmers to life one night a year, seen by her alone. Once a lady, now a huntress, Ro does what it takes to survive, just like the rest of the kingdom plunged into despair never before known. But a beast has overtaken the castle; a beast that killed the prince and holds the castle and kingdom captive in his cruel power. A beast Ro has been hired to kill. Thankful the mystery of the prince's disappearance has been solved, furious the magical creature has killed her hero, Ro eagerly accepts the job to end him. But things are not as they seem. Trapped in the castle, a prisoner alongside the beast, Ro wonders what she should fear most: the beast, the magic that holds them both captive, or the one who hired her to kill the beast.

More from L2L2 Publishing

If you enjoyed this book, you may also enjoy:

Huntress Ro LeFèvre is offered a job to hunt a pest plaguing the Seven Seas. A siren has been sinking the king of Angleterre's ships, and in turn, vast amounts of his wealth. Fleeing heartbreak, Ro gladly accepts, but there's just one problem. The king will credit the Marquis de la Valère, and no other women are allowed on the voyage. Ro will just see about that. Hiring an all-female crew without the king's knowledge, Ro hopes they will follow her to the Caribbean, not take the gold and flee. But when Ro is plunged deep into the ocean by the siren she's being paid to kill, presented the sirens' side of the story at knife point, and pressed to join them or die, Ro must decide whether to complete her mission, join the sirens, or something in between. Before the sirens sink her ship.

More from L2L2 Publishing

If you enjoyed this book, you may also enjoy:

Wisdom may have crafted the worlds by the Maker's design, she may have been at His side since the beginning, but her heart aches. Her sister is gone. Defected, to a group of rebels who loathe their Creator with every fiber in their beings, who plot His downfall. Her new assignment? Fight them. Defeat them. But how can Wisdom fight her sister, when all she wants to do is bring her home? Folly seethes with the pain her new home inflicts upon her at every moment. But she is determined to prove herself to her new master, to become his favorite. Destroying her sister just may be the key to Lucifer's heart. Her plan? Engage Wisdom. Distract her, defeat her. Folly wasn't counting on one minor detail: missing her sister. But Wisdom has orders to thwart her sister. Folly's orders are the same. And both are determined to win.

More from L2L2 Publishing

Candace Marshall doesn't do ghosts. Or zombies. Or vampires. Or mummies. Anything scary, really. When she finds herself signed up for a dare she's gone out of her way to avoid, things spiral out of control. Quickly. Stuck in a mansion alongside a vengeful spirit, a miffed boyfriend, and a room full of people she doesn't know or even like (if she's being completely honest here), she must decide whether to act brave or let the coward within show. Or kill the person who got her involved in the first place.

Ghostly Vendetta is a prequel novella to Zombie Takeover: Book One of the Candace Marshall Chronicles.

More from L2L2 Publishing

If you enjoyed this book, you may also enjoy:

Candace Marshall hates zombie movies. She hates anything scary, in fact. In his usual, not-so-thoughtful way, her boyfriend surprises her with advanced screening tickets to the latest zombie flick, complete with interactive features and a tour. She refuses to watch it, but it doesn't matter. Horror becomes reality when an experiment gone wrong transforms her peaceful town into a mess of slathering zombies. Thrown together with the only other survivor, Gavin Bailey, her favorite actor and secret crush, she somehow fights her way through the mess, making plenty of blunders and surprising herself with . . . courage? But, just when Candace thinks it can't get worse than zombies, it does.

WHERE WILL WE TAKE YOU NEXT?

Hunt with *Kill the Beast,*
Sink into *Silence the Siren,*
Discover *Wisdom & Folly Sisters,*
Shiver with *Ghostly Vendetta,*
and Devour *Zombie Takeover*.

All at
Love2ReadLove2WritePublishing.com/Bookstore
or your local or online retailer.

Happy Reading!
~The L2L2 Publishing Team

ABOUT L2L2 PUBLISHING

Love2ReadLove2Write Publishing, LLC is a small traditional press, dedicated to clean or Christian speculative fiction.

Speculative fiction includes any fantastical element, and usually falls in the genres or the many subgenres of Fantasy or Science Fiction.

We seek stunning tales masterfully told, and we strive to create an exquisite publishing experience for our authors and to produce quality fiction for our readers.

Beast Hunter and Other Fairy Tales is at the heart of what we publish: a fairy tale that turns expected endings on their heads that we hope will delight our readers.

All of our titles can be found or requested at your favorite online book retailer, local bookstore, or favorite local library.

Visit L2L2Publishing.com to view our submissions guidelines, find our other titles, or learn more about us.

And if you love our books, please leave a review!

Happy Reading!

~The L2L2 Publishing Team

www.ingramcontent.com/pod-product-compliance
Lightning Source LLC
Chambersburg PA
CBHW030603310726
48979CB00003B/551
9781943788699